A STAKE IN THE KINGDOM

"Ummm." The Archbishop picked up the goblet, and gulped down its remaining contents – David hastening to refill it from the flagon. He cleared his throat. "Holy Church is never ungrateful. I could see that you are ordained priest. Even though you are young, young. And find you a benefice somewhere. A small living."

"A benefice would be useful, my lord. For the expense of living. In Paris. But without ordination, I think. I do not seek holy orders. All unworthy as I am."

"You . . .? Damnation, boy – what has got into you?" the old man gobbled. "Not seek holy orders? Yet you would have the Church support and sustain you . . .?"

"I conceive myself as able to serve Holy Church very well outside the priesthood, sir. Holy orders hold certain disadvantages. Handicaps. Certain restrictions on a man, shall we say. With regard to women, for instance. I do not see myself as a born shepherd of the sheep, my lord. Unlike your illustrious self! I seek rather a different role in the Church's service. In all humility. And . . . in Paris!"

"The saints grant me patience! What sort of dizzard has John Beaton fathered!"

Also by Nigel Tranter

A Stake in the Kingdom

Nigel Tranter

CORONET BOOKS
Hodder and Stoughton

First published in Great Britain in 1966 by Hodder and Stoughton
A division of Hodder Headline PLC
First published in paperback in 1995 by Hodder and Stoughton
A Coronet Paperback

10 9 8 7 6 5 4 3 2 1

A CIP catalogue record is available from the British Library

ISBN 0 340 63765 X

Printed and bound in Great Britain by
Cox & Wyman Ltd, Reading, Berkshire

Hodder and Stoughton
A division of Hodder Headline PLC
338 Euston Road
London NW1 3BH

PRINCIPAL CHARACTERS

In order of appearance
Fictional characters printed in *italics*

DAVID BEATON: Student at St. Andrews. 7th son of Beaton of Balfour, and nephew of Archbishop James Beaton, Primate.

JOHN HEPBURN: Prior of St. Andrews. Lord Privy Seal. Cousin of the Earl of Bothwell.

JAMES BEATON: Archbishop of St. Andrews, Primate and Lord Treasurer.

Kathy: A kitchen-maid of St. Salvator's College, St. Andrews.

Gilbert Ogilvy: Prior of Restenneth. A son of the 1st Lord Ogilvy.

Cecille de Sancerres: Wife of the Chamberlain of Auvergne. Mistress of Albany—and of David Beaton.

KING LOUIS THE TWELFTH: King of France.

MARY TUDOR: Youthful Queen of France, Sister of Henry the Eighth.

FRANCIS DE VALOIS: Count of Angoulême. Later King Francis the First.

JOHN STEWART, DUKE OF ALBANY: Grandson of James the Second of Scots. Regent of Scotland.

SIEUR ANTHONY DE LA BASTIE: French knight. Lieutenant of the Regent.

Elizabeth Graham: Prioress of Lunan.

LADY MARION OGILVY: Daughter of 1st Lord Ogilvy of Airlie.

ARCHIBALD DOUGLAS, 6th EARL OF ANGUS: Husband of the Queen-Mother. Chief of the English party in Scotland.

WILLIAM DOUGLAS: Prior of Coldinghame, Angus's uncle.

GAVIN DUNBAR: Archbishop of Glasgow. Tutor to the boy King James.

JAMES HAMILTON, 2nd EARL OF ARRAN: Lieutenant-Governor of the realm. Second heir to the throne.

KING JAMES THE FIFTH: A boy of twelve, son of James the Fourth (killed at Flodden), by Queen Margaret Tudor.

QUEEN MARGARET TUDOR: The Queen-Mother, widow of James the Fourth and sister of Henry the Eighth. Married to Angus.

HENRY STEWART OF METHVEN: Later Lord. Now Treasurer. Later married the Queen-Mother.

Patrick Barclay of Collairnie: An Archiepiscopal Chamberlain. Later Secretary to David Beaton.

JOHN STEWART, 3rd EARL OF LENNOX: Powerful non-royal Stewart, but himself descended from a Stewart princess. Loyalist.

SIR JAMES HAMILTON OF FINNART: Bastard son of Earl of Arran.

PATRICK HAMILTON: Lay Abbot of Ferne. Burned for heresy.

MASTER ROBERT CAIRNCROSS: Abbot of Holyrood. Lord Treasurer.

CHARLES DE GUISE: Cardinal of Lorraine.

MARY DE BOURBON: Daughter of Duke of Vendôme. Prospective bride for King James the Fifth.

MARY DE GUISE, DUCHESS OF LONGUEVILLE: Sister of Cardinal of Lorraine. Later married James the Fifth.

PRINCESS MADELEINE DE VALOIS: Daughter of King Francis. First wife of James the Fifth.

JAMES STEWART, EARL OF MORAY: Illegitimate son of James the Fourth by Flaming Janet Kennedy.

POPE PAUL THE THIRD.

PATRICK HEPBURN: Illegitimate son of John Hepburn. Succeeded father as Prior of St. Andrews.

WILLIAM CHISHOLM: Bishop of Dunblane.

JAMES HAMILTON, 3rd EARL OF ARRAN: Regent of Scotland.

GEORGE GORDON, 4th EARL OF HUNTLY: Chief of the Gordons. Son of Margaret Drummond, illegitimate daughter of James the Fourth.

MASTER THOMAS FORREST: Vicar of Dollar. Burned for heresy.

MASTER GEORGE WISHART: Reforming preacher. Burned for heresy.

NORMAN LESLIE, MASTER OF ROTHES: Son and heir of Earl of Rothes.

JAMES MELVILLE OF RAITH: Reforming Fife laird.

PART ONE

Chapter One

THE young man, slender, fine-featured, almost girlish were it not for the strength of jawline, insinuated himself skilfully through the crowd, unobtrusively working his way to the front. In only a minute or two he had gained a position of vantage, where the Market Street of St. Andrews widened out behind the constricted arched gateway of the West Port, without actually giving offence to anyone, even amongst his fellow-students, many of whom had been waiting for hours, his shy smile, murmured apologies and diffident air contributing. David Beaton was like that, a modest-seeming youth who yet knew what he wanted.

He had not attempted, of course, to drag the girl along with him. She was not the shape for insinuating effectively through crowds, protruding in such notable fashion, front and rear, as to interfere with easy passage, and drawing attention to herself by her very contours, especially amongst the male section of any company. So, after hurrying up from the hidden and sheltered nook on the beach, beneath the castle cliffs, deserted this fine sunny June forenoon because everybody was crowded here in the streets, he had abandoned Chrissie — or Katie, was it? — abandoned the giggling creature anyway, without a word, behind the packed throng. He had no doubt that she would be waiting for him afterwards, when it was all over, in the tiresome way of women.

David Beaton saw that he could do still better, latecomer as he was. A little to the right there was a small shrine, erected to Saint Regulus who allegedly had founded St. Andrews, a poor enough thing of clumsy sculpture and faded colours under a canopy. But it was mounted on a stone plinth, and no one of the waiting crowd had had sufficient initiative — or sufficient disrespect for saints — to climb up on this. Edging along inoffensively just behind the front row of watchers, with gentle regrets, the young man reached this plinth and climbed its two steps. He circled a somewhat patched and threadbare arm around Saint Regulus, to hold his position, and so stood, fair head and shoulders above all, his prepossessing smile fairly effectively countering the shocked stares and scandalised mutterings of the godly citizens of St. Andrews.

He was just in time. He knew that, of course. He had heard the trumpets down on the beach, carried on the south-west breeze, and so had regretfully disengaged himself from the person of Katie — or was it Chrissie? — who had been really extraordinarily responsive for that time of the day. Now, he could hear the slow stately chanting of the massed choristers, punctuated by the occasional clash of cymbals, against a faint background noise of many horses' hooves on cobblestones.

The procession, evidently, was nearing this West Port gate into the walled town proper.

The throng stirred, and in the crowded street the Prior's handsomely liveried retainers, aided by the more drab college servants, wielded sticks and staves and the flats of swords to keep the press back and the way open for the cavalcade.

Beaton watched the stress and confusion below him with amused interest, as officious authoritarians manhandled meek citizenry. He moved his position on Saint Regulus a little, so that he was directly above a plump young matron who had been pushed there, and could thus look down pleasantly into the open bosom of her bulging bodice.

There was a pause in the singing and clashing, although shod hooves continued to scuffle and clatter beyond the walls. The four gaily-clad trumpeters, two on the top of each open turret flanking the arched gateway, blew a stirring fanfare; a single singing boy, in vestments, stepped directly above the archway, and his clear, high bell-like treble fluted the *Gloria Patri*; while the Provost of the burgh, fumbling with his chain of office, doffed his bonnet and then put it on again, and stepped out into the cleared space before the gate — to be shooed back peremptorily by a frowning friar in the grey habit of the Franciscans.

The music resumed, fifes, shawms and singers raising the sweet chords of the *Veni Creator Spiritus*, and the head of the procession appeared through the gateway. First came a troop of mounted men-at-arms in helmets, breastplates and the colours of the archiepiscopal See of Glasgow, swords drawn to push aside any inconvenient and presumptuous commonality. Then emerged the sub-Dean of the Cathedral, a resplendent figure on a led palfry, flanked by two acolytes swinging smoking censers of

9

silver, and followed by the first of the choirs, the choristers of the Cathedral, boys, youths and men to the number of four score.

As these passed, chanting melodiously, the young man on the statue raised his own not untuneful voice, to join them in the same strain and tempo—but very different words indeed, lewdly scurrilous in a high degree and no discreet note. Askance and protesting, all around who heard turned reproachful or angry glances—although a few of the younger folk and students sniggered guiltily.

But Beaton's expression was so inoffensive, almost rapt, his beardless delicate features so at odds with the blended subtleties and crudities of his psalmody, that folk somehow had to accept the intervention as essentially harmless, mere high spirits. Even one of the Prior's monks near by, in the white robe of the Augustinians, after eyeing the youth sharply, turned a shoulder and looked heedfully elsewhere.

After a bevy of musicians came a column of Augustin friars; then two stave-bearers, one carrying a tall brilliantly-jewelled cross and the other a heraldic banner, side by side, to lead on the magnificently vested, portly figure of Master John Hepburn, Prior of St. Andrews, Dean of the Cathedral and Lord Privy Seal of the realm of Scotland, mounted on a pure white jennet, richly caparisoned.

As the Provost stepped forward, to dip a knee to the real ruler of St. Andrews, the Prior waved him aside haughtily with a flick of sparkling beringed fingers, and the burgh's representative and chief magistrate retired hurriedly. John Hepburn's heavy-jowled pale face was wholly without expression. It was clear that he was displeased with the entire situation, and only there because he had little or no option.

Young Beaton eyed him thoughtfully, wondered if he should make a notably rude noise as he passed—and decided against it, on grounds of discretion.

This was because, close at the Lord Prior's back rode his personal bodyguard of highly armed retainers, Border moss-troopers to a man and as tough and unscrupulous a company as could be found in all Scotland, despite the fine silver crosses on their breastplates. And they were led by that keen-eyed and sour-faced bastard—legitimated, of course—the sub-Prior, Patrick Hepburn, who happened to be the Prior's natural son and designated eventually to succeed him in this the richest priory in all the land.

Behind the Prior's array came Leslie, Earl of Rothes, who as Sheriff of Fife had to be present on this special occasion, with banner-bearer, trumpeter and men-at-arms, followed by a resounding company of the lesser lords, nobility and lairds of the county and sheriffdom — modest amongst whom rode John Beaton of Balfour, of ancient lineage and broad if not very productive acres, David Beaton's own father.

The young man did not seek to catch his sire's eye, but nor did he seek to hide his sweetly attractive features. As seventh son, he and the Laird of Balfour had little in common save blood and an appreciation of reproductive activities.

After the nobility and gentry rode a single proud figure carrying a great banner that streamed gallantly in the breeze, larger than any other in that cavalcade. This was Sir Andrew Learmonth, Standard-Bearer and Archiepiscopal Secretary to His Beatitude Alexander, Archbishop of St. Andrews, Primate of all Scotland, and recently appointed Chancellor and chief minister of the realm. It was understandable by all, of course, that the Archbishop himself could not be present. He was busy in Edinburgh, with the King, at the new Palace of Holyroodhouse, planning the great invasion of England, projected for this autumn of 1513, once the harvest was safely in — a most necessary activity for the Chancellor if less so for the Primate. Moreover, it would not have been entirely suitable that he should have been present today, in the circumstances; the Archbishop Alexander Stewart was, after all, younger even than David Beaton, little more than a boy, and not in holy orders. Precedence would almost certainly have reared its awkward head and created problems, for as well as being Archbishop, Primate and Chancellor, the youthful Alexander was, of course, the favourite child, albeit out-of-wedlock, of that loving and beloved monarch, James the Fourth, King of Scots. So his standards alone graced this auspicious occasion.

Finally, after a further galaxy of trumpeters, heralds and officers, lay and ecclesiastic, had clattered through the West Port arch, came an extraordinary and magnificent two-horse litter, something like a great four-poster bed borne on poles, hung and upholstered in crimson and purple velvet and with an embroidered canopy above. Lounging in this remarkable equipage was a gross, heavily-built man of middle years, with a round red face and lively black beady eyes beneath a tall archiepiscopal mitre that sat somewhat askew owing to the litter's swaying progress, gorgeously robed in colourful vestments glittering with jewels and stiff with gold. Every now and again he raised a coped arm and two fingers that sparkled with diamonds, to sketch a limp cross, by way of benediction, right and left, upon the folk who knelt in the filth and garbage of the street at his passing, a languid gesture so much at variance with the small darting black eyes. The Archbishop of Glasgow, foremost prelate of the land, though not Primate, whatever else he might be, was not languid by disposition. Apostolic Protonotary, Abbot of Dunfermline, Arbroath and Kilwinning, Lord High Treasurer of the Kingdom, and the richest man in Scotland, but even so coveter of St. Andrews, the Primacy and a cardinal's hat, he was James Beaton, younger brother of the Laird of Balfour, and own uncle of the youth with the arm round Saint Regulus.

David, of course, could not kneel for the apostolic blessing, as did all around him. He contended himself with smiling beatifically instead.

"Mountebank!" he murmured, as though repeating an orison. "Puffed-up toad! Bloated bladder, wind-bag, boy-ravisher, skinflint — God reward and roast you! God guide thy steps to hell! Amen!" That was said, however, entirely without a trace of malice.

The Provost edged forward again, on his knees this time, found that to be quite impracticable, rose to his feet and advanced towards the litter bent double, mumbling, there to proffer an illuminated scroll of welcome to the Archbishop, without so much as raising his eyes to the imposing conveyance. In consequence, he did not hold up the scroll sufficiently high — and the prelate was certainly not the man to bestir himself, lean over and fish for any such offering, or even to have the litter halted for the purpose. The town's representative therefore, had to run alongside the equipage, seeking to keep his head suitably lowered, even to cross himself repeatedly, bonnet in hand, at the same time as holding the parchment, higher and higher, until at length it reached a position where James Beaton's beringed cross-signing fingers could collect it, without his having to change his lounging position, to drop it thereafter into the well of the litter without a further glance.

From the plinth of the nearby statue a peal of silvery laughter rang out, uninhibited and clear above the muttered Aves and reverences of the kneeling crowd. The Archbishop swiftly raised those black darting eyes to meet the amused regard of his nephew. He showed no recognition, made no sign, not even a change of expression. As the litter passed on its way, the breeze off the North Sea, funnelled down between a gap in the tall houses, whisked sufficient of the archiepiscopal vestments aside to reveal to the sharp-sighted that its wearer was also clad in steel armour beneath.

The final troop of men-at-arms, in the See of Glasgow colours, rode in through the gateway. Holy Church was come, in its fullest authority, this day of Corpus Christi 1513, in accordance with the royal command, to seek divine blessing and favour on the projected English adventure, here in St. Andrews the ecclesiastical metropolis of Scotland. King James, romantic, chivalrous and headstrong, had yet an almost superstitious regard for religious niceties and anniversaries. This, the 25th anniversary of his coronation, was to be the occasion for a great ritualistic assault on the Deity, on behalf of the war plans, where He was presumably most accessible — St. Andrews. And by the Apostolic Protonotary, not the boy Alexander, who, none recognised better than his father, was unlikely as yet to have achieved any particular access to the divine ear. But it was equally typical of King James that he found himself to be too busy preparing the plans of action for the campaign to be able to attend personally.

At least, it offered James Beaton an opportunity to cast an eye over St. Andrews again, and make one or two dispositions which might expediate his speedy return here on a permanent basis.

Behind the great procession the crowd broke up, some to surge after it to the castle, some to flock to the Cathedral to await the later service of intercession and dedication, some to go home. David Beaton found the young woman beside him promptly enough, as he had anticipated.

"I hope that you are suitably blessed, hallowed and regenerated, my dear?" he said, patting her shapely bottom. "Badly you need it. For you are, of course, a most wicked, immodest and shameless baggage. An utterly fallen and wanton trollop. Are you not? Bound for hell's fires!"

The girl, a comely and well-rounded wench from the St. Salvator's College kitchens, flushed and giggled at the same time. "Och, Davie . . ." she protested. "What like a thing to say is that?"

"It is the stern and undeniable truth, woman!" he declared severely. "As I am in an excellent position to know! I must say, I fear for your soul. If you have a soul. Have you such a thing, Katie? Or should it be Chrissie?"

"Kathy," she said. She had him by the arm now, and was drawing him towards an alleyway, northwards, between two of the high narrow timber-fronted houses, all overhanging gablets and dormers.

"Where are you dragging me off to, woman?"

"Back," she said, squeezing his arm. "Back to the beach, Davie." Her voice was low, thick and warm.

"On my soul—you are a hot quean! A very bulling heifer, I do declare! So soon, again? Does your mind, Kathy, never rise above your loins?" He shrugged, and smiled ruefully. "Mine now, at this moment, rises just a little higher! To my belly, Kathy—my belly. I am, in truth, hungry. Devilishly hungry, girl—for victual. Food and drink. Just now, I desire meat. Flesh, to put into *me*—not my flesh into you! And I have not a penny-piece to my name, woe's me!"

Still she pulled him along.

He considered her urgent pulchritude. "I am not so well-filled and rounded out as you, I fear," he observed. "Is there a moral here? A parable, perhaps? Here am I, with a mind, an intelligence above the ordinary, a soaring soul likewise. Learned in Greek and Latin, in logic and metaphysics, in philosophy and both civil and canon law. Yet my belly is empty and my bones protrude though my skin, and my skin through my clothing. Whereas you, my dear, have no mind, only a body. If you have a soul at all, it is firm anchored to your scut. You know nothing save what your natural instincts tell you. And yet you swell with fatness!"

"Och, Davie—you talk ower much . . ."

"You think so? Perhaps you are right. I vow I will from now on consider acting, rather than talking. Put my learning to some effect. Yes, indeed—I think so." The young man's fine eyes narrowed. "It is time, probably. But first, Katie — Kathy — I will start with you. I will make a compact with you. A bargain. You will fill up my belly, and I your . . . h'mm, your present requirements. We shall satisfy one the other. In that kitchen of yours, and then on the beach. But . . . the kitchen first. For the delights of the beach are scarce improved by an empty stomach! Take me to your larder at St. Salvator's, Kathy. I'll swear you can find the wherewithal there to stop my bowels rumbling!"

The girl looked doubtful. "It's the time, Davie," she objected. "It's no' the meat. Och, there's aye plenty meat. But the maniciple said we were a' to be back by the Nones bell — a' the maids." She produced another of her giggles. "We'll be needed for the castle."

"You will, will you? Sport for the visitors! Of course — St. Salvator's must not fail in hospitality. You are like to have a busy evening, lass — with benefit of clergy! I wonder that you are so hot for the like activity now! All day. But — save us, there's plenty of time! The Nones bell is not until three after noon. Give me but fifteen minutes in that pantry of yours, and then I am at your service until Nones."

"Haste, then . . ." she urged, hurrying him along North Street.

There was plenty of time, of course. Later by a couple of hours, they lay on a pocket of warm sand in a hidden corner formed by two thrusting bastions of the castle cliffs, only to be reached by scrambling. Even Kathy was sated now, flushed, lying asprawl, her ever exiguous clothing disarranged. David Beaton, beside her, idly wrapping a lock of her sweat-damp hair round his finger, mused aloud.

"Look at those terns, Kathy. Diving for sillerfish in the shallows. Bonnie critturs, are they not? Their bodies white as yours — if a wee thing more slender! Black caps too — though differently sited! But . . . they could teach you a lesson, woman. For they ken where they're going. See them. They don't drift and sleep like the gulls and the jukes — and you! They are busy diving for the wee fishes. All the time. When they're not doing the more intelligent thing still, and diving on one of their own kind that already has caught a fish — to make it drop it. Aye, and catching the morsel and swallowing it before it hits the water again. Now, there's canny, diligent birds. Not like you. Who give

15

yourself to any man today, careless of tomorrow. You're a gull, Kathy – naught but a gull. To be gulled."

She smiled sleepily.

"Most folk are gulls, of course," he went on. "Content to drift through their lives, taking what the sea washes up to them, or doing without. Myself, now – I am not like that. Would you name me gull, Kathy?"

She did not answer.

"Maybe I've seemed something gull-like up till this, I grant you. Maybe I've done what the others have done, drifted with the tide. It's not easy to do aught else when you are studying, mind. You canna go faster than your teachers and tutors. You're tied to the pace of the rest. Aye, I've had to do some drifting. As a result, I have holes in my hose, scarce a sole to my shoes, and not a penny to bless you with. But . . . I am going to change all that. From this day. Aye, I am. You watch me, Kathy, my trollop. Just watch Davie Beaton!" And he tweaked her hair.

"What are you going to do, Davie?" she asked, but lazily, trickling sand over his bare legs.

"Why, I am going to go catching fish, like the terns! Siller fish. But bigger – a deal bigger fish, Kathy."

She actually turned her head to look at him now. "Fish? You're no' going to turn fisher, Davie? You, that's son to a laird? With a' your book-learning? Would that no' be a wicked waste? Your father wouldna have it. He'll give you siller, will he no'? If you're that needing it!"

"My father will not give me one siller piece, lass. I'm his seventh son, mind. And he's not got that much siller, himself. Land, yes – but mainly stones. A castle falling down – more stones! 'If his son ask bread, will he give him a stone?' God, yes – if he's Beaton o' Balfour! With his quiver full, and eight daughters to find portions for! Na, na – I seek bigger fish than my father could give me. And not in the sea, see you!"

"Where, then?"

"In Holy Church, woman. Where else? The well-nourished body of the faithful here upon earth. The Church Militant, that was to be founded upon one Peter, Fisher of Men! Aye – that's where I'll do my fishing!"

"But isna that what you've aye been studying for, Davie? The Kirk? That's why you're here, is it no'?"

"Aye—in a manner of speaking, Kathy. I was destined for the Church, right enough. Like so many another needy laird's younger son. A living somewhere, and the cure of a few souls. But, after this morning, I have decided otherwise. That the Church can do better for me than that. Mind, the idea has birled in my head for long. But today signed and sealed the matter. Today I looked upon the *Ecclesia Domini*, the Church as master. And lost my taste, of a sudden, for the Church as pastor! Do you not agree with me, Kathy? Master or pastor? I vow I know which *you* would prefer!"

"I dinna rightly take your meaning, Davie . . ."

"A pity. Here it is, then, woman. I looked upon my uncle. My father's brother. A boorish and stupid man, my Uncle Jamie, of a low cunning if a quick eye. A hearty oaf—little more. And of a notable meanness. Sixth son of my grandfather, you'll note. Yet there he rode, in state like any king, jewels dropping from his crass person, an earl clearing his path, lords in his train, all of St. Andrews falling at his feet. Treasurer of the realm, high on the Privy Council, he was the son of a poor laird too—and now the richest man in the kingdom, so they say. If a stupid man can achieve that, at forty-three, what might not an intelligent man achieve? And a deal earlier? Myself, for instance."

His companion did not attempt to answer his question. Instead, her hand slid down his person, persuasively.

Gently but firmly he removed that hand, his eyes focussed far away over the sea that was no bluer than themselves. "Would you call me a fool, Kathy?" he went on in an even, almost dreamy voice, as though speaking to himself. "No? Then you would not expect me to act like a fool? Conversely, *not* to act, when the way lies open and clear before me, would be equally foolish? Almost you could say it was my duty. I have been given wits. It is my duty to use them, eh? To myself. To my Maker, who gave me those wits. Even—who knows?—to this realm of Scotland. For auld Scotland is going to need the wits of all her sons who have any, I think! Aye, before long. Do you love our Scotland, Kathy?"

"Eh? I . . . I dinna rightly ken, Davie. I mean, it's no' a thing . . ."

"Aye—you dinna rightly ken very much, wench! Save what your blood tells you. But even that should make you love the land that bore you. This fair, bonnie land, scarred with a thousand wars and deeds of treachery. But still lovely. Still lovelorn. Betrayed by so many who owe it much. Menaced by that vicious English hog, Henry Tudor, who covets all. Governed by fools . . . like my Uncle Jamie! Even her King — gallant, reckless James Stewart! A fond fool too, despite his great heart. A bairn, playing at war! Against butchers, devils!"

The girl sat up now, to stare at him, open-mouthed. Never had she heard David Beaton, or any man speak so. His dreaming voice had changed suddenly to vibrant harshness, his delicately attractive features tensed and twisted.

In a moment he was as abruptly himself again, sinking back. "Folly indeed!" he said, with a little laugh. "There are more kinds than one! I must be on my guard, eh? Walk warily. Watch my steps, and tread as a cat treads. A cat — aye, that is apt. The crest of our house, see you, is an otter. As a bairn I ever thought it a cat — for I never yet saw an otter. I have ever called our heraldic otters cats. So now you shall see Davie Beaton play the cat! Only — you shall not see it for long, Kathy — no' for long, you *or* St. Andrews. For this town and college will not hold him much longer — by God's Mother, it will not!"

"You mean . . . you're leaving the college, Davie? To become a priest? Is that it?"

"Who said aught of becoming a priest, girl?"

"You said . . . the Church?"

"The Church, yes. But did I say priest? Priests, I think, have too many . . . limitations!" And he ran his hand over her swelling bosom, smiling.

"Och, Davie — you talk that much! Siclike spate o' words. If you'd but speak plain . . ."

"Aye, Kathy — plain talk it is, then." He lifted to his feet, agilely, without warning, to stoop to draw up trunks and tattered hose. "It's back to St. Salvator's with you — for the Nones bell will be ringing any time now. Come — make yourself as decent as you may. If you would walk the streets with Davie Beaton — who is hot bound for high places in Holy Church!"

Without waiting for her, he started to scramble over the rocks.

He had to judge his timing carefully that evening — like all the rest of the operation; for all depended upon it. After the inevitable

18

banquet, which would go on for hours, not only would the Archbishop be quite unapproachable, but he would be hopelessly drunk. On the other hand, immediately after the long service in the Cathedral he would be weary. David cared nothing for his uncle's weariness – but being a man of gross habit, he would probably sleep for a while. And a man new woken from sleep, and dressing to preside at a banquet, was unlikely to be at his most susceptible to reason.

It had to be immediately after the service, therefore, when the weary prelate sought only peace and respite. That meant that his nephew must be waiting in the castle.

Gaining access to that great stronghold on the cliff top, one of the most secure houses in Scotland, would have been quite impossible on a normal occasion for any student, ragged or otherwise. But because of the arrival of so large a retinue and the evening's great feast, huge quantities of food, drink, fuel and horse fodder streamed into the castle, the drawbridge was permanently down and the portcullis up, with parties and groups of carriers constantly coming and going. Many students, having been granted a holiday for this day of intercession, were lending their services as extra porters, and nothing was easier than for young Beaton to join them. He entered the fortress, past the steel-clad guards, with a column of others, bent almost double under a load of hay. Once having deposited this in the stable-court, he had no difficulty in detaching himself and finding his way to the kitchens, where many extra hands were enrolled for the occasion. There he fetched and carried willingly, learning the plan and layout of the castle's interior. With a tray, a flagon of wine and two goblets, he diverted his steps eventually to a small garderobe in the thickness of the walling near to the Archbishop's chambers, and, hidden there, settled himself to wait. It amused him to perceive, out of the tiny arrow-slit window, that he was in almost exactly the same position as he had been two or three hours earlier, with Kathy, but perhaps some hundred-and-fifty feet higher.

There was no question as to when the Archbishop returned to the castle, the procession's approach being heralded once again by music. Eventually David was even able to hear his uncle's heavy tread on the stone flags of the corridor outside his hiding-place, the clanking of the armour he habitually wore beneath his canonicals sounding clearly. The youth waited for five minutes more, and then emerged into the passage, carrying tray, wine and goblets.

Two liveried men-at-arms guarded the Archbishop's door, but they evinced no surprise at David's appearance, and on his announcement that he bore special wine ordered by his lordship, they let him past without demur.

The richly appointed outer room was empty, but an inner door to the bedchamber was open, and David saw therein his uncle, sitting on the great bed, being helped out of his armour by a manservant. He waited outside until the servitor was finished, and James Beaton, in shirt and trunks, lay back with a sigh. Then, as the man came out, the youth moved in.

The servant looked surprised, glanced back at his master, and then would have taken the tray from the young man. But David shook his head decidedly, and raised his voice.

"My lord Archbishop," he said. "Uncle James — I greet you warmly. And seek your blessing."

"Eh . . .? What's this? What's this? The prelate opened his eyes. "A God's name — what's to do?"

"Your nephew, my lord. David Beaton. From Balfour. At your service."

The Archbishop sat up, frowning. "God's teeth!" he complained. "You, is it! What do you want, boy? Why are you troubling me? I am weary. Another time . . ."

"I shall not detain your lordship long. The matter is urgent. And private." And he looked at the waiting servant.

"On my soul! Here's insolence, by the Rude! How did you win in here, boy?"

"That is not important, my lord. What is important are the tidings I have for you. For your privy ear. The sooner you hear them, the sooner I may leave you in peace, Uncle."

James Beaton huffed and hawed, scratching at his great protruding belly. Then he waved a hand dismissing the servant, who retired quietly, closing the door behind him. David turned back after him, reopened the door, and watched the other pass through the outer door, before returning to his uncle.

"You are devilish wary — as well as insolent, Nephew," the older man growled, his little black eyes busy. "What's this mummery? Out with it."

"No mummery, my lord. And in this St. Andrews, it behoves a man to be wary. In especial if he is Archbishop of Glasgow!"

"Eh? Are you crazed, boy? Or trying to cozen me? If so, you tread a dangerous path. I warn you . . ."

"Dangerous, yes, Uncle — in thus coming to you. But it was necessary. A danger I accept — for my duty, and love of you, my father's own brother. And, h'm, my father in God!" David, having set down the tray, was pouring wine from the flagon into the goblets, both of them. He took one and raised it to his own lips, to sip, eyeing the Archbishop over its rim.

That man's eyes all but popped out of his head at this extraordinary behaviour. The small pursed mouth between the heavy purple-red jowls opened and shut as he sought for words.

David came forward with the second goblet. "You see — you may safely drink it, Uncle," he said, with his sweetest smile. "*This* flagon, at least!"

"What are you saying? What is this? Are you trying to tell me — me, James Beaton — that, that . . .?"

"That you are in danger? Aye, my lord, I am. But, of course, that is not new, is it? Else why would you wear armour under your robes? There have been attempts on your life ere this, have there not?"

That shaft struck home, at least. The older man, staring at him, involuntarily clutched his arms closer to his person, as though vulnerable. David was using those God-given wits to some slight effect.

"Drink this, Uncle," he went on, holding out the cup. "Since it is tasted, and safe. I brought it as token — that this night you watch for other wine, less certainly vouched for."

"Who . . .?" the prelate demanded. "Who do you speak of, boy? Who would do this? Seek to poison me . . .?"

"Need you ask? Who rules in St. Andrews? Not the laddie Alexander, love-son of the King, who we see but seldom, and knows not a brief from a breviary! Who *rules* here? Who acts behind the title of Archbishop? Who wields the power behind the Primate? Who would occupy his place, if he could? Who sees in the Archbishop of Glasgow the main danger to his hopes, the man who *should* be Archbishop of St. Andrews and Primate? Need you look so far, Uncle?"

21

"You mean . . . Hepburn?" That was but a whisper. "John Hepburn?"

"Who else? Prior of St. Andrews, Vicar-General, Dean of the Chapter, Lord Privy Seal of the kingdom — and your host this day! I think he does not love you, my lord!"

"But . . . but . . . this is madness! Hepburn is a hard man. And powerful. But — what is he? To aspire to the Primacy! 'Fore God — he is not even a bishop!"

"Were you ever a bishop, my lord? Did you not rise straight from Abbot of Dunfermline to Archbishop of Glasgow? How, you yourself know best! But with less powerful backing than Prior Hepburn. He is cousin to his chief, the Earl of Bothwell, that was Lord High Admiral, the King's friend. Cousin also to my Lord Home, the Chamberlain. Half the Borders back the Hepburns . . ."

"Aye. They are strong, damn and scorch them! He has great friends. But . . . how could this thing be? What good to Hepburn my death? Alexander Stewart, the King's bastard, is Primate. He is young, and of rude health. How does the insolent Hepburn think to step into *his* shoes? Tell me that, boy!"

"As I heard the plot, it was simple enough. Bothwell, Home and his other friends, to work on the King to give Alexander high office in the state. To remove him from the archbishopric. Make him Earl of Carrick. He is not in holy orders — so the matter is simple. King James, who ever needs money, only appointed him archbishop, as a boy, in order to gain the revenues of this rich see. Alexander cares nothing for the Church of the Primacy — he would be a soldier. And Hepburn, who is already rich, desires the power rather than the money. He would divorce half the revenues to remain with Alexander and the King, so long as he gains the archbishop and the Primacy. Is that not potent aid to preferment!"

"Suffering soul of God!" James Beaton cried, rising to his feet, to stride the chamber. "Here is Zamiel! Beelzebub! Satan himself, in guise of man! May he burn everlastingly — the cunning, wriggling serpent! Aye — and now the King *has* made Alexander Chancellor of the realm, youth as he is! I see it all, to my woe . . .!"

"Aye, my lord. You see your danger. But do you see also, if Prior Hepburn is outwitted, how greatly nearer to the Primacy you become, yourself, than you may have thought?"

His uncle halted in his pacing, to gaze at him. "By the Mass — you are right! That is true. A pox — you have a head on those bit shoulders, Davie, womanish as you seem!"

The young man almost frowned, but inclined his head modestly instead. "A family heritage it must be, Uncle!"

"Aye. Maybe. But — how did you learn of this? This plot? When none of my own people have told me aught of it."

"Oh, just a bit here and a bit there. A word in this ear, a hint in that." He was nicely vague. "I hear things, in this St. Andrews. And when my own flesh and blood is concerned, my lord . . ."

"Aye. I'ph'mm. And this of the poison?"

"That was but a rumour, a whisper on the air. There may be naught to it. But I deemed it wise to warn you. Even at some risk to myself — womanish as I may seem, Uncle!" His blue guileless eyes rose to meet the other's beady ones. "It may be some other method that will be attempted. Or on some other occasion!"

The Archbishop grunted, gripped plump fists, and resumed his pacing. "You have long ears, I perceive. Keep them open then, Davie. In this St. Andrews. And get me word swiftly if you hear aught else. I will see that you do not lose by it."

"It would be a pleasure, my lord. But, alas — it will not be possible, I fear. For I intend to leave St. Andrews. Forthwith."

"Leave? What do you mean, boy?"

"I intend to leave here," David repeated gently. "With your aid, Uncle. For my safety. And betterment."

"Eh? What's this? What's this?"

"In my, h'm, investigations. On your behalf. I fear that I may have made an enemy of my Lord Prior. No light enemy for a mere student of this college. You will understand my plight. No doubt it will be reported to him, even now, that I am with you. I fear that I have implicated myself. So I must seek your aid."

"But . . . are you finished with your studies?"·

"Far from it. There is much that I would learn yet, and must. But not here."

"Where would you go, boy? To Aberdeen? Or to my Glasgow?"

"I had thought of France, my lord. Paris. I should be safe from the Prior there, I vow — and could continue my studies to best effect. Paris the best school of all, for a churchman. Do you not agree?"

The older man snorted. "You fly high, on my soul! Paris,

23

indeed! Have you considered the cost of it? A deal of money would be needed to send you to Paris. I wager your father has more to do with his siller!"

"No doubt, sir. I had not thought of my father. I believed that *you* might aid me."

"Me! Sakes, boy — have you taken leave o' your senses? In this world's gear, I am a poor man. Aye, nourished only on the same barren acres as yourself, Davie."

"Is that so, my lord? I had thought otherwise." David's mild gaze was rather noticeably fixed now on the prelate's hands, where rings of diamonds and rubies sparkled brilliantly.

The other did not fail to perceive the direction of his nephew's glance. "These!" he exclaimed, waving his hand. "These belong to Holy Church. The . . . the trappings of my office. Holy Church may be rich. But I am not."

"No? Rumour is not always reliable, then? But, Uncle — it matters not whence comes the siller. Does it? Holy Church is rich, yes — and I, her humblest servant, need help if I am to serve her more surely. As I can, and will. In Paris. The Church owns half of the best land in Scotland — and more than that of the wealth. And you control a deal of that, in the archdiocese of Glasgow . . ."

"Tush, boy — the Church's goods are not to be squandered on beggarly students who would pleasure themselves in far places."

"That is scarce my object, Uncle. And I conjectured that the Church perhaps might feel some gratitude towards this beggarly student who has just much advantaged her greatest ornament in Scotland? Perhaps preserved his life."

"Ummm." The Archbishop picked up the goblet, and gulped down its remaining contents — David hastening to refill it from the flagon. He cleared his throat. "Holy Church is never ungrateful. I could see that you are ordained priest. Even though you are young, young. And find you a benefice somewhere. A small living."

"A benefice would be useful, my lord. For the expense of living. In Paris. But without ordination, I think. I do not seek holy orders. All unworthy as I am."

"You . . .? Damnation, boy — what has got into you?" the older man gobbled. "Not seek holy orders? Yet you would have the Church support and sustain you . . .?"

24

"I conceive myself as able to serve Holy Church very well outside the priesthood, sir – as many another has done. Holy orders hold certain disadvantages. Handicaps. Certain restrictions on a man, shall we say. With regard to women, for instance. I do not see myself as a born shepherd of the sheep, my lord. Unlike your illustrious self! I seek rather a different role in the Church's service. In all humility. And . . . in Paris!"

"The saints grant me patience! What sort of dizzard has John Beaton fathered! And why Paris, a God's name?"

"I have more reasons than one for choosing Paris to complete my studies. Good reasons, I think. Furth of Scotland, I believe I may best serve myself, the Church, even Scotland itself. And Scotland, I say, will be a good country for a young man to be furth of, very shortly!"

"What do you mean?"

"I mean what you have been praying and interceding about today, my lord. King James's projected invasion of England. In the cause of the Auld Alliance between his realm and France. I see only ill to come of this, divine intercession notwithstanding."

"You do, puppy? *You* see it!"

"Aye, Uncle – I do so. King James is a bold and gallant prince – but no soldier. His notions are of the tourney and the lists – not the battlefield. He dreams of chivalry and crusades. And for France's sake challenges Henry Tudor his good-brother. On English soil. Henry will not play at tourneys, Uncle. Henry will fight differently. And Henry will win. Because Henry fights for victory, at all costs – not for honour and chivalry and such foolery. Henry the Eighth is a killer, my lord. And the killer will ever beat the shining knight."

James Beaton was looking at the younger man with a strange admixture of impatience, offence and a dawning if unwilling respect, in those black eyes. "Go on," he said heavily, hoarsely.

"None will halt the King in his project. We know that he is dead set on it. The Queen has tried. Bishop Elphinstone has tried. Angus has tried – for his own reasons. Therefore it behoves wise men to look to their own situation, should there be disaster." David paused, suddenly to beam that winsome, heart-catching smile that was probably, next to his quick wits, his most precious asset. "Does it not, Uncle James? For myself, since the King is calling upon all young men in the land to join in this folly of

25

his, to march with him, I would prefer to be furth of Scotland before harvest! I have no desire to be a soldier. In especial, a dead one!"

The other's breath came out in a long exhalation. "So-o-o!" he said. "And Davie Beaton, bejant o' St. Andrews, prophesies disaster!"

"Why, yes. Do not you, Uncle, who are a shrewd man of action? Bishop Elphinstone who — barring yourself, to be sure — has the wisest head in this kingdom, believes it so they say. I am content to accept the good Bishop's view — in particular when it marches with my own! Moreover, so believes Prior Hepburn."

"Ha! You say so?"

"Yes. He tells his bastard so, the sub-Prior. What he learns at the Privy Council table, as Lord Privy Seal. And his son tells a peculiar friend of my own. Hence sundry informations of mine."

"Devil flay him!"

"Undoubtedly. But he is a man of some wits, seeing further than his nose. He sees that if King James suffers heavy defeats in England, there will be great changes here in Scotland thereafter. Much will topple. And on the ruins thereof, nimble men may climb! If they are prepared. John Hepburn foremost amongst them."

James Beaton was no longer huffing and protesting. He was standing at a window, looking out over the wrinkled sea, thoughtfully.

"My lord — King James is well loved. But if he suffer such defeat at the hands of Henry, there will be much unrest. And much hatred for the Queen, who is not loved and is Henry's sister. And the heir to the throne is a sickly, year-old bairn. As I conceive it, the man who is *next* heir would become of a sudden of much importance to Scotland. And who is he? John, Duke of Albany, the King's cousin, who lives in Paris. A Frenchman in all but name. They say that he does not even speak our language. Does it not strike you, Uncle, that it would be of advantage for the head of the Church in Scotland to have some especial link with my lord Duke of Albany, in France?"

The other licked thick lips, but said nothing.

"I speak French passing well," David Beaton added, modestly. He won a grunt out of the Archbishop. "So do many. In the

26

Church. Allowing that there is something in what you say of the situation, there are notable men that I could send to Paris. Abbots, bishops even . . ."

"Aye. But could you trust them? As you can trust your own flesh and blood. To send private word. To speak *your* private words?"

"Shrive me—should I trust you? For delicate work? A callow youth, scarce dry behind the ears!"

"Surely you must, Uncle. When the callow youth has for long kept close secret certain knowledge. Knowledge, which if known to sundry other folk would grievously prejudice the position and good name of my lord Archbishop of Glasgow."

"Eh? What . . . what are you saying, boy?"

"I think particularly of an occasion four years back. When as Abbot of Dunfermline and Bishop-elect of Galloway, you preferred and sought the archbishopric. Sought the aid of the Earl of Angus, leader of the English faction, in gaining it. When Archbishop Blackadder died. I was but a laddie then—thirteen years. And small. I am not of large build, even now. But with long ears. And so could hide behind the arras in the laird's private chamber at Balfour Castle. When you had my father act for you. With the Lord Gray acting for his friend Angus. Och, I mind it all, fine."

James Beacon came to sit down heavily on the bed again, lips moving wordlessly.

His nephew came and sat beside him companionably, confidentially. "I mind you were to join the English faction. And moreover grant to Angus certain Clydesdale lands including the Priory of Blantyre, in the archdiocese of Glasgow, should you gain the archbishopric. With his aid. Other matters too my father offered, on your behalf. To excellent effect, I think—since gain it all you did!" He laughed. "Even as a laddie I was much excited. I could scarce keep from crying out, I mind—to hear such great matters discussed in my own house. So you see, Uncle, how well you can trust me, your loving nephew. That I have never opened my lips on the matter in all these years."

The Archbishop emitted an odd sound, midway between a curse, a prayer and a strangled groan.

"Do you not commend my judgement, my good lord? That I held my tongue. And still hold my tongue. Save to you. After all, if, let us say, the Prior Hepburn was to hear of such a compact, would he not misconstrue it? Believe only ill of you. And in his churlish way, use it to his own advantage. And your hurt. *He* would not hold his tongue, as I have done. Who knows who he would tell . . .?"

"Enough!" the other got out. "Fiend sieze me — no more of it! That is all by and done with. Long ago. Angus Bell-the-Cat is a traitor, and I want none of him. It was a mistake. I was misled as to his intentions . . ."

"Precisely, Uncle. I am sure of it. And your secret, as I say, is safe with me. Especially in Paris. Where I study to serve you, and Holy Church — aye, and Scotland too — with all my heart. And with some small benefice, that I may be clothed and fed as is suitable for the nephew of so illustrious a prelate. Nothing large — not yet. Nothing so fine as a sub-priory, like Hepburn's son. Or even a sub-deanery. Just perhaps a chantry. Or a small rectory. I am sure that Glasgow has hundreds such in its gift. Is it agreed, my lord?"

The seconds ticked past on the handsome chronometer by the four-poster bed, and David Beaton swung his slim legs in their tattered long hose in time to their passing, encouragingly smiling to his purple-visaged relative.

"Aye," the other said, at last. "So be it. *Necessitas non habet legem!*"

"Amen," the young man nodded. "*Bona si sua nôrint!* I vow you have struck the best bargain that the archdiocese of Glasgow has ever made!"

Chapter Two

DAVID BEATON trotted his fine bay mare down between the rolling dusty chalk hills into the town of Dieppe on a golden morning of early November 1514, his servant at his heels. He hummed a tuneful melody as he rode, smiling and giving friendly *bon jour* to such citizens as he passed, especially the women. Nor did he fail to gain suitably gratified acknowledgements in return from the good folk — for it was not every day than an obvious gentleman of position, young and of considerable attractiveness —

28

once again, especially to women — troubled to notice and smile upon ordinary folk, in particular a young gentleman so well turned out as this.

David was notably well-dressed, without being flashy or gaudy, in doublet and breeches of good mulberry worsted, the doublet with silver buttons and stand-up collar framing a small lace ruff. He wore a short cloak of mulberry velvet, lined with crimson taffeta, long riding-boots of soft leather and a slender sword. On his fair wavy hair he wore a flat cap of the same colour, with a single glowing jewel in a golden clasp, and round his neck a plain small crucifix of gold, on a chain — the only indication of his churchmanship. The bay mare he bestrode was suitably fine, a handsome present from the Duke of Albany.

With his well-armed and mounted servant behind him, and the led horse, he by no means shamed the University of Paris, of which he was still a senior student. It might be that he had cause for some slight singing as he rode down into Dieppe.

A number of ships lay in the harbour. At the waterfront David asked a mariner, in unaccented French, whether the *Jonet*, of Leith, was yet in port — to have the vessel pointed out to him, moored actually at a nearby quay. A shouted enquiry, thereafter, to the ship itself, produced the information that the passengers from Scotland had landed last night and were gone to the Coq D'Or inn, in the Rue St. Jacques.

At the hostelry, David, asking for Master Gilbert Ogilvy, was told that the Scots travellers had left, save only Monsieur de Rennes. This puzzled him, until it was conceded that Monsieur de Rennes was a priest, and the enquirer was led to a chamber to meet a youngish man, strong and square in both features and build, wary of eye, clad in clerical travelling wear, who admitted, in good Scots voice, to being Gilbert Ogilvy, Prior of Restenneth.

David bowed gracefully. "Welcome then, Master Prior — welcome to fair France. I am David Beaton, come to conduct you to the Duke of Albany, in Paris."

"Beaton . . .?" The other looked surprised. "You are not the Chancellor's nephew? The Rector of Campsie? So young . . .?"

"The same," David smiled. "I hope that my lack of years does not offend, sir?"

"No, no. Och, never think it," the cleric declared hastily. "I but looked for someone older. Without especial thought on the matter. To be so deep in a delicate business, so trusted by the Chancellor. You will forgive me . . ."

"Nothing to forgive, I assure you," David's laughter was silvery, unfeigned. "I perhaps look something young, even for my nineteen years. It has been remarked upon before this — sometimes in less than complimentary fashion! I have even had my masculinity doubted — although, see you, I think few *women* would make such mistake!"

"H'rr'mm." The Prior cleared his throat, in some evident embarrassment. "I would never . . . believe me, no such thought . . ."

"To be sure, sir. I did not dream it. Clearly you are not afflicted so. A trouble I find too common amongst certain of our good fathers in God! I rejoice — since we have two days' journeying together. And nights! To the Duke."

"Ah . . . ummm." Gilbert Ogilvy's honest features cleared. "Two days? Do we go to Paris, then? I had doubted, in the present situation, if that would be possible. I believed that I might have to meet the Duke in some secret place."

"Thronged Paris town can be more secret than some quiet country village, sir. We ride there openly. You to visit the good Master George Henderson, of the Scots College. King Louis will not object to that. Thereafter you will see the Duke, privily."

The other shrugged wide shoulders. "It is for your decision. The Archbishop said that I was to put myself entirely in your hands in this matter, Master David. You are close to the Duke?"

"Pleasingly. He is a worthy and excellent man — though something lacking in vigour! Not to put too fine a point on it, Prior Ogilvy — lazy! Of good parts and wits, but lacking fire, if you understand? A pity. My uncle cannot now write to him directly, under the new dispensation. So all communications to him come through myself. You see before you the humble link, therefore, between Scotland and her Regent, unlikely as it may appear. For the Scots resident envoy, Bishop Leslie, is watched at all times by Louis's minions."

"Extraordinary!" Ogilvy declared. "When Scotland laid down the flower of her land, for France and her ingrate king! It is scarce to be believed. After centuries of the Auld Alliance."

"Flodden field changed all. Here as in Scotland," David said curtly. "Great is the power of Henry Tudor. And his venom!"

He changed to a quick smile. "But . . . you had a fair voyage, sir? No trouble? From either storms or the English? Good. And my uncle? He is well? Of good cheer?"

"Well in body, yes. And of as good cheer as can be any true man in our unhappy and betrayed country." The Prior spread his hands, with an almost hopeless gesture. "But . . . wine and meats? Sit in, Master David. I was about to eat. Join me. You will be weary?"

"Not weary. I have ridden only some nine or ten leagues today, from Neufchatel-en-Bray. But I shall have one bite and sup with you sir, with pleasure. Before we set out. A moment, if you please while I see my man settled below." A quick smile. "One of the Duke's men, I should say — lest you esteem me more blessed than I am!"

When he returned to the Prior's chamber he brought with him more wine and food.

"So the times are ill, in Scotland?" he asked, sitting to the table. "Ever since wilful, foolish King James led almost a whole realm to valiant disaster, to annihilation, at Flodden, times have been ill. With the best of the land slain. Are they worse now?"

"Aye, worse. Much worse. You know this, of the Queen?"

"I know no good of Queen Margaret. I know that, scarce recovered from the birth of her posthumous child to the King, she hurried into unseemly marriage with young Angus, Bell-the-Cat's grandson. I know that, according to the King's testament she was Regent and guardian of the baby king only so long as she did not remarry. Testament agreed by the Privy Council. So that Albany was forthwith declared Regent of the kingdom, and summoned to Scotland. I know that she has divided the country, set her face against Albany — and also, of course against my uncle, as Chancellor . . ."

"Aye — all that. And more. But there is worse now. She has entered into secret league with her brother, with Henry of England himself. The plot was uncovered, just in time. She was to flee to England, taking the young King with her. Henry thereafter to be guardian and governor of the King and Scotland both! With the aid of the Queen and Angus. Foul treachery . . . !"

"But it is not so? It was discovered? Stopped?"

"Aye, God be praised! So the Estates of Parliament have set up a Council of Regency, to rule until such time as the Duke of

Albany reaches Scotland. To consist of the Chancellor-Archbishop, and the Earls of Arran, Huntly and Angus . . ."

"Angus! On the Council of Regency? After such plot?"

"Aye. The Douglases are too strong to be kept out — the sorrow of it! The young King is taken from the Queen's keeping, and held at Stirling Castle, under the care of the Lord Borthwick, a safe man. And Queen Margaret is under watch at Edinburgh. Henry, in his wrath, has sent Dacre burning and slaying across the Border, and five towns are in ruins, the country there wasted. God help the land where a babe is king! So — you understand why I am here! To show the Duke of Albany why he must hasten to Scotland. Forthwith, and at all costs."

David nodded, sipping his wine thoughtfully. "It is none so easy. Since King Louis made peace with Henry Tudor, and married his young sister, he is in Henry's pocket quite. He will not allow Albany to leave France. He claims him as a French citizen, a peer of France. He says that he requires his services here. He gives in to Henry on every hand — not only in this matter. The old fool is quite besotted with his child-wife. I do not think that France will long stand it. But meanwhile, Albany is held fast. He is not a prisoner, of course — but watched closely."

"Is it not possible for him to make a secret move? To win away by guile? He is Regent of Scotland, next heir to the throne. Scotland needs him to desperation . . ."

"No doubt. But, as I say, he lacks fire. He is not the man to stake all on such a throw. Moreover, he is well content in France. He is, indeed, more Frenchman than Scot. Born here, he cannot even speak our language. His mother was French. As is his wife. Between them they have brought him the entire rich province of Auvergne. Scotland, I fear, draws him but little. He sees her troubles as but sorrow and danger for himself. I like him well — but could wish that there was more of Stewart to him, and less of de la Tour!"

"God be good! Then what are we to do?" Ogilvy started up, his blunt and candid features eloquent with dismay.

"We must do what we can. Use our wits." Beaton rose also. "Never despair, Master Prior. There is ever a way round every mountain. If we use the heads the good God has given us. So, if you are ready, let us start on our way round this one . . .!"

As they rode southwards through the flat Normandy country-side, so much more bland than that of Scotland, so much less rugged, David took the opportunity to point out that they would follow, this first day, the bank of a river that bore his own name — the Bethune. His family, of Norman-French origin, had used this spelling, although custom in Scotland usually corrupted it to Beaton. This he felt impelled to reveal, when he discovered that his companion came of a still older and more illustrious line than his own — being a younger son of the Lord Ogilvy of Airlie, first lord but thirteenth of his line, and sprung of the ancient Celtic Mormaors and Earls of Angus who had long predated the Douglases.

It was Ogilvy's first visit to France, and he was interested in all that he saw, noting that everything was on a bigger scale than in Scotland, save for the contours of the land itself — the towns, the churches, the great houses, all larger, richer, with, conversely, the state of the ordinary folk still poorer, more wretched. Corpses hanging in chains at every cross-roads and outside each church, in particular concerned him.

David explained that these were misguided and presumptuous folk who clamoured for reform in Holy Church, smitten by the infection started by Wycliffe and the Lollards, Huss, Jerome and Savonarola. The Sorbonne, his own university at Paris, had recently taken a strong line on these heretical teachings, and the Council of the Lateran had decreed stern measures. Defecting and rebellious priests and monks were to be burned, of course — but burning was a slow and inefficient way of disposing of people, and the commonality were to be more conveniently, if less spectacularly, hanged.

Ogilvy stared at his informant. "But . . . for what?" he asked. "Is Holy Church hanging men for saying what all know to be true? That there is much amiss? Much ignorance and folly and greed. Did not the Council of Pisa admit this three years ago?"

"Aye. But it is one thing for a meeting of bishops solemnly to discuss the like in council. Altogether another for the common folk to shout it aloud at church doors all over Christendom!" He smiled. "The one is progress, the other anarchy. One of God, the other of the Devil! Not so, Sir Prior?"

"Sin is sin, and error error, by whomsoever propounded," the other said heavily.

"Ha – a dangerous doctrine!" The younger man laughed. "My learned tutors here would be shocked at such sentiments, Master Gilbert, from a churchman. I counsel you not to voice them, here in France."

"The great Erasmus himself says as much . . ."

"And Erasmus is now verging on heresy! I prophesy that he will be proclaimed anathema before another year's out!"

"He is the greatest scholar of our day."

"No doubt. But scholarship and true faith might here conflict."

"Did you say true faith or blind faith, Master David?"

"Let us say just faith, sir. For simplicity's sake!"

"I would not have thought that you were one thirled to simplicity," the Prior countered. "I would say that, young as you are, you are a man of learning, of intelligence. You cannot approve of ignorance in the clergy, of superstitious relic-worship, of the shameless sale of indulgences and the like? These direly weaken Holy Church, and should be put down."

"True. But put down by whom? There's the rub, Master Gilbert – put down by whom! The follies of churchmen are to me the greatest wonder on earth. Yet only the Church keeps the world from utter barbarism. This is undeniable. So at all costs the Church must be sustained, its authority upheld. That authority is being sapped by those who attack the Church's leadership. Reform must come from the leaders downwards. Not from the mob, upwards. That way lies disaster. Remove the foundations of the most noble building on earth and it will collapse. Rebuild it from the top and it will grow the more glorious."

Ogilvy eyed the other curiously, who spoke with such decision and authority. "You are a strange young man," he said. "So certain. Whence comes this certainty?"

"I would not name it anything so fine. Say that I see my way before me – a little further than do some! That is all."

"And you intend to go far, on that way?"

"Why, yes. I do."

It was Beaton's turn to consider the other man, as they rode on in silence. He seemed an unlikely choice to be sent on this secret and delicate mission, a simple, honest man, master of only a small priory in Angus, of no high standing in the Church, however lordly his late father. Moreover, speaking only a word or

34

two of French. David thought that he divined why he had been selected, by his uncle. For inconspicuousness, and on account of Bishop Leslie, the Scots resident at Louis's Court. Leslie was of the Queen's party, appointed before the Archbishop gained power as Chancellor. He was doing nothing to expedite the departure of the Duke of Albany for Scotland – the reverse rather. The arrival of any senior prelate from Scotland, another bishop for instance, would almost certainly have concerned him. He would have enquired, questioned, probed. But this undistinguished prior could visit the Scots College in Paris without attracting undue attention.

"My uncle has chosen no happy time to play Chancellor," the younger man observed, presently, changing the subject. "And on this Council of Regency. Holding Angus, Huntly and Arran together, I vow, will be a task to tax even supple wits!"

"Aye. They bicker wickedly. An unedifying spectacle for the realm. But the Archbishop has his wiles. He plays one against the other, and so, precariously, holds the state in some balance, from day to day."

"The state, yes. But what of the Church? Can he hold the Church, when Forman has the Primacy? That sly interloper."

"Forman is a danger, yes. A slippery snake. But he holds only the name and title of St. Andrews and the Primacy. The Pope could do no more for him than that, against the Queen and Parliament. Hepburn as Vicar-General, still holds the power. And the revenues. Hepburn I believe to be the bigger danger. But, there again, he has Gavin Douglas against him – Angus's uncle. He desires the Primacy, also. With the Queen's backing. You heard that he had gained the bishopric of Dunkeld? Hepburn wanted that for his brother. So there is much bad blood. Since Flodden, and the slaying of so many bishops and abbots, there has been such an ignoble scramble for benefices and high appointments as has never been seen before in all time, I do believe! It was execrable, deplorable . . ."

"But foreseeable," the other pointed out, reasonably.

"Eh? Should we foresee that men, responsible men, ordained servants of God, should behave like common hucksters?"

"I fear we should. Since they always do. Is it not wise to take men as they are, Master Gilbert – not as we would have them to be?"

35

"Are you not a wee thing young, my friend, to hold such philosophy? Or do your French tutors teach you that, also?"

"It was a philosophy that I came to, of my own accord, as a laddie, some years ago," David declared, but gently, modestly. "But . . . we were talking of my uncle. How he fares?"

"Aye. Happily, despite these place-seekers, the Chancellor has the support of the great mass of the clergy, honest, God-fearing men. So he holds Church and state, both. But by a slender grip. He needs the Regent. Scotland needs the Regent."

"To be sure. The pity that the Regent does not greatly need Scotland!"

Two days later, in mid-afternoon, they rode down into Paris.

Ogilvy was much impressed by the size and bustle of Paris, and the dominating proportions of the Cathedral of Notre Dame, although the narrow crooked streets and lanes of the old city compared unfavourably with those of Edinburgh or even Dundee, and the smell, lacking the clean sea breezes of Scotland, was appalling. He was still more impressed, however, by the premises to which David Beaton conducted him, in the central Marais area. Here, in the Place de Ste. Genevieve, they turned off the street into a private cobbled court flanked on three sides by the tall six-storeyed facades of what was apparently a single establishment. Servants came to take their horses as they dismounted, and their own attendant dealt with the baggage as though entirely at home. David led the way in at a noble heraldically-decorated doorway, with every appearance of familiarity.

This familiarity, however, took on a somewhat strange, almost furtive aspect, as the younger man almost hurried the Prior across a wide marble-floored reception vestibule, ornamented with statuary, and up a handsome stairway beyond, not exactly whispering or on tip-toe but sufficiently nearly so as to give an impression of being where they ought not to be. Ogilvy was beginning to question the situation, to enquire where he had been brought, when he was interrupted. From below, the sound of a high clear voice, urgent, authoritative, floated up to them.

"Dav-eed! Dav-eed! *Mon cher David! Mon ange — mon petit ange adorable!*"

A woman had emerged from an inner door down there, to come almost at a run to the foot of the stairs, arms outstretched. She was a magnificently-made creature, probably in her late thirties, all flashing eyes and flamboyant gestures, high-coloured, deep-bosomed, in a notably low-cut gown of the height of fashion.

At the flood of words, David muttered something, and turned back downstairs. Uncertainly the Prior paused, and then followed him.

"So you are back, my heart, my little pigeon!" the lady continued, climbing a couple of steps to embrace the young man bodily, with much vigour, to fasten her rich red lips to his, and so to remain, emitting mingled and smothered moans and endearments. Over her heaving shoulder, Beaton's eyes caught those of the Prior, in apology, even embarrassment. It was not often that either fell to be expressed by David Beaton.

When he could free at least his lips, he began, "We are just new in from the road, Cecille. Straight from Dieppe. A long journey. Today we have ridden from Gisors." All this in French. "Here is Monsieur . . ."

"How I have missed you, David, my heart! *Mon Dieu*, how I have needed you! Endless days, desolate nights! *Miséricorde* — how could you do it to your little Cecille!"

"The Duke's business — as I explained. But . . . here, my dear, is my friend Monsieur Ogilvy, Prior of Restenneth, in Scotland . . ."

"Ha, Monsieur — welcome! Welcome to the Hotel de Sancerres. If you are a friend of my enchanting David. My house is all yours!"

Ogilvy bowed, somewhat doubtful. All the spate of talk was beyond him, being in French, but the general drift of the lady's eloquence was clear enough.

"This is Madame de Sancerres," David introduced, in English. "Our very kind and, h'm reliable hostess. I tell her that we are much indebted to her."

"Hostess . . .?" the other repeated. "You mean — that I *lodge* here?"

"Indeed, yes. In the Hotel de Sancerres. Thanks to Madame Cecille."

The lady burst forth into a further tide, in which solicitude for her guests' weariness, care for their immediate needs, and demands for David's almost equally immediate attentions in her boudoir, were inextricably compounded.

When the men managed to tear themselves away, Madame clapped her hands, and immediately two liveried servants materialised, to conduct the Scots to their rooms, with voluble instructions.

On the second floor, David paused. "A pity she heard us," he said. "My room is on this floor. It seems that you are to go higher. I am sure that you will find it most comfortable. We shall meet again later."

"But . . . I do not understand," Ogilvy declared, detaining him. "What is this place? How do we come to be here? In this . . . palace?"

"I thought it best. Both convenient and safe, you understand. None will spy on you here. Cecille can be something of a trial. But at least she is to be trusted. And keeps an excellent table."

"But who is she? How comes it that we are received thus? I had thought to go to some inn."

"This is where I lodge," Beaton told him. "It is convenient. Both for the university and the Hotel d'Albany."

"You lodge here? You, a student!"

"Why, yes. It serves me very well. Cecille is demanding — but the rewards are . . . commensurate! And Monsieur de Sancerres is entirely accommodating."

"God's mercy! Here's a coil! There is a husband . . .?"

"Ah, very much so. All is most respectable. Cecille, you must understand, was a mistress of the Duke's. Monsieur is one of his gentlemen. Chamberlain of Auvergne, no less. The Duke has now tired of her — but they remain good friends. If the truth be told, she has tired of him also. Preferring myself. Meantime. Which serves us all very well. Myself in especial. I live here a great deal better than I could in any student's lodging-house, you will agree. And at no cost to myself. Other than some slight occasional weariness of the flesh! A small burden that, is it not?"

The good Prior blinked, and said nothing.

"And now the benefits are yours, sir. Here you will be both comfortable and secure. King Louis has spies everywhere — but not in the Hotel de Sancerres."

"Indeed? Is that so? When shall I see the Duke? And where?"

"That I must discover. It may require some arranging, you understand. Since the Duke himself is watched closely. His wife, you see, no more desires him to go to Scotland than does King

38

Louis. So that private meetings, even in the Hotel d'Albany, are difficult. Happily she considers me as harmless. Is even grateful to me, over Cecille. I will seek to arrange something with the Duke . . ."

They came deliberately late to the Hotel d'Angoulême, two nights later, so that the ball was already well started and all the important guests received. The royal coach stood waiting in the great forecourt, all others being banished round the back. David and the Prior arrived modestly on foot. Ogilvy's modesty did not end there, for he was dressed in most retiring, not to say drab, apparel for such an occasion, and not in clerical garb — in some of Monsieur de Sancerres' dullest clothes indeed, far from a glovelike fit on the Scot's square, stocky figure.

The King of France's Scots Guard thronged the forecourt, but David happily knew not a few of these, his countrymen, and they passed on to the great doorway with some raillery but without challenge, Ogilvy keeping his mouth shut. A paper, signed by the Duke of Albany, gained the latecomers easy entrance past the Count of Angoulême's major domo.

In the vast and crowded reception rooms beyond, Gilbert Ogilvy gazed around him at a magnificence undreamed of in Scotland. By the blaze of gleaming crystal-hung candelabra by the hundred, reflected endlessly in scores of great wall-mirrors, the wealth, pride and beauty of France seethed and eddied to the soft music of orchestras in wall galleries above, in a galaxy of rich wear, jewellery and powdered flesh. All the Court was here to-night, and many others, for this great masque given by Francis of Angoulême, heir to the throne, in honour of the man he loathed, King Louis the Twelfth, and his new young English bride, Mary Tudor.

The two belated and most humble guests made their unobtrusive way through the highly scented chattering press in the outer salons, engaged in the unsuitable business of inconspicuously gaining the more rarefied inner sanctuaries reserved by custom for the most important and illustrious. It was not too difficult for Ogilvy to pass unnoticed, being of unexceptional lineaments and a build that some might have dubbed plebeian; but David Beaton was a very different proposition, slender, graceful and so very youthful-seeming, of the sort of fragile good looks calculated to draw the speculative attention of men and the adoring gaze of women.

Twice on their way through the great apartments the younger man was caught up by determined ladies to take part in set dances trod to the synchronised music of the orchestras. On these occasions Ogilvy effaced himself amongst the anything but retiring statuary with which the rooms were lined.

The ornate entrance arch to the fourth of the series of salons was flanked by two officers of the Garde Ecossais, one of them exchanging a few words in braid Scots with David.

This final chamber was less crowded than the others. Moreover the groaning tables here had chairs drawn up behind them, and at these certain resplendent figures sat. There was more formality, less chatter.

Stepping within, David bowed low in the general direction of the topmost table. Ogilvy followed suit.

There was no mistaking King Louis. He sprawled on a special high gilded chair, facing down the room, a heavy, obese man with leaden eyelids and pendulous cheeks, dressed in royal purple but in a style more suitable for a slim twenty-year-old than a man who seemed at least ten years older than his fifty-three years. Yet strangely, although he showed every sign of dissolution, self-indulgence and decay there was nothing about him of lethargy and heedlessness. On the contrary, although he lolled there in ungainly sprawl, the sprawl seemed to be all physical, nothing mental. Indeed there was something undefinable, almost of tension about him. His heavy eyes never roved from a fixed stare.

In a shadowed corner, David nodded towards the monarch. "His Most Christian Majesty," he mentioned. "In a fever of fear, hatred and desire."

"Eh . . .?" Startled, the Prior looked at him. "Fear . . .?"

"Aye — fear first and foremost. Then hatred. Desire last. When he would fain have it first!"

"I do not take you," the other said bluntly.

David nodded again, this time towards that section of the room where the formal measures of a pavane were being danced. "Yonder the cause of all Majesty's troubles!" he said.

It was obvious to whom he gestured. Amongst all the glittering couples, one pair stood out for comment, the man young, dark, dashing and handsome; the woman younger still, a mere slip of

40

a girl, thin, wiry, eager, probably the youngest person in all that company and certainly the most vehemently alive.

"*Vive la Reine!*" David murmured. "Although, perhaps that prayer would be better said for her husband! He requires it, I think!"

"So! That is gross Henry's other sister?" Ogilvy commented. "A minx, I jalouse."

"You are charitable, as becomes your calling, Prior Gilbert!"

The new Queen of France was not beautiful, and of no more figure than a boy, but there was no denying her strong animal attractiveness, her almost febrile magnetism — a magnetism which she was at present directing fully and frankly upon her gallant partner.

"Our host, Francis of Angoulême, cousin and heir to Louis," David went on. "Smitten, would you say? Hip and thigh. An intriguing situation."

"She is vastly different from her sister. Our Queen Margaret."

"Aye — Margaret is otherwise. A fat slug. Or better, a white, slow-worm. Whereas this is a dark, darting asp! They say that she is insatiable — and I can well believe it. In that at least she is like her brother, bluff and bulling Hal! A notable family, the Tudors! Louis has been wed to her now for six weeks — and is but half the man he was! I would say that he is killing himself to keep up with her!"

The dance finished, Count Francis escorted his partner back to the King's side, where he handed her over with an ironic bow, the Queen seeming to relinquish his arm with reluctance. But once seated beside her husband, she quickly transferred her attention to him, leaning against him, stroking his hand, all but rubbing herself on his velvet and gold — an extraordinary sight. Louis responded with an eagerness that was as pathetic as it was undignified.

Francis of Angoulême strolled amongst his guests, back to a small table where sat a tall, thin elegant man in black and silver, to whom a portly cleric stooped and talked, with an uneasy admixture of deference and pawky familiarity. The seated man was fine featured, pale, with large intelligent eyes and a sensitive mouth, over a chin which but for the small black beard might have been weakly. There was a dignity about him, but also a langour, both unusual in a man of thirty.

"Albany," David mentioned. "And that with him is our Scots ambassador, Bishop Leslie – God rot him!"

Ogilvy looked perturbed. "Leslie!" he exclaimed, involuntarily moving back further into his corner. "The last man I'd have see me here!"

"Never fear – he will not look the road you're on, that one. He notices only those in highest places, and judges men by the clothes they wear! Myself, being my uncle's kin, he avoids in case smitten with the pox!"

As Angoulême came up, the Bishop backed away bowing, the dark man nodding briefly. The Count made some remark to the Duke, and laughed wryly. He glanced over directly towards Beaton and Ogilvy for a moment, before sitting down.

"He looked at us," the Prior muttered. "As though he knew."

"He knows, yes, does Francis. He is quite safe. Anything to counter cousin Louis finds him ready. He is Albany's friend."

"How am I to have word with the Duke ? Here?"

"Wait, you. We will manage it, in time. It must be done so as to draw no attention. Not in this room, I think. There are too many eyes concerned to watch. The King himself. The Bishop. And see that proud-faced beauty with the flat chest, who talks with Stanhope, the English envoy? That is Anne de la Tour, Countess of Auvergne and Duchess of Albany. I do not say that she does not love her husband – but she is Louis's best spy, in this matter."

There was another dance, in which the Duke partnered his wife. As the couple paced the stately rhythm past the two watchers, Albany inclined his head to the younger man and let his fine eyes rest for a moment on Ogilvy. The lady, in turn, smiled regally at David, her glance sliding over his humdrum companion as though he did not exist.

She was not the only lady in this inner chamber to acknowledge young Beaton's attractive presence. King Louis appeared to be past dancing, and this time his Queen was partnered by her rather stiff countryman, Sir Thomas Stanhope – who gave no impression of enjoying the experience. As they sailed by, her great glowing, hungry eyes found David's, and held them deliberately, unwaveringly, until a phase of the dance turned her back.

"You observe?" he said. "Even your humble servant!"

Francis de Valois was not dancing this measure. He strolled by, and as he passed, he threw a casual word to Beaton. "After this. A masque of sorts. In the Grand Salon."

They waited for a while, and then drifted through to the second and largest apartment, where a space was being cleared in preparation for a further entertainment. Here they took up a discreet position in another corner, and refreshed themselves from the bountiful provision on one of the laden tables.

Presently liveried menservants began to go round extinguishing most of the candles in this room, to the delighted squeals of protesting ladies whose modesty came promptly under assault. Guests flocked in from the other salons, and after a while there was a great way-clearing, bowing and curtsying in the gloom, announcing the arrival of the royal couple.

High piping music thereafter heralded the entry to the cleared space of an extraordinary troop of dwarfs and monkeys, a crazy crew, the apes clothed and the dwarfs naked, who proceeded to dance and caper in fantastic and obscene fashion to the wild fluting of three Pan-like figures, horned and hairy-legged. The largest monkey was dressed in purple and wore a golden crown, while clutching tightly by the hand the smallest of the female dwarfs – and was led by her to and fro at the run, in the lewdest pantomime and gestures, producing gasps and trills of excited and alarmed comment, loudest amongst which was the high clear laughter of the youthful Queen Mary.

"Only Francis de Valois would have dared this," David said. "He is devilish sure of himself."

The arrival of two young women wearing bishops' mitres, magnificent open copes, and nothing else, bearing episcopal croziers and leading each a bear on a gilded cord, produced further shocked acclaim and feverish argument as to its symbolism. It was while this was at its height that the Duke of Albany, sauntering through the chattering press, found himself, as though casually, at David Beaton's side.

"Ha, my lord Duke," the young man greeted. "Count Francis excels himself tonight, does he not?"

"I hope that he does not *exceed* himself!" John Stewart, grandson of James the Second of Scots, and now Regent of that realm, spoke in French. "Francis knows no moderation." He turned, lowering his voice. "And this is . . . our friend?"

43

"Master Gilbert Ogilvy, Prior of Restenneth, privy envoy from the Council of Regency, my lord."

Albany nodded, and with a raised finger signed against Ogilvy's incipient bow, dark as it was in this corner.

"I regret, Monsieur Prior, that I must greet you thus, like some furtive wrongdoer," he said, still in French, but keeping his eyes fixed on the spectacle in front. "Circumstances demand it, I fear. What news do you bring me from my lord Chancellor?"

At the other's flustered incomprehension, David intervened to point out that the Prior spoke little French, and that he must interpret.

It required no stressing, to Ogilvy, that what he had to say must be said briefly and succinctly as well as low-voiced. It was a strange way to deliver the message and essay the task for which he had travelled six hundred miles.

"Your presence in Scotland is desperately needed, my lord Regent," he began. "The realm is split in twain. In three, indeed. The Queen's party, and the Douglases, are wholly gone over to the English cause. And Angus, on the Council of Regency, betrays all to King Henry."

"I have told my lord Duke all that you have told me," David mentioned. "He knows of the general situation."

Ogilvy nodded. "Henry seeks to intimidate all who would resist his domination. By sending Dacre on savage raids over the Border. The land is defenceless before him, after Flodden. There is great misery and scathe. It is fierce persuasion — but effective. With some. My Lord Home, the Chamberlain, has been persuaded."

"Home!" Albany muttered, when this was translated for him. "Home I believed the strongest man in Scotland. Next to the Archbishop. The only man who came well out of Flodden. The King's friend. And he hates Queen Margaret."

"Aye. But he has been persuaded to the English party, nevertheless. His lands lie all along the East March of the Border. Dacre's attacks hit him hard. He it was the Chancellor-Archbishop hoped would lead the realm's defence, lacking your lordship's presence. The only experienced soldier we have remaining alive. But — he is sold to Henry."

The Duke tugged at his small beard, frowning.

"He is great with Prior Hepburn — who also was against the

English cause, formerly. But it is said that he now offers Hepburn his rich Priory of Coldinghame, and support, with the Queen, for St. Andrews and the Primacy. To have Forman put from it. In return, Home to be Chancellor in place of the Archbishop, and guardian of the young King. The Queen to be Regent again."

Albany shrugged at that, but made no comment.

"That is not all. Always there were two parties, the English and the French, playing against each other. Now there is a third. Arran desires the Regency also . . ."

"Arran!" That was David Beaton.

"Arran, yes — chief of the Hamiltons. He is also in cousinship to the young King, next heir after the Duke. With the Duke's continuing absence, he sees himself as Regent. He is a vain and foolish man — but the Hamiltons are strong. And Scotland looks for strength today, to counter the English and the Douglases."

Even in that poor light it was evident, as Beaton quietly translated the gist of this, that Albany was now much disturbed. Rivalry from the Queen was one matter; but rivalry from Arran, the Duke's own protégé, was altogether another.

James Hamilton, Earl of Arran, was the son of the Princess Mary, sister of King James the Third; therefore he was, like Albany himself a grandson of James the Second. A cocksure man of no great wits and alternating energies and lassitude, he had been given command of the Scots fleet by his cousin James the Fourth just prior to the fatal English invasion, with the object of making a diversionary attack on the West England coast to draw away some part of Henry's forces. Instead, on apparent impulse, he had sailed off to Ireland, presumably on some project of aiding an Irish revolt against the English, and was still burning Carrickfergus and feasting with Irish chiefs when Flodden was fought and lost. As a result he had not dared go back to Scotland, and had eventually sailed for France and put himself under the protection of his kinsman Albany. Now, only a few months returned to Scotland, with the Regent's blessing, he had got himself into the temporary Council of Regency, and was, it seemed, aiming still higher.

"This is insufferable!" the Duke said. "How serious is the danger?"

"It could be serious indeed. He angles for Huntly's support —

45

Huntly to become Chancellor, if *he* gains the Regency. Huntly won over would leave the Archbishop isolated on the Regency Council. Already he has to take most decisions for the realm's governance alone. He cannot fight Angus, Arran *and* Huntly! They all have armed men by the thousand. He has only the Church's support. And Parliament's for what that is worth. If Arran can get Forman's support, the new Primate, then Archbishop Beaton is lost. And your Regency with him, I fear, my lord Duke. Civil war in Scotland."

There was a pause, while Albany digested these unpalatable tidings.

At last the Duke spoke. "Tell the Prior to inform his master that I will make every effort to come to Scotland. That I will use all diligence and despatch. But . . . it is most difficult. It will mean outwitting Louis and his spies. It cannot be done overnight. I am, after all, Admiral of France!"

"How soon, may I tell the Archbishop, that he may look for you, my lord?" Ogilvy persisted. "For how long must he hold Scotland, alone? May not I give him some date, at latest, for his comfort?"

"Tell him that I do not know. Cannot say," Albany declared. "So much has to be considered. It is now November. Before it could be contrived, it will be no season for sailing the seas. It cannot be before the spring. But, meantime, I will send lieutenants. Sound men who know my mind, and can be trusted. From France, here. Anthony, I think—de la Bastie. Yes, I shall send the Sieur de la Bastie, forthwith. Tell the Archbishop."

"But . . .!" Ogilvy began, when David stopped him with a gripped arm, shaking his head.

The Regent, after a moment or two, strolled on amongst the now restive throng.

"Saints aid me! What good is that to tell the Chancellor?" the Prior demanded, louder than he intended. "Wait until the spring! Some Frenchman to be sent . . .!"

"Hush you, friend," David urged, drawing him away. "It is none so ill tidings to bear. Better than I feared. The winter months may bring much plotting, but little action. My uncle will hold out until the spring, I have no doubts. And de la Bastie is a good man. A soldier, with a sound head. Acting with the Regent's authority, he will serve Scotland well. And aid my uncle. Myself

46

it was who suggested to the Duke that he might be sent. Come — we shall gain nothing more here . . ."

Chapter Three

IT was David Beaton's turn to ride in proud procession into a Scots town that waited to do honour to the illustrious — humble as was his position in the cavalcade, on the face of it, even though he rode at the Duke's side. The waiting crowds in Stirling's streets knew nothing as to the identity of the modest-smiling slight figure so close to the long-awaited Regent — probably most took him for a page or personal esquire; indeed, even later, after the first reception at the town's gates, when the enlarged procession was welcomed before the castle itself by the Chancellor-Archbishop and the Earl of Huntly, as representing the Council of Regency, only two people were in a position to recognise the most youthful member of Albany's entourage — and one of these, at least, was less than agreeably surprised. Yet, had it not been for this unknown young man with the almost maidenly expression, it is probable that this eighteenth day of May 1515 would not have been one for Scots to celebrate at all.

Not all of Scotland was celebrating, of course. In a country so torn with faction and the ambitions of power-hungry men, such a thing was impossible. But at least the common people rejoiced in the long-delayed arrival of the Regent, in the hope at last of some stable and lawful government and authority — as did most of the representatives in Parliament of the burghs, the Church and the lesser barons and gentry. It was the great lords and the high-ranking clergy who saw little cause for joy this sunny spring noontide, and were conspicuous by their absence from the scene.

The Duke's ships had sailed up the Clyde into the harbour of Dumbarton early that morning, from France, in fine style, to the booming of salute guns from the ancient fortress. It had not, after all, been a furtive journey and arrival; indeed the reverse, Albany sailing, with flags flying and a flotilla of galleons in escort — the same ships with which Arran had absconded to France eighteen months before — as Lord High Admiral of France, with even French troops abroad to consolidate the authority of the Duke. And all this could be said to be David Beaton's doing, rather than John Stewart of Albany's—for he it was who had smitten the King of France with enthusiasm for the venture, for the revival of the Auld Alliance with Scotland, for the dream of a grand coalition of Christendom against England, allied with hatred of Henry Tudor. Albany, as ever, had been less enthusiastic.

If such a resounding reversal of the international situation seemed too much to accredit to any such slender youth, perhaps the aid given by a still younger and more slender person ought to be acknowledged—that of Mary Tudor, Queen of France. For, of course, that aggressively sensual sister of King Henry had in fact struck a major blow at her brother's cause by wearing away her ageing husband to his grave after only three months of hectic matrimony. The dashing Francis of Angoulême had thereupon become King Francis the First, and the way was cleared for a wholesale and wholesome change in the direction of French policies. David had thereafter made the most of his opportunities. Already on good terms with Francis, who was but little older than himself, his intimacy with the Duke, Francis's friend, had ensured him ready access.

At the jousting-ground before the castle entrance, high above the steep climbing streets of the town, where the late King had delighted in knightly prowess, a resplendent company was drawn up to receive the Regent. If it was less so, and notably less elaborate than that which had signalled Archbishop Beaton's entry into St. Andrews for the Intercession at Corpus Christi two years before, there was ample justification; those days were gone, and times were out of joint indeed.

The Lord Lyon King of Arms signed for his heralds to sound a fanfare, and James Beaton stepped forward, flanked by Huntly and the Lord Drummond, Keeper of Stirling Castle. The Archbishop looked all Chancellor and little prelate today, dressed in full armour lacking only the helm, with but a mitre painted on his breastplate and the arms of the See of Glasgow embroidered on his surcoat.

"*Exulate, justi! Omnes gentes, plaudite!*" he cried, after a swift and doubtful glance at his nephew. "Welcome, my lord Duke— welcome in the name of the Most High God, His Son and His Saints! On behalf of our true and lawful prince James, King of

48

Scots and of his whole realm and governance, I give you greeting. Today, this auld Scotland of ours opens a new chapter in her long story. Aye, one she has awaited long, long. Pray it may be a bonnie one, and glorious, to the comfort of all true men and Christ's Holy Church!" And he rapped steel knuckles on his armour to emphasise his point. That was a long speech for James Beaton, who had never preached a sermon in his life.

The Duke, all in black as usual, bowed gravely, and then turned first to the Sieur Anthony de la Bastie, who had come to Dumbarton to meet and escort his master, and then to David Beaton. He nodded.

The younger man raised his voice, and in his most mellifluous and bell-like tones translated his uncle's welcome into French.

Something like consternation siezed the assembled company, as it dawned upon them that their long-awaited saviour could not even speak their language.

Albany made a brief and dignified reply, in French — which it might have been noted David translated at rather greater length.

This need for interpretation seemed to cast something of a blight over the reception, as eloquence dried up all round. The ceremonial was largely dispensed with, and quite quickly a move was made up to the castle itself.

Dismounted, and walking behind the group of principals, up between the outer and inner baileys, David found his arm taken. He turned, to discover Prior Ogilvy at his side.

"Gilbert!" he exclaimed. "Here's joy! I had not looked to see you here."

"Nor I you! A deal more wonderful, is it not? But — it is good to see you, David, nevertheless."

These two had become good friends before David had finally bade the other farewell again at Dieppe quay five months previously.

"I persuaded my professors to grant me short leave of absence from the Sorbonne, Gilbert. I pined for a sniff of the good caller air of Scotland again. Also I desired a word with my uncle. Madame de Sancerres is desolate!"

"I believe it! Her loss is our gain. But . . . you have been longer than we looked for in getting the Regent here? When we heard of the death of King Louis, at the turn of the year, we looked to see the Duke speedily, all restrictions removed."

D   49

"Aye. But all the restrictions were not of Louis's making. The Duchess worked against the venture, to the end. She has not come with her husband, you will note. Albany himself was loth to move. And when he heard that Arran had indeed risen in arms against Angus and the Douglases, he took it that they would destroy each the other, and that my uncle therefore would more readily ride the storm between them. It required all my efforts to move him. Indeed, it was more King Francis whom I moved, in the end, than our Regent!"

Ogilvy shook his head. "That scarce augers well for Scotland, then. For a strong hand is needed here."

"Is Anthony de la Bastie not proving his worth?"

"He is a bonnie fighter, yes. In many ways he has already become as the Chancellor's right hand. But, being a stranger, folk eye him with suspicion. And speaking the language but feebly, he misses much, and makes mistakes . . ."

The Prior's point was illustrated there and then. The group in front had been endeavouring to converse, as they walked, in poor French and poorer Scots, the handsome de la Bastie seeking to provide the necessary link. But now Albany turned back, to David, speaking fast.

"My lord Archbishop," that young man said. "The Regent does not understand how it is that the young King is not here. He believed him to be kept here, in Stirling Castle. In the care of the Lord Borthwick. It seems that he is in *Edinburgh* Castle. In the Queen's hands. How comes this?"

"Aye, the Queen-Mother has him," James Beaton growled. "She took him from here. Contrary to the expressed will o' the Council and Parliament. It was ill done. She holds the bairn at Edinburgh, and will not give him up."

"But how can that be?" Albany demanded, when it was retailed to him. "*Took* him from here, you say? From this great fortress? You mean that the Queen laid seige to it. I see no sign of battery?"

The Archbishop coughed, and glanced first at Huntly, then at the Lord Drummond, and finally at his nephew. He looked almost glad of the young man's presence now.

"There was no siegery," he mumbled. "The bairn was yielded up. It was something of a mistake. A misadventure. My Lord Drummond here, the Keeper, didna rightly understand the

Queen's intent. Borthwick was decoyed away. Explain to my lord Duke, Davie, that my lord was misled in the matter. That he but intended to let a mother see her bairn. The Queen was ower sly for him . . ."

Clearly there was something here that smelt badly, and the Archbishop did not wish it uncovered. David made the best of it that he could, to the Duke. De la Bastie, however, chimed in with a more realistic if less comfortable version, in French, that set the Regent frowning and glancing around him suspiciously.

It was an unfortunate start to co-operation – even though it emphasised David Beaton's potential usefulness.

It was, as a consequence, some time before uncle and nephew saw each other alone. Once again the interview took place in the Archbishop's bed-chamber, although on this occasion David was summoned thither by the manservant.

The Chancellor went into action without delay. "I'll trouble you to explain yourself, Davie," he said sternly. "How come you here? I gave no instructions for you to return to Scotland. You are neglecting your studies. I didna give you the Rectory of Campsie to squander on siclike ploys."

"No? Why *did* you give me it, Uncle?" David asked, at his sweetest.

James Beaton humphed and hawed, and did not pursue that line. "You neglect your studies," he repeated heavily. "You are not yet of full age. You shouldna have accompanied the Duke without my permission."

"The Duke has found me useful. As I think have you, my lord?"

"That's as may be. I'll no' deny that you have your uses. In France. Here, it is otherwise."

"Even here I may make shift to serve you. In that matter of the Lord Drummond, for instance!"

"Yon rogue! I would have his head, if I could! But he has powerful friends. I may not name him traitor – yet!"

"Then his misadventure was not entirely innocent?"

"Innocent! By the Rude, he planned it all. Had Borthwick lured away. Brought the Queen here. We know it all – but dare not say it. That is the state our Scotland is in today, boy!"

"I do not wholly see this," David said. "Drummond is, or was, the father of Margaret Drummond, the late King's favourite

51

mistress. Some say his secret wife. Why should he aid the Queen? He hates her and all her house. The Douglases also. Because they caused the death of his daughter by poison, and her unborn babe with her. Who might have been heir to the throne, King of Scots now — if they were indeed married. Why should Drummond yield the young King up to his mother?"

"Not for love of her — for hate! He only *appeared* to join the Queen's party. He knew that she intended this flight to England, with the two bairns. *I* stopped that. It was his aim that once in England, Parliament would declare the throne vacant, abandoned. The supreme power then to be established in Arran. Either as King, or Governor of the Realm. His plan failed — but we dare not yet offend him, though he has cost us dear. So delicately are the scales balanced in this realm today."

"So! Then, I brought you the Regent in good time, my lord!"

"*You* brought him!"

"I did, yes. For he would by no means have brought himself! Or should I say that I prevailed upon the King of France to send him? With those ships and French soldiers."

The older man snorted his disbelief. "Faugh, boy — d'you take me for a fool!"

"No, Uncle. I take you for a man who must perceive well where his advantages lie — since the scales balance so fine! And of those advantages, I put it to you, the new King of France is one of the greatest. The King — and David Beaton! For I have the King's ear."

The Archbishop stared hard at his nephew, weighing, assessing. Although a man with his limitations, James Beaton was no fool — or he would not have been where he stood that day.

"By the Mass — you value yourself high!" he said, at length. "You'll need to prove to me that I should do the same, I promise you!"

That was at least a concession. David nodded. "That is why I am come back to Scotland. To further prove my value. To you, my lord. And to the realm. In more ways than one — for I assure you that the Duke of Albany would not be here today had I not laboured to have it so. If you do not accept that, at least accept that he intends his visit here to be of short duration. Of months only. That he intends to return to France."

"What! A pox—return to France? Now that he is come? Are you crazed, boy . . .?"

"Return, yes. After a few months. So he promised his wife. None know this but myself, I think—not even King Francis."

"But . . . but this is impossible! The Regent cannot govern Scotland from France!"

"His heart is there. He is an honest man, but lacking fire. He has no love for power. The pity that he should have been born to this position. But he has an excellent head. With strong men around him, he will rule well."

"If he is here! How can I keep him from returning to France?"

"It will be difficult. But it may be achieved. By returning *me* to France, my dear uncle. As your envoy."

"Christ God!"

David smiled. "I do not ask that I should be accredited Scots Ambassador to His Most Christian Majesty! Not yet, at least! It might look strange, while I am yet under full age, and still at my studies. But a privy letter to Francis to that effect will serve. Albany will agree. He thinks more highly of me than you do, my lord."

"This is beyond all . . .!"

"Not so. It is but good sense. Accepting what is in fact already the case. As I say, I have the King's ear now. But I shall need some authority, however secret. Hitherto, you see, my access to King Francis has been through the Duke. Now that the Duke is no longer in France, I shall require some position at Court— for kings are not to be approached by all and sundry. In especial, by foreign students! Since I cannot yet be Scots Ambassador, if you and Albany send me with some assurance of your confidence and authority, however secret, Francis will no doubt give me some sinecure appointment. To enable me to approach him readily. To the benefit of all. Especially of my Uncle James!"

The Archbishop was speechless.

"Is it not simple, my lord? You wish the Regent to remain in Scotland. He does not. You cannot command him. But Francis can. He is a French citizen, Admiral of France, and commands French soldiers here. The King of France can command that he stay in Scotland. The King of France must be persuaded so to decree. Can you send anyone, other than myself, who could so persuade Francis? Unknown to the Regent."

David did not wait while James Beaton moistened lips so much thicker than his own.

"Bishop Leslie, the present Ambassador, is a lickspittle and a pompous fool. Albany dislikes him and Francis scorns him. Now that the Regent reigns here, he should be replaced — for he is of the Queen's party. But — I would propose that he be left in Paris meantime. With the title of ambassador. While in effect it is I who fill the office. Better that than to send a new envoy, who would not be content to be but a cipher. Is it not so?"

The Archbishop found a hoarse voice. "Sink me — you are bold! Brazen! But — where's your proof, boy? You *say* that you are thus close to King Francis. How do you prove it? Why should I believe you?"

"If you do not accept the fact that I have brought the Duke here today, as proof, I think I can convince you otherwise. The other reason why I came to Scotland." He paused. "A more personal matter, Uncle James. Though now Chancellor of the realm, you still seek the Primacy? The Archbishopric of St. Andrews?"

"By the Saints, I do! It is mine by right. I am senior prelate. Apostolic Protonotary. Only the evil wormings of that snake Forman balked me of it, while I was looking to the needs of the realm, after Flodden field. But he sits none so secure, the viper!"

"That is true. But other than you think, perhaps. I have learned, through King Francis, that Henry of England has made a league with the Pope. Forman is to be ousted. Gavin Douglas, now Bishop of Dunkeld, Angus's uncle and the Queen's friend, to be put in his place and elevated to the Primacy. The Archbishopric of St. Andrews to be made pendant and subservient, for all time, to the See of York. And the English Primate over all!"

"God's death — no!"

"But yes. King Louis was in the plot, so Francis learned of it from his envoy in Rome. He suggested that I warn you. For the project is still forward. They but await the best opportunity."

"But — this is beyond belief! And not possible. For the appointment lies with the Scottish Crown, not with the Pope. He can veto the nomination — but he cannot himself nominate."

"He does not have to. The Queen nominated Gavin Douglas before, when she was still Regent. He was excluded from the office by the stratagems of Forman, Hepburn, and I have no doubt, yourself, Uncle! But the nomination by the Crown still stands. They have waited, in the hope that the Queen would gain the Regency again. But lacking that, they will act on the old nomination, declaring Forman's incumbency void. And you, Uncle — you, if you stand out against it, will be threatened with excommunication by His Holiness!"

James Beaton unburdened himself in a stream, a spate, of cursing, varied, comprehensive, imaginative, until his breath failed him.

"All this, I dared not commit to any letter, since it involves the Most Christian King's name, and credit with the Holy See," David went on. "I had to bring it to you in person. Forthwith. Do you now, my lord, doubt my closeness to His Grace of France? Or my devotion to your cause? Or my sufficient reasons for coming to Scotland?"

"No. No, not so, Davie. It was well done — aye you did right," the Chancellor agreed thickly. He was clearly much shaken. "Gavin Douglas! This is treason! He would sell our ancient independence to the English. It must not be!"

"Now that you are warned, it need not be. You have the remedy in your own hands."

"How can you say that? What can I do? A Douglas — and protected by the Pope!"

"It is simple. Arrest him. Not for this, of course. The Pope's name must not come into it, or you are lost. Arrest on another charge!"

"But what . . .?"

"What sins may a highly placed churchman commit that would damn him? Few indeed! Is it not so, Uncle! But there is one that would stain his name, were he innocent as a babe. Heresy. Have him arrested, my lord, on accusation of heresy, the new heresies of Erasmus and Jerome. Of the Frenchman, Farel. Who deny the efficacy of indulgences, relic-worship, and the like. The Church's most profitable practises. This is worse than treason, worse than the sin against the Holy Ghost, since it hits His Holiness and his friends in the pocket! It matters not whether Douglas is so minded or no — most men of intelligence are, to be sure! Accuse him of it. I have seen how it is done in France. Arrest him, hold him fast, and trumpet aloud the charge

55

— but do not bring him to trial, of course. His name will then stink of heresy — and it will, it must be, anathema to the Holy See. After that, Pope Leo will not dare to support him for the Primacy. Then he can be released, untried. *Laudate Dominum. Beati immaculati!*"

The older man blinked, and then actually grinned, in reluctant admiration.

"It is perhaps sore usage for a high churchman. But we are dealing with a traitor, who would sell his country to the ancient enemy. For such, no usage is too harsh." David Beaton was not smiling; indeed his fragile-seeming features were set, tense, almost austere. "Auld Scotland suffers from a routh of them!"

"Aye. I'ph'mm." The other looked at him, slightly askance. "As you say."

Then the young man was his smiling self again. "Forgive me if I forget myself, my lord! So now, Uncle, may I return to Paris and my studies, with your . . . your blessing? And a letter to King Francis?"

"M'mm. Aye. Aye. Davie — that will be best."

"Splendid! There is but the one other small matter — the question of siller! Being about the Court of France costs me more than the revenues of my living of Campsie cover comfortably. I must be decent in clothing and person, you will understand. I think perhaps some other small benefice would better the situation. Not *too* small. I would not suggest anything so fine as a lay-Priorship, for instance. But . . . a Provostship, perhaps? Or a rather more prosperous Rectorship? You are Abbot of Kilwinning and Arbroath both. Something there, perhaps?"

The Archbishop tugged at his chin, beady eyes busy. "I'll consider it."

"Yes, Uncle — do, I pray you. I plan to sail back to France in two weeks or so. After I have visited home, friends in St. Andrews and the like. If I can, by then, do so as better than the poverty-ridden Rector of Campsie, I conceive that your lordship's affairs and interests with the King of France will go the better!"

If the look that passed between Chancellor and nephew was not wholly avuncular, at least they understood each other.

The Lady Prioress's welcome of the two men was warm, even

hearty — but although she was unaffectedly glad to see Gilbert Ogilvy, who was obviously an old friend, she made no attempt to hide the fact that she was still more interested in his young companion, and by no means wholly because he was the nephew of her superior in God, the Archbishop-Abbot of Arbroath. Indeed, it did not take her long to despatch Gilbert off in the care of a rosy-cheeked nun, to interview his two sisters in some other part of the sprawling establishment, while she herself laid her hand on David's arm and insisted that he accompany her forthwith to view her peaches, nectarines and figs in the great garden which seemingly was the pride of Lunan.

They moved out, past sundry dipping and cross-signing maids and women, into the pleasance, sheltered by tall hedges of beech and clipped yew, by grass paths, trimly kept, and banks of spring flowers, to the magnificent double walled garden. Here, within a cunning arrangement of lofty, mellow, red-sandstone walls, set as a diamond within a square, the breeze off the nearby sea did not penetrate, and all was warm and fragrant and delectable, loud with the hum of bees, the cooing of pigeons and the scent of flowers and raw red earth. Two nuns worked there, with dibble and spade, their heavy habits cast off because of the warmth. Both were promptly flicked away, banished, by the imperious finger of the Lady Prioress, her hand removed from David's arm only for a moment to do so.

"You like my little garden, Master Beaton?" she asked, in a deep throaty voice. "A pleasant simple place, where it is possible for a little to flee distractions and perceive again . . . essentials!"

"Ah, yes." David nodded. His nod had sufficient direction to include a group of statuary in the centre of the garden. "So I see!" The group represented an entirely naked and notably well-endowed young man holding out an apple to a buxom and equally unclothed female, whose posture, smirk, and even the direction of her gaze, left small doubt as to her co-operative attitude.

The Prioress laughed aloud. "You must allow us poor cloistered women some small indulgence, sir," she said. "For my innocents, I name it Adam receiving the apple of discord from Eve. None, I swear, has yet noticed that there is no bite taken from the apple! Apt, is it not, for such a sequestered Eden as this? At least, so thought your revered uncle, my Lord Abbot, when I

57

showed it to him. Marry, my bun is still sore with the nipping he gave it that day!"

David smiled. "My uncle is a prelate of most catholic tastes!" he agreed. "No doubt you forgive him, Reverend Mother?"

"Forgive? Guidsakes — I'd forgive and absolve more than that! As becomes my calling and vocation!" The lady chuckled, and squeezed her companion's wrist. "Save us — it's hot in here!"

The Prioress's habit was of finest black velvet, discreetly edged with silver, and far from heavy. Nevertheless, she threw it wide open down the front, so that only the girdle of chased silver, from which dangled the symbolic bunch of keys, held it to her sides. Beneath was revealed a brief shift of white lawn, trimmed with delicate lace, which did little to cover a swelling bosom or shapely calves in white silken hose. She fanned herself with her hand.

David bowed in acknowledgement. "I burn also," he declared gallantly. "But not from the sun!"

"Hout!" She rapped his fingers with the ivory beads which hung, with the jewelled crucifix, at the other side of her girdle. "You are a liar, young man! But I absolve you also, like your uncle. Mind — I've seen the day . . .!"

"That I believe. But yesterday it would be? Or, equally, tomorrow. Or, indeed . . . today! Were you so minded."

Elizabeth Graham stood back a little, to consider him — and no doubt allow him to consider herself — the better. "You have a more subtle touch than the saintly Archbishop, Master David, I see! Is this what you learn in France?"

"I have learned a thing or two in Paris, yes," he admitted modestly. "But I started out with, shall we say, some native appreciation!"

"Aye," she nodded, slowly. "As well I'm no' a young quean — or I might think to seek safety outside this garden!" Smiling, she moved to link her arm in his again, and walked on. "Come — try your wiles on an old woman!"

"I have a sister no younger than you, lady — and looking older!"

"I do not believe you. But, go you on — you are going finely!"

The young man rose to her frank challenge. He was well used to attracting older women — but this was the first time that he had found himself in the position to play the man to a nun. Not that the Prioress Elizabeth seemed notably elderly or pious; thirty-five or so, he guessed, a well-built not unattractive woman, if a little on the strapping side for David Beaton. Moreover she had an undeniably rousing voice.

Gilbert Ogilvy had told him of her on their ride from Arbroath Abbey. She was the natural child of the former Earl of Crawford by the daughter of a local Graham laird – which lady had eventually married an uncle of Gilbert's own, so that to some extent they were connected. Being approximately of an age, they had grown up in fair companionship. What more natural than that the two young Ogilvy sisters, Janet and Marion, should be sent to her Priory of Lunan during the awkward years of adolescence, with their father dying young and the lordship of Airlie passing to an elder brother.

They came to a rustic seat set in an enclave of clipped privet, private, secluded, facing a fountain where water spouted and tinkled over bathing nymphs in marble. The Prioress sat down, and patted the seat beside her.

"Come, tell me of your France," she invited. "And of how the ladies there treat a young man with the face of an angel and the heart, I swear, of a satyr! How do they defend themselves against Scots Davie Beaton? Or do they try?"

"I find the French ladies kind," David admitted. "But nothing more pleasing than those at home." In sitting, he laid his arm along the back of the seat behind his companion, and his fingers came to rest lightly on her shoulder, within the open habit.

"God pity us – we are all the same!" Elizabeth Graham said – although with little of sorrow evident in her deep voice. "Though I had heard that the Frenchwomen were more . . . artful!"

"Perhaps they have need to be." Gently he stirred his fingertips over the warm soft-firm flesh of her shoulder.

"Ha! You say so? And you are young enough to prefer our artless simplicity?"

"To be sure. The true lily requires no gilding." His fingers crept lower.

"And yet, I think, you return to France? Did not Gibbie say? Shortly?"

"Alas, yes. To complete my studies. At the Sorbonne."

"You study more than women, then?"

"Aye – less rewarding subjects! Civil and canon law, both."

"You would be a churchman, then? Like your uncle?"

59

"A churchman, yes – but only of a sort. And not like my uncle!" he told her mildly.

She turned to consider his face, so close to her own. "What means that? James Beaton is a notable man – and Scotland needs him sorely."

"James Beaton is a blundering bull. Where Scotland needs a fox!" he amended promptly.

She stared at him. "And you? You plan to be that fox? In holy orders!"

"I do." He had not ceased to caress the swell of her left breast. "But not in holy orders."

"No . . .?" The Prioress was silent for a little. Then she nodded. "I see that I must watch well where I tread, with young Master Davie Beaton! Who sees so clearly where *he* treads."

"Is that a sin, Reverend Mother?"

"The seeing perhaps, no. But the treading could be – depending on whom you tread! I have a notion that you could be quite without mercy, boy. Ruthless."

"Only when duty made that necessary, I think."

Suddenly Elizabeth Graham shivered under his touch, a brief but comprehensive tremor of the flesh. She drew away a little.

"A . . . a gliff of cold air," she explained, slightly breathless. Then she laughed, and reached up to stroke the hand that stroked her. "Marry – here are deeper waters than my garden calls for! A place for the quiet shallows, is it not?"

"Undoubtedly." He bent, to brush his lips over her hair.

"Elizabeth! Where are you, Elizabeth?"

"Damnation!" the Prioress said, starting up.

Gilbert Ogilvy and a young woman came around the shrubbery into view. The girl was laughing gayly, but at sight of the Prioress and David her laughter died abruptly. Her brother's blunt features firmed to a sort of stolid expressionlessness.

"There you are," he said. "We looked for you. To seek your permission for Marion to come hawking with us. Along the cliffs. My man waits with a new gerfalcon. The ride and the sea winds will do Marion good."

"No doubt," the Prioress answered. "Though, Guidsakes – she looks well enough lacking that!"

With that verdict David Beaton agreed. The girl with Ogilvy looked very well, indeed could scarcely have looked better, in

60

evident health as in sheer loveliness, as witnessed her gleaming golden long hair, her shining cornflower-blue eyes and clear flawless skin. She was a slim, long-legged creature of perhaps seventeen, dressed not in a nun's habit but in a simple and plain country gown of dark green homespun, the close-fitting bodice cut square and low to show a clean white linen blouse, the full skirt shorter than was the fashion. Her features were winsome to the point of beauty, delicately but proudly moulded and chiselled, and she carried herself with a lissome straight-backed grace that caught the breath — at least, David Beaton's breath. The comparison between Marion Ogilvy's appearance and that of her stocky, plain brother Gilbert, was almost ludicrous.

The young man at the Prioress's side bowed low.

"Here is David," the Prior announced. "Master David Beaton, Rector of Campsie. And now also of . . . of Cambuslang, is it, Davie? Aye, Cambuslang. And sub-Provost of the Cathedral of Glasgow."

"Save us — all that!" Elizabeth Graham cried.

The younger woman looked at David with undisguised interest, but inclined her fair head only coolly, unspeaking.

"What of Janet?" the Prioress demanded. She had pulled her habit together again somewhat, but casually. "She more requires the sea winds than does this . . . this hoyden, does she not?"

"Janet is scarce herself this morning, I find. Some slight woman's sickness. She keeps her room," Gilbert said. "We must needs ride without her."

"In that case, since you two men now lack a female, I shall take Janet's place and come with you!" Elizabeth Graham laughed her loud throaty laugh. "The saints witness, I need that ride and sea air more than any! And Marion will thank me, I vow!"

The girl smiled, but still said nothing.

"It will be a pleasure, Elizabeth," Ogilvy said, but doubtfully.

"I go put on some clothing more meet for horseback. You too, child. Praise be — I have not done the like for years! I shall enjoy this day. Come, girl . . ."

As the women went off, Prior Gilbert shook his head. "Elizabeth was ever of a commanding nature," he declared. "Always she would have her way. As a boy, many things I suffered because of her cantrips. I never learned how to tame her."

"Perhaps you should have wed her!" David suggested. "Some man should have done so, I think."

"H'rr'mph!" Gilbert set off, stalking past the ranked and trained fruit trees, for the gatweay.

"Your sister is very fair," the other observed, coming after him. "And young."

"My father was thrice married," the Prior said shortly. "She is youngest of the family."

Presently the ladies appeared, well-mounted and dressed in serviceable riding-habits with thrown-back hoods and long soft-leather boots, both riding astride. Gilbert took the hooded falcon from his waiting servant and dismissed the man to go try his luck with the Prioress's nuns and their kitchen.

Lunan Priory stood in a small, pleasant and sheltered green valley where only a single bend separated the river of the same name from its confluence with the blue waters of the great sand-fringed Lunan Bay, some eight miles north of Arbroath, in Angus. The Priory, like Gilbert Ogilvy's own establishment of Restenneth, a dozen miles inland, was but one of the many such appendages of the princely Abbey of Arbroath, that was the second richest religious house in all Scotland. Thanks to the phenomenal piety of King David the First, that sore saint to the crown, four hundred years earlier, and to the bad consciences of most of his successors, fully half of the best land of the country was in the hands of the Church, so that in poverty-stricken and feud-torn Scotland, Holy Church was in fact relatively more wealthy and powerful than anywhere else in Christendom, the Papal states of Italy included. Of all, only the semi-royal Abbey of Dunfermline was richer than James Beaton's Arbroath, with its tens of thousands of broad acres.

On the wide firm sands of the Bay, which stretched southwards for an unbroken couple of miles to the soaring cliffs of Red Head, they gave the horses their heads, by mutual consent. Quickly their cantering mounted to a headlong gallop as it became apparent that no hanging back was demanded by the women. Even so, youth told — but David discovered that he was having to spur his hardest to keep up with Marion Ogilvy, who rode as though born to the saddle, bearing herself with the same unconscious grace and assurance as on foot. With lips-parted and glowing-eyed enjoyment, she raced, her long heavy golden hair, come loose from its fillet, streaming out behind her, uncaring for her habit blown back to reveal long shapely thighs. The young man, never better than a full head behind her, knew that he had never in his life seen anybody at once as lovely, vital and challenging, and promised himself that he would have her, whatever the cost.

They reached the cliff-foots near the tiny nestling fishing hamlet of Ethiehaven, some way ahead of their seniors, and laughing, drew up their steaming, quivering mounts on the climbing turf.

"You ride like a wind-goddess!" the man panted. "You are beautiful. Fairer than any goddess." It was not often that David Beaton spoke thus abruptly, without premeditation.

She widened already wide eyes at that. "Do not cozen me," she said.

"I do not. I would not. It is true. You are most lovely."

The laughter died from her eyes. "Why do you say this? Is it your habit, with women? A French custom, perhaps?"

"No. I but say truth. What must be said. Believe me, I mean it. I . . . I have to tell you."

"Why?"

He waved a hand, almost helplessly. Seldom had he felt at a loss, like this – and never with a woman. "I do not rightly know. I but . . . felt it necessary. I had to pay my tribute. Do you blame me for that?"

"Blame you? No, not blame. I only wonder at you. Perhaps I should not. My brother has told me of you. Of your popularity with the French – in especial the ladies! Even in the garden, back yonder, I could not fail to perceive your success. With the Reverend Mother! I should not be thus surprised, I see!"

David cursed inwardly. So Gilbert had been talking! Warning her against him, no doubt. "That is unfair," he complained. "My admiration, esteem, is true. Sincere. Do not judge me by hearsay. You do not know me . . ."

"Nor you me, Master Beaton! Your immoderate praise is only for my appearance – and on a horse . . .!"

They got no further before her brother and the Prioress rode up, the latter loud in her exclamations, reproofs and glee, railing at Marion as a baggage and David as disloyal.

As they mounted the steeply twisting cliff path above the

surging tide, Gilbert led the way with his sister close at his side or heels, while David had to partner the Prioress – and try as he would thereafter to arrange it otherwise, the two women maintained this grouping. The dizzy cliff-top track never allowed more than two abreast – and such two were never David and the girl.

The coastline of Angus, at Red Head, rises in sheer beetling precipices to almost three hundred feet of scored and pitted rose-red sandstone, sea cliffs as high as almost any on Scotland's rugged seaboard. Here, amongst the ledges and crannies of the towering crags, legions of seabirds roosted, gulls, kittiwakes, puffins and above all the great and powerful gannets, the black-and-white solan geese with their six-foot wing span and long pointed beaks. It was against these that Gilbert sought to pit his fine new gerfalcon.

Far and wide the glittering, wrinkled sea below them was spouting and boiling with the diving of the huge birds, as they plunged sheer from a height of two hundred feet and more at fish in the depths beneath. How they spied their silver quarry at that height, and managed to aim their arrow-like attacks directly down upon them, with the fish's swift movement and all the refraction of the water to counter, was not to be known – but it was an exhilarating scene to watch from the lofty perch. When Gilbert unhooded his gerfalcon, however, and prepared to fly the cold-eyed savage brute at the busy fishers, Marion cried out on him to let the bonny birds be. When her brother named her chucklehead and pigeon-heart in consequence, David found himself, somewhat to his own surprise, siding with the girl and pleading for the gannets. His unlikely partisanship was entirely unrewarded, either in influence on the Prior or sign of gratitude from his sister, while Elizabeth Graham hooted her scorn and declared him fraud and imposter.

The falcon, released, soared up and up in spiralling ascent, until it was little more than a dot in the pale blue of the sky, there to hang motionless.

They dismounted, waiting. The bird remained on high, not even circling.

"Tush!" the Prioress cried. "The brute's lazy! Over-fed. A big, proud bird, but dull. Like certain fat churchmen I know! Communing with heaven on a full belly!"

"Not so," the Prior objected. "His stomach has been emptied twice this morning, with swallowed tow on a thread, to make him hungry and angry. Give him time. He selects his prey."

When the gerfalcon did stoop, it did so without warning and at a pace to almost elude the gaze of the watchers, dropping out of the sky at over a hundred and fifty miles and hour. Wings tight folded, it flashed down past many higher gannets, to smash bodily on to a large white circling bird about a hundred feet above the waves, in a cloud of white feathers.

Out of the jerked open maw of the gannet, that died even as the air was smashed out from lungs and body, a silver-gleaming live fish was expelled also. This fell twisting and turning towards the sea—but it was left far behind nevertheless by its late attacker. For the dead solan and its killer, linked as one by talons deep buried in flesh, drove downwards at a speed little diminished from the original stoop.

With a great splash falcon and prey hit the water and disappeared beneath the waves, while the fish was still falling.

"Foul fall me—he's down!" Ogilvy cried. "Never have I seen the like. To hold on . . . under . . .!"

"You may have a kill—but you have lost your gerfalcon, Gibbie!" the Prioress exclaimed.

"No! See!"

There was a seething disturbance of white water a little way from the spot where the birds had disappeared. The gerfalcon still clutched the dead gannet and was endeavouring to rise with it, out of the sea.

"God be good—have you ever seen the like! What spirit! What a heart! He will never do it. That goose is twice his weight. Fifteen pounds and more. It is impossible!"

It was—although the falcon took a deal of convincing. At length the fierce predator, its flapping growing slower, heavier, appeared to perceive the futility of its efforts, and unclenched its great talons. But now it was near enough to exhaustion to have difficulty even in forcing its own weight into the air, from the clutch of the sea. Belabouring and thrashing, in possibly the first ungainly motion of its life, it went dragging over the surface until at last some larger wave seemed to lift it clear, and it was able to beat up into the air.

"The saints be praised!" the Prior said. "I feared I had lost

E

him." He produced a white bone whistle, and blew on it, thin, high and clear. "He is trained to come to this call."

But the falcon, trained or no, was otherwise minded. At first its upward spiralling was laborious, weary, but suddenly it seemed to regain its strength and vigour in the freedom of its own element. Abruptly it soared upwards in apparently effortless ascent, but in mid-climb swung off, approximately level with the cliff-top, in a swift side-slipping turn. It drove directly, furiously, upon another circling gannet, not diving from above but boring in from below.

Thereafter ensued a savage and relentless struggle. To and fro, up and down, in and out amongst the other wheeling, screaming birds, scattering them far and wide, the gerfalcon pursued its new quarry, never for a moment diverted from this one unfortunate fowl. Plunging, banking, darting, they swooped through the air, only feet separating them — for the solan-goose is no mean performer of aerial acrobatics, with enormous power in its great wings. All the other fowl of the air fled the scene in shrilling alarm.

Gilbert Ogilvy blew and blew on his whistle — for this was no way for a trained falcon to behave, especially as the contestants were drawing ever further away, out to sea. At last he ceased, sighing.

Marion spoke. "You have quite spoiled a bonny morning," she said. "With your killing and your hatred." It was the first remark that she had made since the falcon was released.

With real surprise her brother looked at her. "Why do you say that? Because one bird, that was killing fish, has itself been killed?"

"More like because all eyes have been held by yonder handsome falcon of yours, this past while — instead of by a certain handsome minx with golden hair!" the Prioress declared, laughing.

Marion flushed and bit her lip. "Not so, Reverend Mother. I . . . I . . ." Confused, the girl turned away.

David Beaton's eyes had not, in fact been wholly preoccupied with the falcon. Nevertheless he did not so assert. Instead, he mentioned, smiling, "From envy, *as* from hatred and the rest, good Lord deliver us!"

"Ha! Does that cock crow?" Elizabeth Graham cried. "A variable bird! A very weather-cock, perhaps!"

"That crows to great Aurora's self? Possibly."

"What nonsense is this you talk?" Gilbert complained. "Can you see my falcon? I cannot, now. This is bad. It looks as though I may have lost it . . ."

"You are well quit of it, then, I would say," David told him.

"Eh? How can you say that? A valuable bird. All the way from Sweden. With long training behind it. Enormous power. And a great heart . . ."

"A fool!" the other said briefly.

The Prior blinked. "It killed with perfect judgement . . ."

"For what purpose? Killing without purpose is folly. The gannets kill fish to live. You and your falcon kill for the killing. It was a waste of life."

"Yet you would not hesitate to kill, I'll be bound," the Prioress said. "Kill more than gannets! You cannot fool me, boy!"

"Life should not be taken, save for a set purpose," he went on, levelly, still not looking at the older woman. "I abhor waste. And wasteful folly. I said that falcon was a fool. It killed for no purpose. If it had been to fill its belly, it would have killed a puffin or other lesser fowl. Which it could have carried and devoured. It clung to the gannet thereafter, out of hate. Hate also is waste, and folly. It clung, even into the sea, almost to its death. Yet Gilbert praised its stout heart. *I* blame its lack of head! Then in further blind fury it turned on the first flying gannet it saw, not from above where it could have won, but from below, blinded by ire. And pursued only that bird, when others were easier. More folly, more waste, squandering its power! That gerfalcon, on my soul, is like . . . is like my Uncle James!"

As always when betrayed into one of these indiscretions, so seemingly out-of-character, David swiftly and skilfully recovered himself, concerned to put his companions at ease again. Smiling, he made the point that, like chancellors, falcons must weary of goose-chasing eventually, and return to their perches. If the creature did not come back to Gilbert's wrist, it would home in time to its loft at Restenneth.

Gilbert allowed himself to be coaxed away, but on the ride back, despite David's efforts to engineer it, no fine gallop developed back across the sands of Lunan. It was not until they had returned to the Priory precincts indeed, and the sub-Prioress had come hurrying to meet Elizabeth Graham with the news that Sir James Carnegie of Ethie awaited her to discuss the vexed subject of rents for his Inchock grazings, that the young man achieved his aim of being alone with Marion, by accompanying her, with the Prioress's horse, to the stables, waving away the stableman.

"I had to speak with you. Alone," he told her, almost hurriedly and with little of his accustomed aplomb. "You have held me at arm's length this whole day."

"Held you? Why should I do that, Master Beaton? Hold you, either near or far?" But she did not look at him as she said it.

"I but meant that you are cold to me."

"Should I be warm?"

"No. But . . ."

"You expect it of women, I think? Then savour the change, sir — for they say that change is lichtsome, do they not?"

He looked at her sidelong. He did not know why he had to go on, to plead with this chit of a girl. Never had he done the like before — wanted to or required to. It was not only her extraordinary loveliness that challenged and provoked his manhood; it was, unlikely as it seemed even to himself, something vulnerable, tender, and in need of protection about her. In their exchanges, heaven knew, she sounded no shrinking, defenceless maiden. Yet even in her restraint towards himself, her repelling words, there was nothing of arrogance, of cold certainty. Essentially he knew her to be warm, gentle and lacking something of armour. Without being able to put his finger upon it, he was aware that there was something about her which he felt called upon to protect. If only she would allow him.

"Why do you misjudge me so?" he asked. "Gilbert is my friend. Has he spoke so ill of me? And if he is my friend, should not his sister also be my friend? Is that so amiss?"

He seemed to touch her, there. "What do you want of me?" she asked low-voiced.

"Only that you do not build a wall against me, Marion."

They led the horses into their stalls and busied themselves with attending to the beasts, David notably more swiftly than the girl. He came to watch her in her stall, wordless for a little. "Tell me," he jerked, at length. "This place? You do not intend . . .? You are not thinking to become a nun? To take vows?"

68

"I have not yet decided," she said.

"No!" he exclaimed. "Do not even consider it. You must not! It would be a wicked waste!"

Surprised, she looked up at him. "Why do you say that?"

"Because . . . because it is not for you. You are too beautiful, too desirable. It would never serve. A flying in the face of God's providence, against His clear intention . . ."

"*Against* God? How can you say that—you, a churchman? When a woman takes vows, surely she gives her**self** *to* God. Chooses God, rather than the world."

"Think you God gave you . . . what he has done, to have you hide them behind a nun's veil and habit? You are one of the fairest of His creation. Created to give, not to hold back. To delight the world, not to deny it!"

Troubled, she flushed. "I think you forget yourself, Master Beaton," she whispered.

"No doubt. But is that so great a fault? In face of what *you* would do if you were to take this wicked step? You would be insulting your Maker, I say!"

"Is that not . . . near to blasphemy?" she gasped.

"It would be—were you to bury and mortify the finest gifts God has given you! He requires that we use our gifts—our endowments, wits, opportunities, abilities. Is that not our most acceptable worship? Think you God Almighty will discover mean and secret joys from seeing *you* closeted and shut up? Like the loveliest of flowers plucked and locked in a box to wither?"

She swallowed. "You are a very strange man, I think," she said slowly. "And a very strange cleric."

"I am no cleric," he assured her. "At least, no priest. I desire no holy orders. I can serve the Church better without them. But why do you think me strange? Because I would have beauty bloom and delight, rather than hidden to fade?"

She shook her head. "You are too clever for me, with all your words. But . . . naught is yet decided. We were sent here, Janet and myself, to learn knowledge and skills. To take vows only if we so elect. When we have had time to consider it. We are not true novices, like the others. Gilbert would have us become so—but I think our mother would not. Nor, I believe, the Prioress . . ."

"Then Gilbert is more a fool than I thought him! In this. And the Prioress has some particles of sense. As indeed is evident,

She herself, I swear, should have been a wife and mother . . ."

"And you made it evident that you thought as much, I swear!"
That was all but impelled out of her.

"Ha!" He smiled — the first for some time. "You think so? I but
played her game with her. A little. No harm in it . . ."

"Then I'll thank you, sir, not to play the same game with me!"
Marion exclaimed and, finished with her horse, made for the
stable door.

He caught her arm as she hurried past him. "Marion! Do not
spurn me. With you I do not play."

His clutch and her pace combined to swing her round, her
riding-boots catching on the straw of the stable floor, so that she
stumbled and all but fell against him. Quickly his other arm
went round her.

"No? Then unhand me!" she panted.

Swiftly he bent his head, taking her by surprise. But even so
his lips found only the corner of her mouth before she jerked her
head away. Her free hand came up, to slap his face vigorously,
and she twisted free of him.

Blazing-eyed, breasts heaving, she glared at him — and he
groaned aloud at her proud fairness, her desirability, and the
botch he was making of his assault upon her.

"Forgive me!" he cried. "Do not judge me too hard. You
send me dizzy, distracted. And my time is so short! I have no
time to be delicate. Do you not see it?"

"I see only that behind your fine talk you are but an oafish
libertine, after all!" she threw back at him, walking away across
the cobbles of the stableyard.

"It is not so! You must see. Heed me. It is all because my time
is so short. I cannot either say what I would, or say it as I
should . . ."

"That last is true, at least! But . . . time passes for you no
faster than for others."

"I sail again for France in three days! Tomorrow I must take
the road south for Glasgow and Dumbarton. And I shall be
away for long, long."

Something of the urgency of emotion in his voice penetrated
to her, and she slowed her walk, to look back.

"Tomorrow? Then — if your time is short here, your time with
the obliging French ladies will be the longer, will it not?"

"God be good—how can I make you understand? I cannot go away to France leaving you thus. Thinking so ill of me."

"I fear that you can, and must, sir . . ."

"A plague on it—can you not even call me by my name, girl! Just once—as we part for so long. Sir, you say! Master Beaton! Always this!"

She found a little pity for him, then. "Very well," she said. "I bid you farewell, David. Farewell, and Godspeed."

He calmed himself with a long sigh. "Aye. For that I thank you. Thank you, Marion Ogilvy. And, I pray you—do not altogether forget me."

"I do not think that I am likely to do that!"

"No? Then I can hope. You cannot stop me hoping. That you will come to think more kindly of me. One last word, Marion— hear me. Do not, I charge you, I beseech you, let them make a nun of you. Do not take the vows, by all that's holy!"

Troubled-eyed, perturbed, wondering, she looked at him. "Goodbye, David!" she said, and turning, almost ran for the house.

Chapter Four

DAVID BEATON slipped in at the back of the crowded philosophy lecture-room of the Sorbonne, making a minimum of disturbance. Only a few men noticed the arrival of the Scots Ambassador, and of these none objected to his presence. Many of them, indeed, had taught him until comparatively recently, all connected with the theological schools of the University knew him, most accepting him as a young man of liberal mind. Any difficulty had been in getting past the watchful men at the door—but they too had esteemed him a man of reason and broad views, certainly no reactionary.

The speaker, a middle-aged, powerfully built man of leonine head and vigorous gestures, was in full flood and held the close attention of all—even though by no means all his audience appeared to agree with all that he was saying. He had a bundle of papers on the reading-desk before him, and beat on these vehemently every now and again with the palm of his hand.

". . . no fewer than ninety-five!" he was declaiming. "Ninety-five indictments, accusations, as well as propositions. He sets them forth lucidly, unchallengably, damningly! They are irrefutable. No honest man can deny it. Doctor Luther nails each lie, each shame, each folly. Holy Church must right these wrongs. I say. Or perish!"

"Holy Church cannot perish, Ricaud!" somebody near the front called out. "Christ's chosen body on earth can no more perish than can His risen body in Heaven!"

"Are you so sure, Doctor de Crouy?" Ricaud threw back at the interpolator. "If the body is growing corrupt, rotten, could not Almighty God raise up a new body on earth? For His son? Would you limit the All Highest?"

"Not so. But I question the authority of this Saxon, this monk Martin Luther, to decide and declare when the good God is finished with his sacred body and requires a new one!"

"Well said! The man is a mischief-maker, like all . . ." The rest of this supporter's remarks were lost in a storm of objection and abuse from all over the great room. It was clear that the majority of those present were in sympathy with the speaker, Doctor Jules Ricaud.

When he could make himself heard, that cleric, professor of Aristotelian Ethics and a canon of Notre Dame, went on. "Luther is no mischief-maker, but a sober scholar and teacher, erudite as any here present. He teaches my own subject, at the University of Wittenberg. I went there myself, to visit him, to question him. I found him entirely honest and rational."

"Can an Augustinian – and a *German* Augustinian – ever be rational?" a wag demanded, amidst laughter.

"He is sufficiently rational to ennumerate ninety-five propositions against abuses prevalent in the Church today, *messieurs!*"

"He disobeyed the Pope's command to go to Rome, Ricaud. To speak to his propositions," the doubting de Crouy insisted. "Do you condone such mutinous contumacy?"

"Yes, I do! When he learned that he was to be imprisoned and handed over to the Inquisitor! Would *you* have gone, de Crouy?"

"I would not have presumed, in the first place, to assail His Holiness."

"And yet, you too have voiced criticims of the Holy See. Or you would not be attending this meeting, my friend."

"Criticism of details, of enactments, of matters of church government, yes, but attacks upon the person of His Holiness — no!"

"Pope Leo has made no secret that he shares in the proceeds of this shameful traffic in indulgences. He gave the Archbishop of Magdeburg entire authority to sell indulgences and pardons for sins, without confession, repentence or any other condition save the payment of money — half of all the moneys to come to himself! This is the kernel of Doctor Luther's protest — for he, and others, have refused to absolve sinners holding these certificates of indulgence. And so has incurred the Archbishop's and the Pontiff's ire. I say that he is right, entirely justified."

Again the storm of applause.

"If we, who teach, who seek to counter the ignorance of so much of the clergy, excuse and condone such abuses, how can we hold up our heads? How can we retain the respect of our students? We know that such things are not confined to Saxony or Rome. That they occur here in Paris likewise. Is it not so?"

He had the meeting almost wholly with him now.

"What does the Wittenberger suggest?" he was asked. "How are these abuses to be rectified? When they have the blessing even of the Holy Father?"

"The Church must cleanse itself. Set its house in order — God's house. If the master of the house will not do so, then his children must see to it. So says Martin Luther. So say I. We must start with the feet if the head will not heed. And here, in the Sorbonne, we have both the great opportunity and the great duty, in teaching the young and the enquiring. We can effect much, *messieurs*. We must speak out. In this reform of Holy Church, the coming generation of the clergy here in France will take their tone from us. Echo what we now teach. Great then, I say, is our responsibility."

"The Cardinal will not favour this, Ricaud. And few of the bishops," de Crouy pointed out. "All who turn to the Holy See for preferment will look askance."

"It may be so. They must be guided to look elsewhere, therefore. For their preferment. To the King rather than the Pope."

There was a noticeable stir of excitement throughout the room.

73

"King Francis has already challenged the power of the Pope — challenged and won. In the Concordat of 1516, two years ago, he gained much power of independent appointment to the Church in France. He must be encouraged to use such power. To the full. For the benefit, the well-being, of all Holy Church. He is a courageous monarch, and of an independent mind."

Men looked at each other as new vistas opened in their imaginations.

These general principles enunciated, Ricaud went on to enumerate, illustrate and amplify the more important of Luther's ninety-five points. Fairly quickly David Beaton had enough of this, as did some others. When a grey-bearded philospher sitting near by got up to leave, muttering, David rose and slipped out, less conspicuously, behind him.

He had what he wanted, required, he believed.

David rode south, the next morning, by the placid slow-flowing Yonne, for the Forest of Fontainbleau, in very different style to that other journey, nearly four years before, when he had made his semi-secret way to Dieppe with Gilbert Ogilvy, on borrowed horses and with one of the Duke of Albany's grooms as sole escort. Now, mounted on his own handsome bay, with his manservant at heel, and dressed well and fashionably, he rode with a glittering group of a dozen of the Garde Ecossais, the King of France's personal Scots bodyguard, under his friend John Durie, Younger of that Ilk, Ensign, as became the dignity of the accredited Ambassador of Scotland to the French Court.

David had graduated from unofficial to official resident envoy earlier that year of 1518, soon after the completion of his studies at the Sorbonne and just after the Regent Albany had made his long-threatened return to France from Scotland. Despite his youth — he was still only twenty-three — he had been envoy in all but name for three years; but now, thanks to Bishop Leslie's unpopularity, his own friendship with the Regent, and his uncle's position as Chancellor — not to mention his ability — he had risen straight from University to represent his country in her most important overseas position, with her partner in the Auld Alliance. He had, of course, planned it so years before.

If his personal situation was thus excellently improved, however, the same could not be said of the political situation, either here or at home. Scotland was in a ferment again, after a period of comparative peace and fair government, not only on account of the Regent's return to France but because the Queen-Mother, still aged only twenty-eight, had managed to flee over the Border into England, minus the young King, and was from there threatening invasion with a mixed army of English and Douglases, to claim the Regency. While here in France matters had been going less than well for the dashing King Francis. After his early triumphs, wherein he had won back Milan at the brilliant Battle of Marignano in 1515, and his successful Concordat of Bologna with the Pope a year later, things had gone badly. The old Emperor Maximilian had claimed Milan as an imperial fief, and Charles of Spain, who was expected to succeed him in the Empire, had backed him up. Faced with this confederacy, Pope Leo de Medici had changed his direction, and Francis now found himself circled by hostile powers. In consequence he felt bound to come to terms with Henry Tudor of England — to the inevitable detriment of Scotland's interests.

Despite these international preoccupations King Francis, a young man of high spirits and enthusiasms, rather similar to the late unfortunate King James of Scots, by no means gave way to gloom and despondency; on the contrary he still kept the gayest Court in Europe. He was now building a vast new palace in the Forest of Fountainbleau, his favourite hunting-ground thirty-five miles south of Paris, spending much of his time there, either in the chase or in personally superintending the work of construction.

David rode through the dappled miles of the green glades of Fontainbleau in the early afternoon, strangely enough for this fine August day, something low in spirit. It was no failure to appreciate the loveliness around him, the leafy solitudes, the bird-song, the scent of wildflowers crushed by their horses' hooves; the reverse, rather. The trouble was that this place reminded him all too strongly of home, of Fife and the forests of Falkland and Lindores. Truth to tell, despite his successes here, and his admiration for France, he was heart-sick for Scotland. David knew well his weakness, this inordinate and inconvenient love of his native land, which so frequently betrayed itself, and him. And reminders of Scotland nowadays also had come to be reminders of Marion Ogilvy and his futile longing for her. Almost three years had passed since their meeting, but her extraordinary, uncanny hold on his mind and affections had not slackened, try as he would to shake it off. He had sent messages to her through her brother—once had actually written to her directly; but without response. His only consolation was that Gilbert indicated, rather plaintively, that neither of his sisters had yet brought themselves to the taking of vows, lamenting that until the more spirited Marion did, the elder Janet never would.

David berated himself as every kind of fool—but still longed. He was not of the nature to eschew all other women in the meantime, of course.

He ran King Francis to ground, with his master-of-works, considering the excavations for the artificial lake which was to front the palace, and planning the piping for fountains. His Most Christian Majesty greeted his visitor with wry goodwill, dismissing the Court officials who ushered him into the presence.

"Welcome, David!" he exclaimed. "If indeed you are well come? For, on my soul, most often in these days you seem to bring me only headaches and problems! Is it such has brought you all these leagues from Paris?"

"Ill news, Sire. The Sieur de la Bastie has been slain."

"Name of a Name! Slain? Anthony! My sorrow!"

"All true men's sorrow. The Homes slew him. A murder. You will recollect that the Earl of Home, who was Chamberlain and also Warden of the East March, sold himself to the English. The Regent had to have him executed, just before he returned to France, for he had been aiding Henry's Dacre to ravage the Scots Border which he was appointed to protect. My lord Duke, requiring a sound man in this most vital position, with serious invasion threatened, appointed de la Bastie, his lieutenant, to the task. The Homes have not forgiven that—for the Wardenship is all but hereditory in that family. A company of them, under Home of Wedderburn, ambushed the Warden, cornered him alone in a bog of the Merse, slew him there, and cut off his head. Wedderburn rode with the head, tied by its long plaited hair to his saddlebow, and hung it publicly on the market-cross of Duns—as warning to all who would counter Home on the Border!"

"Dear God—my poor Anthony! He was true of heart. One of my most gallant knights."

76

"He was even more than that, Sire, with respect. He was the Regent's right hand. And so my uncle's also, with the Regent gone. His loss is desperate for Scotland, with Arran and the Queen both openly claiming the Regency. And the Regent here in France."

The King pulled at his small pointed beard, saying nothing.

"It is near to civil war in Scotland, Majesty," David went on. "Allied to English invasion. Dacre burns and slays at will on the Border. A strong hand is imperative, to save the land from anarchy. My uncle the Archbishop-Chancellor's hand is insufficiently strong. He urges your Grace, pleads with you — send back the Duke of Albany."

Francis shook his head. "I cannot," he declared. "He is here of his own will. My friend. With leave of absence from your Scots Estates. I cannot order him against his will and rights."

"He is one of your Grace's citizens of France. Your Admiral. And you are bound, are you not, by treaty, to sustain with all your power the good government of the realm of Scotland?"

"No doubt, David. But I must be the judge of what is necessary for that good government." The monarch spread his hands in very Gallic gesture. "Why is the good Albany so necessary to Scotland? So essential? You said that a strong hand is needed. You know as do I that Albany's hand lacks strength. His mind is divided. He is more scholar than soldier. He does not desire power. Why should he be so necessary to Scotland?"

"Because, Sire, of who he is. Of his blood. To the Scots, blood is of supreme importance. He is a Stewart of the royal house. The nearest to the throne, now that the Queen's second son has died. His position is sure, undeniable. Where all else is unrest and uncertainty, he represents stability to the people. He may not be strong, as you are strong, Sire — but he has excellent wits and all know he is honest. In these three difficult years he has ruled Scotland well. Few, even of his enemies, will gainsay it. There has been as nearly peace as was possible. And now that he leaves — this! He should go back, Sire."

"Then apply yourself to the Duke. Not to me."

"Does Your Majesty think that I have not tried?"

The King kicked at a clod of earth. "I regret it," he said. "But I have more urgent problems nearer home. You know it well, David. Placed as I am, with the Emperor, Spain and the Pope

77

arrayed against me, I must treat with England. I have no choice —
little as I love Henry! Or his sisters. Or his jackal Wolsey. Henry
would have me hold Albany here, if necessary in ward! That I
will not do. But I cannot *send* him back. I must keep Henry
from joining the ring around me — or France is lost. Already she
feels the hurt of it."

"That ring can be broken, I think, Your Majesty."

Sharply the other looked at him. "What do you mean?"

"That these enemies of yours make but uneasy allies to each
other, Sire. And only united do they menace France. Separate
them."

"Separate them, says my young Scots friend!" Francis cried.
"Think you this is some game of cards that I play? Separate the
Empire, the Holy See, and the Most Catholic Kingdom of Spain!
With England coveting much of France and likely to join them.
Spare me your callow advices, sir!"

David flushed, but persisted with only superficial diffidence.

"All humbly, Your Highness, I submit that you have the
weapons to achieve this separation, in your hands."

"What weapons? What could achieve such miracle!"

"One man's name could achieve it. Skilfully used. That man —
Martin Luther."

"Luther? The German monk?"

"The same. Sire, heed me. Luther's teachings are sufficient to
divide all Christendom. They will do so, *are* doing so — believe
me. Use the threat of them rightly, and you can affect the
dividing."

"God's name — what are you saying?"

"Do you not see it, Sire? Luther is a Saxon, a German, and he
is defying the Pope. His views are spreading like a contagion. He
has the support of his own Elector, Frederick of Saxony. Likewise, it becomes clear, of many of the other Electors and princes
of Germany and the Low Countries — the backbone of the
Empire The Emperor himself may not approve of him — I know
not. But I do know that, ageing and failing as he is, he dare not
offend his Electors. Nor dare Charles of Spain, if in due course
he would be elected Emperor himself. Do you not see it?"

The King was searching the younger man's face. "I see something, yes. Something in what you say. But . . . I do not see what
may be done. Or how."

"Privily support Luther in Germany and the Empire. Aid his cause by every secret means amongst the Electors and princes. But publicly put down his cause here in France with a strong hand. Turn Luther into a burning issue, a stone for stumbling. Make it so that men take sides openly. So you will divide your enemies. The Emperor for him, the Pope of course against him. And Charles of Spain so torn between his Catholic duty and his ambitions to be Emperor that he does nothing. So the alliance against you is broken."

"Save me — this is beyond all!"

"But not beyond Your Majesty's ability to effect. Moreover, Henry of England has already chosen to cross swords with this Luther. He has penned a treatise against his ninety-five points — to which Luther has replied with scant respect! So that Henry too takes sides. He will accordingly bless you if you come out strongly against the man's teachings here in France. Put down his adherents."

"But . . . shrive me, I have nothing to put down! How can I do all this when there is nothing to attack? It would be but fighting with shadows!"

"Substantial shadows, Sire! I was at a gathering of some scores of them, last night. The majority of the teachers in theology and the divinities in your University of the Sorbonne favour Luther, I found. More than that, they intend to further his cause."

Francis was astonished. "Is this truth? I have heard nothing of it."

"Truth," David nodded. "Would I lie to Your Majesty?"

The King laughed shortly. "That I do not know, either, David! I deem you capable of lying, on occasion, even to me — if your case was sufficiently pressing!"

"I am sorry for that," the younger man said simply. "I had hoped that Your Grace thought better of me."

The other laughed, clapping his shoulder. "Come, my friend — do not take it amiss. All of us engaged in affairs of state must lie at times. I know that *I* do! But this, then, I have to accept as sober fact?"

"Yes. As you will discover, Sire. For they intend to use you in their designs."

"Use *me*?"

"They esteem you, and rightly, to be a prince of wide

sympathies and bold courses. Moreover nowise in thrall to His Holiness. They would seek to encourage you, therefore, to run counter to the Holy See. And so to further Luther's revolt."

"As indeed well I might! For the truth is, David, that I much agree with what this Luther says. Condemn, with him, much that he condemns."

"So must all thinking men, Your Grace. But surely it is not the man's cry for reform that is to be condemned, but his methods for effecting those reforms? The works, not the faith, that is at fault?"

Francis shook his head. "I cannot split such hairs with you, David. I am no religious, no theologian."

"Nor in truth am I, Sire. But I have been taught to discern cause from effect, the gulf between intent and practice. Here is well-intentioned menace, the plague of destruction under the innocent cloak of reform."

The monarch poked doubtfully into the dug-up soil. "I say you pitch it altogether too high," he objected.

"I must, of course, concur in Your Majesty's views. But have you considered what is the greatest single danger to your throne Sire? The greatest danger to the throne of any and every monarch? It is not assault from without, nor yet treachery from within – for in both of these the people will, in the end, come to the realm's aid. It is anarchy that is to be feared above all. For anarchy leaves authority, the Crown, defenceless. And this Luther spells anarchy."

"Reform need not be anarchy, surely, my friend?"

"Reform from the top down, no. Reform from the bottom up, yes! Doctor Ricaud last night gave away his entire cause, uncovered the rot in the tree, when he declared that they must start with the feet since the head would not heed. That way lies disaster for the Church. And if men learn anarchy in the Church, for how long will thrones be safe from it?"

He had the King silent at last, a man all but convinced.

David played his trump card. "If Your Grace was to inform Pope Leo that he had your fullest support against Luther and his disciples, provided always that he decreed that Milan was no imperial fief but a papal state under perpetual lease to the Crown of France – then I swear he would agree. And at his age, would the Emperor Maximilian risk excommunication for the sake of Milan? I think not."

Francis, who for Milan had fought Marignano, was overcome quite. He smiled, chuckled, laughed aloud. "You have thought of everything, David!" he cried.

"Not everything, Sire—but enough, perhaps," the younger man answered modestly. "I have thought, for instance, that the Cardinal Wolsey, Henry's Chancellor, will stop at little to gain nomination as the next Pope. Assurance of your support in his hopes will make him your friend—and make him urge his monarch against any objection to your sending of the Duke of Albany back to Scotland. Where also the Luther heresies fall to be stamped out!"

"Mary Mother of God—you would not bargain with *me*? France!"

"Heaven forbid, Sire! I but foresee the good results of your royal actions."

"I see well why they wanted you, young as you are, to be Scotland's envoy! But watch, Master Beaton—watch! Or one day that clever tongue of yours will go too far. Even for an ambassador!"

"I pray not, Your Grace. That day I shall deserve my fate! But, meantime, I have won you Milan again, I think?"

"At a price, yes. And won a reluctant Regent back to Scotland! Come—no more of this, David, before you have me committing myself to the saints know what! It is thirsty work, combating anarchy, is it not? This way—to my pavilion yonder, and a draught of wine, for sweet mercy's sake . . .!"

PART TWO

Chapter Five

IT was with mixed feelings that David Beaton gazed out over the tossing grey waters of the North Sea, veined with dirty white, towards the towers and spires of St. Andrews half-veiled by driving, chill rainstorms. He alone of the passengers from France in the two galleys braved the unpleasantness of the heaving deck, buffeted by gusts, cloaked against the wet and cold, occasionally wiping rain and salt spray from his face. Was this what he had looked forward to, for so long?

It was Christmas Eve of 1524, and no time to be sailing northern seas. But he had been delayed and delayed. He had planned it all differently from this. He had been trying for months to get away. He had intended to bring with him so much better aid than was contained in these two small ships. He had thought to sail for Leith, the port of Edinburgh, the seat of government – if government was a word that could be applied to Scotland in these unhappy days – but a wise preliminary landfall and call at Dunbar, at the mouth of the Forth, had given him warning that events had moved on, and badly, and that disembarkation at the Capital would be disastrous. The Archbishop was at St. Andrews, all but beleagured apparently. There he must go.

It made a strange homecoming indeed for the young man who for years had all but pined for Scotland. He had been home once or twice, as an envoy must, in these last years, but only for brief and urgent visits. Now he had burned his boats. This was the end of a chapter. He was come home for good – or ill. Yet at great cost to himself, and doubting his welcome.

For David Beaton had resigned the appointment of Scots Ambassador to France, not been dismissed or replaced. Indeed, his resignation, sent by letter to his uncle some six weeks before, remained as yet unanswered with no word of replacement.

That David, not only of his own free will and decision, but against the advice of many, including the King of France, should have so reversed his own fortunes, thrown up so much that he had

striven and planned for, would surprise more than the Chancellor
—if, in fact, Chancellor the Archbishop still remained. It might
seem to be an act of folly, of self-injury, wholly out of character.
From occupying an assured and influential position, almost
absurdly lofty for so young a man, which moreover he could have
retained almost indefinitely, he had turned himself into an
impecunious private citizen again. He had not done so, needless
to say, without much thought.

There were numerous reasons behind his action. Albany had
given up the Regency and returned to France, finally, for good or
ill. King Francis had foolishly gone to war against the new
Emperor Charles, and was even now campaigning in North Italy
from his base at Milan—a development David, as a hater of war,
much deplored; the King's desire for the Scot to accompany him
on this adventure had indeed precipitated this return home. But
basically, essentially, David was here because he loved Scotland,
felt that he had been too long an exile, and believed that in her
present straits he could aid her more effectively at home than in
France. The recognition that perhaps he was wrong in this only
sharpened the piquancy of the situation.

And Scotland was in straits indeed. She had been, of course,
for over ten years now, since Flodden Field and the succession
of a baby to the throne. But never so ill as now, with Albany gone,
the English party triumphant, the young King James the Fifth
allegedly reigning without a Regent but in fact controlled by his
mother, with whom Arran had joined forces. To all intents Henry
Tudor was now ruling Scotland at last, with the English Ambassador, Magnus, the most powerful man in the land. It was to this
that David Beaton had elected to return.

Even on a wild Christmas Eve, the armed French ships created
some small stir in St. Andrews harbour. David left everyone
aboard meantime, to prospect the situation ashore on his own.
Halfway up the well-remembered steep track from the shore to
the town, a clanking picket of men-at-arms, their steel breastplates painted with the mitred arms of the See of St. Andrews,
met him and challenged him without undue respect.

"I seek the Archbishop. The Chancellor," he told them. "Is
he here? In St. Andrews?"

"Aye, he is. Your name and business, sir? Are you one o' the
Douglases?"

85

"Douglas? Lord—no! I am from France. The Archbishop's nephew. But—what of Douglas? Why name that name?"

"The Earl o' Angus is here. With his brother, Sir George Douglas, expected. And others. Frae England," the leader of the picket informed. "These ships . . .?"

"Angus! Here? In St. Andrews? What folly is this? What brings Angus here?"

The man shrugged. "Dinna ask me. Come—I'll take you to the castle."

"Is Angus there? At the castle? Does the Archbishop receive him? Surely not. He was in England. With King Henry. How comes he here?"

The soldier would make no comment, amplifying nothing, obviously fearing to commit himself, although a minion of the Archbishop's. David perceived nevertheless a sufficiently eloquent comment, however involuntory, on the state of Scotland in 1524.

He found it as well to have an escort, for the approach to the castle postively bristled with armed men, many with the Red Heart of Douglas on their armour.

There was a difference about the ̄castle ̄itself. ̣ New defensive works were in evidence, walls and towers had been strengthened, and the flag that flew from the great central keep now quartered the arms of Beaton with those of the See of St. Andrews. James Beaton had at last gained his ambition, the Primacy and St. Andrews, on the death of Archbishop Forman two years before.

There appeared to be little of the accustomed Yuletide preparations about castle or town. The place seemed more like an armed camp. Even the inner courtyard was full of horses.

David found the Great Hall noisy with men, few of whom looked like churchmen. Armour, helmets and weapons lay about everywhere, amidst billowing smoke from the two huge fires which had everybody coughing. Enquiries for Prior Ogilvy, the Chancellor's secretary, produced only blank stares; but a private room off the Hall itself was indicated as containing the Archbishop's presence.

In this small chamber, richly hung with arras and with a more effective log fire blazing brightly, three men sat round a table littered with flagons of wine, goblets, meats and papers. All glanced up frowning at David's entrance.

"God's death — you!" James Beaton half rose to his feet, more corpulent, more purple of face, for the passing of the years.

"Myself, undoubtedly, my lord," David bowed. "My patrilineal greetings, Uncle. My respects to you also, my lords. I hope that my intrusion will be pardoned — but I have left sundry Frenchmen waiting down at the harbour, important men, envoys of the King of France. Also, I have letters from King Francis and the Duke of Albany."

All three stared at him, his uncle blinking rapidly, a younger, good-looking man haughtily, and a smoothly assured middle-aged cleric with shrewd interest.

"My nephew," the Archbishop got out, sinking back into his chair. "Davie. Master David. The Resident. In France. Here's . . . here's a surprise!"

His guests reacted differently. The younger snorted, but said nothing. The elder inclined his head civilly.

"Master Beaton's fame is known to all," he said, in a rich and carefully modulated voice. "The surprise is, I am sure, a most pleasing one."

"My lord Earl of Angus. And Master William Douglas, Prior of Coldinghame," James Beaton muttered, moistening thick lips.

David bowed again. "My surprise is even greater than yours, my lords, I think!" he said. "It is a notable day that finds my lord of Angus in St. Andrews Castle!"

The Earl glared. "My lord Archbishop — we were discussing privy matters of state, I think!" he said curtly, harshly.

The Chancellor plucked at his chin, frowning in turn. "It may be that a few minutes interval will no' hurt our discussions," he jerked.

"Undoubtedly," Prior William agreed soothingly, glancing at *his* nephew.

David considered Angus with interest. This was his first meeting with the notorious Archibald, sixth Earl, grandson and successor of the still more infamous Bell-the-Cat, husband of the Queen-Mother and head of the great House of Douglas, the most powerful noble in all Scotland. He was younger than the other had been apt to think of him, a tall and handsome man in only his late twenties, narrow-featured, high-browed and undeniably distinguished-looking, but with a thin-lipped mouth which, allied to flaring nostrils and a hot pale blue eye, spoke of a fiercely proud and ruthless nature little tramelled by self-control. Angus, like his grandfather before him was the leader of the English party. Having quarrelled irrevocably with Queen Margaret, Albany had managed to unite the rest of the nation against him and his Douglases, and he had been forced to flee for the last couple of years to Henry's Court in London. That it should be here in James Beaton's house that this menace to Scotland's integrity should have turned up, intrigued David as much as it alarmed him.

"My lord, privy matters of state have been my daily business for years, as this realm's representative with the Court of France," he mentioned, mildly enough. "There are few matters so privy that it has not been my duty to know them!" He paused, to let that sink in — lest Angus be under any misapprehension as to his knowledge of his treasons and treacheries. Or, for that matter, that Prior William should esteem him ignorant of the part he had played in the death of the Sieur de la Bastie, and his extorting of the Priory of Coldinghame from the Homes, in consequence. "My presence therefore should not incommode your lordship."

His uncle eyed him uneasily. Admittedly this was not like David Beaton, to push himself in, to force his company where it obviously was not wanted. That he did so proved louder than his words his suspicions and hostility towards Angus. The Douglas, of course, had played into his hands by mentioning matters of state — for until he was actually replaced as ambassador, David was still an important servant of the state, while, whatever he had been, Angus was at present something in the nature of a renegade, an outlaw.

"My lord discusses with me the safety of the young King, Davie," the Chancellor declared hurriedly. "The laddie has been held as good as prisoner, in yon cauld dreich Castle o' Edinburgh up on its rock, this long while. It's no' right and proper . . ."

"We fear for his health and well-being, Master Beaton," the Earl's uncle put in reasonably, amicably — although his glance was on Angus rather than on David. "It is a grievous danger for our young liege lord's health that he should be detained thus. In draughty durance. It is against all nature. And taxing even to grown men — as my lord Archbishop and myself can vouch, from sore experience!" He smiled.

David could scarcely prevent a smile also. This was a cunning and smooth rogue, third son of the late Bell-the-Cat, who had been in and out of imprisonment for offences innumerable all his days. He was also twitting James Beaton with the immuring of his own more scholarly brother, Gavin Douglas, here in the Sea Tower of St. Andrews Castle, those years before when, at David's suggestion the Bishop of Dunkeld has been held on a charge of heresy in order to prevent his elevation by the Pope to the coveted Primacy and Archbishopric. And, again, he was drawing attention to the humiliating incident of only a month or two before, when the Chancellor himself had been thrown into a cell of Edinburgh Castle by the Queen-Mother, for onward passage to an English prison, only escaping by undignified means.

But there was cause for other than smiling here, David perceived all too clearly. That these three should be hypocritically concerning themselves with the twelve-year-old King's health in Edinburgh Castle could only mean one thing — that some plot was being put forward to detach him from his mother's and Arran's keeping. King Henry, having gained what he wanted, control of Scotland, without Arran's aid, had now discarded the Douglas. Bishop Gavin, his uncle, had died of the plague in London — but this other and less reputable uncle had presumably been the link to bring together Angus and the Archbishop. Was Uncle James himself up to mischief? David smelt danger, trickery, treachery. He must walk warily.

So, in his own way, apparently felt the magnificently dressed Angus. He jumped up from the table. "Fiend take me — Douglas did not come here to gossip with . . . clerks!" he exclaimed. "When you are of a mind to resume our privy talking, my lord — come seek me!" He stalked out of the room into the Great Hall, slamming the door behind him.

"Archibald was ever hasty," the Prior observed philosophically, into the succeeding silence. "A man of action, rather than of words. But with his virtues." He sat back. "Well, young man — I hope that you have brought us good tidings from France?"

"Yes and no, Master Prior. Tidings are seldom all good. Or all ill. Are they? The letters, and the French envoys, will explain all, no doubt. To the Chancellor."

The other eyed him blandly but at the same time keenly, closely. "And my lord Duke?"

"He is well."

89

"Excellent. But . . . does he propose to return to Scotland?"

"That you must ask the Chancellor. Hereafter."

William Douglas sat for a few moments expressionless. Then, nodding he rose to his feet. "So be it, my friends. I shall await your further confidences, my lord Archbishop. And meantime shall go seek cherish the good Archibald's patience – with scant hopes of success!" With this affable warning, he left the Beatons alone.

"Davie! What's the meaning o' this?" the Chancellor demanded, the moment the door was closed. "By the Mass – here's no way to come breaking in! Before yon Angus, of all men! How came you here, at all? From France? Lacking my summons. This is ill done, man – ill done."

"Is it, Uncle? I'd say that it was not ill-timed, at anyrate! You would seem to be on the point of being swallowed up in the bloody maw of Douglas!"

"Not so. No, no, man – I but converse wi' them. We parley. We debate . . ."

"As well parley and debate with a lion in the arena, as with Angus! He will play with you, then turn and rend you. As he has done all others. And Scotland with you. He has always been your enemy, the enemy of all true men who would preserve this realm. How comes he here? In your house?"

"It was necessary, Davie. There was nothing else for it. Matters run so ill in Scotland today that I must turn even to the Douglases. There are three factions in the land, with Albany gone – the Queen's, Arran's, and Angus's. I canna fight them all. Arran has thrown in his lot with the Queen, and they hold the young King tight. Henry has prevailed, and James is erected to reign. Without a Regent. Because I refused to recognise that erection of a laddie of twelve years as lawful, I was thrown into prison in Edinburgh. Arran got me out – for now he's married to your cousin Janet Beaton. The weak fool thinks to rule, through the King! While, God pity him, he will not see that it is Henry Tudor who rules – through the whore Margaret Tudor, the King's mother!"

"All this I know, Uncle. Indeed, it is why I am come home from France. To aid you. But ill as it is, here is insufficient cause to cherish the viper of Douglas to your bosom."

"Wheesht, Davie – you babble like any bairn! Where else can

I turn? Henry, no longer needing Angus, has thrown him over. The man is hot with insult and anger. He burns with hate against his wife, the Queen-Mother. As well he might! She is talking of divorce. You know that she has taken to her bed that popinjay, young Henry Stewart of Methven? The filthy harlot! She would marry *him*, now. Worse, she has already nominated him Chancellor, in the King's name!"

"God be good—Chancellor! Can she do that? Are you no longer this realm's chief minister, then?"

"Aye, praise be—I'm still Chancellor! By law. But only just. It requires the Privy Council and Parliament to unseat the Chancellor. And the woman and Arran havena dared to risk calling these. No' yet. But there's no' that much time, Davie. I've got to hold the Church. For the Church can swing both Parliament and the Council. And I have my enemies in the Church too. The Hepburns in especial. John Hepburn hates me. He's now appointed Bishop o' Ross, with his bastard Patrick succeeded him here, as Prior o' St. Andrews. *Here*, mind—in my own backyard! They'll bring me down if they can. There's a wheen Douglases in the Church too—and this William o' Coldinghame is the chiefest o' them, now that Gavin's dead."

His nephew nodded, mind busy.

"I've *got* to hold in with the Douglases, in this pass," James Beaton went on. "Angus can move enough voices in Parliament to hold the balance. He, with his friends Erroll, Crawford and Huntly, controls the North-East. And he can put ten thousand men in the field! He may be traitor and scoundrel—but I need him, man. I need him. If I'm to stay Chancellor."

"And that is essential," David agreed crisply. "At all costs you must remain Chancellor."

"I'm glad you see it! Tell me how I'm to do it, boy, lacking Douglas?"

"That I'll turn my mind to. Give me time. But . . . what is this of the young King? This sudden fear for his health! I never heard that he was a sickly youth. Is it a plot? To gain his person?"

His uncle glanced round the empty chamber, and even involuntarily lowered his voice. "No' so loud, man—for sweet mercy's sake! 'Tis but a suggestion. A matter for discussion. Angus believes it possible that the King could be delivered out of his mother's hands. By guile. For the weal of King and realm both. So that Henry Tudor would no longer control both . . ."

"Archibald Douglas to control them instead! Think you that a better fate? For either?"

"It would break Henry's grip. For the moment. Now, through Magnus the English envoy, he appoints whom he will to the rule in this realm. It must be stopped, or we are no more than a province of England. He has petitioned the Pope again, to put down my Primacy, and to lower this See of St. Andrews to a bishopric and place it under York!"

"Aye. Henry does not change. But I say the answer never is for the Chancellor to turn brigand. To be a party to seizing the King's person. You say that you must hold the Church. You will not do so thus."

"What, then? Since you see so clearly, new come from France! Angus puts forward this ploy. I dare not offend him."

"You dare not lose the respect of the Church and the burghs, the people, either! Or you lose all. Temporise with Angus. Do not commit yourself to his follies. Use your strength, not your weaknesses."

"Strength! What strength have I got? In this pass?"

"Your strength is in your spiritual authority. Use it. And in the support for it in the many small, not the few great. In the Church and the burghs. Use that also. Call a Parliament. Quickly as may be. You can do it, as Chancellor. The Queen will not dare to withhold the King's consent. She will hope that such Parliament and Council will remove you from the Chancellorship and elevate her paramour, this Henry Stewart. We must see that it does not. Parliament is still the voice of this realm. Use it, while it will still speak for you."

"Christ God—here is an almighty hazard! A chancy venture, man. To risk all on such a throw . . ."

"Better that than to ruin your name and credit by seizing the King. If you failed with that, it would be highest treason. If you fail with the Parliament, you lose the Chancellorship; but you are still Primate. Still leader of the Church. You will not fail with the Parliament, I think. We must see that you do not. There is much that you can do. You can excommunicate! A mighty weapon, skilfully used. And you are still the wealthiest man in Scotland, are you not, Uncle James?"

The other darted a swift glance at his nephew at this thrust, but said nothing.

"It would be foolish to underestimate your advantages, see you," David went on. "I think perhaps you have not fully exploited the strengths of your position. I have been discovering the powers of the Primate and Archbishop. You take precedence before all others under the King. You may levy customs. You have the authority to coin money. Siller, Uncle! You are ultimate heir of all confiscated property within your regality and spiritual dominion. Did you know that? You can pronounce anathema. On my soul, Uncle James — you are a very fountain of power, of one sort and another! If you will but use it." He smiled winningly. "It is, I must confess, to aid you use it that I am come home!"

James Beaton huffed and gobbled in mixed astonishment, perception and apprehension.

"So be of better cheer, my lord Chancellor, Primate, Archbishop and Uncle! We shall do great things for this Scotland, I promise you. I shall require some little subsistence and delegated authority, of course. But nothing that you will not recoup yourself for, a score of times!"

"What word have you brought me from France?" James Beaton growled.

"Little enough to gladden your heart, I fear. King Francis has fully committed himself to war with the Emperor, and has no troops or treasure to spare for Scotland. I did my best to move him against such folly. He has sent one hundred of his Garde Ecossais — as a token, as a guard for yourself and such French officers as are still in Scotland. They are down in the galleys. That is all."

"God's blood — one hundred! And I need ten thousand! Is this the best you could do, man?"

"The best. Gained with some difficulty, I assure you.

"And Albany? Does he return?"

"There also, I can bring you no joy. Nothing will move the Duke. He will not come back. He says that even if the young King James died, he would reject the throne. He is willing to serve Scotland in France. He could be useful there. Moreover, see you, he is still Lord Admiral of France — and Francis requires him in his war. He has had enough of our troubles. And he was ever more French than Scots."

"Aye. So that — that is all you have brought me from France, Nephew! Naught but heartbreak and an end to my hopes!"

"Not so, Uncle. I have brought you three envoys, very gallant. One hundred trained soldiers, who can be trusted. And myself." David laughed. "And, sink me — I think that I, and my wits, are the best of it!

"You esteem yourself highly, man! Always you did that."

"I know my worth, yes — I would be a fool otherwise. And so, I swear, do you, Uncle! Since you are no fool, either. You have profited by my wits, in the past. Now, I am going to be still more useful. But for that I require some small authority and subsistence. That it is in your power to grant me. And to your benefit." His voice altered. "Where is Gilbert? Prior Ogilvy, your secretary?"

"Ogilvy? He is no longer such. Secretary. He is returned to his Priory of Restenneth. A true man. But insufficiently agile of mind."

"Ha! That I can believe. Gilbert will be happier at Restenneth. Who replaces him?"

"No one man, Sundry clerks . . ."

"Good! Then you have a new secretary, my lord Chancellor! To wit, Master David Beaton, lately Ambassador to the Court of France! But — lest that seem insufficiently to resound, too great a fall in glory . . . name him David, Lord Abbot of Arbroath!"

"Sacred soul of God!" That ejaculation rose from a shout to a squeak. James Beaton gagged and choked. Thick fingers jabbed and weaved protest and affront that his lips failed to form. He stepped back from his nephew as though he had been struck.

"Come, my lord — it is none so high a price to pay, for your rescue!" the younger man claimed, smiling. "For all I can do for you. The labourer is worthy of his hire, is he not?"

"P'plague and blister you! You ask . . . you ask . . .? Arbroath! You are crazy-mad, boy! Arbroath . . .!"

"Arbroath, yes. One of your many abbeys. Uncle. Which you hold personally. I am not crazed, I assure you. Arbroath I desire — for my own good reasons."

"Fool! Presumptuous! Insolent! Do you know what you ask? Arbroath is the second richest abbey in all Scotland. Seat for a mitred abbot. Superior of a dozen lesser priories and houses. Its granges the most fertile in the land. Its revenues princely . . .!"

"Ah, yes. And do you need all this, with so much else, Uncle? Do you grudge a little for your kin? You do? Then we must come to some compact about the revenues. If they mean so much to you. One half, perhaps, to you. And if I manage the abbey, I swear they will rise. But I want Arbroath."

"A God's name—why Arbroath?"

"Say that it appeals to me. That if I am going to be an abbot, I will be a mitred one, for a conceit! More important, it carries a seat in the Estates, in Parliament. And you are going to need me there, Uncle. When you call that Parliament, it will serve you to have the Lord Abbot of Arbroath speaking in your cause!"

"Guidsakes . . .!" the older man muttered. Then he raised a pointing finger. "But . . . it's no' possible, Davie! You're no' in holy orders. You canna be a mitred abbot and no' a cleric. It's no' possible."

"To God all things are possible. And to the Primate and the Pope, most things! Including this. I can be abbot *in commendam*. Without becoming a priest."

"On my soul—no!"

"On your soul—yes, my lord! If the late and lamented Alexander Stewart could be Archbishop of St. Andrews and Primate, *in commendam*, at seventeen, I can be Abbot of Arbroath."

"He was the King's son. In bastardy."

"And I am the Archbishop-Chancellor's nephew, legitimate!"

"The Pope would never confirm it."

"I think he would. The Holy Father is somewhat beholden to me. In the matter of the putting down of the Lutheran heresy in France. And knows it well."

When the older man was silent, David clapped his wide steel-covered shoulders, almost affectionately.

"Is it a compact, Uncle?" he asked, smiling. "I think that I know too many secrets for you to wish me . . . discontented! Is it not so?" And though he laughed, he tightened his grip.

The Chancellor groaned, raised hunched shoulders under that grasp, and let them fall. Almost imperceptibly he inclined his bullet head.

"Excellent! You will have no cause to regret this day, I promise you, my lord. Now—with your permission, I shall go bring up the envoys. And your fine guard."

James Beaton cleared his throat. "What . . . what am I to say to Angus?" he asked dully, flatly. He seemed to have become an old man in the last few minutes.

"Angus? Tell him that you have had important word from France. Say that all is changed. That it will not be necessary to consider seizing the King. That Parliament will command that the King be placed in good hands. In a council of governors—one of whom shall be the Earl of Angus! And do *not* tell him, meantime, that Albany does not return. That will keep the Douglas quiet, I think . . ."

Chapter Six

DAVID rode fast, and alone, without the escort of a score of the French guard which he had allocated to himself as Chancellor's secretary. His fine white stallion's hooves rang on the iron-hard ground, for frost had the land in its grip; but the great and fertile vale of Strathmore lay smiling under the pale and brittle sunshine. Colour, muted but exhilarating, was everywhere, in the deep red-brown of tilled land, the ochres of winter pasture, the bottle-green of the pines, the purple and gleaming white of the naked birches, and backing all, the hazy blue majesty streaked with dazzling snows of the vast mountain barrier that closed off all the north and west. David rejoiced in it all, rejoiced to be a-move again in Scotland. Rejoiced also in that this fair terrain which he rode over was now largely his own, part of the far-flung domains of the great Abbey of Arbroath. There was much to be improved, of course—but it was indeed a goodly heritage.

He was making towards that potent mountain barrier, or at least for its foothills. Already the land was beginning to lift to the Braes of Angus, green even in early January. To his left, down in the strath, rising ground allowed him to glimpse the grey roofs and turrets of the castle of the Lord Glamis, while beyond him, northwards, beyond the smoky huddle of Forfar town the woodlands of the Priory of Restenneth showed darkly.

Skirting Kirriemuir to the south and beginning to climb in

earnest, David came presently to the jutting prow of land, soaring high in the shape of a sharp wedge, where the headlong streams of the Isla and Melgam Waters united — a wedged promontory crowned by the proud sheer walls and dizzy towers of the Castle of Airlie, seat of the Ogilvys, descendants of the ancient Celtic mormaors, lords of this land before any Norman came out of France.

The drawbridge was down, and two kilted gate-porters, broad-swords in hand, awaited the arrival of the single rider on the steaming stallion. David, challenged in the soft Gaelic, shook his head and replied in Lowland English that the Abbot of Arbroath sought leave to enter the house of the Lord Ogilvy of Airlie. In especial he sought the presence of the Lady Marion Ogilvy.

Marion herself presently appeared in the gateway to interview the visitor — for the present Lord Ogilvy was a mere boy, her nephew, studying in far-away Bologna. She came with the servitor, hurriedly tidying her silver-gold hair. And David Beaton's heart turned over at the sight of her.

As well it might. Marion Ogilvy had used the years since their last — and first — meeting, to develop from a lovely girl into a still more lovely and attractive woman. Now aged twenty-four, she was quite breath-taking in the sweet excellence of her features, the bloom of her skin, the sparkle of her eyes and the proud splendour of her figure. If the man had been cherishing a dream all those years, at least it had been no mere mirage. The actuality was still more enthralling than the memory.

"You!" she cried, startled, as he bowed, her hand up to her breast. "I . . . I did not know! I thought . . . I . . . I . . ." She halted, flushing, at a loss.

David's carefully rehearsed speech deserted him. "Marion!" he jerked, hastening forward. "At last!" He stopped, biting his lip. "Marion!"

Still yards apart, they stood and gazed.

"Calum said Abbot," she got out. "I thought . . . I looked for . . ." Helplessly she shrugged. "I believed you in France."

"I returned. But eight days ago, I would have come sooner, but . . ." He paused again. This was not what he had meant to say, or how he had planned to greet her. "I hope I see you well," he ended stiffly, lamely.

"Yes. I thank you. Well. And you, also?"

"To be sure. Never more well. I am glad to be home. In Scotland. And in the same country as you! I rejoice to see you."

She inclined her head, and they considered each other doubtfully, while the two Highlandmen looked on with interest.

It was a long time since David Beaton had found himself embarrassed and tongue-tied. Almost angrily he sought to throw off the strange effect of her, all but shaking himself, to start again—and wavered wildly between curtness and almost unctuous suavities in consequence

"Come. Give your horse to Calum." She turned, to lead him into the inner courtyard.

Walking beside her, close now, he could barely keep his hands off her. He had lived with the image of her so long, and they had been close, close, in his mind. It seemed all wrong, somehow, a denial, that he could not take her to him, as he ached to do, as he had done a thousand times in his dreams.

"You did not become a nun," he said. "You will not? Now?"

"No."

"For that, I thank God!"

At the fervour in his voice she looked at him strangely, sidelong, but made no comment.

She took him through the great vaulted Hall and up a narrow turnpike stair beyond into a smaller room above where a cheerful fire blazed and red-berried holly branches glowed in pots. She took his long travelling-cloak and flat velvet bonnet with the curling ostrich feather.

"I will get wine. Food. Have you ridden far, Master Beaton?"

"Only from Arbroath. Across Strathmore. A pleasant trot, no more. In this frost."

"Aye. It is a bonnie day for riding," she agreed, with a little sigh. Then she raised her brows, smiling. "My—you are fine!" she said.

He was. He had dressed in his finest daytime clothes from Paris to come to visit her, crimson velvet slashed with gold, short trunks and long silken hose appearing out of the tops of his high soft-leather riding boots.

"As befits no less than the Lord Abbot of Arbroath, Knight of the Order of St. Lazarus of Jerusalem, and secretary to the

Chancellor of the realm!" he declared, sweeping her an elaborate, flourishing bow.

The young woman was looking at him wide-eyed. "How comes this? An abbot! Are you now . . . a priest, Master David?"

"Not me! Never think it. Do I look like a priest, Marion? Do you perceive a tonsure?"

"I have never heard of an abbot who was not priest."

"It is possible to be one without the other. *In commendam*, as the phrase is. You would not wish me to be priest?"

"I? Wish it? No. I mean . . . why should it concern me?"

He shrugged one padded shoulder, a French habit which he had picked up. "I would wish that it might," he said.

She turned away. "I shall fetch you refreshment . . ."

"Do not trouble with it," he told her. "I was not two hours on the road. And seeing you again, after all the years, is sufficient refreshment."

She frowned and smiled in one. "You have not changed a great deal. In those years. My Lord Abbot!"

"I have not changed," he agreed, levelly.

"You must have wine, at least," Marion said hurriedly. "At this Yule season." She left the room.

He paced to the window, to gaze out and down over the swooping prospect, the frightening drop into the deep ravine directly below, the white rushing torrent, and the thrusting, jumbled hillsides that rose beyond. But he saw little or nothing of it. He cursed himself and his folly. His weakness over this woman, in the first place. And given the weakness, his inability to behave towards her as he would, as he planned, his halting feebleness. That he, who could hold his own with kings and princes, outwit statesmen — aye, and take his way with talented and beautiful women innumerable — should be reduced to stammering confusion by this slip of a girl form an Angus glen, daughter of a lofty line though she might be! It was beyond all bearing. He must do better. Assume some authority. He was a man of authority now, was he not? Let him prove it, then. Women did not want slaves — they wanted masters!

Marion's return, her warm winsomeness and above all, the damnable effect she had on him of somehow seeming to demand his protection, by no means buttressed his fine masculine resolution. Nevertheless he did change his tune considerably, and over his wine and oatcakes endeavoured to take a fairly vigorous initiative.

"You said that it was a bonnie day for riding, Marion—as it is." he asserted. He had not failed to note something of wistfulness in her voice when she had acknowledged that. "You are a bonnie horsewoman, likewise. That I know. Come riding with me, Marion Ogilvy—this sparkling morning!"

Her blue eyes widened in astonishment—for this surprising invitation was shot at her almost as a command. "Riding? With you? Where?" she wondered.

"Why, anywhere. There are no sands here—but there are hillsides a-plenty. Or . . . ride to Restenneth, to see Gilbert. If you would so wish. But, come riding."

"Alone? With you . . .?"

"Why not? Bring one of your people, if you must. But we would ride better lacking them, I swear! See, Marion—you sit a horse more nobly than any woman I have known. You could not do that if you did not delight in it. As do I, myself. Often have I thought of our ride across the sands of Lunan Bay. The memory was like a breath of good Scots air to me, many a time, in soft, complaisant France. I came today, to take you riding again. So have I thought of it, dreamed of it. You will not deny me? Will you refuse the new mitred abbot his first command? Did Elizabeth Graham so teach you, at Lunan Priory? To spurn the prerogative of Holy Church, Marion Ogilvy!"

She smiled, then. Even sketched a tiny bow. "Very well, my lord. If you so command . . ."

Presently they were riding down the winding track from the castle—and no escort trotting at their backs. At the foot, where they must ford the Isla and turn left, southwards, if they were to make for Restenneth Priory, the girl slightly in the lead, made no attempt to do so, but rode on along the riverside, upstream. Well satisfied, David followed on, northwards, into the hills.

For a couple of miles they weaved their way amongst the haughs, water-meadows and scattered woodlands of the rushing Isla, by a narrow bridle-path, the man content to trot at Marion's heels, admiring her superb carriage in the saddle, the easy grace of her sway to the bay's movements—and the frank line of her long limbs, for she rode astride, as before. Where the river-valley narrowed in abruptly between lofty steep braes, they paused to admire the splendid waterfalls of the Slug of Achrannie, seeming to steam in the frosty air. Then, hardly speaking, she put her beast to the high enclosing bank of grass, gravel and frozen earth on the right, a stiff climb that seemed an unlikely route to be taking for a pleasure jaunt. David held his peace.

At the top it was to emerge upon a totally different scene. The trees thinned away and the land fell gently over grassland to a noble loch, embosomed in the hills, roughly circular in shape and more than a mile across, the snow-streaked summits reflected in its calm ice-fringed waters.

"Lintrathen!" the young woman called to him. "Where our race was cradled." Without pause or warning, she dug in her heels and was off down the grassy slope, quickly passing from a canter to a full gallop, her mount's hooves beating out a stirring metallic tattoo in the crisp air.

The man did not attempt to make a race of it, pleased to retain a position close enough to savour all the verve and spirit and sheer joyous appeal to his sense; his was a complicated nature — but at that moment he was entirely, essentially and uncomplicatedly happy.

They thundered along in splendid style, spattering clods, startling waterfowl, Marion's hair escaping from its coif to stream out like a banner. Perhaps a thousand yards of loch-shore they galloped, leaping three incoming burns in their stride, one of them large enought to make a major jump, and then, at the head of the loch where the Melgam Water flowed in, Marion alarmingly and without pause drove headlong through the shallows in a spectacular splashing that sent up showers of icy water, David following, after the merest involuntary falter, in mixed trepidation and exhilaration. On and up the rising slopes beyond she went, but as the hillside steepened she slackened rein to let her bay make its own pace. Gradually the speed eased to a canter and a clambering trot, until finally she drew up beside an ancient moss-grown standing-stone a couple of hundred feet above the waterside.

Panting, flushed, eyes aglow, breasts in a tumult, she laughed to him as he came pounding up, all strain, wariness and defensive caution gone.

"I am sorry!" she cried. "Did I frighten you? At the river?

It was wicked of me. To lead you through that. To soak all your fine clothes . . ."

She got no further. Straight up to her he rode, swinging his stallion round in a rearing curvet, so that he actually jostled her steaming bay. Without pause or word he leaned over, swept an arm around her to draw her to him, and bending, fiercely kissed her parted lips. He held her so, mouth on her's.

When she broke away, partly by the movement of her horse, it was to turn and gaze at him, wide-eyed, gasping, wordless as himself. For moments they stared, eyes locked, and then, as the man raised an open hand towards her, urgent in both command and pleading, she suddenly twisted her mount's head around and was away again, at speed, up towards the ridge of this grassy hill.

As, frowning, he rode after her, he perceived that she did not now ride upright, carefree, but bent low in the saddle, head down. Undoubtedly she was no longer laughing.

It was almost half an hour later, and they were deep into the hills that formed the watershed between Glens Isla and Prosen, before arrival at the snow level forced Marion to pull up, as her bay slithered and faltered, breaking through the frozen crust. David came up beside her.

"You take a deal of keeping near, in your Angus hills, Marion Ogilvy," he said, a little breathlessly. "Are we bound for Aberdeen? Or where?"

She continued to look straight ahead of her, over the snowfield towards the lofty summits of what were now mountains. "You should not have done that. Back there, at Lintrathen Loch," she said. "It was ill done." She spoke calmly, levelly.

"Was it? I say not, Marion. It was the most natural act in the world. It was not done—it happened." He raised his head, smiling grimly. "At least it was better done than that last time! I do not apologise for it."

"Once you asked me not to build a wall against you. It seems that a wall is necessary."

So she had remembered that. "You would wall yourself away from me? Why?" When she did not answer, he went on. "You must fear me, then? Do you fear me, Marion?"

"Fear you? No—I do not fear you, I think."

"Perhaps it is yourself that you fear?"

Thoughfully she considered that, and him. "Perhaps," she said. "I would not be here if I was afraid of you," she said. "Would I? Although perhaps I should be. Afraid. What do you want of me, David Beaton?"

Challenged directly, he hesitated, searching her lovely face and his own heart. Other women had challenged him, and he had not doubted how to answer them, how to act. But this was different; this was no game, no series of moves on the age-old, well-played chequer-board of the sexes.

"If I answered you truthfully, I suppose that I should say *you!*" he told her, at length. "That it is you I want — all of you. That I desire you, long for you, need you. All that is you, I covet. That is truth. But only part of truth. For it is much more than that, Marion. I would cherish you. How can I explain it? I need you — and believe that you need me."

"How can this be?" she asked. "You have seen me only one day before this. Years ago. When I was very young. Yourself not so greatly older."

"Is time important? The greatest events of all may take place in an instant — and endless ages drag on meaning nothing. That one meeting, at Lunan, was sufficient. For me. To perceive you as my destiny. Since then you have never been far from my mind. Always in my heart. In Paris and Rome and Madrid — wherever went David Beaton, there went Marion Ogilvy also. Can you understand? How can I tell you? You have been with me all those years. I cannot now treat you as though you were a stranger."

"Were there no women in Paris, and Rome, that you required this pale shadow from Scotland?" she asked, her voice uncertain.

"Pale shadow! I am no man to be content with a pale shadow, on my soul! You can never be that, however far from me. It was the other women who were the pale shadows." He shrugged. "Yes, there were other women. Many. I would not deny it. I am a man who requires women. As I require meat. Wine. And good talking. They are an appetite. Something to enjoy, to appreciate. But . . . you are different. You are part of me."

"I think not," she said quietly, and turning her horse's head, she set it at a walk back whence they had come.

He reined round after her. "I am sorry if I have offended. Spoken too frank," he said urgently. "You asked me what I wanted of you, in honesty. If I have answered too honestly, forgive. Bear with me. There is so much to say. Forgive me if my tongue runs too fast."

"Too far, rather than too fast," she amended, though not ungently. "When you say that I am part of you, then you commit me. I cannot be part of you, and remain my own woman. You see it, do you not? I cannot be part of you, or any man, unless I will it so. I *will* not be so used, made thrall of."

"Thrall? Save us – it is *I* who am in thrall, if you could but see it!" He threw up his head, almost angrlly. "Back there we spoke of danger. You being in possible danger – from me. I declare that it is myself that is in the danger, not you!"

"I do not understand . . .?"

"Danger is ever to the vulnerable, to he who has most to lose. It is you who have entered me – not me you. You are whole. I am wounded, stricken. Think you I would have chosen it so? Think you that this wound does not endanger all? My whole life?"

"I think you speak wildly. Great swelling words . . ."

"I speak sober fact. I intend to do great things in this Scotland. That, God knows, needs great things done for it! Think you that entanglement with you, with any woman, will aid me in that? Placed as I am?"

She stared, at his harsh, almost brutal words. She did not answer.

"I must work within the Church – where women have little place. Only through the Church can I rise – as my uncle has risen. But further. Higher. Stronger. For James Beaton is not strong, as I see strength. To entrammel myself deeply, to the heart, with a woman, can only hinder and restrict me. That is certain."

"Then – of a mercy, untrammel yourself, sir! Instead of seeking to entrammel me!" Marion exclaimed, with an access of spirit. "For I seek nothing of you."

He shook his head. "It is less simple than that, woman! Do you think that I have not tried? My mind, to free my heart? I have had years to debate the issue. I am no callow, lovesick youth. I know myself . . ."

"But, it appears, for all your much talking, you do not know *me*!" she asserted warmly. "Learn this, at least – that I will aid you, with all *my* heart, to be free of me! Of this hindrance and impediment to your fortunes! Which I never sought nor suspected." Involuntarily she urged her bay to increase pace.

David groaned, part-despairingly, part-humorously. "Have mercy!" he cried. "To think that I am esteemed to have a nimble tongue! Have you understood none of me? Must I speak to you as I would at Court, or to statesmen – picking my words, schooling my lips? I speak to you from the heart. And what I say, what I have discovered, is that the heart of me is stronger than the head. That I *cannot* be free of you. That I do not wish to be. That, seeing you again today, in the flesh, but embroils me deeper. Whatever the cost."

The young woman did not speak for a little. "This cost," she said, at length. "It is no concern of mine. But I see that you have set your heart on high position. On vaunting power. To me it seems that if this is what you lust for, it behoves you to be single-minded in the pursuit!"

He frowned. "You do me less than justice, Marion," he complained "That word lust . . ."

"I said that you lusted for power and position. It is true, is it not?"

"Not as you mean it. The power I seek is not for my own glory. It is to aid this realm. This Scotland of ours, so sore stricken. I see so clearly what she needs – and see no one concerned to give her it. Save only, after a fashion, my poor foolish Uncle James! On every hand I see men concerned only for themselves, greedy for power to give themselves lands and wealth . . ."

"And are you not?"

"I seek these, yes – for what I may do with them. In Scotland's cause. Is that so strange? Can you not understand it?"

"I can understand you loving Scotland, yes. And seeking her betterment – as must all who have not hearts of stone, I think, in this present sorry pass . . ."

"But not for me to act on it? To effect something? You think that I esteem myself too highly? That I am immodest – Davie Beaton, the son of a poor Fife laird! But what virtue is there in modesty if it prevents a man from doing what he knows he *can* do, and is his duty? I tell you. I see my part otherwise."

She sighed. "You may be right, David. It is not for me to say that you are not. But what can you *do*? For a start. One man—and young. Even with your uncle so high?"

"I can prevail upon the Chancellor to call a Parliament. In the King's name. As is his right. And in that Parliament, as Abbot of Arbroath, I can speak."

"I see." She all but pulled up her horse, to face him. "Now it becomes more clear. And will Parliament work your purpose?"

"That is to be seen. There has been no true Parliament for long. But, in name at least, Parliament still rules this unhappy land. The Church is strong in it—or should be. If it will speak now, for the right, with no uncertain voice, then we may yet confound King Henry Tudor of England. And all who do his will in this realm!"

Something of the shine came back into the girl's eyes. "Pray God you are right!" she exclaimed. "In that, at least, Davie Beaton, I am with you."

"Aye. And I am glad. For if you, others with you, Marion. You see? There you spoke from the heart. You are of no faction or party. That, I say, is the true voice of Scotland. That is the voice with which, Heaven willing, Parliament will speak. If it has opportunity. That opportunity I will give it—if one man can!"

They rode on again, both fallen silent now, and with less of barrier between them—until, that is, they topped the long ridge of Coul, and looked down upon Lintrathen Loch again, and constraint once more raised its head.

As they trotted past the spot where David had so unceremoniously embraced and kissed her, Marion's gaze now fixed firmly ahead of her, the man spoke.

"Am I forgiven?" he asked.

"Does it matter? Is it important enough for forgiveness? You said that it was not done—that it only happened. And you sought no pardon. Do you do so now?"

He stroked his chin. "Perhaps not. Only—I would not have you to think ill of me."

"I do not. For that."

"No? You say not? But . . . for the rest?"

"Say that I try to understand. For I would not have you think so ill of me, either."

"You mean that, Marion? That it matters to you? What I think of you?"

"What do you wish me to say, David?"

Once again her directness brought him up short. "I . . . I do not know," he admitted ruefully. "I am being a fool. I dread what you may say. Yet cannot have it left unsaid. Marion — your heart? Is it given to some other man?"

"No," she said simply.

"I thank God for that! Then — is there room in it for Davie Beaton?"

She nodded. "Not only David Beaton can cherish memories. Of a day of breeze and sea and sailing clouds. And things said and unsaid."

"Marion . . .!" He kneed his stallion closer, and reached out to grasp her arm.

"No," she said, and gently but firmly put his hand from her. "That is not the way of it, David. That way resolves nothing. Let us cherish this day also. And think on it. Think long. We are not bairns. And there is a deal to think on."

"I have had too long for thinking. Years."

"And yet — you are less than single in your mind, are you not? Whatever says this heart you tell me of."

He frowned. "I tell you. My heart has overborne my head. Quite."

"Overborne — but not silenced. *I* have to think of that. And so do you. Before next you come riding to Airlie."

Chapter Seven

DAVID BEATON, dressed for the first time in the splendid full robes of a prelate of Holy Church, sat in his appointed place in the Great or Parliament Hall of Edinburgh Castle, his lips moving soundlessly. Perhaps some around him—and there were many who not infrequently glanced in his direction — conceived the new so innocent-looking Abbot of Arbroath suitably to be at his devotions; others may have assumed that he was rehearsing a speech. In fact, he was counting. Counting heads. And not for the first time that dull late-February morning. Only, this must be the final count — for the fanfare of trumpets from outside had just heralded the approach of the royal party from the palace-quarters of the Castle, near by. No more belated attenders were likely to appear now. It was going to be a close matter.

In front of him, in this section of the Hall set aside for the Lords Spiritual, sat, in order of precedence, four bishops — and there could have been twelve. In brand-new magnificence, even greater than David's own, lounged Gavin Dunbar, the King's tutor and preceptor, recently appointed at the Queen's instigation directly from his classroom to the second place in the Scottish hierarchy, as Archbishop of Glasgow, James Beaton's former position. No question how his vote would go. Next to him sat his own uncle, of the same name but very different character, the Bishop of Aberdeen, a true and saintly man. Then there was the Bishop of Dunblane, an ignoramus but a creature of the Douglases. And lastly, Ross, only Bishop-Elect but none other than John Hepburn, lately Prior of St. Andrews, James Beaton's old enemy.

Scant comfort there.

David's own category of lesser prelates, mitred abbots, could have shown nearly a score. In fact there were but seven present, other than himself — with the addition of Patrick Hepburn the Bastard, now Prior of St. Andrews, whose Priory was powerful enough to carry a seat in Parliament. The Abbot of Scone was a Queen's man, while the Abbot of Paisley was a Hamilton, a son of Arran. William Douglas, so lately and ingloriously Prior of Coldinghame, had been hastily promoted Abbot of Holyrood for the occasion, by the Primate — but even so there could be no more than five favourable votes here. All the rest had elected to stay away.

Across the Hall, in the Lords Temporal stalls, sat eight earls and eight Lords of Parliament. There were three more earls to come — but still that represented less than half of the adult peers entitled to attend. At the best of it, David could not see the Chancellor gaining more than nine or ten votes there.

He did not waste much attention upon the third of the Estates, the burgesses, on their hard wooden benches at the bottom end of the Hall — for although there were more of them present, three of four from each royal burgh, only one from each could vote. And only Edinburgh, Stirling, Linlithgow and Dundee had responded to the summons — together with the great ecclesiastical burghs of St. Andrews and Coupar. Of the score and more of others, none had dared to send representatives.

Threats and bribes had done their work. There would be no more than forty votes in this Parliament. There had been promises of sixty — and could have been over one hundred.

As the clanking of armour and grounding of pikes sounded outside, the great doors were thrown open and all men rose, to the high neighing of trumpets that flooded the half-empty Hall. Preceded by pikemen in the royal livery, the Lord Lyon King of Arms and his lesser heralds led in the procession of state, consisting of those high officers of the realm who were not either imprisoned, banished, or afraid to appear, the Dempster, the Clerk-Register, the Justiciar, the Treasurer and the Lord Privy Seal. Then in full armour, earl's robes thrown back from it, strode in the Earl of Erroll, Great Constable of Scotland, bearing the Sword of State — a key figure, of doubtful allegiance. Behind him, walking side by side managing to turn each a shoulder away from the other in mutual disgust, came James Hamilton, Earl of Arran, Lieutenant-Governor of the realm and second heir to the throne, bearing the sceptre; and Archibald Douglas, Earl of Angus, holding the crown—and holding it almost tucked under one arm, as though it was his private property. The Douglas, much the younger, taller, and better-looking, also wore steel beneath his furred robe; but Arran, thin, cadaverous, middle-aged, was sumptuous, indeed over-dressed, in cloth-of-gold and jewellery, garb fit for any king.

As these paced well into the Hall, there was a special flourish of trumpets, and into the succeeding silence the Lord Lyon announced the person of their gracious sovereign lord, the High and Mighty Prince James, by the grace of God, King of Scots, Duke of Rothesay, Earl of Carrick and Lord of the Isles.

Young James Stewart, aged twelve, after a moment or two of delay, came on in something of a rush as though pushed from behind, taking extra long paces, eyes darting left and right from under down-bent brows. He was well-built for his years, broad rather than tall, with a hint of his father's good looks in more than his long red hair. But his royal appearance stopped there. His carriage was hesitant, jerky, his expression furtive, and his clothing probably the least fine in all that chamber, and worn with no grace. Long-strided, as though stepping over obstacles and counting them as he paced, he made for the gilded throne.

David Beaton, whose first glimpse this was of the child who had been practically a captive since birth — and whose representative he had been in France — knew an access of pity to complicate his other emotions.

Close behind the King came his mother. Margaret Tudor was now aged thirty-four, and looked older. She had always been stocky, fleshy and plain, even when as a girl of thirteen she came to Scotland as bride for the reluctant and dashing James the Fourth; now, grown heavy, with her hair greying prematurely and her puffy features pasty, only her dull-glowing dark eyes revealed that here was a woman of some spirit, who could hate with a smouldering intensity and whose rages were as notorious as her lasciviousness.

David wondered anew that anyone so physically unsavoury could be so concerned with her own body. Her brother, Henry the Eighth, was similarly gross — but at least he had a certain animal attractiveness. Margaret was undoubtedly one of the Auld Enemy England's most effective disservices to Scotland.

When the crown, sceptre and sword were placed on the table before him, the boy King moved round to mount to his throne. The Queen-Mother took his arm and more or less propelled him into his tall chair. Then she moved her own lesser chair, placed close behind his, closer still and forward, and sat down, near enough to touch her son.

With murmurs and exchanged glances, the assembly sat down. The Lord Treasurer, a young man of effeminate appearance and dandified clothing, laid his purse-of-office on the table, and went, not to the seats of the other officers of state, but up the royal dais, to stand at the Queen's shoulder, immediately behind the King — Henry Stewart of Methven, second son of the Lord Avondale, the Queen's present paramour, whom she would have had sitting in the still vacant Chancellor's seat directly opposite, had she been able. Glares from all around, especially from Angus, Margaret's husband, followed the simpering lordling to this lofty and un-suitable stance.

Erroll, Arran and Angus now stalked to their earl's seats. That the two latter had to sit side by side and close together was a misfortune which both of them contrived not to notice.

A single blast on a trumpet was the signal for everyone to rise again to their feet — everyone except the King, that is. Even the Queen-Mother made the gesture of raising her heavy thighs from her chair and crouching thus, most uncomfortably, frowning. A side door opened and the dazzling figure of the Chancellor, President of the High Court of Parliament, entered.

It was obvious now why Henry Stewart had chosen to stand, from the first—so that he would not have to rise to his feet for the man whom he had been appointed to supercede.

Dazzling was the only description of James Beaton that grey morning. He wore the most magnificent and colourful robes that even an Archbishop might aspire to, alb, cope, pallium and stole, all so encrusted with jewels and gold as to make his every movement a blazing scintillation. Holy Church was today preaching one of its more telling lessons.

The Primate paced to his appointed solitary seat between the Lords Spiritual and Temporal and directly opposite the royal dais. The Clerk-Register came to sit below him, at the clerk's table with the pens and paper. The Archbishop bowed to the King and raised his hand. He uttered a prayer, extraordinary for its brevity. He sat down—and the Parliament of the Three Estates of Scotland was in session.

The ceremony of the Fencing of Parliament was followed by the Clerk-Register reading out the royal summons, signed by the young King only after an epic struggle of wills. Then he read out the names of the Lords of the Articles appointed by the last Parliament, whose period of office and responsibility was hereby ended. This was a sort of executive committee appointed to carry out in detail the broad decisions of each Parliament, which itself made only the one sitting. It was noticeable that of the ten names read out, five were missing.

Almost before the clerk was finished, the Queen-Mother, the only woman present, stood up, gesturing towards the Archbishop. She—nor anyone else save the King himself—could speak until the Chancellor gave his assent. Deliberately now he kept her waiting, leaning forward to speak to the Clerk-Register, before, at length, he nodded.

"My lord Chancellor, my lords and barons," she said, ignoring the burgesses. "This Parliament is untimeous and unnecessary. I do regret, as does His Grace, the inconvenience and cost to which you have been put, to attend it." She spoke slowly, forcefully, but with a high-pitched voice at variance with her appearance—and despite twenty-one years' residence in Scotland, she had not lost her English accent. "The Lords Articular just named, with whom I sat, were well able to conduct the affairs of this realm. There has been no great event, no disaster, no threat to the realm. I move that the said Lords Articular be re-appointed, forthwith."

She sat down amidst a stir of excitement. Never had challenge been thrown down so swiftly, a trial of strength that could end the proceedings before they were begun.

Angus jumped to his feet, hardly waiting for the Archbishop's permissive nod. "My lord Chancellor," he exclaimed. "With the greatest of respect for Her Highness my consort, I move to the contrary. Douglas has not come here from afar for such device. We have come to right the realm's business." No swords, other than the Sword of State, were permitted within the Parliament Hall — but the Earl managed to beat his sheathed dagger metal-lically against his plate-armour as he sat down.

At his side, Arran rose. "I support the Queen's Highness," he declared shortly. "I call a vote."

"My lord — you will await my permission to speak. And address such speech thereafter to this chair!" James Beaton said heavily.

The Hamilton glowered at his new wife's uncle, but kept his seat, refusing the indignity of repeating himself.

The Hamilton Abbot of Paisley rose. "My lord Chancellor — I humbly seek your favour, to support Her Highness and crave the vote of this assembly," he said smoothly, bowing all round.

"Damme, my lord — let them have their way!" the Bishop of Dunblane roared. "Let us see who supports Douglas!"

David Beaton bit his lip. This was damnable — utter and complete folly. To vote at this stage, at all. And to make the vote for or against Douglas. All might well be lost on this one throw. But, the motion moved and seconded, he could do nothing about it.

Nor could the Chancellor. Red in the face and frowning darkly, he was forced to put the matter to the test. "Answer Aye or No," he growled, repeating the Queen's motion. "And think you well ere you judge!" he added ominously. "My lord Arch-bishop of Glasgow?"

"Aye."

The Chancellor swallowed, gave the impression that he might

even spit, at this prompt slap in the face for himself, the Primate, by the new Archbishop.

"My lord Bishop of Aberdeen?"

"No."

The Chancellor nodded commendingly. "My lord Bishop of Dunblane?"

"No."

"The Bishop-Elect of Ross?" That was indeed spat out, even the lordship omitted.

"Aye."

"My lord Abbot of Scone?"

"Aye."

"My lord Abbot of Arbroath?"

"No."

"My lord Abbot of Lindores?"

"No."

"My lord Abbot of Paisley?"

"Aye."

So the time-honoured procedure of calling each vote by name went on. The Lords Spiritual, with a final Aye from Patrick the Bastard, came out with six supporting the Queen and six against —Holy Church's testimony patently blurred.

After Arran had said Aye and Angus No, Erroll the Constable, in obvious agitation, glancing from the Queen-Mother to the King and then to the Chancellor, blurted out an Aye. As did the Earls of Lennox, Eglinton and Cassillis. Those voting No were Argyll, Crawford Morton and Rothes.

Six to five for the motion.

The Lords of Parliament, led by the Lord Forbes voted five to three against the Queen.

Sir John Stirling of Keir, the only Knight of a Shire present, voted for the motion.

Now there was only the burghs. Edinburgh, dominated by the cannon of this great Castle, controlled by the Queen-Mother, voted for her. Stirling, in the same position, did likewise. As did Linlithgow, a Hamilton town. Dundee, in Angus, cast its vote against. Coupar, dependent for all things on its great abbey, voted as did its Abbot, against. St. Andrews, the last vote, swithered and twisted as though grilled on hot iron, its representatives peering from its Archbishop, whose burgh it was, to its Prior, whose Hepburn servitors and mosstroopers from the Borders, ruled its streets. The Chancellor had to thunder at them for haste, with sufficient of threat in his bull-like voice, to extort a hesitant No.

Nineteen for, nineteen against.

James Beaton held up his hand to still the mounting clamour. "Silence, I say! Your Grace, my lords — in this equal division it falls to me, as President, to give my casting vote. I vote No! The motion is in defeat. Hereby declared."

In the uproar, David wiped his brow and found it wet — although the Hall was far from warm.

Queen Margaret, whom previous Parliaments had given power, when she was Regent, to attend and to move, but not to vote, was on her feet again immediately. "My lord Chancellor," she grated. "I have further motion. That this Parliament appoints for itself, as is its right, a new chancellor forthwith, your lordship being of sere age! I name the Lord High Treasurer, Henry Stewart of Methven!"

Everywhere men gasped and exclaimed. Here was war to the knife, with a vengeance! And shrewd thrusting. It was lost on none that the Tudor woman's stroke was masterly. She was a true sister of Henry of England! On such a personal issue, James Beaton could not vote. There would be no casting vote to save him.

David groaned in spirit. Had he been a fool in forcing this Parliament? A presumptuous fool? Had he precipitated the disaster he sought to avoid? Played into the Queen-Mother's and English party's hands?

This time, however, Margaret Tudor had overplayed her own hand. In nominating the weak and wilful stripling, Henry Stewart, to the position of chief minister of the realm, she offended certain of her own supporters. Erroll was the first to show it. Other lords followed his lead. This motion was defeated by twenty-three votes to fifteen.

The Queen, angry and lowering but unbowed, appeared to be determined to retain the initiative. She rose again to declare that in the appointment of new Lords of the Articles it must be accepted that the safety and wellbeing of the King's Grace was all important. It was being said that evilly disposed men were plotting to capture, hold and wreak their wicked wills upon their sovereign lord, contrary to all right, law, humanity and the weal of the

114

realm. Her information was reliable. Let them be sure that every man appointed Lord Articular was such as would not thus take the law into his own hands.

Despite his concern, David could not but admire the English-woman's ability. She was making suspect not only the Douglases, whom all knew to be capable of an attempt on the King, but also the principal motion of the day, the real reason for the calling of this Parliament. This podgy, unappetising woman, he perceived, was the true foeman for his steel — if only he was given opportunity to use it.

James Beaton grew more and more restive under his glittering cope. Angus was clanking almost sufficiently to drown his wife's high voice. At length the Chancellor could bear it no longer. As she paused, momentarily, for breath and to glare at her husband, he broke in, loud-voiced.

"All that Your Highness declares is noted. Will be considered in our deliberations and decisions. These decisions we must now reach."

There was more than a murmur of agreement from many of the lords. Reluctantly Queen Margaret resumed her seat.

"First, let us deal with the matter of the panning, making and selling of salt. Master Clerk — you will speak to this . . .?"

There followed a number of simple and non-controversial issues dealing with trade, crafts and commerce, of more interest to the burgesses than to the lords — although the Church had certain trades almost in her own hands, and was concerned to retain her monopolies. These were disposed of expeditiously, while the Lords Temporal fidgeted and talked aloud. It was the Archbishop's method of reducing the temperature and countering the effects of the Queen's warnings.

Then the new Lords of the Articles were chosen, this time six from each of the three Estates. This was an innovation, suggested by David himself. Normally there were only nine or ten — but apparently there was nothing to preclude a greater number being appointed. As anticipated, the opposition was unprepared for this, with insufficient nominees thought of. In consequence although the two factions were so evenly divided in the assembly, the Angus-Beaton party found themselves with a majority of ten to eight Lords Articular, David himself emerging as one.

While the Queen's people were still gnashing their teeth over this tactical defeat, the Chancellor caught his nephew's eye.

"My lord of Angus has now a proposal to make, concerning the health and welfare of our lord the King's Grace," he said.

The company was as though galvanised. Even the young monarch sat up interestedly. He was known to admire his hot-blooded and high-handed step-father.

The Douglas rose. He was a man with little use for either finesse or eloquence, esteeming these to be but suitable devices to fall back upon for those who lacked power to act more effectively — clerks, churchmen, weaklings and the like.

"I say that the King's Grace is kept mewed up in this Castle of Edinburgh, to the scathe of his health and person," he barked. "It's an ill place, cold, windy and dreich. I move that he be enlarged. Removed to the new palace of Holyroodhouse. For his weal. Forthwith. I move that a high council be appointed to look to his better welfare. I move that this council be of four. Myself. The Chancellor. My lord of Argyll. And . . ." He turned to look at his neighbour in the earls' seats, smiling thinly, ". . . my lord Arran." He sat down.

The Primate had to beat on the arm of his chair to still the tumult. Lords were jumping up everywhere. He perceived none of them. "The lord Abbot of Arbroath will speak," he said.

David rose, to await quiet. He was only too well aware of the dimensions of his task, self-allotted as it was. The motion could hardly have suffered a worse introduction, especially after the Queen-Mother's revelations of a plot to gain possession of the King's person. Angus himself should never have spoken to it — but the Douglas had insisted. It had been thrown at the Parliament as a Douglas command rather than any motion for debate, a *fait accompli*. Moreover, it should have been divided into three distinct motions, carefully spaced, each only moved after the other had been accepted. Nothing could have been better calculated to arouse resistance, even outside the Queen's faction, than this.

"Your Grace, my lord Chancellor, my lords and burgh's representatives, members of this High Court of Parliament," he began, at his most modest, diffident, deferential, sounding almost in awe of the company he kept. "I rise most aware of my lack of years, my inexperience, my effrontry in raising my faltering voice in this august assembly. That I do so at all, arises only from my conviction that in France, where these years I have been His Grace's all unworthy resident envoy, I was privileged to learn certain principles relative to the governing of a state, that seem to bear on our present problems. I plead your charity, therefore, and pray that you will bear with me."

Men glanced at each other, and shuffled their feet. What way was this to talk, in Parliament? Like a novice in a nunnery!

"The first principle in matters of state, which of course you all know well, is that the realm is our mother and the king our father, each one for the love and protection of the other. Earthly mothers and fathers, alas, come and go. But these two, the realm and the kingship, are God's appointed order, enduring, ever-lasting."

The Bishop-Elect of Ross blew his nose loudly, scornfully. His Beatitude of Glasgow turned round in his seat to inspect the speaker haughtily. Others were restive.

"You consider, my lords, that I speak like a bairn, of first principles? Unsuited to your more mature minds. It may be that I do—so I pray you, have patience. But . . . are we not here dealing with first principles? For here is a realm and a king, our auld Scotland and our liege lord James—whom God defend! And the one does *not* cherish the other, protect the other. Nor the other the one." With the utmost of hesitation, he coughed. "I say that any man and wife who so flout both God's ordinances and first principles must perish. Any realm and monarch the more so."

There was no shuffling of feet now. Men leaned forward rather, in their seats. Here were strange words indeed from the Chancellor's pretty nephew, who was supposedly supporting Angus's motion. He had not actually named Angus and the Queen-Mother, but few could doubt his allusions—certainly not the scowling Douglas and his heavy-browed wife, who glared at each other and the speaker with equal animus.

Having thus personally dissociated himself from Angus and his supporters—who of course could be relied upon to vote for the motion anyway—David went on to develop his theme for the less committed.

"The realm to cherish the monarch, and the monarch the realm—or perish! That is God's law. And our duty, who conduct the affairs of this realm of Scotland. But has Scotland cherished its monarch? All humbly I say that she has not. The worse in that the monarch is of tender years. She has neglected her duty. She has left the care of the monarch to his earthly mother. In despite of her duty. The realm has failed King James, has it not?"

Disturbed, men of all views stirred uneasily, the Chancellor amongst them. The Scots Parliaments were unused to oratory and dialectics. Meeting in infrequent single session, with broad issues to be promulgated in short time, it was more of a court for publishing decisions of majorities that had been decided elsewhere, than a debating chamber. This strange young man's flood of words were not like the Queen's, plain declarations and accusations. They went round in circles, as though to ensnare the wits of his hearers. This was no way to address his betters.

David bowed towards Queen Margaret, smiling. "None will question the devotion and ability of the gracious lady, the Princess Maragaret Tudor, Countess of Angus, the King's mother, who has borne our rude Scottish ways, in order to cherish her son in our midst. When undoubtedly she would have been better content and at ease in her own England. This we must acknowledge, with gratitude – but decide to relieve her of the burden, forthwith."

Now some of his hearers were seething – including the gracious lady in question – some grinning, some looking thoughtful.

"My lords, this realm has suffered great things these last years, since the death of our liege lord's beloved father, and so many of our brothers, on Flodden Field. We blame the English, who raid and rape and rob, who slay and subborn and seduce, who threaten our Borders and steal our honour." He paused for a moment, to let his suddenly ringing words throb on the air. "But is the blame not our own? May it not be God's judgement on this people for having failed to cherish its Lord's Anointed? For having failed to show to this, our sovereign Lord James . . ." and his hand shot out to point to the wide-eyed boy in the gilded throne, ". . . that love, care and devotion which was our due service, and should have been our joy! Is the blame not ours, my friends?"

He was playing on emotions now, unblushingly but skilfully.

The Auld Enemy, patriotic fervour, the fatherless child, the luxury of vicarious self-chastisement – all these chords he blended to potent effect.

He looked along at his fellow prelates. "My lords Spiritual – we, I fear, must be most aware of the short-comings of Holy Church – or better, of us her unworthy servants – in this matter. If the realm is mother of the people, the Holy Church is mother of the realm, of all realms. Yet has not the Church equally failed to guide and lead in this matter of God's will? The Church has scarce raised her voice. Two men indeed have striven nobly to cherish and upraise our prince, and these the loftiest of our number. But these have had to act alone, and as individuals, not as the authoritative voice of Christ's body on earth. My most renowned kinsman, my lord Chancellor, the King's chief minister; and the most eminent scholar, now Archbishop of Glasgow, the royal tutor and preceptor. These have indeed well served the Church and the monarch – but has the Church well served them? I pray you, my lords Spiritual, to speak now, with the clear voice of your high calling."

There was no hiding the discomfort amongst the clergy, thus assumed to have a corporate voice – and the voice of God Almighty, at that.

David smiled almost shyly all round. "I greatly thank you, Your Grace, my lords and burgesses, for having heard me out so patiently, my stumbling and inadequate words. It but remains for me to say, what we all know, that what we decide here is not for this party or that, not for present gain or any man or woman's upraising, save that of the King. It is for the very life and preservation of this Scotland of ours, which all would die for. That has remained independent, God be thanked, for six centuries, but today is in dire danger. Danger today. And danger tomorrow – for if the King's Grace is not cherished by the realm, as he should be, happed at all times by the good and proper care and advice of true counsellors, how shall *he* come to cherish his realm aright when he reaches man's estate and full kingship? If indeed this ancient realm is still independent that day! Think well on that, my lords."

He paused for long moments, dramatically.

In a different voice he added. "I commend the motion to your wisdom and judgement. With this addendum – that to the council

119

who shall cherish the King in our name is added my lord the Archbishop of Glasgow."

David sat down amidst a furious hubbub of exclamation, question and concern. None present, undoubtedly, had ever heard the like. None, even the Chancellor himself, was quite certain as to reaction, to the fullest implications – none save the only woman present, that is. She rose at once.

"We . . . we have listened to words amany, my lord Chancellor. A great wind of words. None of which alter the case – which is that the King's Grace is my son, and must remain in my care. I . . . I . . ." The Queen-Mother was actually trembling with fury, so that her words were barely distinguishable. "'Fore God – enough of this! I move against this wicked motion!"

There was silence now in the Hall, as men eyed each other, and waited. The Chancellor also waited, shrewd little pig-like eyes busy.

The moments passed. The calculations and speculations in men's minds were almost to be heard. The Earl of Arran stared straight ahead of him. He had never loved the Queen, and he was nominated, however sourly, for this governors' council of the King. How would the vote go? He dared not be in the minority. Gavin Dunbar, Archbishop of Glasgow, had his head bowed, as though in prayer. However much the Queen-Mother glared at him, he did not speak.

When it was evident, at length, that none of the more lofty supporters of the Queen were going to commit themselves to seconding her, John Hepburn, Elect of Ross, did so, curtly.

"I sustain Her Highness's move," he declared. "We have heard enough of folly!"

Stewart, Lord Avondale, stood up to speak, Methven's father – but James Beaton affected not to see him.

"I call the vote," he said loudly. "My lord Archbishop of Glasgow? How say you?"

Gavin Dunbar's normally bland and rubicund face was flushed and tense, a man torn. A year ago he had been but a humble scholar, nephew to the Bishop of Aberdeen but a mere tutor to the boy King. Now he was Archbishop, and being proposed for the governors' council – which would make him one of the chiefest in the land. This undoubtedly had been David Beaton's most brilliant device.

He looked up, at last. "My lord Chancellor — may I speak?" he asked his flute-like voice strangely rasping yet hesitant. "My name has been named in this matter. My person is therefore, by no choice of mine, involved. In such circumstance it would ill become me to vote. I shall abstain." He did not once look in the direction of Queen Margaret.

The sigh that ran round the chamber might have taken its origin from David's breath of relief.

The Chancellor nodded grimly. "Very well, my lord. It is noted. You, my lord Bishop of Aberdeen?"

"Aye."

"My lord Bishop of Dunblane?"

"Aye."

"The Bishop-Elect of Ross?"

"No."

"My lord Abbot of Scone?"

There was a pause as that prelate nibbled his finger-nails. His dilemma was evident to all. Hepburn of Ross's vote could be ignored; he was a soured and disappointed man, fobbed off with this most remote bishopric when he had aimed at the Primacy. He would vote against James Beaton on any and every issue. The Abbot of Scone's position was vastly different. He was a Queen's man — but he was senior abbot and in line for a bishopric. Glasgow, more Queen's man still, had seen fit to abstain. Was the Queen's star in the descendant? Dare he vote contrary to both archbishops? Could he take the responsibility of leading the note of discord in the voice of Holy Church?

The Abbot groaned. "Aye," he said, barely audibly.

Parliament knew its fate decided, by that word.

Thereafter only Prior Hepburn of St. Andrews voted for the Queen amongst the lesser prelates, the Hamilton Abbot of Paisley abstaining, lacking guidance from his father Arran.

That earl, leading the Lords Temporal appeared glad to follow Glasgow's example. He abstained. After Angus, Erroll voted Aye. The die was truly cast.

While the burghs were still voting their Ayes, the Queen-Mother rose from her seat, jerked something at her young son, who cowered as though he had been slapped, and without a glance at the Chancellor swept out of the Hall, Henry Stewart, rather embarrassed, trailing after her.

James Beaton, ignoring this discourtesy, announced the result of the vote as twenty-two for, ten against the motion. Never had there been so many abstentions in this most decided of assemblies.

After that, the rest was little more than a formality. It was agreed that two or more of the five governors must remain with the King at all times, waking and sleeping; that the removal to Holyroodhouse would be forthwith; that the Queen-Mother should have access to her son at all times, but that any attempt to remove him furth of the realm, by any whatsoever, would be branded as *lese majesty* and earn a penalty of death. More to the same effect.

The young King listened to his fate with interest and no signs of distress.

It was agreed, almost without discussion, that Angus should be appointed Warden of the East and Middle Marches of the Border since he now clearly was at bitter enmity with England anyway, and was the only man strong enough in those parts to keep the Homes, Hepburns and the rest in order.

The new Lords of the Articles were sworn in, the Clerk read out the summary of decisions taken from his papers, and these were brought over to the King to be touched by him with the sceptre, so to become law, and the Parliament of February 1525 broke up.

For better or for worse, the tide of history was turned.

In one of the ante-rooms thereafter David found his uncle, with Angus and the Earl of Morton, another Douglas. "My lords," he said, bowing, and leaving comment to them.

Angus considered him with those pale hot blue eyes. "You, Master Beaton," he jerked. "What are you? Friend or enemy? I know not which. You speak too many words for my liking."

"I am sorry if my words offend your lordship," David said. "But if so, at least allow my actions to speak in my favour."

"Aye, my lord — you'll no' deny that the laddie saved our cause for us, this day," the Chancellor declared. "I doubt we'd never have got the vote, lacking him and his words."

"There are words and words! There were some spoke yonder I did not like the sound of!"

"My lord — there were many there to move, with differing tastes in words. It was necessary that a majority be moved to vote for your motion. By whatever words. They were, were they not? And . . . not by any words of yours!"

Morton guffawed, slapping his knee. "That's good, Archie!" he said.

The other left it. "Being other than a clerk, I prefer deeds to words. Heed that, Master Beaton. Also heed that a word which mocks Douglas, spoken where or by whom, is dangerous!"

"I will remember, my lord." David turned to his uncle. "The King's person? Will there be any difficulty, think you? The Queen-Mother . . .?"

"Whether she will or not is no matter," Angus interrupted shortly. "Douglas will attend to that! Throughout all yonder talking, my men have been coming into this castle. Three hundred are now within the walls. Another three hundred keep the streets of Edinburgh. A thousand wait six miles away at Dalkeith. The King will ride to Holyroodhouse, never fear. With Douglas. Words or no words. I said I prefer deeds, you'll mind!"

"I see," David said quietly.

Chapter Eight

IT was mid-October, with turning leaves and a golden haze over the land, before David Beaton once again rode north amongst the Braes of Angus on his fine white stallion.

This visit was not unannounced, like the last. The previous night, on David's arrival at Arbroath — which itself had not seen him since January — Gilbert Ogilvy had sent a messenger to Airlie informing his sister of their coming. In consequence, Gilbert now rode alongside, but not too close to the curveting, sidling stallion and its moody rider. Perhaps this partly added to David's irritation.

It was, in a way, his own fault. In April, before leaving for France, he had installed Gilbert, while still retaining his Priory of Restenneth as Bailie and sub-abbot at Arbroath, to carry out his ambitious plans, ideas and reforms for that great and lax establishment. It had scarcely been possible for him to deny his friend's assumption that they should together make this

123

visit to his old home and sister, however strongly David had hinted to the contrary. After all, only a dozen or so miles away, the fellow could visit Airlie any day! The new goshawk which he had brought him from France, now perched on Gilbert's wrist, was David's only hope and consolation.

Marion was waiting for them in person at the gatehouse of Airlie, a strangely unlikely guardian of that fierce battlemented and gunlooped wall, drawbridge, portcullis and machicolation for the pouring down of blazing pitch and boiling water. She embraced her brother, and held her hand to David. But her smile was warm.

"Welcome, my lord Abbot, Articular . . . and any other lord-ships you may now possess!"

He kissed her hand fervently, and held it thereafter sufficiently long for her to have to disengage it gently. "Eight months!" he said. "An eternity!"

"Nine," she amended, mildly.

He blinked. "Is it? So . . .?" He paused. "Can you blame me if it has seemed beyond all calculation? But at least, you have used it well, Marion — to grow still more beautiful, more desirable."

Gilbert Ogilvy cleared his throat.

The young woman laughed. "You have indeed been back to France, by the sound of you, David! For further lessons!" Her smile died. "But . . . I cannot say the same for you. That you have used the months so well. You look tired, weary."

"As I told him," her brother agreed. "He does too much. It is folly."

"Is it folly to labour to save Scotland, Gilbert!"

The old Lady Ogilvy, Marion's mother and Gilbert's step-mother, had lately died, and the girl was now acting as chatelaine of Airlie until such time as the young lord should return from Italy. On this occasion David did not have to coax her to take to the saddle; she seemed fully prepared for it. Moreover her brother candidly announced that why he had come was to try out the new goshawk on the herons which frequented Lintrathen Loch.

So, after refreshment, they rode off up Isla-side. This time there was no racing or galloping. Indeed Gilbert took the lead.

"You are quiet, David. Less full of life than I have known you," Marion put to him, presently, as they trotted past the falls of the Slug of Achrannie. "Have matters gone ill with you? Or it is here, at Airlie, that things are . . . different?"

"Eh? Dear God—no! Not that, I promise you." He lowered his voice. "To see you again . . .! It is so much of joy and peace as to leave mere words lacking all value."

"This, from Davie Beaton!" she said. "Here is wonder! It was not peace I brought you, when last we met, as I mind it!"

He nodded. "Nor will it be again, I think, in a little! If I know myself. But, meantime, it is my . . . salvation."

"Then, I think, matters must indeed go ill with you. And yet— you ride higher than you have ever done, do you not?"

"I' faith, it is not with me that things go ill. Not with myself, but with the realm. What I fight for."

"Your Parliament, then, did not prevail? As you hoped?"

"Aye, it prevailed. But we had to sup with Satan. In the form of Angus. And now pay the price."

"And now Angus holds the kingdom, as well as the King?"

"Nearly so," David admitted. "He rides over all, rattling his sword and shouting. All in the King's name. And few fail to bend the knee and touch their bonnets!"

"But not David Beaton?"

"No."

"Angus is only one to five, governing the King?"

"But the others are not strong men. Indeed my Uncle James is the strongest of them—and he is no Hercules! He is Chancellor now only in name, with the Douglases doing as they will in Scotland."

"We hear the echoes of that, even here in these valleys. Terrible things. But this is Douglas country, so we suffer less than most. Douglas has not yet come chapping at Airlie's gate, praise be!"

"By God—if ever he does, he will not live long to regret it, that I swear!"

"Davie—that does not sound like a prelate of Holy Church!" Marion charged, only half-smiling.

"It is the truth, nevertheless."

Marion sought to change the subject somewhat. "At the least, David, King Henry's sway is past? You have loosed the English hold?"

"At a price, yes. And Henry Tudor is an angry man. In especial, since I went to France."

"Why did you go? Gibbie told me that you had gone. But not why. I feared . . ."

"It was necessary, Marion. King Francis, you will know, suffered a great defeat at Pavia. In Italy. In his war against the Emperor over Milan. And was himself captured, on the field of battle. It was folly indeed — all folly. Worse indeed than I warned him of. Thus the Emperor Charles, who is also King of Spain, became supreme in Christendom. Which does not please Henry, whose fear of Spain is great. To seek preserve the balance, Henry has to treat with stricken France. With captive Francis's mother, who has become Regent. Someone had to go, from Scotland — and quickly. I went."

"To what purpose?"

"Our Auld Alliance. Our ancient mutuality of support, with France. Why Flodden was fought. I had to ensure that Scotland's interests were not thrown to Henry, by distracted France. Thank God I succeeded there. With Albany's aid. We have greatly to thank the Duke. The French refused to ratify the treaty with Henry unless Scotland was included. He has had to sign what is in truth a three-year truce. That he will not raise hand against this realm for three years. That at least is gain."

Impulsively Marion reached over to touch his arm. "For that all Scotland must thank you!" she exclaimed. "Only you could have done it, I think."

"That I would not claim. But it has tied King Henry's hands. For if he breaks his word and sends his armies raiding and slaying into Scotland again, his treaty with France is at once also broke, and the Channel is open to the Spanish fleet. So, on top of losing his control of young King James, Henry Tudor is an angry man." He found a smile. "I am assured that he thirsts for the blood of one, David Beaton!"

"Like some others!" Gilbert, who was now listening to the talk, interpolated.

"Perhaps. He has turned his wrath against all Scots dwelling in England. He has taken all their goods and wealth, and forced all to leave his domains, walking on foot with white crosses marked on their clothing. The act of a savage tyrant. What think you he would do to me, if he could lay hands on me?"

126

"David — you are making enemies! Angus. King Henry. The Queen-Mother," Marion said. "You must be careful . . ."

"I take precautions, my dear. As witness the Queen Margaret. Save us — she is almost my friend now, because of the good care I take! At least, shall we say that she hates Angus worse! Indeed, I acted as her ambassador also, to Paris and Rome. Peddling her divorce."

"David!" Shocked, Gilbert pulled up. "You did not? Pander to the woman thus?"

The other shrugged. "Why not? She will never return to Angus. She already beds with young Stewart. Hers is no marriage. If ending it will aid the realm — then end it I say."

"It is still a marriage in the sight of God."

"Is it, my good Gibbie? The Pope, it appears, is prepared to think otherwise."

"Then the Pope greatly errs!"

"Ha! Here we have major heresy! On the part of the Prior of Restenneth and Baillie of Arbroath, no less! Contesting the infallibility of the Holy Father. A serious failure."

"You may mock, David — but you know that I speak truth."

"Truth is so many-sided, Gilbert. I know that His Holiness is persuaded that if it is in the best interests that Margaret Tudor and Archibald Douglas be no longer joined in holy matrimony, then he will pronounce that they are not. Despite Gilbert Ogilvy's truths!"

"And is it in these best interests?" Marion intervened.

"I believe so. Angus is the King's stepfather. Take that away, and he loses something of his hold over James. Once divorced, also, he can never again claim that he is acting in the Queen's name. And Margaret will become discredited in the sight of most men; as a woman divorced she will never be considered a suitable keeper of the young James. Again, King Henry is known to be hot against her divorce. Which speaks in its favour!"

"Are such reaons worthy, David?"

"Worthy? Is the subject a worthy one? Are either Angus or Margaret worthy? The reasons are valid, at least. This realm will profit."

As they neared the loch, the squattering and uprising of wildfowl set Gilbert in a fever of excitement to try out his goshawk. When a couple of herons flapped up lazily from the rushes at the farther end, nothing would do but that the hawk be released at once.

It was a well-trained and businesslike killer, that French goshawk, and it disposed of its first heron with a minimum of fuss and delay, bringing the larger bird down amongst the reeds and waiting with its kill, impatiently plucking out feathers until retrieved. Then doing the same again, in identical fashion. At the third sortie, however rapt was the proud Prior at this uncanny precision and efficiency, the idle spectators had had enough. David raised a single eyebrow at the young woman, and she smiled, nodding.

"Gibbie," she said, "you may be well content with your slaughter. But for us, who prefer our herons otherwise, the sport begins to pall. You will not miss us if we ride on for a while?"

They spurred off, round the loch.

Fording the shallows of the Melham Water in modest style and without a drenching, they trotted side by side up the green hill. Near the standing-stone where before they had made dramatic halt, as with one accord they turned to look at each other. The girl was a little flushed, but she kept her head high and her lovely eyes were clear and steady. It was she who spoke.

"I charged us both with a task, here. That day," she said, as though forcing the words. "To think. Long and deep. Perhaps . . . despite the months, you have not had time for that? Against all your other so great thinkings and actings, David?"

He glanced away. "I needed no time," he answered. "But, at the back of my mind, I have thought of little else."

She considered him for a moment. "And your decision?"

"As it was then. That my love for you is rivalled only by my need for you. That you are part of me — even if I am not yet part of you."

"Part of you! That again. But . . . part of your head, David? Or only your heart. That was the stumbling-stone, was it not?"

"Part of *me*, head and heart both. Of eyes and hand and sinews. Aye, and of loins too! Part of me, woman — all of me, do you hear!"

She looked down, saying nothing.

"And you?" he asked, in turn. "What of you? Have you had long enough. What think you?"

She swallowed, and then laughed a little breathlessly. "I think

128

. . . that we are still in plain view of brother Gibbie!" she said, and touched up her horse.

Off like the wind she went, the man left some way behind, northward into the crowding hills.

He did better today than formerly — or perhaps he had his stallion to thank. At anyrate, he caught up with her in less than a mile, in a quiet foothill valley amongst scattered thorn trees, where sheep grazed. She did not look at him as he drew alongside — but neither did she pull her mount away.

His arm reached out, to encircle her. David Beaton was not a large or muscular man, nor practised in this sort of thing; but somehow in that moment he managed to do what had to be done, and swept the young woman bodily from her saddle and over to the front of his own. Possibly Marion's agility and proficiency on a horse contributed — for she was not so foolish as to resist. At anyrate, in one spirited if complicated movement she was within his arms and the stallion was sidling, double-burdened.

For the second time he found her lips, and on this occasion she did not seek to free them. Indeed, after a moment or two, her hand lifted to hold his head surely there, against the horse's prancing.

By unspoken consent, recognising that the saddle of a restive horse was less than ideal for their present urgent needs, they slipped to the ground. A drift of dry fallen leaves beneath a thorn tree attracted the man, and Marion allowed herself to be drawn thereto; was in fact the first to sit, pulling him down to her frankly.

"This, then, is the answer to your long thinking!" he said thickly, his lips against the proud column of her throat.

"Some of it, Davie — some of it!" she whispered, as she stroked his hair. "Hold me close, my sweet. For it was long, too long."

Nevertheless, when presently his hands, as eager as his lips not satisfied merely to hold, to caress, commenced to grope and pull at her clothing, she shook her head slowly, almost regretfully, and closed her fingers over his.

"No Davie," she said. "Not that, my dear. Be content. With . . . less. For this present."

"Content! How can you talk of content, woman? Now! Think you that it is contentment that I find in you? You are all delight,

I   129

rapture, challenge. I want you, desire you, need you, in every smallest part of me. And you talk of content!"

"I know it, David. For I am in like case — I confess it to you. But still I say be content. With what you have. Be patient. As must I."

"Have I not been patient for long enough? All these years . . ."

"If for years, a little longer. Bear with me, Davie. For . . . does not my whole life hang on it?"

"Your life . . .?" That gave him pause.

"Aye, my life. If not yours, then that is where we are different, you and I. It is my life you hold in these hands, David Beaton."

He drew back a little, to search her face that was grown even more lovely with the glow of love.

"You would have me give myself to you, Davie. And my heart would have me do so, I admit. But — I have a head also. And I must use it. As you, no doubt, have used yours."

"Now, Marion? Use it now? At this moment?"

"If I do not use it now, I think I need never trouble to use it hereafter! See you, Davie — I am no woman to try and rouse and provoke a man, and then to withhold. But . . . I said that we must both think deeply, those months ago. Have you so thought?"

"I told you, my heart. That my love for you is the best and strongest of me. That I want you, need you, must have you. Whatever the cost."

"Ah — there it is, Davie! Whatever the cost! Cost, for you, there must be. With me. Marriage, for a churchman, is cost indeed!"

He drew a long breath. It was the first time that word had been mentioned between them.

"That price I am prepared to pay," he said evenly.

"Oh, David!" she exclaimed, with a sigh, and sat up. "Do you not see why I question and doubt? Marriage should be a joy, a glory — not a price to pay. So I fear and falter."

"It is not the marriage that would lack joy and glory, Marion. It is the folly of men in their view of it. There is the rub."

"And you would marry me, despite that cost?"

"Yes."

"Tell me something of it, David. That cost. I know but that marriage is frowned upon in churchmen."

"I care nothing for frowns," he said. "It is what it could prevent me doing that troubles me. In priests and those in holy orders, it is forbidden. I have resisted taking orders — but I am still a churchman. Such power and authority as I possess springs from that. Lacking the Church, I am but the impoverished seventh son of a Fife laird."

"And marriage could lose you this?"

"Marriage could prevent me from going higher. In the Church. And higher I must go if I am to do what requires to be done for this Scotland. There is the kernel of it, Marion. My uncle is an ageing man and less strong than he seems. In will as in body. He will not be Chancellor for ever. And once he goes, my power to aid this realm ends — unless I can rise before it. Under his wing. In the Church. So that I may then act in my own right, not his. Do you understand, Marion?"

"I understand," she nodded. "Some men wed the Church, as they say. You, I think, would wed Scotland!"

"I would wed only Marion Ogilvy. But God knows, Scotland needs men to cherish and sustain her. Men in high places. And look where I will, I do not see them."

"I know it also, David. Do not doubt it. Perhaps I may be able to do something for Scotland likewise, woman as I am. In this pass."

He looked at her doubtfully.

"Do I have it aright? Your marriage, to me or any woman, if known to all, would injure your advancement? And so your ability to fight for Scotland, in her trials?"

"That is so. But it is a hazard that I am prepared to face."

"How if your marriage was secret?"

"Eh . . .? Secret? You mean . . .?"

"If it was not known, meantime? Or only to a few. Until such time as these troubles are past. Would that serve?"

"Marion — do you know what you are saying? What this would mean? For you?"

"I do, yes. For I have though much on it. But . . . I must be sure of *your* mind. Sure that you do not shrink from the marriage itself, only the consequences of men knowing of it. Sure that whatever we do is right in God's eyes, whatsoever it may be in men's."

"But, lassie — think well! I live and move at all times — or most — in the eye of men. If they are not to know of my marriage, what of you? How shall they see you?

"I believe that I can bear it . . . if I am named concubine! So long as *I* know that I am wife!"

"No!" he cried. "Not that! I will not have you so sacrifice yourself."

"It need not be so ill, Davie. You say that you live and move in the eye of men. That I have no wish to do, even as your wife. I have no love for cities and palaces and courts. My place is here, in this good land of Angus, where I may breathe the clean air of hills and sea, where I do not have to be a play-actor or other than myself. I would not come with you to Edinburgh or St. Andrews or the like, Davie—so none would point the finger of scorn at me there. And here—why, here I would be your wife."

He rubbed his chin, frowning.

"Are you ever asked if you are wed, David?" she pressed him.

"Asked? No—no, I think not. I cannot think of it being put to me . . ."

"Save by one of your ladies, perhaps? So—why should it be asked now? A churchman, you will be taken to be unwed. As are others. Who pries into their private lives? I know of a score hereabouts who have their mistresses, with children a-many. Bishops too, I have heard. Holy Church, it seems, is more concerned with other failings!"

"Aye—the folly of it! That it should be more fitting for a churchman to live in open sin than to marry! But—all this is of little matter. For I cannot let you sacrifice yourself."

"Even for Scotland's sake?" Marion smiled. "In truth, I do not think that I am a self-sacrificing woman, Davie. After all, I am requiring marriage, am I not, before I give myself to you? Many women would not—many women indeed *have* not done so! My sacrifice is only in respect of other's notions. The shadow and the sound, not the substance."

David rose to his feet, to pace up and down amongst the rustling leaves.

The girl watched him. "Do not fret yourself, Davie," she said. "It is better so. And, who knows—it may not be for long."

"I cannot decide, here and now," he told her, almost roughly. "I shall have to think on it. I never conceived of this."

She got up. "What did you think on, all those months?" She sighed ruefully as she moved to her horse. "Only affairs of the realm, I vow! Who but Marion Ogilvy would yield her heart to a

132

churchman who meddles with the state!" Lithely she mounted to the saddle, unaided. "Come, Davie — or Gibbie will be looking for us."

He came trotting after her presently. "We were so happy," he said.

She held out her hand for him to grasp. "We still are that, Davie. Are we not? What has changed? Only that you need more time to think than do I. But what of that? I am but a woman. Moreover, we have plighted our troth, have we not? Is that not sufficient happiness for one day?" Almost like a child she humoured and soothed him.

And almost like a child he rode by her side, holding her hand, a man with heart and head too surely balanced for any ease of spirit.

Chapter Nine

For a churchman, David Beaton seemed to spend a deal of his time in the saddle these days. When he had visualised his career, often as he had done so in the past, it had never been as a determined horseman, spurring urgently about Scotland. His wits, he had anticipated, would be the busiest part of him, rather than his buttocks and heels.

On this occasion, he had managed to dispense with the half-troop of the French Guard which were so apt to clatter and jingle at his heels, wise precaution as they were for a traveller in a Douglas-dominated land; but in this, his own territory and almost under the walls of his great Abbey, he believed that he could risk riding alone, and had left the soldiers at Arbroath, his mission being entirely personal and private.

Seven miles on his way, and trotting unhurriedly now down the long slope of Idvies Hill — for it would probably be inconvenient for all concerned if he arrived at Restenneth Priory before the appointed hour of noon — he had just come in sight of the hamlet of Letham, and his own great grange there, one of the largest of the Abbey farms, when the fast tattoo of hoof-beats behind him twisted him swiftly round in his saddle, a sound calculated to make any man tense himself in 1526.

Two horsemen were flogging hard-driven beasts a quarter of a mile in his wake. His hand dropped automatically to his sword — for it would be foolish to assume that their evident concern was not with himself.

Then he recognised the Archbishop of St. Andrews' colours, dusty as they were, worn by one of the pair, a servitor of his uncle. Sitting his stallion he waited, cursing to himself.

The men thundered up, reining in their lathered mounts in a spatter of clods and spume. The one in half-armour was well known to David, young Patrick Barclay of Collairnie, one of the Archbishop's chamberlains.

"My lord Abbot!" he cried. "God be thanked we've come up with you! Pray it is not too late! You must return. The Chancellor commands. It is Angus and the Douglases. They have struck. We have ridden hot-foot. From St. Andrews. Crossed the ferry to Broughty. Hoping to find you at Arbroath . . ."

"Wheesht, Patrick — wheesht! Peace, man. What's this? Angus has struck! Angus is forever striking something or somebody! What is it this time?"

Barclay made a great effort. "Angus has seized sole control of the King. At Edinburgh. He declares that there is some ancient law, some edict, whereby at fourteen years the monarch is of age to rule. Wholly rule, without governors or council . . ."

"But this is folly! James will not be of full age for seven years! There can be no such law."

"Angus says that there is. And the King was fourteen a month ago. He has declared it a new reign. All decisions taken before are proclaimed abolished. All appointments revoked. In the King's name. The council of governors dissolved. The Archbishop no longer Chancellor. His arrest ordered. On charges of treason. A parliament called for next month. Angus himself meantime acting Chancellor. And Douglases taking over every high office."

"Dear God — the snake! The treacherous viper! But . . . what of Argyll? There were always to be two of the governors with the King. My uncle and Arran left Argyll with Angus in Edinburgh only a week since. After their own duty with James. Argyll, with his Campbells, could have prevented this. We trusted Argyll . . ."

"My lord of Argyll fell of a sudden direly sick. Vomiting blood. Poison, it may be. Angus brought in the Archbishop of

Glasgow, in his place. And he has agreed with all Angus does. When Archbishop James is brought down for treason, Archbishop Gavin to have the Primacy!"

"Aye! Gavin the Tutor flies a high hawk! But the quarry has beak and talons of its own! My uncle is not convicted of treason yet!"

"No. But a great force of Douglases is riding against St. Andrews. Some say that Angus himself is with them. To take the Archbishop. They slept at Cupar last night. We rode at dawn to seek you. To bring you back. With every man that you may raise."

David frowned, tugging at his small pointed beard. He turned to look northwards, where rose Dunnichen Hill. Just beyond that, only four miles away in the shelving vale of Rescobie, was Restenneth Priory, his destination. More than his destination — his fate, his gamble with fate, his testing, temptation and fulfilment in one. For he rode this day to his wedding, at noon.

"Devil seize it!" he groaned. "Not that! Not now!"

"We thought to find you sooner. At Arbroath Abbey . . ."

"Yes. Go back to the Abbey, Patrick. Take my guard. Summon in my name every man who can bear arms. From there. From the town. From every grange and house in the Abbey's demesne. Take every horse that will carry a man. Take fishing-boats from the havens of Arbroath and Auchmithie, for such as may not ride. To sail for St. Andrews. On my orders. Here is my ring, for authority."

"Aye. And you, my lord?"

"I cannot come with you now. I have pressing affairs. Elsewhere. I shall come . . . later."

"But . . . my lord! Even now the Douglases may be in St. Andrews. There is no time to be lost."

"Then do as I say, man. Do not wait for me. So soon as you have gathered a fair company, ride with them for St. Andrews. I shall bring on the latecomers. The officer of my guard, John Durie, will aid you. Go, now."

The other pulled round his weary mount's head, sketched doubtful salute, and with the servitor spurred back whence he had come.

Set-faced, David Beaton rode on northwards, down the hill of Idvies.

At Restenneth, where Gilbert Ogilvy had gone the previous

day, all was in readiness – although there was no aspect of the abnormal about the establishment, no suggestion that this was in any way a great occasion. The Priory was a comparatively small one, of a dozen canons and not many more lay brothers, set on a green promontory jutting into Restenneth Loch, a cloistered, sleepy place, where the lapping of waters, the quacking of wildfowl and the tolling of the hour-bell, set the quiet tempo of life.

In one of the bare and functional cells of the cloisters, he changed from his travelling clothes into a fine cream satin doublet and short trunks, with long white hose, by no means his grandest apparel but suitable as a judiciously quiet wedding garment. Thereafter he slipped across the grass-grown precinct amongst the strutting pigeons, to the modest church with the tall broach spire, from which the sound of chanting already emanated.

The canons and a small choir of singing boys were in their places, and constituted all the congregation. But the little church by no means seemed empty, so full was it of flowers and fronds and green branches, their scent mingling with that of incense and candles. If at David's unobtrusive entrance the chanting faltered somewhat and grew uncertain, perhaps the singers were scarcely to be blamed. Never could those hoary walls of red sandstone have witnessed a stranger scene than that of the slight and slender young man in cream satin who waited modestly, almost shyly, to the side of the chancel steps, and yet who was singers' Father in God, one of the greatest prelates of the realm. And waiting for a woman, to be wed!

Exactly as the Angelus bell began to ring overhead for noon, with equal lack of flourish or pretension, the vestry door at the far side opened, and three people emerged – Gilbert Ogilvy himself leading the bride, with the Prioress Elizabeth of Lunan pacing behind as attendant.

Almost involuntarily David started forward. Although this must have been far from the wedding of her dreams, Marion looked radiant, serenely happy. She was dressed all in white, silk barred with narrow bands of velvet, a long close-fitting bodice, tight-sleeved, to mould her splendid figure, with high upstanding collar rimmed with pearls, and a wide full skirt sweeping to the ground. Against the white of it, the silver-gilt of her hair under the brief pearled cap, peaked in front, and the honey-colour of her skin bronzed by sun and air, glowed warmly.

In contrast to the faltering at David's entry, the singing now promptly grew louder, more wholehearted. All here knew and loved the young woman — not only in that she was the Prior's sister but because most of the company could claim her in some sort of relationship, however distant. The Priory was more or less hereditary in the Ogilvy family, and its shelter a haven for the less fortunate members, the illegitimate in particular.

David moved on to the altar steps ahead of his bride, and there turned to hold out his hands to her. She took them shining-eyed, and he had to restrain himself from going further and enfolding her in his arms there and then, as sufficiently valid witness before God and man that this man took this woman in very truth. Gilbert's honest square face was stiff as he made his way round behind them to the altar; but Elizabeth Graham smiled openly.

Hand in hand they turned, and knelt, as the Prior raised his voice.

David Beaton was scarcely aware of anything of that ceremony save that Marion was at his side, warm, loving, and his own. Presumably he made the necessary responses, acted as was required, playing the bridegroom at least well enough for Gilbert Ogilvy presently, and with something of a sigh, to pronounce them man and wife.

The wedding feast in the Prior's apartments thereafter, although attended only by the four of them, made considerable demands on David, at least. For more reasons than one, he would have dispensed with it, could he have done so with decency. But Gilbert, and Elizabeth Graham, had gone to some pains in the matter. Moreover, this was Marion's day, and she must have it as little spoiled as might be. He therefore exerted himself to seem at his happiest, wittiest, most carefree, doing justice to the fine fare provided. If his gaze always returned to his bride's fair and winsome face, that was as it should be — even though the smile was apt to die from his lips, and his eyes grew sombre too often, as he did so.

Marion used her own eyes, and had her thoughtful moments also.

Thereafter it was necessary to visit the large refectory of the establishment, there to accept the good wishes of the monks and lay brothers, and to watch an entertainment especially devised for the occasion, portraying episodes from the history of the Ogilvy family. David stood as much of this as he was able, and then, rather abruptly announcing his thanks, declared that they had a sizeable journey to make and prayed to be excused the remainder. The Prioress Elizabeth made considerable play with this, in a roguish way, but otherwise it was accepted with suitable respect.

Changed back into his riding clothes, and waiting for Marion, David had a private word with her brother.

"So soon as we are gone, Gilbert, assemble every man fit to use a sword and a lance," he directed shortly. "Ride with them to Arbroath without delay. Collect others from Letham and Conon Granges as you go. All who are able, I say. Accept no excuse. We need every sword that we can raise. Have all assemble at the Abbey. To be ready to ride for St. Andrews at dawn."

"Dawn! And you?"

"I will be there."

"But . . . what of Marion?"

"Not a word of this to her. Meantime. She shall have this day. And night."

Gilbert said nothing.

They said farewell to the others, David steadfastly refusing to say where they were going. They rode off alone, eastwards, on the road to Brechin, in the late afternoon, strangely enough leaving Elizabeth Graham in tears.

Marion broke a long silence. "Well, Davie," she said. "It is done. I am yours, now. All yours. And you mine – but not all, I fear. You mostly mine, shall we say? Are you happy?"

He nodded. "Happy. And you?"

"Happy," she agreed. "Indeed, I think that I am happier than are you. For there is something amiss, is there not?"

"What could be amiss on this day of days, my heart?" he asked, lightly.

"I do not know. But you are not wholly yourself. As though some part of you was otherwise. Not as I have known you . . ."

"Would you expect a man to be as he has always been but an hour after he has been wed to the fairest woman in the land?" he demanded.

She smiled. "Where are you taking me, David?"

"Wait you," he said.

"Must I? It is much to ask of a woman. Do you perceive, my lord Abbot, that for the first time in her life – or since she was a small child – this woman is being taken she knows not where. Alone. And by a man!"

He laughed, for the first time for a while. "You are in the care of Holy Church, my daughter! Let that suffice you."

"I do not know that I am the more emboldened."

"Ha – a doubter! Lacking faith. We shall have to cure you of that!"

Riding across the desolation of Montreathmont Moor, David presently turned off by a bridle-path due eastwards, further intriguing Marion.

As dusk was falling they came into sight of the purple-blue plain of the sea, from the high ground above the Grange of Inverkeilor. Marion drew up, to gaze at it, gleaming-eyed.

"Look yonder!" she exclaimed. "What makes me so love the sea? I am glad, glad you bring me to the sea, Davie – for part of my heart is there, I think."

"That is why I brought you, woman! For I covet all your heart!" he told her, deep-voiced.

They trotted down to ford the Lunan Water, but now, instead of riding on towards Inverkeilor, Lunan Priory and the great bay, David turned right-handed, to climb gently through shelving pasture-land, south by east. The girl, who knew the area so well, wrinkled her brows.

"Where . . .?"

"Wait you."

Crusie-lamps were being lit in the cot-houses that crouched in the folds of the green, shadowy land, hiding from the winds off the sea. But away beyond these, outlined against the wan glimmer of the water, standing high on a grassy table of land and hiding from nothing, rose a tall, proud battlemented tower, square and stalwart in rose-red mellow stone. Four storeys it soared to a parapet and walk, with a crowstep-gabled garret and caphouse above, and all ablaze with lights in every small window this dove-grey evening.

"The Castle of Ethie!" Marion cried. "Sir James Carnegie's house. The fairest in this land! Do we . . . do we go there?"

"The Castle of Ethie," David agreed. "Come."

Through sloping parkland they rode, where cud-chewing cattle awaited the night, and up to the lofty tower on its airy plinth. A moat barred the approach but the drawbridge was down, and their horses' hooves drummed hollowly on its timbers and into the courtyard defended by turrets and gunloops. No man showed, no sign of life, other than those innumerable blazing candles.

Before the great oak and iron-studded door they pulled up, and David aided the wondering girl to dismount. Then he strode to the door, drawing his sword with a flourish, and beat on the echoing planks with the hilt of it. After only a moment's interval the heavy door crashed wide – but no man appeared within.

Sheathing his sword, David turned and caught up Marion in his arms. In laughing protest she clung to him, as he paced, somewhat unsteadily, over the threshold, to set her down only a few feet within. Then he stepped back, panting a little, outside again.

"Your permission . . . to enter . . . Ethie Castle . . . my lady!" he exclaimed. "David Beaton seeks . . . your shelter this night."

Wide-eyed she considered him, the laughter dying on her lips. "Why, Davie – what is this?" She glanced about her, within. "Where is Sir James? What play is this?"

"No play, lass. I seek your permission, as Lady Ethie, to enter your house. As is seemly."

"But . . . Davie? What . . .? How . . .?" Bewildered, she stammered.

"A wedding-gift, my dear. Ethie is all yours. Not mine – yours. Bought from Sir James. It is not Abbey land, see you. The only estate on this coast that is not. It is now the property of the Lady Marion Ogilvy, every stick and stone and turf of it, yours and only yours – right to the cliffs of Red Head where we stood one day, years ago, and watched a gerfalcon kill a gannet, and knew it folly. The two of us."

"Oh, Davie! Davie!" Tears starting to her eyes, she ran to him, and threw herself into his arms, to gasp incoherences into his breast.

"Weeping is it? Tears! Come, lass – here's no way to hansel your new home!"

They climbed from the stone vaulted vestibule up the winding turnpike stair to the Hall, where a log fire blazed in the great open hearth and the long table was set, at one end, for a meal. Still no other person, no servants, revealed themselves, although most evidently hands had been busy, and recently.

He led her up three flights more, to the very topmost storey, where, within the battlemented parapet-walk, the entire garret floor was made into a long and narrow bedchamber, its walls hung with tapestries, its floor carpeted with white sheepskins, its dormer windows looking out over far prospects of land and sea. A great canopied four-poster bed occupied the farther end, mirror reflected the mellow candlelight, and a small fire flickered its welcome. Midway, a curtained door, which David opened, led out on to the stone-flagged walk, sixty airy feet above the ground.

"My heart!" Marion reached out her hands to him. "It is all a wonder, all beyond my dreams. You have though of everything. So much thought and regard and care . . ."

"So much love," he said, and in the open doorway took her to him, gently yet masterfully. She parted her lips to his.

As passion grew between them and they strained body to body, fingers clutching, the man it was who presently, regretfully, drew back a little.

"My sweet, my beloved — here is joy, bliss, heaven!" he murmured. "But . . . perhaps we go too fast? I must be patient. I am hungry only for you. But . . ." He smiled. ". . . the belly must be served — as well as other parts! A meal awaits us below. Perhaps . . . ?"

As though to his signal, a bell rang faintly, deep within the castle.

Down in the Hall they found cold meats and sweets and wines set out for them in abundance, and David ushered the girl to the great chair at the head of the table.

"This is not for me," she protested. "This is no woman's seat. *You* must sit here."

"Not so," he assured, pressing her down into it. "Your place. Now, and ever. This is your house, not mine. You are mistress of Ethie. See — there is the proof of it — that it is your chair. These papers on the table, signed and sealed. These are the titles and charter, of the barony, fortalice and demesne of Ethie, with the mill, the haven thereof, the cot-town, fishings and all other pertinents whatsoever, in the name of the Lady Marion Ogilvy, to have and to hold." He sat down near by.

She shook her head, helplessly. "But why, Davie? Why have you done this? So much. It is all beyond belief . . ."

"It has been my dearest wish — or shall we say, my second most dear? For long. That day I rode along the cliffs of Red Head, the day I lost my heart to you, I saw this castle queening it here. I do not say that I decided there and then to have it for you. But I saw it as something most desirable, meet for you. I have linked it with you ever since, my dear. In my mind. I swear, if old Carnegie had not been of a mind to sell I would have hounded him out of it in some fashion — even though it demanded a Papal bull!"

"But why for *me*, Davie? Why in my name? Since now, your house is my house . . ."

"No. There's the rub, Marion. In our case, the pity of it, that is scarce true. All that is mine, cannot be yours. Arbroath Abbey is mine — but you can have no part of it. And the like. This has vexed my mind. But this house here is yours, wholly. Do not think that I fail to perceive what I am costing you, marrying you thus. Secretly. A churchman. I have wrestled with this long. It may be a sin — a sin against you. That you may live to rue this day, Marion, is my greatest fear. Deep in affairs of state, as I am, there will assuredly be times when to be bound to me will be to your scathe and hurt, not your advantage, God knows . . ."

"And think you I shall flinch at that?"

"Perhaps not, stout-heart! But this house will, at the least, give you some surety, some abiding place. I have taken you from the strong castle of Airlie. I must needs see you in no less sure a house. Whatever *my* fortunes, none can take this from you . . ."

"Davie! You sound as though you fear ill times indeed. Foresee only evil . . .?"

"No, no. Never think it, my love." He reached out to clasp his hand over hers. "But . . . it may be that at times David Beaton may seem but a poor husband to you. Who deserves the best that this land could raise. Then . . . Ethie may warm your heart a little, I say."

She gazed at him, wide eyed.

He raised a laugh, and poured out wine for them both. "Come — this is no talk for a wedding-night, the saints be witness! Eat, my dear. Drink. Is all this provision to be wasted? Here is lobster in malvoisie . . ."

Presently, looking around amongst the shadows of the Hall and its hangings, Marion said, "Davie – I have not seen man nor maid since I entered this house. Save only you. I have not heard a voice . . ."

"Am I not sufficient? Did we not have enough of company at Restenneth?"

"Surely. But – there must be servants? All this. All things most perfect. Yet I have not seen a one . . ."

"Nor shall you, my pigeon. Not this night. I have my own notions as to a wedding-night – and seek none other's company than one! I have been at too many otherwise, where something inward and true and lovely has been debased to a shameful puppet-show for leering oafs and skirling women. That a man may use his mistress in private, but must make public display of bedding his wife, I will not have!"

In some small confusion, Marion addressed herself to her viands.

When David saw, in a while, that she was only toying with her food, he pushed back the cushioned form on which he sat, and came round to stand behind her.

"Sweeting – your heart is not in this, I think," he said softly. "We shall leave it . . . for a better place!" And he raised her up.

A horn lantern was now waiting for them in a niche of the stair landing. David took it and led the way up. More than once he turned to look back as she followed at his heels – but she kept her eyes downbent.

Two silver lavers, with warmed water for their washing, steamed beside the fire in their bedchamber. Marion made something of a business out of that washing, taking an unconscionable time about it, her back turned to the man. Patiently he waited, smiling a little.

At length, when she could make no more of it, and merely stood there, he came to turn her round to face him, to look into her troubled eyes.

"See now – here is none so desperate an occasion, my love," he told her. "Smile again." He shook his head over her. "So much loveliness."

His hands ran down the warm curving excellence of her, in moulding caress, knowing, lingering hands that pressed her to him. She did not resist, but she was tense within his arms. He kissed

143

her, but this time her lips did not part for his, although he sought skilfully to stir them. She was trembling again – but with a tight tremor now, not the loosened eager quivering of before.

David raised his head, drew back a little, and ran his fingers through the heavy coils of her hair. Then he took her hand. "Come," he said. "We shall improve on this also."

He led her over to the great bed – and it was as though her feet dragged on the sheepskins. But there he only leaned forward and, still holding her hand, snuffed out the candle that stood beside the bed, with a nip of the fingers. He took her over to the candle which burned in the first landwards-facing window, and extinguished that also. Then on to the next window, and so round the long room.

By the time that they came to the last window facing the sea, the young woman was accompanying him more freely. With the final candle dowsed and only the mellow subdued flickering of the fire enfolding them, the chamber and the night, they stood close, to look out over the battlements to where the sea was but a vast presence, an emanation unseen but potent. The faint unceasing roar of its swell breaking along the rockbound coast came to them, to mingle with the quiet whuff and splutter of burning aromatic birch-logs.

"It is none so ill here, Marion lass, in this chamber which I built for you, in my mind, by the edge of the sea. Is it?" he whispered. "So many years abuilding. For this moment. None so ill?"

She whirled round abruptly, to cling to him, to clutch, almost to shake him. "Oh, Davie – forgive me!" she cried. "Bear with me. I am so foolish, so sorry a bride! But . . . I fear to fail you. I know so little of, of this matter. Nothing to the point, indeed. Only what silly girls whisper together. I did not know that it would be thus, with me. I am ignorant. And afraid, Davie. Afraid, not of you – never think it. But of myself. That I may grievously disappoint. Bring you no joy this night . . ."

"Mercy on us – is that all!" he exclaimed. "Foolish indeed, my jewel! Of all the worries of the world, here is the least, heart of my heart. For you, of all women!"

"No – it is not so! It is not. Cannot you understand me, Davie? It is you, of all *men*! You, who know so much. Who have had so many women. Clever women. Women of experience, bold

and practised. French women. And I know nothing of it, nothing . . .!"

"Preserve us—you need know nothing, girl! Nothing that your
own body does not tell you. Your body is a glorious one—that, at
least, my experience tells me! It will serve you, and me, right well,
I promise you! It is you, Marion Ogilvy, that I seek this night—
you, all of you and nothing other than you. As you are. No other
woman on this earth." He was unfastening the back of her gown,
deftly, unobtrusively, as he spoke. "Knowledge is a small matter.
Besides, I have knowledge enough for us both—for we are one
now, woman! One, joined in wedlock. What you have to give
us now is infinitely greater than any knowledge, my beloved,
never fear."

He had her gown loose now, and eased it from her shoulders so
that only her arms in the sleeves held it up. "Will you help me,
dearest! I need it, you see."

"Why . . ." She swallowed, and drew her arms free of the
stiffened cloth, so that the heavy gown slipped to the floor and she
stood in her short white shift. "Why, yes," she mumbled. "If I
can help you, Davie dear—I will."

"You can. And must."

The thin shift, in turn, dropped away.

The man groaned aloud at the sight of her, in the ruddy glow
of the firelight. "Dear God—you are glorious! Glorious, woman!
Oh, Marion—at last!"

His hands alive, he swept her up in his arms and strode with
her to the bed, with an end to words.

Marion Ogilvy thereafter became just and only Marion
Ogilvy. And thought no more about being gentled.

Presently, panting, exhausted, he lay beside her, lips brushing
idly against her damp brow, hands slowly stroking.

"To think . . . that this was the woman . . . who feared!" he
murmured "Who knew nothing. Who desired that I be gentle!"

"Was I . . . was I . . .? So forward? Wanton? Shameful?"

"Shrive me—what now? Shame is no word for the marriage-
bed. But yes, my love—you were wanton! Joyously wanton,
praises be—deliciously wanton! A woman, all woman, utterly and
gloriously woman!"

"Oh, Davie—it was a wonder! A rapture! You are so strong.
So much a man. And yet so kind . . ."

At some hour through that timeless northern night that was never wholly dark, David, lying on his side and considering all the rich and sleeping loveliness beside him, sighed to smother what was almost a moan, and carefully eased himself over to the edge of the great bed, and up. Quietly he found his scattered clothing on the floor, and dressed himself. The young woman, one arm outflung and fingers curled, hair spread wide over the pillows, breathed deeply, evenly, a faint smile about her slight parted lips.

He leaned over her, gazing down, mouth tight, brows furrowed. At length he kissed her on the brow.

She stirred, and opened her eyes. The smile widened — and then faded, as comprehension came to her and she saw how he stood and how he was fully dressed. Alarm dawned in her eyes, and she made to sit up.

He pressed her back gently. "My love," he said, "this is an ill trick to play on a bride. On any woman. On so glorious a bed-fellow and the heart of my heart. But it must be so, I fear. I must leave you, Marion."

"But . . . but, Davie! Why? Leave me? You cannot be so cruel!" That was a wail.

"Think you it is less cruel for me? Marion — Angus is risen. He has taken the King. Ordered the arrest of my uncle. The Douglases march. Even now they assail St. Andrews. I have to go. I am raising every man that I can, to oppose him. To save the Chancellor. I cannot myself hold back."

"Angus! The Douglases! Oh, Davie — fighting! War?"

"Aye. In some measure. We must withstand Angus. We cannot allow Scotland to fall into his hands, without a blow."

She gripped him tightly. "No. No. Not that. But — you will take heed? Be careful, Davie? For my sake, if naught else . . .?"

"That I will do, never fear. I will count the hours until I may win back to this chamber."

"Can I not come with you, Davie? Not to fight, but to be near you, at the least? I can ride as well as any man. I need no soft living . . ."

"Would you be named camp-follower as well as concubine, Marion Ogilvy."

"I do not care, for that . . ."

"I believe you would not! But *I* would. And you are my wife

146

now, woman. You will do as your husband says. You will stay, either here or at Airlie. As you please. There are servitors below, armed. Three of them. They will protect you. Escort you to Airlie, if so you wish . . ."

"No. I shall wait here. In this house you have given me. I shall be here, at Ethie, when you come back to me, Davie. Here I shall feel the closer to you."

He all but choked, and swept her to him. He held her close — then almost fiercely thrust her from him, all that fair white perfection of desire and appeal. Jumping up, he turned and all but ran from the shadowy room.

Chapter Ten

IT was no more than seven miles from Ethie to Arbroath, and the first crimson bars of the sunrise were staining the vast grey levels of the pewter sea as David Beaton and Gilbert Ogilvy rode out of the gates of the great Abbey and took the road to the south.

Behind them, led by the Deemster bearing the splendid banner with the mitred arms of Arbroath, came a large if somewhat motley company numbering just under one hundred, monks, lay-brothers, tenants, craftsmen and servants, young and old, armed with a variety of weapons and mounted on every conceivable sort of steed, from chargers to pack-horses, from palfreys to ponies. This was, of course, the scrapings of the Abbey barrel, for Patrick Barclay, with the French Guard, had taken almost twice as many the previous evening.

David, dressed in gleaming half-armour now, with the magnificent black cloak, lined with green satin, of the Order of St. Lazarus of Jerusalem, thrown over it, the handsome green Maltese Cross of the Order picked out in emeralds on the shoulder, fretted as he rode. To have to hold in his stallion to the pace of lumbering carthorses and short-legged garrons was trying in the extreme — especially when a part of his conscience nagged at him that he was twelve hours late. Too late, perhaps. Gilbert made a silent, not to say morose companion this grey morning — although admittedly he looked more apt as a warrior than a prior. It was perhaps significant that he did not once ask after his sister.

Jingling and clattering through the sleeping land, they went by Muirdrum and the Granges of Barry and Monifeith, church lands all. But long before they reached Monifeith, David himself had ridden ahead, making for Broughty and the ferry.

Here, at the first narrows of the great Tay estuary, the Lord Gray's massive castle stood on its thrusting rock and dominated all, controlling the ferry to Fife and levying toll and custom on all shipping using the river. But the Abbey of Arbroath was his best customer, and although Gray was known to be a friend to Angus, it was barely conceivable that he would seek to hamper the Lord Abbot. The ferry denied them would entail a vast circuit of the estuary, by far-away Perth, adding sixty miles to their journey.

But no flag flew at Broughty Castle, intimating that its lord was not in residence, and David had no difficulty with the ferry steward – who was indeed prepared for this second contingent, having been warned of its coming by Barclay of Collairnie the previous evening. A sufficiency of fishing-craft and boatmen were requisitioned and in readiness. Routed from their beds in the haven under the castle walls, they were standing to their boats by the time that the Abbey company put in its appearance.

With the early sun dispersing the morning clouds, they made the mile-wide passage across a calm sea to Ferry Port on Craig on the Fife shore, where another stark castle frowned on their little fleet but did not interfere.

The township, rising to the new day, was agog with rumours. The Douglases were coming. They were in St. Andrews. They had put the city to sword and flame. The Chancellor-Archbishop was dead. Or fled. Or a prisoner. David, noting that no pall of smoke clouded the sky to the south, where eight miles away lay St. Andrews town, asked for news of his own advance party. That they had passed through Ferry Port the night before, heading in the direction of Tents Muir, was all that he could ascertain.

Lacking sure news, he likewise chose to move southwards into the sandy anonymity of Tents Muir, a huge waste of bents and dunes rimming the sea, rather than use the accustomed road by Forgan and Leuchars. By so doing there was the little estuary of the Eden to cross, but this was a shallow basin which could be forded at low water – and the tide was on the ebb.

A favourite haunt of his student days, David led his straggling

148

squadron through the maze of sand-hills and reedy hollows, amongst the teeming rabbits and the darting wildfowl, mile after twisting mile until the estuary opened before them and, two miles beyond, the towers and spires of St. Andrews rose between blue sea and blue sky.

But it was not the sight of that fair and ancient city, intact apparently and certainly unburned, that held their gaze. Much nearer at hand were men, many men, horsemen in headlong gallop, flight and pursuit.

No prolonged inspection was necessary to establish the situation. Coming hotfoot from the direction of the town, and clearly making for the cover of this sand-dunes area, was a large party, scattered and strung-out. Behind them came a larger band still, twice as many, riding down stragglers from the first as they came – and even at a distance the red splashes on the breastplates of these latter proclaimed the ominous Bloody Heart of Douglas. Although the fugitives bore no such easy identification, amongst them rode sundry individuals wearing the blue and white colours of the King of France's *Garde Eccossais*.

"By the Rude – it is our own people!" David cried. "Yonder is Barclay. And John Durie!"

"Save us – what now! Douglases – in hundreds!" Gilbert exclaimed. "What can we do? Can we save them? We must try. Come . . .!"

"Wait!" David commanded. "Not so fast. This early sun is in their eyes. They will not have seen us, I think, in these dunes. Let *them* come on. No man fights his best in soft mud!"

As Gilbert protested that their friends were dying, David marshalled his alarmed and nondescript company. The host of hunted and hunters came thundering down to the mud-fringed tideline of the Eden-mouth, tending to close in and bunch as they made for the line of barnacled posts which marked the site of the low-water ford. Into the glutinous slime the first horses plunged. From a headlong gallop every beast was slowed to a floundering scramble as horses slithered and slipped. The chase became promptly no more than a confused mêlée. Friend and foe inevitably became inextricably mixed, and most were much too busy keeping their seats and controlling their mounts to make more than a gesture at fighting.

Amongst the dunes of Shelly Point, that thrust out towards the

149

ford on the north, David Beaton insisted on waiting, silent, hard as it was to watch friends in distress. He waited until not only were most of the fleeing churchmen across the river but the first of the Douglases also. At this point, as so often in estuarine streams, the mudbanks were nearly all at one side, the Eden having cut in close round the little promontory of Shelley Point.

At length he drew his sword and raised it high. "A Beaton!" he shouted. "A Beaton!" his far from gruff voice cracking a little in the process. He spurred forward his restive stallion.

If the echo of his clarion-call was somewhat ragged and half-hearted at least it had the benefit of complete surprise for the enemy. Down upon the ploutering, scrabbling mass of horsemen in the river rode David's five-score heroes — and undoubtedly the preoccupied Douglases would have been paragons indeed had they taken time to note that there was a certain lack of enthusiasm in the suddenly advancing cohort, and the proud streaming banner of Arbroath the best of them.

Apart from student affrays, and on occasion when he had been beset by robbers on a French road, this was David's first actual battle. He knew fear — but it was mainly that his judgement might be at fault, that his followers might fail in their part and his plan miscarry. Sword waving, cloak flung back from his armour, with Gilbert Ogilvy, yelling now, close at his side, he drove down directly upon the trio of plumed and bonneted — as distinct from morion-helmeted — horsemen who were obviously the leaders of the Douglas host.

These, staring, were furiously seeking to rally and order and concentrate their men. But it was an all but impossible task at that moment. The actual area of the ford was not wide, a mere twenty of thirty yards, and inevitably the majority both of the flight and their attackers had plunged in on either side of it. Not that the water was so much deeper there; it was the bed of the stream that was different — firm shell and gravel at the ford, which was merely an extension of Shelly Point, and soft silt elsewhere. Horsemen caught therein, however fierce and valorous, were bound to be less than single-minded, angry though they might be.

The fleeing churchmen were a nuisance, of course, getting in the way, cluttering up the river. Some of them indeed were roughly jostled and even unseated by the charging newcomers.

But, since the majority were in the mud, astride the ford, and David's last orders to his people had been to maintain a solid and compact wedge-shaped phalanx behind him, holding to the centre of the ford itself, there was less of collision than there might have been.

The three Douglas leaders being themselves close together and squarely on the ford, were in good enough state to fight. David drove at the oldest of the trio, a heavy man of middle years in finely chased armour with a heraldic breastplate. His sword was of the massive, old-fashioned two-handed variety, twice as heavy and half as long again as David's, such as the younger man's slender wrists could never have wielded. One blow with that, and it was unlikely that a second would be required. Only speed would serve against it.

He required that speed from the first moment. Whirling like a windmill, the great blade flashed within inches of David's head as he came up, before ever he was within striking distance of his shorter weapon. Swerving in the saddle violently, he was all but unseated in avoiding the stroke.

Desperately he recovered himself, dragging round his stallion's head, Gilbert jostling on the far side of him. He sought to thrust in under the Douglas's guard, but the older man's reach was too much for him, and the wind of that furious steel again fanned his cheek.

He had to use his wits quickly—or he would have no wits left to use. Behind him Gilbert had engaged another of the trio, and the Deemster was successfully using the Abbey's banner and staff as a lance to keep the third man and his whirling blade at a safe distance.

David tried a feint, pretending a thrust at the other's throat, but ready for the swinging response, and instead jerked back his point to stab in low, below the breatplate immediately the stroke was past. But the Douglas was a master of horsed swordery, on a trained mount, and a driving knee sent the beast rearing to one side. David's point rang only on armour-plating. Again he recovered himself with a mere inch or two to spare.

But the rearing horse had given him a notion. As the brute came down and his own stallion curveted round, with a back-handed swipe he brought down the flat of his sword over the creature's broad rump. It swerved, whinnying in fright, just as its master raised both hands for a terrible downwards-chopping drive. The Douglas could not stop his heavy weapon in mid-blow. Thrown off balance by the abrupt movement, he almost fell out of the saddle with the weight of the stroke, only superb horsemanship keeping his seat. As he wavered, David, leaning over managed to stab his point under the suddenly unprotected arm-pit.

It was not conventional sword-play without a doubt – but it was effective. The Douglas toppled sideways, the sword falling from his hands to splash into the water. With a crash he followed it, his mount careering off wildly.

Panting, David was staring down at his bloodstained steel when a loud yell at his back swung him round. Not a second too soon. Another Douglas, seeing his leader fall, had spurred in to avenge him. His savage lunge slashed a long rent in David's flying cloak.

It was Gilbert's shout that had saved him – and it was Gilbert's swift vigour that saved him again. For so affected was David by the sight of the first blood he had spilled in anger that he could by no means have recovered his wits in time to parry a second blow. His new brother-in-law's readier blade did the business for him, driving in to fell the attacker efficiently.

There was fighting all around them now, but it was a struggle of movement – with the motion distinctly southwards. The Douglases were falling back.

It was scarcely to be wondered at. The mud was their undoing. Two of their leaders had fallen. And the first Arbroath contingent was now reforming on the firm north shore, and some were even re-entering the fight.

Ensign John Durie materialised at David's side. "My thanks!" he panted. "Here's bonnie fighting. They were too much for us . . ."

"Keep them moving!" David jerked. "Quickly – bring your others back. We must not let them gather their wits." He raised his voice. "Forward!" he shouted. "Forward! A Beaton! A Beaton!"

Durie, with much more soldierly lungs, took up the cry. There was a general surge onward amongst the churchmen, accompanied by triumphant yells. The enemy moved away the faster, with no sign of a rally.

David left Gilbert and Durie to lead the pursuit. He himself swung a little unsteadily out of his saddle and jumped down into the mud-brown water. He stooped, to grasp the shoulder of the grey-haired man who, face down, lashed feebly there, dragged down by his armour, in a growing patch of cloudy red. Stumbling, he pulled his half-drowned victim to the shore.

There was no prolonged chase by the churchmen, exhilarating as it was to pursue the dreaded Douglases. The nearness of St. Andrews town, where there were more of the same, in plenty, turned them back quickly. Jubilant they returned to the river-mouth.

David had discovered that the man whom he had brought low and then rescued was Douglas of Whittinghame, a Lothian laird of broad acres and distant cousin of Morton's. His wound was not a vital one, but he had lost a lot of blood and his lungs were full of water. One of the monks, skilful in such matters, worked on him. When some protests developed over this waste, David pointed out that a Douglas hostage might be valuable.

The rejoicings of victory were short-lived. The Abbey contingents had fully a dozen wounded, and the first party over a score missing. Patrick Barclay explained that his company had arrived to find St. Andrews fallen and wholly occupied by the Douglases. They had scouted around the vicinity, seeking news of the Archbishop-Chancellor, and had had skirmishes with small groups of the enemy. Then, returning by Leuchars, they had run into this large force under Whittinghame. Outnumbered and nearly trapped, they had taken refuge in flight, making for this wilderness of Tents Muir . . .

"Yes, yes," David interrupted impatiently. "All this I could guess. But what of my uncle? What of the Archbishop? Has his castle held out?"

"The castle, they say, was never held. The Archbishop found that Prior Hepburn's men were inside. They were everywhere, within the walls. Treachery. They would declare for Douglas at the first blow. So, when he saw no aid coming, he slipped away . . ."

"Sieze you, man — to the point! Is he alive? Taken? Or free?"

"They say that he won clear. In the darkness. That he had a boat waiting in the harbour. That with only two or three companions he sailed away. So there was little stand against Douglas. It was wise, I suppose."

"Where is he gone? Is it known?"

153

"The Abbot of Balmerino — we saw him at Leuchars — said that my lord was for Stirling."

"Stirling! Fiend take him — the Queen-Mother is at Stirling! Holding that Castle. He would never go to her!"

"Where else is he to turn, my lord Abbot?"

Durie intervened. "They say that Lennox is with the Queen, there. That he is against this taking of the King, and has quarrelled with Angus."

"Lennox . . .?" John Stewart, third Earl of Lennox, was head of the most powerful and senior non-royal branch of the great House of Stewart. His influence, especially in the West, was substantial, although he was a man of retiring habits and no ambitions, too honest for his station and the times in which he lived. "The Stewarts, eh . . .!" David stroked his tiny beard.

Gilbert Ogilvy spoke up. "Lennox or none, here is no place to linger, I say. When those Douglases reach yonder town, they will not be long in coming back, I think, with many more."

David clapped his mailed shoulder. "You are right, Gibbie. No profit for us here, now. Is Angus himself in St. Andrews?"

"I think not," Barclay said. "There has been no word of him. Morton is spoken of . . ."

"Aye. Then we waste our time here. Where Angus is will be decision — nowhere else. Come — we ride."

"Where, my lord? Where do we go?"

"To Stirling," David announced briefly. "Some of us."

At the northern end of Tents Muir, with the mouth of the Tay in view again, there was a parting of company. David took the fittest, toughest and best-mounted of his people, to the number of some four-score, and sent all the rest, with the hostage and the wounded, under Gilbert, back to Arbroath.

The reduced company, notably faster-moving now, rode westwards, well south of Ferry Port, to strike the little-used road which followed the south bank of Tay. This went by Church lands all the way to the Ochil Hills, belonging to the Abbeys of Balmerino and Lindores and the Priory of Abernethy, a pendicle of Arbroath. This roundabout route was necessary if the great Douglas-dominated lands of central Fife were to be avoided, especially the area around Loch Leven where one of the most powerful branches of the House was based.

By mid-forenoon next day they were hidden in the woods of the Abbey Craig of Cambuskenneth, with the soaring rock of Stirling and its royal castle rising out of the level plain of Forth less than two miles away. The abbot here was one of the Queen's party, but David risked sending on a messenger to enquire of him the situation in the town, and whether the Archbishop had in fact come here.

The word brought back was much to the point. It was from the sub-Abbot, the Abbot himself having been summoned to the castle by the Queen-Mother, in consequence of the arrival there the previous night of the Archbishop of St. Andrews. The Earl of Lennox was also there, as of course the Earl of Mar, Keeper of the fortress. Some sort of council seemed to be in progress.

David delayed no longer. Tidying up his travel-worn force to make the best show possible, he led them at a jingling trot across the levels, over the causeway of the Forth, and Stirling Bridge, to the gates of the town, banners flying. None sought to hold up so impressive seeming and confident a company.

Up through the cobbled streets of the grey climbing town they clattered, to the same stern ramparts where years before David had introduced the Duke of Albany to the problems of Scottish government. Here it was less simple, the guards allowing no unauthorised entry. David haughtily announced the Lord Abbot of Arbroath, Lord Articular, to see the Chancellor of the realm and the Queen Margaret's Grace.

After some little delay they were admitted to the fortress. Leaving his men with Durie, and hurried instructions, in the outer court, David with Barclay the Archiepiscopal Chamberlain in attendance, was led to the royal quarters. He expected to be taken to Mar, the keeper, but it proved to be to a small private chamber that they were conducted—and Patrick Barclay was turned back brusquely at the door thereof by an Englishman with anything but courtly manners.

Margaret Tudor herself was alone in the inner room, sitting by the window. She stared at David heavily, directly, from those dull yet strangely glowing eyes.

"So you follow your kinsman to my door, Master Beaton!" she said shortly. "And like him, seek my help, I have no doubt? The protection of my house?"

"Help, Your Grace? Protection?" David managed to look

155

surprised, even as he bowed low. "No – I come only to convey my respects to Your Highness. And to seek word with the Chancellor . . ."

"Who is no longer Chancellor!"

"I would not have believed that Your Grace would have accepted the events of these last days as of lawful effect, or binding on any?"

She flicked that aside with a gesture of her hand. "Archibald Douglas is a law unto himself. And very effective."

"Aye, Madam. But not a law unto *you*, I think? Nor unto me. Nor to many another, praise God, in this realm."

"He holds the realm in his hand, does he not? Save only this Stirling."

"I think not. Edinburgh and St. Andrews he holds. With much of the Borders, the Douglas lands and his friend Arran's Hamilton country. But there is much of Scotland otherwise minded. Many who will not bow the knee to Douglas."

She searched his face. "You speak bolder than your uncle, Master David," she said.

"I speak but plain truth, Your Grace. Have I your permission to go speak with the Chancellor-Archbishop?"

"Be not so hasty, my friend. Time enough for that . . . if it is my wish."

David paused for a moment. "I cannot conceive it otherwise, Madam. Since that is why I have come. And, with all respect to Your Grace, it is my simple right."

"Your right, sirrah! In *my* house?"

"In any house, man's or God's! James Beaton is not only my uncle and I his secretary. He is Primate of this province of Holy Church. And I am Abbot of Arbroath. Your Grace will not, I think, seek to constrain Holy Church?"

"So – that note the cock crows! Aye, you are bold, Master David. To think use the Church for your personal ends! To me!"

"I used it for yours, not so long since, Madam! To gain you your divorcement."

The Queen frowned, tapping the wall-panelling with her finger-nails, an unlovely, massive woman, whey-faced, without grace, yet with some essential, earthly animal force and attraction.

"Perhaps we are foolish to contend thus, Master David," she said, after a moment or two. "We do not love each other — but we might make more profitable partners than foes, I think?"

He considered her and her suggestion coolly. "Your Highness is gracious. And probably right."

"Come, then, and sit here, by me. Let me hear what you propose."

"I propose, Madam, to confer with my uncle. For that I came . . ."

"Tush, man — do not play with me! You have twice the wits of your uncle — and do not have to be told it! You would do better to confer with me, I vow! We would both draw Angus's teeth, would we not?"

"Aye, that is true." David sat down — and a white lard-like hand, the fingers glittering with rings, reached out at once to take his own.

It demanded all the young man's resolution not to snatch his hand away. The very feel of her, new as he was from Marion's fresh beauty, all but revolted him. He was not abnormally fastidious, by any means — but this woman positively repelled him.

Margaret Tudor, however, was in far from affectionate mood. The fingers that held his gripped tightly, almost fiercely, and the nails dug in painfully.

"You are a pretty man, Churchman!" she said. "But I think your wits are the best of you!"

David would have liked to have retorted that they were matched in that — but contented himself with inclining his head. "I do not aspire to partner Your Grace in any other respect!" he said mildly.

"Ha! Insolent!" She raked with those long nails, savagely. "Watch your words, sir! Remember to whom you speak!"

"I am not likely to forget, Highness. You wanted something from me, did you not? Some understanding?"

The Queen-Mother nodded. "You lifted Angus up, at the Parliament of a year past. At my cost, 'fore God! Now you would pull him down again, I think. With my help, again. Is it not so? That, as least, is what the Archbishop would be at."

"Until I have spoken with my uncle, I cannot accept that this is his policy," he returned. "But — that Angus has acted against

157

the true interest of the realm is only too apparent. Clearly the situation must be rectified. Somehow."

"And you perceive how it may be done, Master David?" Still she grippped his hand.

He hesitated. It had been no part of his intention to discuss what was only a tentative idea simmering in his mind, with Margaret Tudor of all people. Yet, since she was pressing him, there might be little harm in it, and a possiblity of great good. Hatred was this woman's most effective trait – and her hatred for her ex-husband, in the circumstances, might be a strong card, if skilfully played.

"Madam – I perceive one bright thread running through this sorry and tattered Scots tapestry of ours, so far unregarded. One thread, which nimble fingers might stitch into a pattern, a stout and effective pattern, more potent even that the Red Heart of Douglas. That pattern, the Fess Chequey of Stewart."

"What do you mean, man?"

"I mean that here is a grouping of forces and powers which has not been considered nor attempted. I understand that my lord of Lennox is here? With his adherence, I think it might be possible to rally all the House of Stewart. You have wed Henry Stewart and his brother, Lord Avondale, is head of the Lanark-shire Stewarts. The Earl of Moray, your late royal husband's bastard by Janet Kennedy, is young – but he has great lands and power in the North. And he has been reared by his mother to hate the name of Douglas."

Margaret Tudor was leaning forward now, her heavy figure alert, her grip on his hand steelly despite the white and puffy fingers. She did not speak – but there was no question but that she perceived the possibilities of his proposal.

"The Stewarts are a great and scattered race – although, to my knowledge, they have never united hitherto in any cause," David went on. "But there is no reason why they should not, I think. The Earl of Atholl can field thousands. The Earl of Buchan is old and donnert, with no heir – but he has stout bastards amany. My lord of Innermeath . . ."

"That old fool Buchan is no friend of mine! Nor Innermeath – a sour devil!" the Queen-Mother exclaimed.

"To be sure. The thing will have to be done featly, discreetly – for few of the Stewarts love Your Grace, I fear!" David paused, to emphasise the point. "But Lennox, now—Lennox is senior amongst them, and esteemed of all as honest. This of Lennox, his coming to Stirling to you could be an ill day for Angus. For there are a multitude of Stewarts—Stewarts of Roysth, of Traquair, of Garlies, of Ardgowan, and the rest. All over the realm. Aye, and Appin, the Highland branch."

"No doubt. But how is this miracle to be worked? You say that they do not all love me. But nor do they love each other. They have nothing in common, save the name."

"Save the name!" he nodded. "And the fact that it is the King's name also. In no other land than this, possibly, would it serve. But in Scotland name and blood means much. If King James Stewart will appeal to all other Stewarts soever to deliver him from the evil grasp of the Douglas. And if Stewart, Earl of Lennox, principal scion of the House, is the first to rally to his cry. Why, then I think you will see your miracle, Highness."

"God's death! This will require a letter from my son, the King?"

"Yes. That would be best. I think that it might be achieved. Angus cannot sit over him all the time."

"What need? His writing can be forged."

"Not so, Madam. Then His grace would deny it. Angus's denials would signify nothing. But the King's, young as he is, would be harmful. I say . . ."

The door was opened, and unceremoniously in came Henry Stewart of Methven, the Queen-Mother's new and third husband. Dressed in the height of extravagant fashion and with more wine in him than he could conveniently carry, he stopped abruptly at the sight of David Beaton sitting there hand-in-hand with his wife. David would have withdrawn his hand—but firmly, deliberately, Queen Margaret hung on to it.

"W'what's this? A pox—what's this?" the young man cried. "Slay me—it's Beaton! Unhand my wife, you . . . you snivelling clerk! D'you hear me?"

"Henry—be quiet! You are drunk!" Margaret Tudor snapped.

David managed to free his hand, and stood up. "Have I to congratulate you, sir, upon attaining the married state?" he asked coolly.

"You are imp-impudent! Leave us. Leave us, I say."

"Henry—do not be a greater fool than you may help! Remember whose presence you are in! I give audience to the Abbot of Arbroath . . ."

"Audience, is it! Shut in here, and holding hands!"

"Silence! Enough! Think you to have bought me? Me, the Queen? You will keep your place, Henry – or by the Rude I will teach you it!"

Stewart had sufficient wits left to turn his attack wholly upon Beaton. "I do not like churchmen," he declared thickly. "Nor, I believed, did Her Grace! They creep. They crawl. No woman is safe from them."

David smiled. "Her Highness, nevertheless, is safe from me, sir!"

That produced glares from husband and wife both.

"We discuss affairs of state," the Queen-Mother said. "Have you aught else to say on the matter, Master Beaton?"

"Only, Madam, that as to the letter we spoke of, the Archbishop of Glasgow might help. Your friend, Gavin Dunbar, Tutor! I cannot think that he can be entirely happy in opposing you, to whom he owes all his preferment!"

"Another treacherous and ungrateful clerk!" Methven jerked.

"Aye – Gavin!" Margaret Tudor nodded. "I swear that his head lies uneasy of a night! Angus will prove a harsh taskmaster. Gavin has proved a broken reed, indeed – but he might serve for this, of the letter."

"What letter? What is this you speak of?" the young man demanded suspiciously.

"Nothing that need concern you, Henry," his new spouse snapped.

Doubtfully, mistrustfully, Stewart looked from one to the other. "You would gammon me? Cozen me?" he wondered. "Burn me – I'll teach you otherwise! You'll not play with Henry Stewart . . .!"

"God forbid!" David exclaimed fervently, but still with that smile. "Madam – with your permission I will retire. Go seek the Chancellor. Leaving you to . . . to your felicity!" And he bowed.

David found his uncle in one of the most insignificant chambers of the fortress, little better than a cell indeed, in an old and semi-ruinous tower, Barclay his Chamberlain already with him. David was shocked at the older man's appearance. Something of the meanness of his quarters seemed to be reflected in James

Beaton. Here was a man dejected, broken, his clothing awry, his person unkempt. Almost, his gross and bulky figure appeared to have shrunk.

The younger men exchanged quick and pregnant glances. Then David came over to clap the Archbishop's bent shoulder.

"Greetings, my lord," he exclaimed heartily. "It is good to see you. But . . . on my soul, here are sorry quarters for the Chancellor of the realm!"

"Aye, Davie—but I am no longer Chancellor," James Beaton said dully, flatly.

"To be sure you are! You do not accept Angus's trumpetings and proclamations as lawful and valid, do you? In the eyes of all true men you are still Chancellor of Scotland, I say."

"The King's signature appoints Angus in my place . . ."

"A signature forced from a fourteen-year-old boy by his gaoler! Only a lawfully constituted Parliament can confirm such change of office. You still have the seals of office, do you not?"

"Aye. But . . . scant use they are to me!"

"At least, holding them, you deny them to Angus. But, Uncle—the Chancellorship is not all. You are Primate, Apostolic Notary and second person of this realm. Ranking above all, under the King's Grace. Above all lords spiritual and temporal. Above Angus. Or Mar, here, the Keeper. Or Margaret Tudor herself, who is but relict of a former monarch and married to a nobody. You are the head, and voice, of the Church in this land. That none can take from you, save only the Pope. And I think we can ensure that he will not do that! Save us, Uncle—what have you lost? St. Andrews Castle, that is all. And that can be recovered. God-a-mercy—are you not still the richest man in the land?"

The Archbishop looked up from under heavy brows—but at least there was something of a gleam in his little piglike eyes, even if it was only the gleam of re-awakened avarice endangered. "Och, aye. I'ph'mm. Well—maybe. Maybe not. I'll no' just say that, Davie. Forbye, what little I have is in the main in lands and houses. What good to me in this pass? Angus, in the King's name, can *take* them . . ."

"You can bestow some on others, before Angus has time to take. Others judiciously chosen. To win back again in due course. Also, as Archbishop and Primate, you have the authority to coin money. The only man who may, under the Crown . . ."

"Aye—but what use? Where's the siller to come from? Am I to coin money out of iron, boy?"

"Not so. The Church is rich in silver. And gold. Plate. Chalices. Candlesticks. Pattens. Crosses. Censers. Images. Fonts. The accumulations of centuries. *You* are the Church, my lord! Take what you need. The Church can and will fight against the tyrant and the despoiler."

James Beaton licked thick lips, glancing almost furtively at Patrick Barclay. "Aye. M'mmm. Well." He shook his grey bullet head. "But, Davie—it's men. It's no' siller that will save the kingdom. It's men. Armed men. More men than Douglas and Hamilton can throw against me. Monks and servitors and ploughmen wi' swords are well enough—and I hear you did right well wi' the like at Tents Muir. But we need thousands. Trained fighting-men. To overthrow Douglas in battle . . ."

"Agreed, Uncle. Although I would ever counsel against meeting Angus's power in battle. That is to fight on ground of *his* choosing. Better that we should choose our own. Using our wits rather than our swords. There is no virtue in bloodshed. If men must die, let it be the selected few, to save the many. Did not Christ Himself teach us that? He that taketh the sword! Swords there must be, more's the pity. But the threat of the sword may be more potent than the sword's use, see you."

"Shrive me, man—do not speak me in riddles!" his uncle charged peevishly. "What's your purpose?"

"It is simple, my lord. Merely that you gain a sufficiency of swords to threaten Angus."

"How, Davie—how?" The other's voice rose almost to crack. "How may I do this? Where are these swords to come from?"

"Rally the House of Stewart. To rescue James Stewart, the King. A holy war to save the King's Grace from Douglas. There are thousands of Stewarts. And two of their leaders are in this castle today. Lennox and Avondale, Methven's brother. Think of the others—Atholl, Moray, Buchan, Innermeath and the rest."

The Archbishop stared ahead of him, unseeing. But his massive shoulders were no longer bowed.

"It would be a most notable project, my lord," Patrick Barclay put on. "And there are three Stewart bishops, are there not?"

"If my hands were not tied here . . .!"

"Who dares tie the hands of Holy Church?" his nephew

162

demanded. "Here are only bonds of straw, Uncle. Burst them! First of all, send for Mar, the Keeper of this castle. As second person of this realm and Primate of Scotland, demand the best quarters in the house. Forthwith. Demand servants. Messengers. Paper and ink. In the name of Holy Church. Your Guard to surround your person. I have them in the Outer Courtyard. Then require the Earl of Lennox to attend on you. Not here. In better quarters. The Abbot of Cambuskenneth to act your chaplain and notary. Send for Lindores, Balmerino, Abernethy — all abbots and priors within reach. Establish your own Court here . . ."

"But the Queen? What of Margaret Tudor. She queens it here . . ."

"She has not true authority in Stirling Castle. She is only a private citizen. Mar owes no allegiance to her — only to King and Parliament. The King is a captive — and *you* represent Parliament. Moreover, the Queen-Mother has two great weaknesses. She hates too hard. And she dotes on young men. We shall play on these."

James Beaton drew a deep and quivering breath. "Aye . . .!" he said.

Chapter Eleven

DAVID BEATON was, on the whole, of a cheerful and sanguine nature, however cynical at times were his views of his fellow-men. But this grey September day he was depressed, and could not find the wherewithal to shift his depression. For practically everyone around him was in high spirits — and they were many. He was weary, of course, tired from endless days in the saddle, scouring the length and breadth of Scotland.

He was still in the saddle, although now no lone courier but one of a great host, a host proudly led under many flaunting banners — and all but a few of them yellow with a blue-and-white diced band across the centre, the Fess Chequey on gold of the House of Stewart.

The great concourse, more than five thousand strong, was in fact the proof both of David's success and his failure. Success in his scheming and planning; failure in the abandonment of his policy. It was a triumph that all these men should be assembled under the leadership of the Earls of Lennox and Atholl; but little short of a tragedy, in David's opinion, that they should be here, riding towards Linlithgow, in battle array.

It was the old story, of course, of it being more simple to raise the Devil than to lay him again. Not that it had been anyways simple raising these five thousand Stewarts, and others. They represented a great expenditure of time, patience, energy, money, and sheer cajolery, over the intervening two months. David had spared neither himself, those whom he could command, nor his uncle's fortune, in the process. And now, to have all jeopardised by impatience, by pride, by folly, however gallant.

Strangely, it was the moderate, honest and normally mild Lennox's fault, in the main. He it was who would not wait – not even for the young Earl of Moray coming from the north with another two thousand, or for Stewart of Garlies who was on his way from far Galloway with five hundred more. With the simple and single-minded John, Earl of Lennox, David's efforts had been all too successful. His young monarch had written to him, beseeching him in the name of God and Saint Andrew to come deliver him from the violent hands of Douglas. Asking not how this letter had been obtained, Lennox became afire to rescue his prince. Counsel of caution and delay found him deaf – or at least, the despairing cries of young James Stewart sounded louder in his ears. Nor would he acknowledge the claims of churchmen, however authoritative, to constrain him, the chief scion of the Stewart stem. God would uphold the right and the cause of His Anointed, whatever the craven fears of clerics.

So they had marched, and David Beaton was a prey to fears.

They had left Stirling early, and now were nearing the valley of the Lothian Avon, only a couple of miles from Linlithgow. Angus had held the young King in the royal palace there much of the summer, avoiding the stinks and odours of Edinburgh's narrow streets and its Nor' Loch during the hot weather. It was known that Angus himself was returned to Edinburgh, eighteen miles away – but it was uncertain whether he had taken the young monarch with him. Hence this ill-advised expedition. This was all Hamilton country, and ever since Falkirk their advance would have been observed and reported on. Not that Lennox and

Atholl would have sought any secret and underhand approach, anyway. That was the fine Stewart style of them.

These two rode in the forefront of the long and gallant line, a sight to stir the pulse indeed. Lennox was a gravely handsome man, in his early thirties, tall and dark with the great liquid Stewart eyes. Dressed in splendid polished armour, with an old-fashioned heraldic surcoat of vivid colouring, he bestrode a massive charger richly caparisoned as for a tournament. John, Earl of Atholl, known as The Magnificent on account of his princely extravagance, was a huge golden man, shoulder-long hair and silky beard gleaming, black armour so chased and engraved with gold that little of the steel was noticeable. The bonnet with its curling yellow plumes, the sword-belt, even his horse's harness, glittered with jewels. They made a spectacular pair of knightly paladins who would have been hard to surpass on any field in Christendom, riding under their respective banners. They were brothers-in-law as well as chiefs of independent Stewart septs.

Behind them, only a little less resplendent, came the Earl of Cassillis, not a Stewart but cousin to the man who rode by his side, Andrew, Lord Avondale. With them was Lord Innermeath, Andrew Stewart, Bishop of Caithness, Henry Stewart of Methven and the Lord Lindsay of the Byres. There followed a long line of Stewart lairds, too numerous to recount, all vying with the Chief of Appin, who was in full Highland panoply, with his retinue of lesser chieftans. The rest of the Stewarts looked on these last as more or less barbarians but treated them with wary respect nevertheless. Their swarms of bare-chested, kilted followers were the only unmounted portion of the host. Not that the others had to ride the slower on their account.

David rode a little way apart, with a mixed company of his own people, other churchmen from various abbeys and bishoprics, and further oddments, to the number of about four hundred. His column formed the extreme left of the line — and clearly, as far as the leadership was concerned, could be dismissed as more or less valueless.

Linlithgow was already in sight, the towers of its fine palace vague in the autumn haze. But between the advancing host and the town was the River Avon, running in a steep-sided valley. They were still half a mile from this unseen barrier when scouts came galloping back, obviously big with news. Trumpets rang out, calling the army to a halt. David spurred off to the right, with Sir John Stirling of Keir, to ascertain the position.

He found the Stewart lords in some confusion, exchanging high words. The line of the Avon was being held against them by the Hamiltons, Arran, their chief, being in command. They were massed, with some Douglas support, along the far side of the river — but a strong party had been thrown forward across Linlithgow Bridge, and held the bridgehead. They probably mustered little more than half the Stewarts' total.

The dispute was as to tactics. This was the only bridge to span the Avon, up or down stream, for many miles. The river was not notably deep or swift, but the banks were steep on both sides, presenting a serious problem for crossing under attack. Atholl was loudly advocating, demanding indeed, direct assault on the bridge, Cassillis and Stewart of Methven agreeing. Innermeath, backed by Lord Lindsay, declared that this would be too costly — and even though they won the bridge itself, they could be bottled up at the other side, unable to get sufficient men across its narrow passage to break out. They must seek a crossing elsewhere. Around these protagonists, men took sides, whilst Lennox himself remained undecided.

David listened to the argument with ever-growing concern. More than once he tried to make his voice heard, but failed. At length it was Lennox himself who, in his perplexity, turned to the churchman.

"Master Beaton," he asked, holding up his hand for quiet. "What is your advice in this pass?"

"Aye!" jeered Henry Stewart. "What says Holy Church? Retreat, I'll be bound! Run from half our number! Then prayer and supplication, with fasting!"

"The Laird of Methven speaks wiser than he knows, on this occasion!" David said. "I would indeed advise retreat, before we come to blows, to await a better opportunity. But . . ." He had to shout to be heard above the growl that produced. "But since I know that none will heed such advice, I offer this instead. Something over a mile upstream there is the small Priory of Emmanuel. A house of nuns. Under the protection of the Order of St. John of Jerusalem, whose Preceptory is but three miles away. But, on the other side of Avon, my lords. There is much coming and going between the two houses. There is no bridge — but there is ford. A causeway of stones, laid in the river. The Nuns' Ford. It is narrow, for a host such as this, but . . ."

"Ha — a ford!"

"Here's better talking. A ford will serve."

"God bless the nuns!"

"A mile up, you say, Master Beaton?" Lennox said, quietening the others. "Then we need not delay here. If we can move thereto, unseen . . ."

"A moment, my lord," David urged. "Better that we *should* be seen — or some of us. They know well that we are here — or they would not be awaiting us yonder. If we do not appear now, Arran will know that we have gone to try elsewhere. And small doubt that the Hamiltons know the Nuns' Ford well enough, for this is their country."

"I still say let us have at the bridge!" Atholl interrupted strongly. "What are we — men or nuns? To go creeping and scuttling. Put the matter to the test of arms, I say — and see who wins!"

"On a tourney-ground — yes, my lord! But here you fight a river and steep braes, as well as the enemy. But — make an assault on the bridge by all means. With no great numbers. Others to line the crest of the bank above the river. In full view of the Hamiltons. With much ado and shouting. So shall you hold them there. The rest to move back, quietly, and ride to Emmanuel and the ford, unseen. To cross there, and move in behind the enemy. If may be. If opposed at the ford, at least it will cause Arran to break up his array."

There were more shouts of acclaim for this programme than there were growls and scoffs about clerks, faint-hearts and pretty boys. Lennox began to give the necessary orders.

Perhaps half the total force, under Lennox himself, made by hidden ways for Emmanuel Priory under its green ridge, David hurrying ahead with scouts, seeking information. He discovered from the Prioress that, in fact, a picket of armed men had been watching the ford all morning from a clump of hawthorns across the river. Not many of them, but sufficient to prevent any surprise crossing.

This was disappointing news — but at least it meant that if they hurried they ought to be able to get across the Avon more or less

167

unopposed – for from the Priory windows much of the east bank
of the river could be observed, and there was no sign of any large
body of men. Lennox ordered an immediate advance to the ford.

Nearing the water, they could see horsemen spurring away from
a scattering of trees opposite.

The blocks of stone set in the river-bed formed a causeway of
no great width, and were moreover very slippery. The crossing
therefore was slow – and Lennox would by no means wait until
all his people were across before pressing on downstream. Arran
must not be allowed time to make new dispositions.

David accepted the need for haste, but doubted the wisdom
of failing to consolidate the host first, leaving them strung out
behind. When a tributary burn came in from the east, cutting a
ravine for itself, he urged the Earl to wait. Here was a good
defensive position where they could reassemble and regroup.

Lennox would not hear of it. He was not looking for any
defensive position, he cried. He was here to rescue the King –
and that was not to be done by sitting inactive and waiting for
traitors to attack them.

He rode down into the ravine and up the other side.

They could hear the din of strife ahead of them now. Atholl
was evidently making no mere feints at the bridge. In front of
them was a wide area of open grassy banks and braes, where
cattle grazed, a pleasant pastoral landscape where horses could
stretch their legs. The Stewart horses were urged to do so in no
uncertain fashion.

David perceived bullocks doing likewise, presently, tails in the
air and spread over quite a wide front – but the cattle were
coming towards them, not running away. He shouted and pointed
– but none paid him any heed. In a few minutes he could see the
first banners and pennons and lance-tips behind the bullocks.
The sight of these drew yells and cheers from all around him,
but certainly no diminution of pace. This was what fighting-men
had come for.

Cursing, David Beaton reined in, and waved such of his own
company as were near and would heed him, to pull a little way
aside and halt. Horsemen thundered past them, by the score, the
hundred, pointing, waving on, jeering or shaking their fists or
swords at the cowardly churchmen.

Unheeding, David marshalled his group of about one hundred

into an arrow-head formation, tight and compact, with the Abbey of Arbroath's standard in the centre. He gave brief but strict orders as to keeping that formation, each man to automatically support his neighbours. Then they moved forward again, but only at a trot.

Already the main forces had clashed, and inevitably in considerable confusion. The Hamiltons were approaching in line abreast, whereas the Stewart advance was in no formation at all, merely charging masses of men, scattered and outspread. Their initial impetus in most cases carried them through the enemy line, giving an illusion of swift success. But as the Hamiltons reformed, and their rear swung round to assail the Stewarts who had broken through, the latter perforce were split up into struggling groups, some pressing ahead, some turning back, some doing well, others less so. Lennox lost any control that he might have had over his force as a whole, any ability to direct the battle.

There were not a few red-and-white Hamilton banners in evidence, but one was larger than the others and undifferenced by any symbols of cadency—Arran's own, almost certainly. For want of any more certain objective, David Beaton led his close formation directly towards this, himself in the apex, and at a canter now.

They struck the perimeter of the struggling mass of men and horses, yelling "A Beaton! A Beaton!" Although David was in the lead, Patrick Barclay on his right and the sub-Prior of Abernethy on his left were so close behind that their mounts' flaring nostrils were snorting foam on his bent knees. Equally, these two were backed by four others, as closely. It was a most effective formation, giving enormous driving strength and mutual protection—although it meant that the inside men had little fighting to do—until positions were changed either by reforming or by casualty replacement amongst the outer men. Each individual had to consider only a strictly limited front. But it demanded good horsemanship, and no sudden changes of direction on the part of the leader.

David, in fact, drove right through the first mêlée without coming to serious blows with anyone, pressed on as he was by the weight behind him. Men were unseated and horses went down before them, knocked over by the sheer solid boring impact. Inevitably some Stewarts were amongst those who crashed, in their irresistible path, for there was no means of dodging around individuals. But the effect on the enemy was as shattering morally on a wide scale as it was physically on a narrow.

Clear through the seething mass and into the open, where there were only single riders, David sought to wheel round in an arc wide enough not to break his formation. It was less compact now than it had been – but there were no empty saddles, although two or three men appeared to be wounded. Ordering these to be replaced by men from the centre, he drove back again into the fray.

He was making a determined attempt to get at Arran, when he perceived Lennox's own banner in the thick of the fiercest fighting – and it was sagging and swaying alarmingly. Even as he looked, it went down. He could just glimpse the Earl's highly coloured surcoat, tattered in shreds now above his armour. At least *he* was still horsed.

Yelling their Beaton slogan, the churchmen drove in, smiting.

Most men fell back and gave ground, if they could, at the sight of that furious wedge of destruction bearing down upon them. But not all. David was suddenly aware that one man was not only standing fast ahead of them but that there was a lance levelled unwaveringly at his throat.

He had not time, forced on headlong from behind, to take avoiding action. He could only swerve in his saddle – swerve to the right. Throwing up his left arm, he grabbed at the lance as he reached it. He failed to hold it – but at least his wrist ran along its shaft. Over and down he brought his clenched fist – and the lance was under his arm.

Although his opponent relinquished his hold on the weapon at the last moment, there was no possibility of avoiding collision. David hurtled into the man and horse – and mount and rider went down under him in a chaos of flailing limbs. The white stallion tripped and stumbled over the other animal.

David, flung violently forward, clutched and clung round the neck of his floundering horse. In that moment he was preternaturally aware of many things – but most starkly of the pounding, lashing hooves of all his own men's beasts immediately behind him.

Desperately he scrabbled, sought to hold on, to keep his balance.

It was the stallion that recovered, not its master. Somehow it managed to retain its feet, although down on one knee, and staggered up. And on — for there could be no break in the driving pressure from behind. Barclay's strong hand reached down to grasp David, to drag him up, to steady him in the saddle. All as they swept on.

Beaton was bruised, shaken — and had lost his sword. But he had learned a lesson. The leader of such a wedge was in the most dangerous position of all. It was not for him to fight, to do anything other than spearhead the attack and protect himself. That, and control his horse. All else must be left to his supporters.

Willy-nilly they were driving on towards where Lennox had been fighting. But there was no sign of him now, though the press was still thick. Arran's red-and-white standard was some distance to the left.

There was another Hamilton flag, however, almost directly in front — one with a black slantwise bar diagonally across its red, from right to left, a bend sinister. There was only one man who was likely thus to flaunt his own illegitimacy — Sir James Hamilton of Finnart, the Bastard of Arran, that chief's eldest son, although born out of wedlock. He was an able but ruthless man, and a renowned fighter.

David had no desire to cross swords with this grim celebrity — especially now that he had no sword to cross. But there was no halting the impetus of their charge, without endangering all.

As they cut through the battling throng the situation in the centre became apparent. Lennox was down, and a group of Stewarts, dismounted, stood over his body, wielding their swords with the fury of desperation, supported by a broken ring of horsemen. Hamilton of Finnart was assailing them with a determined and savage band of mosstroopers.

The churchmen's arrival from almost behind the Hamiltons changed all. Finnart had to try to wheel his men round, and had neither the space nor the time to do it effectively. In a confusion of rearing beasts, lashing hooves and cursing men, David's wedge was upon them, scattering, overturning.

This time David had no need for protection. He was through almost before he knew it. He raised his hand, to slow down and halt his column.

The wheeling round and return to Lennox was not achieved

without considerable disorganisation of the arrow-head formation. Fortunately Sir James Hamilton himself had been thrown off his horse by the impact, and seeking another mount was in no position to throw in a counter-attack.

Stewart of Murdostoun shouted to David that the Earl was not dead, only wounded, and stunned by being thrown in armour. David formed his men into a ring around the semi-conscious Earl, whilst others hoisted him up into a saddle before his own esquire.

It was at this moment that, above all the shouting and din of battle, dread and ominous, came a chanting roar, powerful, insistent. "A Douglas! A Douglas!" it rang out.

Everywhere men paused to raise their heads, turning towards that sound, friend and foe alike.

They looked eastwards. All along the rolling skyline of the green braes that stretched between Avon and Linlithgow, horsemen were silhouetted, hundreds upon hundreds. In the centre of the mile-long line, amongst a host of Red Heart banners, the Royal Standard of Scotland itself fluttered proudly.

"God be good – see there!" David cried, pointing. "That can only be Angus. Come from Edinburgh. With the King."

"He has us trapped!" Patrick Barclay exclaimed. "The river – we are held against the river."

As the great Douglas host came on, cheering, the Hamiltons rallied everywhere. And, as evidently, the Stewarts faltered and gave ground. With no central leadership, soon it would be every man for himself.

David shouted for his men to close in again, in their original formation, around Lennox. Murdostoun and his Stewarts joined them.

"Back to the ford," he commanded. "The bridge is still held against us. Hold close. None to stray. Come!"

Amongst hundreds of men streaming off the field, mounted and dismounted, in ones and twos and groups, some down towards the river itself but most back in the direction of the Nuns' Ford, the tight body of churchmen at least retired as a disciplined force, a purposeful unit still under the flag of Arbroath. In the panic and confusion, they represented something reliable and sure. And this, ironically, was their undoing. For, in consequence, many flocked to them. Soon they were no longer a close, wedge-shaped company, but an amorphous mass of fleeing men. David was quickly aware that he could have little or no control over them.

And control was vital, for it was a fearsome thing to have to ride along the front of that swiftly advancing Douglas line, harried at the rear and flanks by the Hamiltons. Particularly as the Douglas front appeared to be crescent-shaped, with the horns further advanced than the centre. The southern horn looked like reaching the Nuns' Ford area almost as soon as David's company could do so.

As men perceived this, more and more spurred into headlong flight, doing anything to get ahead, to reach the ford before the dreaded enemy, jostling each other, even riding down their fellows. And the panic was infectious. Swiftly the Arbroath contingent degenerated and disintegrated, until there was only a remnant of a compact score or so around David, Lennox and Murdostoun. Inevitably this group could not ride in formation so fast as did fleeing individuals.

"It will not serve," Patrick Barclay exclaimed, at David's ear.

The other, grim-faced, made no reply.

The Douglases were now very near, and converging on David's party. He debated with himself whether to break away to the right, for the nearest point of the river, to seek to swim their way across somehow. The steep rocky banks told against that. And they would never get the wounded Lennox across.

There was only the one gleam of hope in the situation, that he could see. The underwater causeway at the ford was narrow. Quite a small group of men, if sufficiently determined, could hold that against a host, and so allow fugitives to get across. If they could get there before the first of the enemy. Somebody might have thought of it, amongst the Stewarts . . .

Somebody had though of it—but Hamilton, not Stewart. As the Arbroath party at last came to the final slope to the river, it was to see, with sinking hearts, that they were too late. The ford was held against them by a company of perhaps fifty, in the Hamilton colours, stationary in mid-stream. There was no escape. Everywhere Stewart fugitives were recognising it, and throwing down their arms.

Grimly, David Beaton bowed to the inevitable. "What must be, must!" he jerked. "Now—only to seek make the best of what

173

may not be mended." He pointed to a small green knoll near by. "There. On that, at least, we may yield us with some dignity. No broken rabble."

"God help us—yielding to Douglas!" Barclay said.

They rode to the little grassy mound, and up to its summit—and it was already trembling to the thundering hooves of the advancing Douglas array. Drawing up their sweating, panting steeds, they waited there.

It was Lennox who spoke, in the face of that daunting onslaught, his voice weak, weary. "All is lost, then? Lost!"

"Only the day is lost, my lord," David answered him. "There will be other days. You are something recovered?"

In only a few moments that green knowe was like an island in a sea of turmoil. All around them horses surged and reared, men shouted and cursed, steel clashed and trumpets blared. Silent, the group above stood, motionless.

At length some order developed, and a way was cleared through the milling throng for a burly red-bearded man, well armoured and mounted. He rode part way up the little slope, and waved his sword at them.

"What do you up there, like conies on a warren?" he demanded mockingly. "Think you to escape us there?"

"No, sir," David answered. "We but wait to yield ourselves, since we must. To some man of honour and repute. Are you such, sir?"

"By the Mass—you crow loud, cockerel! I am Douglas of Mains. Is that sufficient for your lordship?"

"I know him," Murdostoun murmured. "A stark, hard man. But of fair estate."

"Very well," David nodded. "I am Abbot of Arbroath, sir. And here is my lord of Lennox, sore wounded. And Stewart of Murdostoun. We yield to you, sir." He took Barclay's sword, and held it out, by the point, to the Douglas.

Mains was clearly impressed by the standing of his captives. He took the sword, and seemed scarcely to know what to do with it. "Lennox?" he said. "Lennox himsel'? And you—you'll be young Beaton? Murdostoun I know."

"Yes. My lord of Lennox is hurt. He needs aid . . ."

"Aye, well. Aye—you are my prisoners." Mains beckoned forward some of his men. "Come, you . . ."

174

Rough Douglas hands presently wrenched the abbot's ring from David's finger, and plucked the gold chain with the tiny crucifix from his neck—the only symbols of his office that he wore. They did rather better with Patrick Barclay, the Chamberlain. The Earl of Lennox, despite his injuries, was most thoroughly despoiled, even his armour being stripped from him.

This process over, they were awaiting the victors' pleasure beneath one of the hawthorn trees when, with something of a commotion and flourish Sir James Hamilton the Bastard rode up. He was a tall darkly handsome man, with fine features, a noble brow, but notably cruel thin lips. He carried one shoulder slightly higher than the other.

"Ho, Douglas!" he cried authoritatively. "Who commands here? You, Mains? They tell me that you have my prisoner, here? The traitor Lennox himself."

"*My* prisoner!" the Douglas growled. "What do you want with him?"

"He is mine," Hamilton declared haughtily. "I ran him through. Unhorsed him. In fair fight. Before ever you saw fit to take the field! I want him."

"And you shall not have him!" Mains roared. "To me he surrendered. You are too late, man!"

"Fool! Do you know who I am? I am Finnart. Son to Arran. I demand . . ."

"Son o' a sort! I carena whether you were Arran himsel'. Or young Jamie Stewart on his throne! Yon's my prisoner—and bides it." He grinned. "You can have his esquire if it suits you!" And he pointed mockingly to the group who stood around the seated Earl, under the tree.

Obviously Hamilton had not observed Lennox—or at least not recognised him without his armour and surcoat. Staring, he jumped down from his horse and strode over to the prisoners.

"So, traitor—it comes to this, does it!" he jeered. "You thought to outmatch Hamilton? To assail honester men? We shall teach you better, I swear!"

Lennox, with the aid of his pale young esquire, got unsteadily to his feet, the better to face the newcomer. "It ill becomes such as you, sir, to talk of honester men!" he declared thickly but with spirit. "Seek you honest parentage first! And to say traitor—you who aid Angus to hold the King's Grace . . .!"

Hamilton's hand shot out, furiously to slap the Earl across the face.

David Beaton started forward, in angry protest. Sir James whirled round on him, in turn.

"Stand back, fool! Whey-faced halfling, whoever you are! Or I will tread you into this turf, like the worm you are!"

At the sheer venomous violence of the man, David involuntorily faltered, but swiftly recovered himself. "You are a mighty man before defenceless captives!" he exclaimed. "Less mighty on the field, when we broke your array . . .!"

It was Douglas of Mains who saved him. As the Bastard's hand fell to his dirk, the older man strode up "Hands off my prisoners, Finnart!" he shouted. "Hear you? These are mine. Douglas's!"

"God's curse on you, Douglas! I told you . . ." With an effort, the dark man mastered himself somewhat. "A pox—you may have this milkmaster, if you want him!" And he jerked a scornful head at David. "But Lennox is my property. Do not meddle with things too high for you, man. I take him. After all, he is my cousin!"

That was true. Lennox was son of Arran's sister.

"For the last time—no!" Mains gestured with his mailed arm to the ranks of watching Douglases, who far outnumbered Finnart's Hamiltons. "Take him—if you dare!"

"Fiends of Hell—dare! I —Finnart!" Handsome features contorted, the Bastard took a quick step forward. His hand fell again to his dirk's hilt. Like lightening he whipped out the gleaming steel. "By the Christ—if *I* may not have him, none shall!" he cried.

Ferociously he lunged, to plunge the dagger into Lennox's breast. Twice, thrice he stabbed. Then wrenched the reeking weapon clear, and contemptuously wiped it clean on the Earl's drooping shoulder as, groaning, he sagged, his knees buckling under him.

A short bark of a laugh, and the Bastard of Arran spat, swung on his heel, and strode back to his horse. Stupified, appalled, none moved save the killer himself. He lifted lithely up into his saddle, despite the weight of his armour, and reining round without a backward glance, spurred away, his men falling in behind him.

David and the squire sank to their knees beside the prostrate Lennox, while Mains lifted his great voice in furious profanity.

The Earl's last breath bubbled out through a flood of blood.

In the confusion and recriminations that followed, David Beaton all but forgot the problems and dangers of his own position.

Presently there was a diversion. With much shouting by mounted forerunners, a resplendent group came riding down from the higher ground—no less than the Earls of Angus and Arran themselves, backed by many of their chief men—amongst whom, evidently unconcerned, was none other than Sir James the Bastard.

Mains went forward to greet them. What passed between the angry laird and his superiors David could not hear. But from their captor's expression and resentful gestures, it appeared that he was gaining little satisfaction from the interview; and Finnart was not summoned up from amongst the other supporting knights and gentry.

They were still talking when Arran dismounted, and leaving the others came pacing heavily over to the hawthorn-tree where the prisoners, with the dead man, still were held. He was, as ever, over-dressed, a thin, lantern-jawed ageing man, with fine features marred by weakness, greying, stooping and melancholy, despite the splendour of his apparel. In silence, though his slack lips moved a little, he came on, large and lachrymose eyes only on the corpse that lay there. All around men paused, to turn and watch.

Arran stood over Lennox, his nephew, head down, shoulders bent.

In the sudden silence, David Beaton alone spoke. "Your son did this, my lord," he said evenly, levelly. "Finnart. Slew an unarmed and wounded man. Unprovoked. In wanton spleen. Your son."

The other did not answer, did not so much as look up. Still he stood, and then suddenly sank down on his knees beside the dead man. His hand, trembling a little, went out to touch Lennox's face. Indistinctly at first, but with growing intensity, he spoke.

"Here is woe! Woe, I say. A victory dear purchased, indeed. The wisest, the stoutest man, the hardiest knight in Scotland! Fallen this day." He choked to silence.

Impressed, perplexed, embarrassed, men looked on at the extraordinary scene.

David turned to consider Sir James. He sat his horse, watching, a faint smile about his thin lips, but otherwise apparently unmoved.

Arran rose to his feet, took off the handsome cloak that covered his armour, scarlet with the ermine cinquefoils of Hamilton, and spread it over the corpse. Then swinging about, he stumbled back to the others, to his horse, looking at none. His esquire aided him up into the saddle. There, he pulled his mount's head round, and without another word to anyone, rode away, esquire and standard-bearer hastening after him. Perplexedly his Hamilton gentry looked at one another, and then, in some doubt and confusion, turned to follow their chief.

Angus, left thus unceremoniously, snorted in disgust, made sundry uncomplimentary remarks to his Douglas henchmen, and then rode over to the group under the tree. He looked down, first at the body of Lennox and then at David.

"So, Master Beaton — I find you in bad company!" he said harshly. "Worse than that — in arms against your sovereign lord the King!"

"Not, so, my lord. I was, as my lord of Arran has just said, in excellent company — until a dastard's dagger did its fell work. And as to being in arms, we are here at the King's own request. And with the authority of the Chancellor of this realm. And the Primate."

"I am the Chancellor, sir. And that for your Primate!" Angus snapped his fingers.

"You say so. But only the King in Parliament appoints the Chancellor."

"The King *and* Parliament so appointed me."

"I think not, my lord. Not a true Parliament, lawfully called. The summons to Parliament must bear the seals of the Chancellor, to be effective and lawful. Was your Parliament so summoned, my lord?"

Angus narrowed both lips and hot blue eyes.

"I think not — since the seals are still in possession of my uncle," David went on. "Until he relinquishes the seals of office, my lord, the Archbishop of St. Andrews is still Chancellor of Scotland."

178

"Faugh! Have done, man!" the other shouted. "The King's seal was on the summons. As was Douglas's! Enough for any man. Think you that the affairs of this realm are dependent upon two trinkets of silver, pocketed by a churchman? But — enough of this. I am not here to bandy words with clerks! Taken in treason." He turned to Mains. "Sandy — have this long-tongued clerk taken to Linlithgow and warded secure. I will deal with him later. See to it. And have this carrion removed."

"My lord — they are my prisoners . . ." the other pointed out. "Lennox was also. That ill Hamilton . . ."

"You will not suffer, Sandy — never fear," his chief interrupted him. "But Beaton is mine, do you hear? Do as you will with the rest. But hold Beaton close. Or, by God's eyes, I'll have your head for him!" He reined round. "Now — where is James? Where is the King?" he demanded. "I said that he was to be here. By the Rude — where is he?"

David Beaton had to wait three days and nights in a damp, dark vaulted cell below a flanking tower of Linlithgow Palace, despite his urgent demands to see Angus, before he was eventually conducted before the man who now ruled Scotland. The Douglas saw him in what had been the previous King's own bedroom, a handsome chamber but never so sumptuously plenished as now. He was alone, and dismissed the guards who brought the prisoner.

David, encouraged by this, waited silent.

"Well, Master Beaton — you seek my face, I am told?" Angus said, after a moment or two. "Have you thought of a reason why I should not hang you?"

"Aye, my lord," David answered promptly. "More than one. Other than that you would not wish to hang a representative of Holy Church."

"Do not think that will save you, man."

"I think it will," he declared, confident without being aggressive. "I do not believe that even the Earl of Angus will risk so offending the Church, His Holiness of Rome, and men of good faith everywhere, by hanging the Abbot of Arbroath. It is not hanging that troubles me, my lord. It is that I should any longer suffer the restrictions of yonder hole where I am penned."

"Ha! You have complaints as to your quarters, my lord Abbot? Is a simple cell not seemly accommodation for a churchman?"

"Lacking light and air and any decencies – no sir. But even were it so fine as this, I would be quit of it, my lord."

"You are hard to please, Master Clerk. So you would be free of us?"

"Yes, my lord. Free of you. And you of me. For the gain of us both."

"What gain can you offer me – Angus? Free or fast?"

"Much. Since I can give you what you require."

"Douglas *requires* nothing from such as you, sir!"

"I say that Douglas does. He requires the Chancellor's seals of office! The Great Seal of Scotland!"

"You . . . you would do that? *Could* you do it?"

"I could. And would."

The other stroked his chin. "You would have me exchange your person for the Chancellor's seals."

"A fair exchange, is it not? Since you may then be Chancellor indeed. And in law."

"But will the Archbishop think it so, 'fore God?"

"I believe that he will take my advice."

"You believe, man! Devil take it – I require more than that! Think you I will let you go on such frail chance? How shall we put it to the test?"

"You still hold Barclay of Collairnie? Chamberlain of St. Andrews? Then send him to me, my lord. And I shall send him to my uncle. You will gain your seals, I warrant."

Angus got up to pace the floor. "Even so, there is more to it than that," he said. "You are in some way Mains' prisoner. No small prize – the Abbot of rich Arbroath, no less! Sandy Douglas will need some accommodation, see you."

"You mean ransom, my lord? Is that the Douglas style – chaffering and merchanding? Very well – let Mains have his price also. Say . . . a thousand merks? No – make it two thousand, and be done with it."

"Sink me!" The Earl stared. "You rate yourself high, Master Beaton! By the mass, you do! Two thousand is . . . handsome!"

"Adequate." David shrugged. "But, if one thousand would serve Mains equally well – why, the second thousand may go . . . wherever you deem best, my lord." Casually he said it.

"Ah. To be sure." Angus looked away. "Barclay to effect this also?"

"Why, yes. If you will but have him brought . . ."

A little later, in an ante-room, Patrick Barclay was delivered.

David explained the situation. Saying "You will tell the Archbishop, Patrick, to hand over the Chancellor's seals of office to you, to bring to me. In exchange for our liberty."

"Mary-Mother—the seals! The Chancellor's seals!"

"Hush, man—keep your words quiet."

"But . . . this is to yield all! To . . . to betray my lord Archbishop! This will make Angus Chancellor indeed . . ."

"He is Chancellor in all but name, now. What advantage for my uncle to cling to the name, in this pass? It will serve him nothing."

"But—will he give them up? The seals? Surrender all to Angus, thus? Would you have him to do so, my lord . . .?"

"Listen to me, Patrick. I have had long enough to consider this well. Three days in a black hole, with naught else to think of! I am of infinitely more worth to the Archbishop and his cause, free, than are those seals—empty symbols now, since that foolish battle. You know it is true. My uncle, these days, is a broken, done man. Without me he will do nothing save wring his hands! If this realm is ever to be delivered from the Douglas thralldom—it is I who must do it. My uncle, of himself, will not, can not. I believe that I can. What use empty seals in this? I cannot fight Douglas from a prison cell!"

"That is true," Barclay conceded.

"Aye. You will bring from my uncle also two thousand merks in silver, Patrick. You understand? As well as the seals . . ."

"Two thousand! God be good—that is a treasure! A fortune!"

"It is the price of our ransom. A high price—but worth it. He can well afford it. I chose the sum. Angus must not misdoubt the power and wealth of Holy Church! It will be money well spent, I think. Money is for spending, is it not? To good effect. My uncle would hoard it—I would not. A doubt or two sown in Douglas's mind is worth a little siller!"

"But—two thousand . . .!"

"The Archbishop may make more difficulty over giving you the money than the seals. Tell him that it is the only way he shall have me back at his side. Collect the siller from the abbeys, if need be, meantime—Cambuskenneth, Lindores, Balmerino.

And quickly — for I would lie here not one hour longer than I must. You understand?"

"Aye, my lord."

"And tell my uncle that I will have him back in St. Andrews Castle, and the Great Seal of Scotland in his hands again, before he is a deal older. So be that he trusts me now."

Patrick Barclay wagged his head, wordless.

Chapter Twelve

IT was on a blustery November night of wind and rain, that David Beaton hammered a swordhilt on the door of Ethie Castle for only the second time. The moisture running down the faces of the little party who waited there was salt now, for all the air here was filled with the spindrift of shattered seas.

When the little shutter in the door's peephole grating was cautiously opened, David called out.

"Greetings to the Lady Marion, of Ethie. Ask if she will receive to her house honest travellers? The Archbishop of St. Andrews, Primate of this realm. The Abbot of Arbroath. And others."

"Hech, me! Master David! My lord! My lord! Och — bide a wee. It's me. Will Fiddes. Bide just now, and I'll draw the bar. No' a minute . . ."

"Not so, Will. Do as I told you. Seek the Lady Marion's permission. This is her house . . ."

As the servitor, one of those left there by David on his marriage night those months ago, hurried off, James Beaton grumbled petulently at the unnecessary delay, and even Patrick Barclay looked sour. They were all tired and hungry, as well as wet.

Presently they heard the great greazed oaken beam being slid from behind the door into its deep socket in the thickness of the walling, chains and bolts drawn, and the massive iron-studded timbers swung open — and still pushing it, Marion came running out, to throw herself into David's damp arms.

"Oh, Davie! Davie! Davie!" she cried, choking. "At last! At long last you are home! Oh, my dear . . .!" The rest was lost, mumbled against his lips, his cheek, his soaking cloak.

He stroked her hair, already blowing wild in the wind, and held her close. When he could, smiling, he chided her.

"My heart, my sweeting—here, come to your door, is His Beatitude the Archbishop, Primate and Apostolic Protonotary. Also his Chamberlain. And two brave fellows of less note but stout hearts. And you do not even see them . . .!"

Marion, gulping, turned to the others. "Forgive me, my lord. Sir . . ." She peered, not knowing which was the Archbishop, for all were equally undistinguished as to dress, muffled in old and inconspicuous clothing, stained and travel-worn. "You are welcome, so very welcome, to Ethie. Come . . ."

Inside, calling for lamps and candles, and sending servants to see to the horses, she led them first into the great vaulted kitchen, where a huge fire of driftwood filled the twelve-foot arched fireplace. There wet gear was removed and hot toddy was produced, while the house was ransacked for alternative clothing. Even so, thereafter, James Beaton had to be aided up the winding turnpike stair, by David and Barclay, past the empty Great Hall, and higher to a lesser private apartment where another fire blazed brightly, and needlework lay where Marion had dropped it.

When food had been brought, and consumed, and they relaxed, oddly clad, before the fire—the Archbishop nodding, indeed— Marion's dammed-back questions flooded forth. What had happened? Where had they come from? Were they in danger, coming thus in darkness? Had they suffered great hardship? Was all lost, and Douglas everywhere triumphant?

"All is by no means lost, my dear. And though the Douglases seem to have gained all, yet their house is built on sand. It can, and shall, be swept away."

A noise, part grunt, part groan, from the Archbishop, seemed to indicate weary dissent, as though he had heard it all before and failed to find conviction. He kept his eyes closed.

"My lord is tired," David mentioned. "He finds traipsing the country in winter scarce to his taste. He has not passed two nights under the same roof in two months. Two such nights here, and he will be himself again, I warrant. Ready for the road again—and Douglas!"

"Two nights? Davie—*two* nights, you say? Mary-Mother— you mean . . .?"

"Aye, Marion lass. I mean that we cannot, dare not, bide

183

longer. We are hunted like coursed hares. I would never have come here, risked bringing down the Douglas wrath on *your* head — save that Uncle James sorely needs such rest and cherishing. Even for so short a time. I cannot believe my link with Ethie is known to our enemies . . ."

"Of course you had to come here!" Marion cried. "This is *your* house. Think you I would hide away in it? That only you would fight Douglas? My name is Ogilvy — and the Ogilvys are no hiders!"

"My heart . . ."

"If you saw, my lady, what Angus does to folk he suspects. Or houses he covets," Barclay put in, "you would understand my lord Abbot's concern. Already we have left fire and death and weeping behind us."

"Even so, sir — right is right, and wrong must be fought." She moved over to the chair in which the Archbishop slumped, bringing him another cushion and a stool for his feet. "My lord — a warm bed awaits you," she said gently. "Better there . . ."

James Beaton shook his head testily. Not yet sixty, he looked an old man, his formerly heavy body sagging and bent, his purple cheeks hollow, jowls hanging limp. Dressed in ill-fitting servant's clothes he made a sorry spectacle.

"Let him be, my dear," David advised. "My lord savours being merely still, I think. And warm. Of late he has enjoyed little of either."

She sighed. "To see the head of Holy Church is such case! The realm's Chancellor . . ."

"Name not that name in my hearing, woman!" the Archbishop exclaimed, with sudden surprising strength of voice.

"Uncle — in Ethie, we speak the lady of the house otherwise!"

"No, no! Oh, Davie — what has brought you to this?"

"The malice and bad faith of men, lass. And of women. For Margaret Tudor is scarce guiltless. When Angus triumphed at Linlithgow, she made haste to make her peace with her former husband, hate him as she does — and threw my lord Archbishop out of Stirling Castle. Not content with that, she sent the Hamiltons word of his whereabouts. When I bought myself free of Angus's grasp, and went seeking him, it was barely to escape with my life at Stirling. And then to find my lord, at last, passing as a shepherd in the Ochil Hills. Since when, in six weeks, we have lurked and skulked—and kept ahead of Arran's bands of hunters only by hairs' breadths. And God's mercy."

"But . . . Arran let you go? And then immediately hunts you again?"

"Aye—that is the style of Archibald Douglas. He had us followed, when he released us. He believed that we would lead him to the Archbishop. When he would seize us again. He let us go, only to lead him to my lord, here."

"Dear God! And what now? Where will you go now—if you leave here? You cannot continue thus, Davie. My lord cannot, certainly . . ."

"France!" That was James Beaton again, in a croak. He had his eyes open now, and pointed a finger at his nephew. "France, I say. A vessel. At Montrose. Or Stonehive. Or Aberdeen. My lord o' Aberdeen will find me a vessel. He'll no' hand me over to Angus. France it must be."

"No, Uncle," David said, shaking his head. "That way lies the end. It is surrender. Abdication. Leave Scotland and you lose all. Play Angus's game, throwing away the power you still have, abandoning the Church . . ."

"Power, man!" His uncle all but choked on the word. "What power have I now?"

"Much power, my lord—if you will but use it, I say. You are still Primate. And the richest man in this realm! How long would you remain either, think you, once you leave the country? You would be proclaimed as having deserted your spiritual province. The Pope would be petitioned to appoint Gavin Dunbar, of Glasgow, in your place. He could scarce refuse—if you had abandoned all. Then Angus would have the Church, as he has all else."

"But what can we *do* here, man Davie?" the Archbishop wailed. "You prate of power. And having the Church. What good is the Church to me in this? What can I do? I cannot go running and slinking more . . ."

"You can write a letter. To Angus. As Primate and Apostolic Protonotary. Or I can write it for you."

"Och, man—you're back to this o' the abbeys. I canna do that."

"Uncle—what use are your abbeys to you now? Or in France? Angus, I have learned, has his weaknesses. One is avarice. I

185

proved that in Linlithgow Palace. He took a thousand merks of my ransom, for himself. As well as the seals. He can be bought, I believe—in some fashion. But, better—he can be threatened."

"What threat can *I* offer to Douglas?"

"A great one. To his immortal soul. Excommunication my lord!"

"Eh? What! Ex . . . excommunication! Precious soul of God!" the other gobbled. "I canna do that, Davie! He's no' a heretic . . .'"

"You can, Uncle. It is in your power. Write to him. Say that by his persecution of yourself he hinders and harms the proper governance of Holy Church. Declare that if he does not immediately call off his pursuit of you, and permit you to return to St. Andrews and the peaceful resumption of your duties as Primate, you will pronounce sentence of Greater Excommunication and Solemn Anathema upon him, to his exclusion from the whole community of Christ's Body and the eternal damnation of his soul!"

"Oh, Davie . . .!" That was Marion, shocked, eyes wide.

James Beaton gnawed the back of his hand, in doubt.

"As well, my lord, declare that you will likewise excommunicate any and all who aid him in works against you or the Church. So that, even if Archibald Douglas will risk everlasting fires, others will not, and will hold back. This would much tie his hands. No priest could serve him, or them, in any way. Gavin Dunbar would no longer dare to aid him, even be in his presence. His Douglas prelates likewise. None may ignore the solemn fulminations of excommunication."

"Aye. But the like has never been done, Davie. Here in Scotland."

"That is no reason to hold back. You have the power. Use it. Or the threat of it. For I do not think that you will indeed have to excommunicate."

"M'mmm."

"With the threat, show the better way. Say that the Church can be kind as well as stern, forgiving as well as harsh. For Angus's aid in restoring you to your proper place at St. Andrews, for the Church's weal, it would gladly make present of the Abbeys of Dunfermline and Kilwinning. These, only on full restoration to you of St. Andrews Castle."

The Archbishop groaned. There was no doubt but that the

parting with his abbeys would be a telling blow. "It is too much," he said.

"Angus is not some petty baron to be placated," David pointed out. "His avarice, like his power, is great. He demands a large price. But Dunfermline has greater revenues than any abbey in Scotland — greater even than Arbroath. He could aspire to no nobler a gift. He will accept it, I vow — with excommunication the alternative! Arran will require to be appeased, likewise. Give him Kilwinning, the lesser place." At his uncle's head-shaking, he charged, "Would you rather, my lord, rule in St. Andrews once more, lacking Dunfermline and Kilwinning? Or be a hunted exile, lacking all?"

When there was no answer to that, Barclay spoke. "Even restored to St. Andrews, no longer hunted — how shall we fare? Angus now rules all. How can my lord do more than sit there, little better than a prisoner in his own house? We shall be held, hand and foot."

"But not wits, Patrick — not wits! We must use them, use guile, since we have little else. My lord must seem to take no part in affairs of state. Nor wish to. Our only concern the governance of the Church. So shall we lull Angus to believe us harmless."

"Would that not be better in any case?" Marion put in, urgently. "To trouble no more with affairs of state, Davie?"

"And fail our land and King, Marion? Sell him, indeed, to the English? For peace and security for ourselves? For that is what it would be. Angus is a friend of King Henry again, and Henry with him. They both need each other. That is why Margaret Tudor rides high again. Angus and Margaret and Henry have agreed that King James shall wed Henry's daughter, the Princess Mary. Have you not heard?"

The young woman bit her lip, silent.

"With James a mere youth, and the masterful Henry his good-father, what hope would there be for the independence of Scotland?"

Into the pause, Barclay said, "It is evil. A disaster. But you cannot prevent it."

"I can try." David amended that. "*We* can try. My lord, even restricted to Church affairs, can still do much."

"Against Angus? And Henry of England?"

"I believe so. The Douglases are strong. But they must have allies, other than Henry. Today they have many. But these might be stripped from them — for none, I swear, love the Douglas. I said that Angus's towering house was built on sand. I say that it can be undermined."

James Beaton seemed to have sunk back into lethargy again, but his Chamberlain sat forward, and Marion's eyes never left her husband.

"The Hamiltons are at once the strongest and the weakest links in Angus's chain. Powerful allies, but doubtful friends. Angus mislikes and despises Arran. That is why I say give Arran Kilwinning Abbey. It will not but make bad blood between them — for Angus will conceive that all should be his. Moreover, the Hamiltons themselves are a divided house, I think. Since the murder of Lennox, Arran cannot esteem his son Finnart the Bastard. Who ever sides with Angus. Here is a soil on which a pretty crop may grow!"

Marion, lips tight, shook her head. But Barclay nodded encouragingly.

"I warrant I know a crop which the Church could harvest with profit from that soil," David went on slowly. "Heresy. There is a certain prelate by the name of Hamilton, is there not? Patrick, Abbot of Ferne, *in commendam*."

"Ah!" the Chamberlain exclaimed. "The disciple of the German, Martin Luther."

"Exactly. A somewhat foolish fellow. I knew him in Paris, where we studied together awhile. I warned him, even then, that he was playing with fire. He now, I hear, prates openly of the Saxon's doctrines. Criticised the Holy See. It is time that the Church took order with Master Patrick, I think — for her own sake. And the fact that he is a Hamilton, and high born — kin to Arran himself — should suit our cause very well. Serve to drive a wedge between Angus and the Hamiltons, if I misdoubt not. Yes, I warrant that would serve."

"What do you propose, Davie?" James Beaton was sitting up now.

"The trial of Patrick, Abbot of Ferne, on a charge of heresy, my lord. Your first act when you win back to St. Andrews. The man is a danger to the Church. It is our good fortune that he is a Hamilton."

"You think Angus would not interfere to save him?"

"In the Church's business? No, rather I think Angus would rejoice. Since Arran would suffer embarrassment. And certainly His Holiness would rejoice—which would be valuable, in this pass. Moreover, it would reassert your authority in the Church, my lord, and serve as a warning to other mischief-makers and self-styled reformers."

"I believe, my lord, there is much in this," Patrick Barclay said strongly. "On my soul, I do!"

"Aye." The Archbishop rose to his feet. "I shall sleep on it. It is a weighty matter, but . . . I shall sleep on it. Where is my bed, young woman?" Both the Primate's voice and his steps were stronger than they had been.

"This way, my lord . . ."

Later, when at last they had likewise got Barclay off to bed, David and Marion clung together in their own upper room. Emotion gripping them, they were silent now. So much to say, yet so little need to say it.

"So long, Davie—so long!" the young woman whispered. "Oh, the endless waiting . . ."

He stopped her further talk with his lips.

For some time they were content to hold each other fast, in that dark room about which the winds howled. But gradually passion took possession of them, and their hands did more than hold and clutch. Swiftly the strong tide of it mounted, once begun—and now Marion was no shrinking doubtful partner. A full-blooded vital woman, she was as eager as he was—and less weary with travel. In moments they were on to the great bed, with clothing only an encumbrance and folly, reserve and modesty things invented by desiccated and envious unfortunates who were only half-alive. Here was fulness, to generous, magnificent overflowing.

At some unknown hour of the blustery night, as they lay awaiting only a further access of fulness, David murmured,

"To think that once you were frightened, my love! Frightened of this! Frightened of *me*!"

"It was myself that I was frightened of, then," she answered slowly. "It was not you, Davie. I was never frightened of you . . . until tonight!"

"Until tonight? What do you mean, sweeting—until tonight?"

"Tonight, down in the Hall there, I knew fear, Davie. Fear of you. Fear for you."

"Fear? I do not understand, my dear."

"I feared, a little, for the man who could so plan and devise. Who could so use other men's weaknesses and failings. Who could use even the Church's most sacred powers to gain his ends. Then I feared you, Davie — never here in this chamber."

"But, my heart — what is there to fear in this? I devise means whereby the good may triumph over the evil, the weak over the strong, the Church over her enemies. Do you not see it?"

"I see a man whom I think could be ruthless."

He raised himself, to lean on an elbow. "There are times when a man must be ruthless if he is to serve his cause. If the cause be sufficiently great. Scotland is to be served. The Church is to be saved. If God has given me the wits to do it. And, through my uncle — who himself cannot do it — the power, it may be. Am I to hold back, for lack of resolution?"

"No," she said. "No. Put so, it is . . . otherwise."

"How else is it to be put, then? To see evil abounding, and to have the means of halting it, and not to seek to do so — is that not sin?"

"It may be, Davie. I do not know. *You* are the churchman, the man who decides right from wrong. I am but a woman, who fears a little. In especial, for this Abbot Hamilton."

"Patrick Hamilton is a fool. And worse — a traitor to the Church which sustains him. This heresy of Luther has already played havoc with the Church, in many lands. In the Empire in especial. All is anarchy in Germany. It sweeps elsewhere like a heather-fire. It must not rage here. Of all this folly and trouble with Angus, that is perhaps the greatest evil — that the authority of the Church is so weakened, that this German heresy is being allowed to breed fast, is not being put down. The Church's leaders' eyes are elsewhere — to their peril. The Church must be purged, reformed, yes — but not so. From above, not below."

"Oh, Davie — so much of problems, of difficulties! Will there ever be an end to it? For us?"

"Who knows! We can but fight for the day, and plan for the morrow. But . . . tonight! My love, my heart's desire — tonight is for other matters! Tonight is for you. And for me. Alone. Not to waste, thus."

"Ah, yes, Davie — yes . . . !"

Chapter Thirteen

IN the college hall of St. Salvator, in St. Andrews, where David had so often sat in days past, a heavy silence prevailed, after much talking, as men deliberated, a silence little resembling the place's usual student bustle. Not that there was any need for deliberation about the verdict. The accused had not only confessed to all the charges, at great length, but had positively glorified in re-affirming his heresy before them all, as though he would convert the very court to his apostasy, refusing and rejecting all induce-ments to a retraction, and even forms of words which would allow him to be dismissed with a purely nominal punishment. Guilty the verdict must be – but hesitation in pronouncing it was understandable, in view of the inevitable sentence.

Most men preferred to eye the Primate rather than the accused – although one at least, the Bishop of Dunblane, was fast asleep, and had been for the last hour.

James Beaton tapped his blunt finger-nails on the long table at the head of which he sat, and the sharp clicking noise of it sounded clearly in the great echoing hall, seeming even to startle some. He grinned suddenly, in something of his old style, and rolled his little pig-like eyes wickedly to the right, to bear on his neighbour at that side.

"Well, my lord o' Glasgow – how say you?" he demanded. "Guilty or no'?"

Gavin Dunbar bit his lip, embarrassed – as he was meant to be. He had not desired to be present at all – but this was the highest court of the Church, and he had been summoned. That Beaton should have chosen to adopt this parliamentary pro-cedure, of seeking each individual's decision – with the second Archbishop, as senior, first – was as unexpected as it was unfair.

He coughed. "It is a matter of interpretation, my lord," he said. "All depends on that, does it not? How we interpret the doctrine of justification by faith only. It is a Pauline . . ."

"Guilty or not guilty, my lord?" the Primate snapped.

"Ah. Umm. Guilty, I fear. Yes – Guilty."

"Aye. My lord of Brechin?"

"Guilty."

"Dunblane? Of a mercy — waken Dunblane!"

Every man of the score and more who sat at that long table, five bishops, six abbot and priors, the Rectors of the Colleges, certain minor ecclesiastics, and two lords as representing the civil power — all these declared Patrick Hamilton, lay Abbot of Ferne, guilty of the sin of deliberate and contumacious heresy, in the first degree, David, Abbot of Arbroath, on the Primate's left, giving the last decision.

"Aye. So be it," James Beaton nodded. He glanced all round. "Then, as preses of this court and Primate of this realm, it falls to me to give and pronounce due and condign sentence on the said Master Patrick for his affirming, confessing and maintaining of the aforesaid heresies of Martin Luther and his followers, repugnant to our faith; and his pertinacity — they being condemned already by the Church's general Counsels and most famous universities. I declare that the said Master Patrick be handed and conveyed to the secular power of this realm, to be burned to the death in the open space before this our church of the blessed Saint Salvator. This I declare in the name of The Father, the Son and the Holy Ghost. And may the same Almighty God have mercy on his soul hereafter!"

Into the quivering silence which followed that dire pronouncement, all eyes at last turned upon the man who sat alone at the foot of the table. Patrick Hamilton was young, of a mere twenty-eight years — he had been titular Abbot of Ferne since his teens, and it is to be doubted whether he had more than once visited the remote Ross-shire Abbey of Ferne from which he drew the revenues. He was good-looking, in a fair and ruddy way, combining a modest expression with a lofty air — for he was high-born, the son of Sir Patrick Hamilton of Kincavil, kin to Arran himself, by the daughter, illegitimate but acknowledged, of no less than Alexander Duke of Albany, King James the Third's brother and father of the recent Regent. The Earl of Angus had been the more happy to acquiesce in this trial, in consequence of the accused's antecedents.

Now, he gave no impression of being appalled by the fate appointed for him. Not that there was in his eyes any of the unearthly shine of the willing martyr. He was calm, composed, quietly assured. He betrayed neither agitation nor resentment or any distress. Obviously he had experienced no surprise in the trial or verdict – or indeed in the failure of his earlier and eloquent exposition of his views to impress his judges. He looked, from the Primate, round the semicircle of faces, and one by one as his level gaze met theirs, glances dropped. All except the last, when his eyes encountered those of David Beaton. That young man stared back at him with a look as steady, resolute and unabashed as his own, interested, almost appreciative.

"Have you anything to say, Master Patrick?" James Beaton said harshly.

"Only Amen, my lord, to your final prayer," the young man answered simply, firmly. "That God Almighty may have a like mercy on *your* souls as on mine."

"H'rr'mm." The Primate pushed back his chair abruptly. "I declare this court adjourned," he announced. "The officers to their duty."

St. Andrews was full that day – as full as it had been on that occasion fifteen years before when King James the Fourth, of gallant memory, had ordained a day of dedication and intercession for Scotland's cause against King Henry and the Auld Enemy – and unfortunately God Almighty had looked the other way. As then, folk had flocked into the town from all around, the students had been given a holiday, and the streets were crammed – for this was fully as great as occasion an that; not for a full century had there been a public burning in Scotland – and that had been a mere foreigner, a crazed Bohemian called Craw who foolishly denied the doctrines of transubstantiation and confession; whereas this was a man of note, an abbot no less, kin to a great lord and the great-grandson of a king.

More than spectators thronged the streets, of course. Douglas men-at-arms were everywhere, the red-heart emblems of their breastplates marking them out from the Archbishop's men, the Prior's men and all others. There were fears that the Hamiltons might try to effect a rescue. And the laird of Airdrie Castle near by had been boasting in his cups the night before that he and others like him would see that the saintly Patrick did not die.

The crowds were greatest, of course, in North Street, where, in the open space outside the church and college of St. Salvator an enclosure had been railed off. In the centre of this the faggots were already heaped high, and out of the midst of them a tall stake of green wood rose ominously. Hereabouts men-at-arms were thick.

The good folk waited impatiently, for it was a chill grey morning, with rain squals driving in every now and again on an east wind off the sea — typical March weather in St. Andrews. Wags grumbled at the delay, declaring that at least once the fire was lit it might be a bit warmer. Pessimists announced gloomily that they had feared this — the day would come to nothing and all would be a disappointment. Rumours circulated that my lord of Arran had won his nephew a pardon from the King; that the entire business was a hoax, play-acting, to intimidate the Lutherans, with no real intention of carrying out the sentence; even that Archbishop Beaton, the old fox — or, more likely, that even more sly nephew of his — had arranged for the victim to be smuggled out of the castle by a postern to the harbour, where a special vessel was waiting to convey him to foreign parts, since it was inconceivable that an abbot of Holy Church should burn.

Cheers of relief therefore, an hour before noon, greeted the appearance of a little procession from the direction of the castle. First came the Provost of the burgh, a new man of rather more stalwart aspect than heretofore. Then the Town Guard, feeble fellows despised by all. Then a strong company of Douglas retainers — real men these, bristling with arms, wolves compared with the sheep whom they all but seemed to drive before them. Behind came a chaplain from the college and then three men bearing burning, smoking torches of pitch-pine. The first was a hulking, grinning individual, only one part human in appearance — the public hangman; the second was Patrick Hamilton himself, dressed possibly for the first time in public in the white habit of the Premonstatensian Order to which Ferne Abbey belonged — but, oddly enough, with the cowl thrown back and a handsome velvet and jewelled cap worn instead; the third was his manservant stumbling along alarmed and miserable, where his master stalked strong and sure. It was a nice thrust to have the guilty man carry his own lit torch. Men-at-arms followed closely.

Driving back the surging, cheering, jeering crowds, to reach the open space, the guards formed a circle round the pyre, while the chaplain muttered a brief Latin prayer, crossed himself rather than the victim, and hurried away, distasteful duty done, to the angry shouts of the throng, who could not see what was going on because of the ranked men-at-arms. However, that was soon put right. Giving the unwilling Provost his own and the Abbot's torches to hold meantime, the hangman climbed up over the stacked faggots, beckoning Hamilton after him. There, removing his robe, doublet and cap, the malefactor handed these down to his trembling servant, with the calm declaration that these were all the worldly goods he had left to bestow, and placed himself in position beside the green stake, fully eight feet above the street's cobblestones, in excellent view of all. There the executioner bound him, with long strips of fresh pigskin, still wet from the newly killed beast — which it was hoped would not burn through before the Abbot. This achieved, the apelike headsman danced a sort of jig up there on the faggots, almost fell off, but recovering himself, laughed loudly, bowed all round, and climbed down.

Hamilton spoke aloud, evidently to his manservant. "What I am about to suffer, friend, appears fearful. Bitter to the flesh. But, remember, it is the entrance to eternal life, which none shall possess who deny their lord."

The crowd showed its opinion of this markedly undramatic statement with catcalls. Some perceived that a chair had been placed within the arched doorway of the church. To it now came to sit the Archbishop-Primate, his armour showing behind his robes. At his back the slighter figure of his nephew and secretary came to stand. Other churchmen appeared at various of the college windows.

The Provost turned and bowed jerkily to the Archbishop. He gained no sign nor acknowledgement. Holy Church did not soil its hands with such inappropriate activities; burnings, hanging, mutilations and the like were the business of the civil power.

After a moment of two, the Provost shrugged and turned back. He raised both torches and his voice.

"So perish all enemies o' Christ's Kirk!" he cried, and threw the blazing brands in amongst the piled faggots.

It was not a very good throw. One of the torches landed in a position where it could set fire to nothing, while the other rolled down the heap of wood and on to the cobbles. The hangman had to retrieve both, to re-insert them in more effective places, with derisory shouts. The manservant's brand also he grabbed and deposited just below the feet of the victim.

A great sigh rose from the watching assembly.

Hamilton's lips moved in silent prayer, and the Provost hurried into the midst of the Town Guard.

After a few minutes, it became only too obvious that the torches did not seem to be setting anything very much alight, and the executioner had to go round picking out choice pieces of tinder and dry fragments to coax the reluctant flames. He was markedly unsuccessful in this — and very vocal, shouting aloud that the wood was all wet and green and would never burn. He obtained considerable advice and comment from the crowd — but it soon became evident that unless something drastic was done the torches which were now burning very low indeed, would die out without burning anything of the pyre itself.

A great cry went up for oil — pig's-fat, tallow, resin, pitch, lamp-oil, anything. The Church ought to provide candles, wits suggested. Missals, lectionaries — all dry enough, in all conscience!

The Provost, appealed to, sent for fat from the college kitchens. While it was awaited, argument waxed fiery enough at least, the citizenry debating whether this might not indicate divine intervention on the Abbot's behalf, or a deliberate attempt on the part of either the Hamiltons or those crooked Beatons to pervert the course of justice and cheat the assembled lieges of their spectacle. The belief that the whole thing was an elaborate hoax gained ground.

When the fat eventually arrived, a new fire was started with flint and tinder. But even so it was a feeble and localised conflagration. A driving rain-squall did not help matters. The hangman pleaded all round for better and drier wood.

More than one hour after the start of the proceedings, James Beaton rose in disgust and clanked away into the Church. David stayed where he was, behind the chair, set of face.

With the Town Guard fetching more combustible fuel, the executioner, incensed now by the jeers of the throng, built up the new wood actually round the feet and legs of the offender, liberally daubing it with pig's fat. This, when it was lit, went up with a brisk, spluttering blaze, and fairly quickly part of Hamilton's clothing caught fire. But the rain had wet it, and it smouldered and smoked rather than flamed. The sufferer was wincing and biting his lips, but not crying out.

After a while it became apparent that even this superficial

topmost fire was flagging, and though the Abbot's lower quarters were now blackened he was far from dead. Indeed he had not as yet emitted a single shriek. Some of the disillusioned crowd had melted away. Others found an alternative interest in baiting the executioner. Two hours after the start, that harassed incompetent was howling for more dry wood, more fat, more tinder, anything which would burn.

This continuing delay seemed even to affect the patience of the victim, for at one stage he suddenly lifted up his voice to cry, "How long, oh God—how long?" Then, perhaps conscience-stricken at his own weakness, he amended his plea. "How long, oh God, shall darkness cover this kingdom? How long wilt Thou suffer this tyranny of men?" This said, he steeled himself to a renewed and patient silence.

By the time that the town's innumerable bells tolled out the Nones hour, and the clergy at the college windows had all departed for the main meal of the day, a rather more effective fire had been kindled, and Patrick Hamilton had uttered his first scream. David Beaton yet stood alone behind the empty archiepiscopal chair.

It still was an interminable affair. The weather grew worse rather than better, and dry fuel seemed to be hard to obtain in St. Andrews after a long winter's firing. Such of the crowd as still remained had begun to chant a monotonous refrain:

"Drown the limmer, dinna burn him,
Or drown the widdyman—that'll learn him!"

Hamilton, although badly charred below, so that it was impossible to tell what was clothing and what flesh, was only singed about the upper half. He was not always fully conscious now, so that sometimes, head fallen forward on his breast, he seemed to sleep—much to the fury of the chagrined hangman, who prodded him with one of the many unburned faggots. But, clearly, he was far from expiring.

Servants brought David wine and refreshment, but he waved it away wordless.

About four o'clock in the afternoon, the wind changed, and there was even a gleam of watery sunshine. It quite quickly had a surprising effect, on the fire as well as on the bored men-at-arms and the remaining spectators. Tongues of flame began to lick and flicker at various points about the dull and smoking pyre.

From the parched lips of the sufferer there burst the fervent exclamation. "Praise be to God!"

The cry was taken up enthusiastically by all concerned. Even David Beaton's lips moved, though soundlessly.

Even so the business was grievously protracted, the main mass of the wood being sappy and incombustible. But there were continuous flames now. When the Abbot's fair head caught fire there was a great shout – but it died when the hair had all burned away leaving a sort of black skull-cap, and the malefactor was still seen to be alive and conscious. More than that, indeed, for his own voice was quite strong, though cracked, as he lifted it up.

"Lord Jesus, receive my spirit!" he cried.

Thereafter the smell as of cooking pork grew stronger. David had put it down to the fat used as firelighter hitherto, or the thongs of pigskin that bound the sufferer. Now he begun to doubt this. He was in the wrong direction for the new wind, and one particularly strong gust had him all but vomiting. He kept his lips and jaw the tighter set.

Patrick Hamilton emitted no actual word after that – although he remained conscious for another half-hour, and his at first bitten back cries and screams became ever more unrestrained and animal-like. Finally even these died away, as at last the fire gained the victory over shrinking but stubborn flesh and sappy wood both.

Nevertheless, the now capering hangman gleefully kept, at intervals, shouting out that the panel, as he called the martyr, was still alive, that he still jerked and twitched.

Actually the March daylight was fading and the Vespers bells beginning to ring for evening prayer, before almost reluctantly the belatedly successful executioner, now streaming with sweat and red in the face, announced that the panel was truly dead quite, to the very small residue of watchers – who had waited merely to go forward and collect fragments of unburned wood as mementoes, or larger portions as welcome additions to depleted fuel stocks.

The wayward lay Abbot of Ferne had taken six hours to die.

The other lay abbot, of Arbroath, who had likewise stood in the one spot for all that time, stiffly, woodenly, turned away at last, to walk as one in a dream, perhaps a nightmare.

Passing through the hall of St. Salvator's College thereafter, he was hailed by his uncle, sitting at meat with the Principal and others.

"Hech, man Davie – there you are! Come you, and sit in," he called. "You must be fair famished. You saw it out, to the last, eh? A bungled business. But at least, we had nae bother with the Hamiltons. Man – you must have a stronger stomach than have I, by the Rude! A little o' that was plenty for me. And you've swallowed six hours o' it! You're a stouter chiel than you look, I do declare, lad!"

David Beaton, pale of face, stalked on and past, without a word, to the surprise of all.

Chapter Fourteen

IN his bedchamber in the Palace of Falkland, in mid-Fife, young King James, newly sixteen, paced the floor excitedly. His basically good-looking features, developing now towards manhood, were enlivened by a tension and interest normally lacking – or at least, successfully repressed usually – his fine Stewart eyes wide instead of narrowed, veiled. His speech came hurried, thick, urgent.

"What if Sir George comes back, sir? he demanded. "St. Andrews is not that far away. George Douglas is an ill man, hard, hard. If he learns of this . . .!"

"Sir George will not come back, Sire," Balfour of Fernie, Keeper of Falkland Forest, assured. "Not tonight. He will be detained in St. Andrews. With the Archbishop. On the matter of a grant of lands. Ever dear to the Douglas heart! My lord Abbot of Arbroath has arranged it. As he arranged for the uncle also, Archibald Douglas, to be detained in Dundee overnight, with an especial doxy. Your Treasurer, Archie Douglas of Kilspindie, is a notable one for the women – and this is an exceptional wench! Do not fret, Your Grace. All will be well."

"But . . . my lord himself? Angus! He may return. He is only gone to Tantallon, in Lothian. And has already been gone four days."

"The roads and the ferries are watched, Sire. My lord of Angus never moves without at least five score of men at his heels, as you know. He will not come within a dozen miles of Falkland without our knowing it. Only James Douglas of Parkhead, Captain of the Royal Guard, remains here to watch Your Grace — and he is the least stark of them all. He suspects nothing, I swear. Indeed, if there was aught of suspicion anywhere, Sir George and his Uncle Archibald would never have left Falkland."

"It . . . it may be but a trap!" the youth cried. "They have never before left me so. With but one of them guarding me. Always there have been three or four of them, at least. It could be a trap. To trick me into rebellion against them. So that they might deal with me the more sorely . . ."

"No, no, Sire. It is not so. Angus and the Douglases it is that are tricked. Master David it is — my lord Abbot — who sets *this* trap!" Balfour barked a laugh. He was a far-out cousin of the Beatons, a tough, youngish man. "That great Yuletide feast at St. Andrews Castle was the setting of the trap. When Your Grace, Your Grace's Lady-Mother, Angus and all the Douglas leaders were feasted for a sennight at the Archbishop's expense. And given costly presents and lands. That was the start of this night's work. Angus now believes that he has the Beatons wholly won over."

"Aye. I believed it myself."

"All men do. It is not the Archbishop's nature to dissemble thus — for he is a blunt man, But Master David is of a different kidney. He has the Douglases lulled. Today is the baiting of the trap. Tomorrow we shall spring it!"

"Must we wait, then?" the King asked, swinging from the doubts to the over-confidence of youth. "Why not ride now? Tonight? Escape in the darkness . . ."

"Patience, Sire. That might be to ruin all," Balfour said. "This palace may hold few Douglas leaders tonight, but it is well furnished with their men! None could ride away from here unchallenged. Every gate and door is held. But this great hunt tomorrow is a different matter. There will be much coming and going. I have seen to that. Tomorrow, early, will be the time . . ."

"Aye." Young James Stewart stalked about like a caged lion. "But what if it is too late? Sir George *might* come back tonight.

He's not a man to be deceived. And if he learns of this, he . . . he will be very wrath. He is the worst of them all, I tell you. Worse than Angus his brother. He said once that he would kill me . . .!"

"No, Sire! Never that!"

"It is true. It was the day of the battle. At Linlithgow Bridge. We were riding from Edinburgh – the Douglases, to the aid of my lord of Arran, and the Hamiltons. They made me ride with them. I rode as slowly as I might, to delay them. Angus rode ahead, leaving Sir George to bring me. He is Master of my House-hold. When still I rode slowly, he vowed that he would hasten me. He said not to think that I had aught to gain by Lennox's victory. Quite other, indeed. He said that rather than surrender my person he would have his men tear me limb from limb! He swore it by a great oath. That is the truth."

Balfour of Fernie shook his head, wordless.

"So it must not fail, Balfour man – dear God, it must not fail!" the young monarch cried.

"It will not fail, Sire," the other assured. "Now – I counsel bed for Your Grace. For we rise before the sun . . ."

Next morning the palace was early astir, for the special stag-hunt that had been commanded in the King's name – and few were earlier up than the King himself. The little town of Falkland too was seething with what passed for a Court, with Fife lairds assembled for the chase, scullions and servants bringing in meats for the night's banquet, huntsmen preparing for the day, grooms watering horses. In the bustle and turmoil, before ever Douglas of Parkhead, Captain of the Guard, and other leading men were out of their beds, James, dressed in the garb of a yeomen of his own Guard, slipped out of the palace with the porters and servitors, and presently was joined in the town by Balfour of Fernie, whose duties as Keeper of the Forest made him respon-sible for the hunt arrangements. He had with him a single groom in huntsmen's costume, with three horses. Unobtrusively, by lanes and alleys, they made their way through the lower part of the town and along the water-meadows and willowy haughs of the Maspie Burn, westwards. Once out of sight of town and palace, they turned their beasts' heads northwards into the forest, and dug in their spurs.

It was as easy as that – as David Beaton had asserted it would be, declaring that all properly planned operations, however ambitious, ought to be easy and simple in the actual carrying-out, the difficulties having been overcome within men's heads beforehand. The King of Scots had won free of the iron grasp of Douglas.

At about nine o'clock, having rounded the great Leven Loch, they came up with a single figure awaiting them on a green knoll not far from the Colvilles' castle of Cleish, in lonely country. It was David Beaton himself. He bowed low to the shining-eyed and transformed monarch.

"I rejoice to see Your Grace — a free man at last!" he exclaimed. "On my soul, this is a fair day for Scotland!"

James actually laughed aloud — and few people had ever seen him do the like, for years. "Aye — a fair bonny day! Bonny! We won clean away, man!" he cried. "Parkhead, Captain of the Guard, was still in his bed! It was bravely done, I say. Was it not, sir?"

David nodded. "Bravely, Sire. The first of many brave doings, I swear. With our king restored to his kingdom."

"Aye." The boy drew himself up in the saddle. "That is so, my lord Abbot. I have to thank you. For this. And my lord Archbishop. You have served me right well in the matter. And the Laird of Fernie, here. It shall not be forgotten." This princely acknowledgement made, James looked around him, rather less confidently, the somewhat bewildered youth again. "What . . . what do we do now?" he wondered.

"All is arranged, Your Grace," David assured. "We ride for Stirling."

"Aye." But . . . is it safe, man? My mother — will she yield it to me? Will she maybe take me in — and then hold me? Hand me back to the Douglases. She has done the like before . . ."

"The Queen-Mother is not now at Stirling, Sire. She has been induced to give up the castle. In return for . . . advantages elsewhere. The debts on her husband's property of Methven have been bought up, and paid off. In your royal name Henry Stewart has been promised a Lordship of Parliament, as Lord Methven. Lord Avondale, his brother, is now Keeper of Stirling, and awaits Your Highness anxiously."

"Avondale! Aye — he is a better man than yon Henry. But, Master Beaton — what then? Can I hold Stirling? Against all the might of Douglas?" James was gnawing his lip, as the problems began to loom up before him. "For God's sake, I must not fall into their hands again! Or it will be the end of me!"

"Fear for nothing, Sire," Balfour reassured him. "My lord Abbot has all in train."

"Yes. I have sent . . . h'm . . . my lord Archbishop has summoned to Stirling, in your name Sire, lords loyal to yourself. Stewarts and others. The Earls of Moray and Buchan. The Lord Innermeath. Also the Earls of Argyll and Eglinton. And sundry bishops. Enough to ensure Your Grace not only of protection at Stirling, but to see to the government of your realm. Fear nothing, Sire. This time we are using wits rather than cold steel — a commodity the Douglas is less rich in!"

"And Angus . . .?"

"We have plans to deal with Angus, also. He must be declared guilty of treason, at once. Forfeited and put to the horn. So that no man may aid him without being guilty likewise. But — time for that at Stirling. Have we your royal permission, Sire, to ride there? It is less than a score of miles ahead . . ."

The little party rode over Stirling Bridge in mid-forenoon, and on David's prompting, King James issued his first free royal command — for the bridge-warden to shut the gates and hold it against all soever as he valued his head. Balfour of Fernie rode ahead to announce the monarch's arrival at the castle, and to order the bells of Stirling to be rung.

Lord Avondale was awaiting them, with the keys of the castle in his hands, and fell down on his knees before his young sovereign, tears in his eyes, as the fortress cannon thundered out their salute. James bit his lip, looked at David Beaton for guidance, and raised up the kneeling Avondale.

"My lord, we accept this our castle of Stirling at your hands," he jerked. "We thank you. And you all, my lords." This to the bowing row of earls, prelates and lairds. "We greet you. Warmly." His voice cracked a little. "I'm free. I'm free, I tell you! Won clean away. Do you hear me? Free . . .!"

"God save His Grace!" David Beaton cried. "God save the King's Grace."

James was not entirely free, of course — but perhaps as free as any monarch of sixteen could be in unruly sixteenth-century Scotland. At least he was more free than he had ever been before – and relished it mightily.

No attack by the Douglases actually developed, although there were rumours and false alarms a-many. This was not quite so strange as it might seem. David Beaton had laid his plans carefully and cunningly. The ferries across Forth were all watched and guarded, night and day, right down to North Berwick and Earlsferry, with parties ordered to deny passage to all Douglases and to sink the boats should the enemy be too strong for them. Thus it took Angus some time to get back to Falkland from Tantallon – and he could not take any large company with him. The only way that the Douglases north and south of the Forth could link up was by Stirling Bridge, securely held for the King – for westwards stretched the impassable marshes of the Flanders Moss. Moreover Archbishop Beaton's personal fortune, and the accumulated funds of Holy Church, were poured out like water, in gifts, pensions, bribes, so that Douglas lairds and supporters were hard put to it to decide on which side their bread was buttered thickest. The Earl of Arran surprised many – but not David Beaton – by rallying to the side of the King against his former ally, at whose door he laid the main blame for the deaths of Patrick Hamilton and the Earl of Lennox, both his nephews. Thus the great House of Hamilton was divided, for Sir James of Finnart remained in sympathy with Angus. Scotland held its breath and watched Tantallon Castle in Lothian, Angus's main seat.

A Court and government gathered around young James. Angus's appointments were all cancelled and new ones made, awaiting the confirmation of a Parliament called for early September. James would have had Archbishop Beaton Chancellor again – and the Primate would have accepted – but David advised against it, and gained his way. He pointed out – to his uncle, at least – that in this unsettled situation they would do better to wield the power without holding the positions. Better sometimes to control the Chancellor than to be Chancellor oneself. He advised Gavin Dunbar, Archbishop of Glasgow, for the position. A man lacking direction in matters of State, he would be the more easily directed; a scholar and poet rather than a statesman, he was at least a churchman, and so in some measure

204

under the Primate's control. Great lords in such high office were apt to grow altogether too great.

David Beaton at first would accept no office for himself, preferring to be entirely free. But the young King was insistent to express his gratitude to the deviser of his escape, and at length he persuaded David to accept the largely nominal though resounding office of Lord Privy Seal. He was surprised and not a little touched, when he received his patent of appointment, to discover that James had personally endorsed the commission as one for life. This young man would have to be watched carefully, he perceived; monarchs could not afford to be too warm-hearted and generous.

As a consequence, David arranged another appointment for himself – as co-preceptor with Sir David Lindsay of the Mount, Lord Lyon King of Arms, charged with the further education of the monarch until he should reach full age.

He was satisfied, meantime.

David had, however, one dangerous, powerful and implacable enemy – Sir James Hamilton of Finnart, the Bastard of Arran. Hamilton, finding Angus inactive, came to terms with his father and re-appeared at Court. He was too powerful, with half the Hamilton clan behind him, to dismiss out of hand. He was intelligent, talented as well as handsome, and utterly without scruple. And he made no secret of his dislike of the Abbot of Arbroath.

The Bastard had, of couse, a sharp and convenient weapon ready to his hand now that Angus was in the shadows – the death of his cousin Abbot Patrick Hamilton. Admittedly he had not himself raised a finger to save his kinsman at the time – but that did not prevent him from claiming David Beaton as the murderer. He was skilful about the business, never challenging David openly enough to bring matters to a head. But everyone knew that these two must one day come to a trial of strength.

Unfortunately, Hamilton exerted a sort of fascination over the young King James, who had a reluctant admiration for his sheer, ruthless power and gallant swagger. He was the undisputed champion, too, at the tourneys and joustings, of which the monarch, like his father before him, was inordinately fond – and at which David Beaton shone not at all. James, then, did in some measure fall under the Hamilton influence, even though well warned against him. It was David's fear that the Bastard would manage to poison the King's impressionable mind against him – and so much depended on him keeping that young man's confidence.

That his fears were not groundless was proved one day when, after the King had signed some papers which David put before him, he turned to him enquiringly.

"Master Davie," he said, "why did you burn the Abbot of Ferne? Did you hate him?"

Blinking, David moistened his lips. "Why, Your Grace – I did not burn Patrick Hamilton. Nor yet hate him. Indeed I scarce knew him. He was condemned by the highest court of the Church. For heresy. And the penalty prescribed for proclaimed and unrepented heresy, in the first degree, is the stake."

"Yes. Yet they say that *you* burned him."

"They say? You mean, Sire, that Sir James Hamilton says it!"

"Well . . . yes. He says that it was your devising. That the Archbishop would not have done it else. That you slew him. Out of hatred for the House of Hamilton."

"I think it ill becomes Sir James to talk of slaying, Sire! After his murder of my lord of Lennox, wounded at Linlithgow. Moreover, Angus could have saved Patrick Hamilton, for he was handed over by the Church to the civil power, after sentence. And Sir James was close to Angus. He lifted no hand to save his cousin." David shrugged. "But, Your Grace – in matters of government, in Church as well as State, those who would overturn due order and authority must be put down. And firmly. Else anarchy and chaos follow. We have seen all too much of it in this realm of yours. It must not happen in Holy Church. Patrick Hamilton was a danger to the Church. And therefore to your realm, of which it is the main support. He openly preached subversion, the doctrines of Martin Luther, and the denigration of the Papacy. All too many were prepared to listen to him. That could not be tolerated. He had to be silenced, made example of . . ."

"Aye, Master Davie – but there are those who say that burning the man was no' the best way to silence him!" James declared, with his own shrewdness. "I've heard it said that Master Patrick's cries from the stake reached more folk than ever did his preachings! I mind Angus himself saying that he counselled that any more burnings would be best done in the vaults of St. Andrews Castle, rather than in the town's streets—where the stink of it offended over many noses!"

David eyed his liege lord carefully, with an access of respect. "Pray that Scotland needs no more such burnings, Sire," he answered sombrely. "It is my hope that the stink of one such, noxious as it was, will be sufficient. That I pray to God—for the stench of it is in my nostrils yet!"

James eyed him strangely, as, with a bow less formal than was his usual, David Beaton left the royal presence.

Chapter Fifteen

"Oh, Davie, Davie! Would to God that I could hold you here! Hold you close, here at Ethie," Marion said, voice suddenly quivering, vehement. "Make you see where lies our true happiness—yours, as mine. Not in courts and palaces and parliaments, not in the places of the great. Not even in your great Abbey of Arbroath. But here, together, at Ethie, by this silver sea, amongst simple things. Each night I pray in yonder chamber that I might turn your eyes away from things far and high and proud, to what you have here, under your very hand . . ."

"Think you I cannot see it? I who made it so? Who chose this Ethie. Who wooed and won you, and brought you here!" Almost harshly the man spoke. "Think you I am so blind, Marion?"

"Aye, Davie—you saw it then, dear heart. It is not this that I cannot make you see—but where lies your true happiness. That you strive and struggle and plan for, endanger yourself. Aye. even I sometimes fear, your very soul! For what? For power and position. Oh, I know that it is so that you may serve the realm and the Church. But must it ever be you who serves? There are so many others who could, who should. Must it ever be David Beaton?"

"There are none so many, my dear, who could do what I can do. I do not boast. It is only truth. For any man to serve his country in high degree three things are needful—position and wit and will. Not many have them all. But all three *I* have been given. Is it God's purpose, think you, that I should throw them all away? You talk of happiness. But there is more than that. There is duty. And honour. And good faith. What happiness would I have if I hid myself here at Ethie, knowing that I could do much to save the kingdom? And if *I* know myself to fail, how happy would *you* be?"

She did not answer him directly. They sat on the cliff-top of Red Head, in the mellow sunshine of the last day of August, gazing out over all the glittering plain of the sea. It was the sixth day of a visit, stolen from the cares and ties of the Court.

"Nothing I can say, then, will keep you?" she asked. "Prevent you from returning to Edinburgh tomorrow? So short a time . . ."

"Short, but blessed." He sighed. "I must go. You know it, my dear. Parliament is called for the eleventh day of September. And there is much to be done. For it means so much, this Parliament. The Douglases are stirring again, and Angus is by no means done yet. Parliament must manage matters aright, or all could yet fail . . ."

"Do you not mean, rather, that *you* must manage the Parliament, Davie?"

"I must watch it, yes. Guide it, if I can. If the King's authority is to prevail, it must have the backing of Parliament If *I* do not assure it, who will? My uncle has lost his will to rule, either in Church or State. He is little better than a done man. Gavin Dunbar is not to be trusted, lacking firm guidance. Abbot Cairncross, the new Treasurer, is a good man, but lacks experience. Abbot Myln, the Clerk Register, is a Queen's man, and to that extent unreliable . . ."

"All the King's government are now churchmen?"

"Aye. James has had enough of great lords. Fleming, the Chamberlain, is a safe man – but his lands are surrounded by those of Douglas. He will not lead in Parliament while Angus lives."

"Angus is to die?"

"He must be brought low, once and for all. Only so shall Scotland have peace. The King has declared him guilty of highest treason, and ordained his forfeiture and death. But the Council and Parliament must confirm it."

"Another death! That you advise and would ensure, Davie? Dear God – you are become, I think, a very merchant of death!"

"Marion!"

208

"Oh, I am sorry, Davie! But is there not truth in it? Patrick Hamilton . . ."

"By the Mass, woman—you too! Must you also name that name to me? Always Patrick Hamilton! 'Fore God—it is too much!"

Marion stared, flushing. Never before had he spoken to her like this.

At her stricken look, he took a grip of himself and shook his head. "Forgive me, lass. That was no way to speak. Bear with me. I have had much blame for Hamilton's death."

"Yet . . . you planned it, did you not? Here in Ethie, you planned it. In my hearing."

"I planned his apprehension, yes. His trial. His downfall. That was necessary. But not his death. Before and after his trial I pleaded with him to recant. He would have been freed. Even a word or two would have saved him. A promise to preach no more heresy. But he would not. He sought martyrdom. I sought to make it easy for him to avoid the penalty for his action. But he spurned me. And now I am blamed for his death. I tell you, I have suffered many things on account of Patrick Hamilton."

"Pontius Pilate, I recollect, also suffered many things on account of a condemned man—and was esteemed no less guilty therefore!" she said evenly.

Abruptly he rose to his feet. "If that is what you think, then let us go from here! For there is no pleasure left in the prospect, I vow!" Then he remembered, and turned back to help her rise. "Och, Marion, Marion—here is no way for us to deal with each other. And you with our child in you! I am sorry, my dear."

"As am I, Davie." She clung to him. "It was unkind of me. But . . . I grow so anxious here. Alone. For so long. I fret. Perhaps the child has something to do with it. I think and think . . ."

"Aye, lass—you are over-much alone. I feared it must be so . . ."

"No, no. I do not bewail my lot, Davie. I would have it so. Here at Ethie is the life I would live. If only you were here to share it more often. Oh, I know that I promised not to meddle in your affairs of State. This role I chose. But . . . six days in as many months, my love!"

"I know, I know, sweeting. See you—I promise to return the

moment that the Parliament is over and its affairs in train. That for sure. It is a compact . . ."

That Parliament, held in Edinburgh on the eleventh of September, set the seal on David's long months of planning and dissimulation and effort—and the expenditure of his uncle's fortune. The treason edicts were confirmed—and no Douglas or Douglas supporter was present, for it was proclaimed that any such coming within six miles of the monarch would forfeit life and lands. Elaborate precautions were taken to see that no armed attack on the Capital took place, and the town walls were manned in force night and day—even King James himself, in full armour, taking turns of duty at the task, and obviously enjoying it more than sitting through the much talking of the Parliament. No assault developed—although there were armed Douglas hosts reported from as near as Sir George's house of Dalkeith, and rumours of Angus issuing forth in wrath from Tantallon were of daily occurrence. The creaking machinery of government gradually gained momentum, decisions were made, the royal appointments substantiated, and Angus was required to present himself in ward, for trial, when summoned. Meanwhile to remove himself beyond Spey and to yield up his uncle and brother, Archibald and Sir George, as hostages.

All this was not achieved without some heat and opposition, of course. Archbishop Gavin, of Glasgow, in the Chancellor's seat, spent an evidently unhappy two days—but the Abbot of Arbroath was never far from his shoulder, and his former royal pupil was only too eager to reverse roles for a change, and frowned furiously on his ex-tutor whenever occasion required. Abbot Cairncross, who now held William Douglas's Abbacy of Holyrood, was a man after David's own heart, and kept the lesser prelates on the right road, whilst Gilbert Ogilvy, now Dean of St. Andrews, did his best with their superiors.

Two discordant voices were apt to be raised—those of Henry, Lord Methven, and Sir James Hamilton of Finnart. But fortunately these tended to cancel out one the other, for they hated each other like poison, never failing to taunt the other with bastardy or effeminacy. That both also loathed David Beaton and all his works was unfortunate—but at least Hamilton had sufficient discretion not to seem to run counter to the King's evident wishes. He gained his reward, for he surprisingly had a flair for architecture and things practical, and was appointed Master of the King's Works and superintendent of the royal palaces – these requiring much attention after the neglect of years.

By the middle of the month David, in company with Gilbert Ogilvy was on his way back to Ethie after seeing his uncle safely deposited in St. Andrews Castle.

It was one of those golden autumns when Scotland is so bathed and stained in colour as to bring tears to the eyes. Marion was at her most lovely and loving – and though David's care for her person was elaborate, she was not yet in fact at a stage of pregnancy to interfere much with their enjoyment of each other. David had to put in some time at the Abbey, but they spent five halcyon days and nights together, before the messenger came.

He arrived one evening at dusk on a weary foundered horse – one of Cairncross's Holyrood men, having ridden night and day from Edinburgh. The word he brought was grievous, infuriating to David. The King, despite all urgings to the contrary, had assembled a large force, an army, from the townsfolk and Lothian lairds, and was now assailing from the walls of Tantallon Castle. Angus had refused the Parliament's demand to yield himself, or his kinsmen, or to retire beyond Spey; indeed, he had proclaimed defiance and declared that he would sweep the present rabble of clerks, churchmen and poltroons around the foolish young monarch into the Forth. Here was James Stewart's answer.

David cursed at the folly of it. This was no better than to play Angus's game. James, in open warfare, was little better than a babe, compared with the veterans of Douglas. David had impressed on him, time and again, that steel should be his last resort. This could mean utter disaster.

David reached the East Lothian coast at North Berwick seventeen hours after leaving Ethie. He found the little town in an uproar – as well he might, for he had been hearing the boom of cannon from ten miles out in the Forth, and here they were barely three miles from Tantallon.

The good folk informed him that the King had brought a mighty host from Edinburgh – some said ten thousand, some twenty – to assail their feudal lord in his tremendous stronghold. That he had sent to Dunbar for the great cannon, Thrawn-

Mou'ed Meg herself with her consort and brood of lesser ordnance, bocards, moyons, double-falcons, quarter-falcons, sakers and so on. But they could roar and belch as they would, they'd never win into Tantallon, the folk declared. Dinging down the walls of Tantallon was just as easy a task as building a bridge out to the Bass — as young King Jamie would discover! Raising his eyes to consider the huge humped mass of the Bass Rock towering over a mile out to sea, David took their point.

He rode round the coast to where the vast pile of Tantallon soared on its cliff-top, directly opposite the Bass — and long before he reached it was pushing his way through the scattered, idle and undisciplined companies of the King's array. The Crown, of course, had no standing forces, other than the small Royal Guard — which, having been wholly Douglas-dominated was now in process of reformation. There were townsmen, train-bands, churchmen's retainers, lords' levies and the like, a host as unmanageable as it was inexperienced.

David had never seen Tantallon before, save at a distance from the sea — for it was a place wise men kept away from. But its fame was only too well known to him, its strength renowned, probably the most impressive private stronghold in the land. It stood at a corner of a proud cliff directly above the waves. Before it were two great and wide ditches, one dry, one filled with water, cutting off all access save by drawbridges, and these were enhanced by a system of earthworks beyond, so extensive and elaborate that no approach could be made closer than nearly a quarter of a mile while towers and wall remained manned. The Bleeding Heart banner of Douglas flew proudly from the keep's topmost turret. It all made St. Andrews Castle look insignificant.

He counted no fewer than sixteen cannon, great and small, ranged in a semicircle as near as the earthworks would allow — but clearly only the larger ones could throw a ball far enough to reach the castle itself. Behind these, safely out of range of Tantallon's own guns, men were everywhere, sitting about, lying, sleeping, playing games, even fighting amongst themselves, hundreds, thousands of bored and idle men. Only about the three or four great cannon was their any sign of activity. Even as David stared, a cannon roared thunderously, belching flame and smoke — with no visible effect whatever on the huge red-stone walls. Indeed, no sign of damage from all the prolonged bombardment was evident.

David found the King further forward than almost any of his warriors. A large stone dovecot stood to the north-west at about three hundred yards from the castle, and screened behind this the royal pavilion had been erected, colourful in red and gold. In it, he discovered the young monarch sitting despondently on a bench alone, red head in his hands, gazing down at the trodden turf, a picture of dejection.

He looked up on the guard's announcement of the newcomer, with a start that was almost guilty. "Sakes — Master Davie!" he gulped. "You! I thought . . . I believed you to be at Arbroath. I did not know . . ."

"I came, Sire, hot-foot." David bowed perfunctorily. "The moment that I heard of this cantrip. I have not paused, praying that I might be in time . . ."

"It is no cantrip, sir!" Indignantly the youth jumped to his feet. "I am come here, as is my right, my duty. To teach this rebel Douglas who is King in Scotland! He must be brought low."

"Aye. Sire — but not with cannon and swords. Have I not told you — only wits will serve to bring down Douglas . . ."

"Wits! You prate of wits — but do nothing! Talk, fine words, are of no avail against Angus, Sir Abbot! I tell you, only deeds will serve now."

"So you waited, Sire, until I was safe a hundred miles away, to effect your deeds?"

Hotly the King flushed. "My lord Abbot — you forget yourself!" he cried.

David inclined his head. "Perhaps I do, Sire. And if so, I crave your pardon. It is only out of love for Your Grace. You knew that I would have advised against this . . . this expedition."

"You are not my only adviser, sir."

"No. Only your Lord Privy Seal. And preceptor. But — your other advisers? The Chancellor — my lord Archbishop of Glasgow? I vow he would not smile on this venture? The Abbot of Holyrood, your Treasurer? Was this *his* counsel? Abbot Myln . . .?"

"Churchmen! All Churchmen!" James exclaimed. "Men of words, not deeds. Must I be trammelled and confined in all I do by such as these? I think that I have too many priests around me!"

"I say that Your Grace is most assuredly right!" a voice said strongly, behind them. "A surfeit of clerks is a grievous burden. I would dispense with some few of them Sire, I vow!"

They both turned. The handsome person of Sir James Hamilton of Finnart, gallant in splendid half-armour, stood within the tent-mouth. He flourished a salute at the King, and smiled mockingly at David.

"Oh, aye, Sir James. H'mmm." The King looked embarrassed. The crash of another cannon-shot came to his rescue.

"Perhaps it was Sir James who advised you to this adventure, Sire?" David suggested.

"Well — he aided me in it. Aided me right kindly."

"Kindly . . .?" David looked at Hamilton, eyebrows raised. "Kindly towards whom, Sire?"

"Sirrah — you will watch your words!" the other snapped.

"That is what I do, sir. And in the King's presence, and speaking to one of his ministers, you will be wise to watch yours!"

"Och — my lords! Sirs!" James looked unhappily from one to the other. "Here's no way to talk. Master Davie — be not so sour . . ."

"Your Grace — Sir James has been many things. Including for years the staunch ally of he whose castle you here assail. But this he is, for certain — a soldier! A man of war. And any soldier could, and should have told you that Tantallon Castle is impregnable to armed attack. Your puissant father tried it, and failed. As have others. None have succeeded. Those walls are twelve to fifteen feet thick. No cannon can breach them. You cannot win close enough for mining, because of the outworks and ditches — and even so the place is built on solid rock. You cannot starve it out, because it can be supplied by sea — victual raised from boats, on ropes, at night. This venture cannot succeed — and Sir James Hamilton, of all men, must have known it. To advise Your Grace so was his plain duty . . ."

"Thus pronounceth the mighty churchman, trained in war!"

"It is not so, Master Davie," James asserted. "Tantallon must yield, in time. Angus cannot much longer defy me. He cannot escape me. My cannon will grind his walls to powder. In the end Douglas will be brought low."

"Not thus, Sire — not thus. If Angus is to be brought low, it will not be by strength of arm. For his arm is stronger still than any other in Scotland. Even the King's. It will be by using a shrewder head."

"Such as Master Beaton's!" Hamilton put in, with a snort.

"If no shrewder may be found. How many days, Sire, have you been battering at Tantallon? Four? With what result? Think you that four more will effect any difference? Or still another four? And what will Angus be doing? They say in North Berwick that he slipped out, two nights ago. Down the cliff to a waiting boat. He could do so easily. It is my fear that he is now assembling a Douglas host to attack you in the rear, while you sit here. Or to take Edinburgh behind you."

"A mercy — no!" the youth cried, staring wide-eyed.

"Rumours! The prattle of cotters and packmen!" Hamilton said shortly. "Heed not this either, Your Grace."

"Rather put the matter to the test. Send forward a herald and trumpets. Demand a parley with my lord of Angus himself. If he is there, and comes, tell him that if he agrees to yield his castle you will permit him to remove himself meantime unhindered, either beyond Spey or into England. If he does not come to speak with his king, then you will know that he is no longer in Tantallon."

"Aye. We can do that . . ."

Thereafter, the herald's summons from before the royal host produced only procrastination at first, and then the somewhat unimpressive figure of one Simon Panango, the castle's resident captain, on the keep's parapet, to declare, in the name of the Earl of Angus, that Tantallon never would yield.

James, nibbling his finger-nails, was much put out. But he would not consider raising the siege and retiring to the security of Edinburgh. Primed by Hamilton, he declared that this would lower his dignity and reputation in the eyes of the whole nation, an open admission of failure. But he would send out scouting parties in all directions, to ensure that no Douglas host came upon them unawares.

Unable to prevail, David fell back upon constitutional niceties. Warfare and the like was a matter for the Privy Council. It had not met or been consulted. As Lord Privy Seal it was his duty to arrange for such meetings. He requested the royal authority to summon the Council.

James could not deny this, but he did refuse to come to Edinburgh to attend it. If his Council did in fact wish to meet, it could do so here before the walls of Tantallon. There again Hamilton's voice was to be detected, behind the King's. It would take a considerable time to gather together the members of the Council.

It took David five days, for he had to ride as far as Castle Campbell in Clackmannan, to ensure the attendance of the Earl of Argyll, as Lord President of the Council, and Stirling, to reach the Earl of Mar, Vice-President — neither of whom was over-eager to heed the pleas of an upstart cleric; five days in which ever more ominous rumours of Douglas mobilisation in the Borders and Douglasdale reached David; five days in which Mons Meg and the other great cannon battered monotonously and ineffectually at Tantallon's walls, and for the King's distraction and amusement Sir James Hamilton turned the besiegers' camp into a tourney-ground and jousting-lists. By the time that a quorum of the Council members assembled, the entire expedition had taken on the character of something between a wapinschaw and a fair, with a picnic atmosphere prevailing, and it was difficult to arouse any sense of danger and urgency.

The majority of the council, meeting in the Royal Pavilion, agreed that the siege of Tantallon should be raised forthwith.

David, towards the end, made a major effort to salve the royal pride, and to give a new and acceptable lead in the greater problem. He pointed out that Angus, while so obviously powerful still, had two sources of weakness. He was avaricious; and he depended upon the support of Henry of England. These both could be used against him with skilful handling. He, David Beaton, had made it his business to discover that Angus had been for years in receipt of a large annual pension in gold from King Henry. In some of the papers taken over by the new Treasurer, details of this had come to light.

Glancing round the company, David could sense discomfort on not a few noble faces present — for Angus was by no means the only Scots lord to accept English gold. Allowing a few moments for this to sink in, with the possibility of other incriminating papers emerging, he went on,

"Your Grace, my lords — we all know that the greatest and most dangerous enemy of Scotland is not Angus, but Henry

Tudor, whose tool he is. I conceive that we may here strike a shrewd blow at both. Let His Grace write to King Henry, his uncle, in favourable and respectful terms. Inform him that he has now assumed full rule and governance of this his realm. Thank Henry for the favours, the many favours, conferred on him during his minority . . ."

At the growl of protest that arose, not least from King James himself, David raised a hand.

"Bear with me, Sire," he pleaded. "In this matter, since we cannot use might, we must use guile. Henry's favours have been sore ones — but Your Grace need not say so today. Declare your obligement, and hopes for a lasting peace between your two realms — which at this moment Henry needs, for he has gone to war with the Emperor Charles. Which means also war with Spain. And he is quarrelling with the Pope. So he requires the goodwill of France, and no trouble with France's ancient ally Scotland. To maintain and further this happy peace between nephew and uncle, however, you would add that you desire King Henry summon his pensioner Angus to England forthwith, where he has lands and estates — and to retain him there. Adding that such a summons would make it unnecessary to inform the King of France, your ally, of the payment of this pension — which is, be it noted, a direct infringement of the treaty between England, France and Scotland. I believe, Sire, that Henry will not refuse. Especially if your royal mother also writes, requesting her brother to recall her former husband, who is now an embarrassment to her."

There were deep breaths drawn and exclamations made, few doubting or hostile — the Lord Methven being loudly vocal. James, who saw himself restored to take the vital and determinate role in it all, was sitting up.

"Aye, Master Davie — my lord Abbot," he said. "That is well thought on. But . . . will Angus go? Will he obey Henry, and leave Scotland?"

"I think he will, Sire. He requires Henry's continued support, since he has lost all other now. And if he offends Henry, he loses not only his pension, of two thousand gold crowns, but his English lands."

The Earl of Arran clinched the matter, "Master Beaton is right," he declared. "So shall we be quit of Angus, meantime.

217

More cheaply than by fighting him. So be he does not catch us here before his castle first!"

That set men in a stir — for the fears of it had never been far from the minds of most of the Council members. The meeting was somewhat hastily brought to a close, and the commands went out to all the besieging host to strike camp.

The retiral upon Edinburgh — which town David had ensured was meantime in a state to withstand attack — was still less orderly and impressive than had been the original exodus. This was because a Hepburn courier arrived to inform the Earl of Bothwell that a large Douglas force, allegedly under the command of Angus himself, was working its way through the Lammermuir Hills in the direction of Bothwell's castle of Hailes, and was now not more than a dozen miles away. This sent the Privy Counsellors scurrying off in some alarm, not waiting for the slower-moving host, and urging that the King ride with them. James would not do so — but nevertheless the feeling of affright was distinctly infectious, and despite the angry efforts of Sir James Hamilton, the major part of the royal force was smitten with an equally urgent desire to avoid any confrontation with the dreaded Douglas in open battle. But even James's stubborn and youthful pride, and Hamilton's resentment, were not proof against the appalling, crawling slowness of the artillery.

The royal party had reached the Esk at Musselburgh, only a few miles from Edinburgh, when the deputy Master of the Ordnance came spurring up behind them with grim news. Angus himself had come up with the artillery-train near Dirleton. They had resisted as best they could, but to no avail. Many of the gun-crews were dead, including John Falconer, the Captain-Gunner. All the pieces were captured.

Young James turned first red in the face, then pale. Tears in his eyes he stared back over the green Lothian landscape, towards the distant cone of North Berwick Law, and raised his clenched fist.

"God's curse upon him!" he cried thickly, hoarsely. "The everlasting curse of God and His saints on Archibald Douglas! On all of that devil's name! Johnnie Falconer — the finest gunner in the land! My cannons! My bonny cannons! I swear . . . I swear in the name of Christ and Saint Andrew that I will be even with them! That so long as I live, no Douglas shall find a resting-place in this my Scotland! So aid me God!"

At the sick and helpless passion of the boy who had suffered so much at Douglas hands, all men were moved. But only David Beaton raised his voice.

"Sire — fear not," he said. "You shall prevail over Douglas. This day will be avenged, its shame wiped out. Believe me. This shall be Angus's last triumph — and a barren one. He chose Henry to serve, not Your Grace. Now he shall pay Henry's price. Write to Henry Tudor this night. I will word the letter for you. And I promise you, by all that I hold dear, that Archibald Douglas will be out of your realm before Yule, and yonder proud castle in your hands. Never shall Angus return, save on your summons. On that I stake my name and repute. The pen shall do what the sword may not. We shall make an end of Douglas, before the year is out."

Silent, set-faced, the King of Scots turned towards his Capital.

PART THREE

Chapter Sixteen

MARION OGILVY sat on a sun-warmed bench under the red-stone walls of Ethie Castle, sheltered from the chill April breeze, and watched her two menfolk at their pacing on the greensward which stretched away from the house towards the cliff-top, watched and smiled a little, toying with the curls of baby Elizabeth on her lap. But her smile was only momentary, and very much for the three-year-old George, who marched to and fro a few yards away, long-strided on plump sturdy legs, fair head bent, chubby hands behind his back, in exact imitation of his father. George loved to copy his father in all things.

David Beaton, further off, had been pacing back and forward, the wind blowing about him, for fully half an hour, features set, gaze seldom lifted from the grass to all the bright sun-filled exhilaration of the morning where gulls wheeled white against the blue, larks trilled, and the waves made lace edging along endless miles of seaboard.

Marion should have been happy, smiling at more than her little son. David had come north hoping for a longer spell at home than had been possible for long. All, for the moment, went reasonably well in the kingdom — at least on the face of it. King James, now almost twenty, was secure on the throne — and largely thanks to David Beaton. Although the latter was now thirty-five he looked ten years younger, figure still slender, almost boyish, features unlined, silky fair hair untinged with grey. Perhaps Marion was grudging, ungrateful, to be thus critical and anxious.

Strangely enough it was his mouth that worried her — those lips which she loved so dearly. David Beaton had always had a particularly sensitive mouth for a man, the sweet curve of smiling lips redeemed from effeminacy by the delicate strength of chin and jawline. But of late, something of the set of those lips seemed to have changed, narrowed, hardened. A tiny thing, barely perceptible — but it worried the young woman.

At length, she set down little Elizabeth to crawl on the grass, rose, and patting the plodding George's bent head, moved over to join her husband at his pacing.

"Davie—my caged lion!" she chided gently. "Is Ethie become so constricting a place for you that you must stalk and prowl as though padding the limits of your den?"

He slowed his perambulations a little. "I was but thinking. I am sorry, Marion."

"Thinking no pleasant thoughts, I swear! By your frown and your tight mouth. Oh, Davie—is that what you came home to Ethie for?"

"No. No. Forgive me, my dear. It is but matters of state . . ."

"But you come here to *forget* matters of state, do you not? To be just David Beaton, not my Lord Privy Seal and all the other lofty things you are. That has been *my* part. To restore you. To keep you thirled to true and honest and simple things. To sustain the man against the statesman. Am I failing in that, Davie Beaton?"

"No. Indeed no, Marion. Never think it. You are all my joy, my consolation. I am foolish, selfish . . ."

"There is more than selfishness here, I think, Davie," she said quietly, firmly. "There is something wrong, is there not?"

"Wrong?" He glanced at her sidelong. "What should be wrong my heart? More than is ever wrong in this realm of Scotland! Where troubles ever proliferate . . . like maggots in a carcase!"

"Maggots in a carcase! That is a strange likeness, is it not? What made you choose it, I wonder? But—never heed. It was not of matters of state that I spoke when I said that something was wrong. It was nearer home than that. Between us, Davie—between you and me. What is it?"

"Nonsense, woman!" he cried, sharply. "Do not talk folly." And then, more gently. "I am just a little tired, sweeting. Concerned a little. Over the news from England."

"I think not, Davie. A hundred times I have seen you tired, concerned over the realm's affairs. But not like this. Here is something of ourselves. You look away from me too often. We know each other, Davie, too well for this. There is something you hide from me."

He had quickened his pacing, so that she had some ado to keep up with him. "I tell you it is not so! Not . . . not what you say. It . . . it is but the English trouble. Henry threatening Scotland again. That, and the arrogant, lawless nobles. And heresy and decay in the Church. They are all linked. Henry would put away his wife, Catherine of Aragon—divorce her, or claim their marriage null, so that he may marry his trollop Anne Bullen. The Pope will not aid him in this—therefore he denies the Pope's authority and claims himself to be head of the Church, in England. Moreover, he covets the wealth of the Church. So he encourages the so-called reformers—and the Bullens are of that faction—the Lutherans and those others, less honest, who would bring down Christ's Church in ruin, for its pickings . . ."

"Yes, Davie. It is wicked. Shameful. But—I know it all. You have told me before. This is not what makes you so strange, I vow."

"But do you not see?" he insisted, almost heavily for that man, maintaining his striding. "Henry seeks to rule Scotland also. Would incorporate it in the English Crown. Aids and encourages revolt in the Scottish Church. It used to be only the nobles whom he bribed. Now it is also churchmen. He is pouring gold into the country."

"No doubt, Davie. But I question whether it is King Henry's shadow that rises between you and me, nevertheless!"

He was silent for a little. "Bothwell has turned traitor," he said, at length, stolidly. "He has gone over to the English. Joined Angus, in England. We have sure word that he has promised to see Henry crowned King of Scots in Edinburgh! So the two great Border houses of Douglas and Hepburn are now against King James . . ."

"Yes, my dear. So you said." Marion touched his arm, and instead of turning with him at the end of their pacing-ground, moved off towards the house. He continued his striding, unchecked.

She skirted the castle proper, making for the stable range within the courtyard. Thereafter she went indoors.

When Marion came back to David's side she was dressed for riding. "Come, Davie," she said. "Horses are saddled and waiting. A ride across Lunan Bay, this fair morning. That ever brings you close to me. Perhaps it will unburden you."

"Riding . . .!" He stared at her. "Now? In your state, Marion?"

"Tush!" she exclaimed. "What state am I in that would unfit me for the saddle? I am but four months gone. I can ride for months yet. What think you I do when you are not here? I range the country, a-horse, pretending that you are at my side."

They rode down the cliff-track, by Ethiehaven, to the beginning of the three-mile crescent of golden sand that lined Lunan Bay.

Marion led the way, in fine style, quickly urging her beast into a full gallop. She did not allow him to catch up with her too easily — indeed they were well into the third mile and not far from the start of the rocks that culminated in Boddin Point, when he reached over to encircle her with his arm. He had not intended anything so ambitious as to transfer her to his own horse, in view of her condition — but Marion intended just that, and came half out of her saddle to meet him. Almost before he was aware that he had done it, David had her sitting before him, his arms around her, and her beast was running free.

"Oh, my love!" he panted. "My lovely, beautiful, adorable love! Was ever a man so blest . . . and so cursed!"

"So! I am a curse to you, Davie Beaton!" Still she laughed, but her eyes were suddenly wary, alert.

"Not you. Not you, my sweeting. You are all that is dear and fair."

"What then is your curse?"

He shook his head. "It is . . . other. Would you spoil this good moment, woman?"

"In this good moment, my dear, there should be nothing between us. Nothing that you cannot tell me now. Is it so ill? Tell me. Best now, when we are so close."

He drew a deep breath, and eased his horse to a walk. "So be it, Marion. This, when I hold all joy in my arms, is the sorest moment of my life. My curse is that I am a churchman — but only half a churchman. My sorrow is that I must be wholly one."

"What do you mean?"

"I mean, my heart, that I must take holy orders."

"But . . . but why? What has changed? You would never be priest. Before."

"All has changed, Marion. Has been changing for long. I have seen this coming — and fought it off. And cannot, any longer. So long as my uncle was a man, however much he lacked, I could work through him, from behind him. He is no longer that, truly a man. He is now but an ailing empty husk, done, spent. He

225

cannot take any decision, exert any authority. And daily men see it more clearly. Yet he is still, in name, head of the Church in this land. And never did the Church require a stronger leader. Nor this realm more require the strength of the Church. I can little longer work from behind James Beaton's person, Marion — since now all men perceive that it is I who work, not he. And the Church cannot, will not, be led by a man who is not a priest."

Desperately groping for the reality behind his words, she stared.

"Do you not see, Marion? Bishops, abbots, priors, clergy — they will not accept their orders from a layman. In the Church, I can only transmit commands — I cannot give them."

"And must you command in the Church? You?"

"You know that I must. Archbishop Gavin, the Chancellor, aspires to the Primacy — and he is a weak man. He will not, cannot save the Church. I can save the Church. And the realm. I believe that I am the only man who can, in Scotland today. But not as lay Abbot of Arbroath. I must be my uncle's coadjutor, not his secretary. I must be able to act, not only move his arms and speak with his voice. The Pope desires it. He would appoint me Apostolic Protonotary in my uncle's place. But I must take holy orders."

"And . . . and priests may not marry!" She said that with a catch in her throat.

"Aye," he repeated grimly. "Priests may not marry."

"Dear God!"

"I said that I was accursed, did I not?"

They rode on for a little, silent.

"And you would be this . . . this Apostolic Protonotary?" Marion got out, at length. "It means as much to you? As this?"

"I must, Marion. It is not a case of what I *would*. I must. Otherwise I cannot be Coadjutor-Archbishop of St. Andrews. And only so can I preserve my uncle's rule in the Church. And if he goes down, before the reformers, the self-seekers and the English party — then the Church goes down. If the Church is to resist this flood, then it must be purged. Much that is sinful and wrong must be cleansed. But from above, not below. This I have been trying to do, through the Primate. But it is not in Gavin Dunbar to do it, to effect it. And if not he, who else will be

Primate? James Hepburn, now Bishop of Moray, Bothwell's half-brother! That knave! There is no choice before me."

Levelly she spoke. "It is as well, then, that you kept our marriage so secret, all those years ago. Perhaps you thought of this, of course? For you were ever far-sighted, Davie!"

He bit his lip. "Marion — what can I say? How can I tell you?"

"You have told me enough, have you not? Although it pains you to say it, I can see you would have our marriage over. Finished. Like . . . King Henry!"

"No! Oh, my dear — do not say it! This is a grievous coil, but it need make little difference in our lives here. Nothing shall, or can, destroy the reality of our union. Here at Ethie all shall be as it has been. Only, in the eyes of the Church, I shall not be married."

"How can that be? When, indeed, the Church married us?"

"There are irregular unions. On which the Church, if need be, can turn a blind eye."

"Ours was not irregular, Davie. Gibbie married us. In all honesty."

"Aye. But even Gibbie knows, I think, where Holy Church's true interests lie!"

"And the others who witnessed it? The Prioress Elizabeth? And the brothers of Restenneth? All here who know us husband and wife?"

"All good servants of the Church. Knowing the dangers that face it. All will keep quiet."

"So — you have thought of all. All is planned," she said wearily. "It could not be otherwise, I suppose. With David Beaton! I am to be mistress. Wife no longer. That you may fulfil your destiny."

"That Scotland may be saved. And the Church. Only that. Only that could warrant it."

"Warrant . . .?"

"Marion, try to understand."

"Oh, I understand, Davie — understand very well. Give me time. Time to accept. As accept I must. There is no choice, is there?" Suddenly she drew a quick breath. "Davie — the children! What of them? What of George and Elizabeth? If we are to be no longer married, they are . . . they are . . . bastards!"

He did not answer that.

"Davie!" she insisted. "Do you hear me? You, who think of

everything. Have you thought of this? Your children. George. Elizabeth. And this one to come. Bastards! Illegitimate!"

"They can be, shall be, legitimated," he muttered.

"Legitimated! Has it come to that . . .?"

"I am sorry, Marion — sorry. I have tortured and racked my wits to discover a way out. And found none."

"No? So be it, then. Get my horse, and let us return home."

"Can you forgive me?"

She turned in his arms again, to search his face. "Yes, Davie — I forgive you. For this is the man I married — or did not marry! This is the man I took, for better or for worse. I should not make complaint — for I knew always that you were of this quality. That you could do the like, if you must. Once we agreed that marriage, for a churchman, was cost indeed. And you said that you would pay that cost, whatever it was. Well — it seems that the time has come to pay that price. And I must pay it also. Aye, I forgive you, Davie. But . . . will our children?"

He bowed his head, and reined his horse around.

Chapter Seventeen

IN the abbot's lodging of the Abbey of Holyrood, so much more palatial than anything in the adjoining royal palace of Holyrood-house, the three men looked at David Beaton with varying expressions, admiring, grim, doubtful. Abbot Robert Cairncross, the Treasurer, was admiring; Gilbert Ogilvy, Dean of St. Andrews, was grim; and Patrick Barclay of Collairnie, Chamberlain of the Diocese of St. Andrews was doubtful. But at least they were all impressed, seriously concerned.

"You recognise, my lord, that this will have the effect of dividing the Church, not uniting it?" Barclay said. "That it will drive a wedge between the regular clergy, the monastic Orders, and the parish priests. That it will gain you no esteem from the majority of the prelates of this land, be they bishops, abbots or priors. And these hold forty seats in Parliament. Can you afford so to offend them?"

"You have no lofty opinion of your superiors in God, Patrick!" David answered, with a faint smile. "I ask, rather — can I afford not to? The Church must be reformed from within, if it is to withstand the blast of would-be reformers from without."

"Aye — but so soon! To signalise your appointment as Apostolic Protonotary thus swiftly, with so harsh a measure. There have been no Visitations in Scotland for long. Half a century."

"To the Church's sorrow and corruption. The more reason that they should be resumed now. Before is it too late."

Cairncross nodded. "I agree. Everywhere the Church is under assault. It is not merely this Luther and his theories. There are many who know nothing of Luther who yet point out scandals, shames and corruptions in the Church, here as elsewhere in Christendom. Holy Church must set her house in order, or she will fall — as she has fallen in Germany, is falling in England. It is no time for half-measures — as they have discovered in France."

"But what of the realm, my lords? If the Church stands divided by your Inquisition — the realm assailed already by grievous division and treachery? With Angus and Bothwell sworn to bring down the King, in England? Is this the time to weaken your own, and you uncle's, authority thus, David? To throw away the support of many prelates. To give Bishop Hepburn the support you will forfeit? Is this the time?"

"It is always the time to do what is right," Gilbert Ogilvy declared shortly.

"You take too short a view, Patrick. And too narrow," David said, from the window. "You look only at Scotland. You must look further. In especial at England. And France. These raids on the Border are grievous. But they are not the worst of Henry's attacks on Scotland. How much worse if he can bring about the collapse of the Church in Scotland. Which is what he seeks to do. He pours in gold, to that end. He trains dissidents in England, so-called reformers, and sends them here. He knows that the Church is King James's surest support and buckler. If he brings it down, His Grace has only the nobles — and God save him from them! Henry's agitators do not preach of Martin Luther so much as point to the failings of churchmen. Particularly the monastic Orders, the abbeys and priories. We must set them to rights."

"Yes, my lord. But . . ."

"Then there is France. King Francis is putting down the reformers with a strong hand, his Huguenots. Yet he is still in uneasy league with Henry, who encourages them. I believe that we can separate Francis and Henry, to Scotland's great benefit. Using, amongst other matters, the weal of Holy Church. We must fight the reformers, therefore, on this score also."

"Fight the reformers, yes. But not your fellow churchmen!"

"Patrick—how better to fight them, man, than by silencing them? By removing the causes of their complaint. The true causes. I have never denied that the Church has grievous faults. Which require to be purged. But from within, by herself. The Holy Father agrees with me. Gives me authority so to act."

"These Visitations, Davie—my lord? Where do we start?" Gilbert Ogilvy demanded, with his usual practicality.

"Where but at my own Abbey of Arbroath! Commence there—and there be most severe. Most offences are already cleansed, as we know. But some small failures remain, I have no doubt. You and Patrick together, thereafter, will visit every abbey and religious house in the land. It will take years. You will inspect, remonstrate, and draw up reports. To present to an Inquisitorial Council on which the Chapter-General of each Order will be represented. These things in especial you will look to. Their accumulated wealth. How much of parish revenues they pay to vicars and curates, and how much they retain for themselves. No curates to receive less than Twelve Pounds in the year. How much, or how little, the rules of the various Orders are adhered to. The due observance of worship, services, choirs and works. The open keeping of women in monastic houses. The hiring of servants to do the work of the monks. The demanding of burial dues and offerings. You will think of many other common failings, I have no doubt. All to be truly reported, with favour to none. There will be wrath and threats, I know —therefore I chose you, Gibbie, for you will be unmoved by such. And no abbot or prelate can have any true complaint—for such Visitations are ordained in the rules of every Order in every part of the Church. Regular inspections by duly appointed officers. As Apostolic Protonotary I appoint you such officers. To report to the Inquisition which I shall also set up, under Abbot Robert here. With the full authority of the Primate and of the Holy See."

They looked at each other. If any wondered how Archbishop James Beaton, who had garnered a greater fortune from the Church than any other man in Scots history, came to authorise this Inquisition, none voiced their thoughts. At least, David Beaton had been instrumental in expending most of that fortune. And his Papal authority was undisputed; there were only seven Apostolic Protonotaries appointed in all Christendom, with undefined but almost unlimited powers. How David Beaton had persuaded the Pope so to appoint him was a matter for speculation.

"How will my lord of Glasgow look on this, David?" Cairncross wondered. "If he was to move against it, it would be difficult to carry through."

"He will not dare to come out against it, I think. He will not controvert the Pontiff's authority. Also, as Chancellor, he needs me, and knows it. Moreover, Gavin Dunbar, whatever he lacks, is honest, after his fashion. He has little to fear from such investigation . . ."

An urgent knocking at the door heralded a monk, somewhat flustered. "My lords—His Grace!" he exclaimed. "His Grace, the King. He is here. Would speak with you . . ."

The King himself thrust the man aside, and strode into the tapestry-hung chamber.

James, now within weeks of attaining his majority, had become a well-built, good-looking and lusty young man, with a wary eye to counter his impulsive nature. Careless in dress, easy in manner, he yet had an undeniable air of authority about him.

"Master Davie," he exclaimed. "They told me that you would be here. With Master Robert. There is evil tidings. From the Border. Invasion again. A great raid. Angus and Bothwell together. With Percy of Northumberland. Burning and slaying. Jedforest and Teviotdale are ablaze. It is not to be borne! I *will* not bear it!"

The others had risen, and were eyeing the angry young monarch with concern.

"The Laird of Buccleuch . . .?" David asked.

"The word is from him. He has fought, and been defeated. There was treachery again. With the Turnbulls and Armstrongs. You must call the Council. At once. We must raise a host. To go punish these traitors. I myself will lead it . . ."

"Aye, Sire. But to what purpose?" David put to him. "You have done the like twice already. At your royal approach, the raiders slip back over the Border into England. They know that

231

you cannot follow them there, the King of Scots, without provoking Henry of England to outright war."

"Then war let it be, by God! Am I to stomach this?"

"No, Sire. But war with England is too high a price to pay to be even with Douglas and Hepburn. As your royal father proved at Flodden! Send a host, yes. Burn some Douglas and Hepburn castles, some Turnbull and Armstrong peels. Hang some of the Border mosstroopers who aid these treacherous lords. Send somebody after them into England if you will, to burn and slay in turn, to teach them a lesson. But do not yourself go, Sire. Or seem to countenance it. If Henry crossed your Border, in person – that would be different. A declaration of war. But he does not. He sends Northumberland, and uses your rebels. Do not put yourself in the wrong, before all the princes of Christendom, by setting a foot in England, however righteous your cause."

"But, man – am I to bow before him? Knuckle to Henry, like the vassal he would have me?"

"Not so, Your Grace. But there are better ways of striking back at Henry Tudor than with a sword."

"More words, my lord Abbot!"

"Aye, words, Sire. Words can be potent things. Particularly French words!"

"Eh . . .? French? What mean you?"

"I mean, Your Grace, that King Francis can hit Henry more shrewdly than you can. Send me to France. I know King Francis. He used to honour me with his friendship. I believe that I can detach him from his alliance with England. That would hurt Henry a deal more than any armed expedition over the Border."

"You think it possible? How could it be done? They have been allied now for many years."

"Henry, Sire, has frequently proposed your marriage to his daughter the Princess Mary. Rightly, you have always rejected this – for he would but use his daughter to assail you, to undermine you, as he has used your royal mother, his sister. But King Francis also has a daughter, Madeleine. Now nearing marriageable age."

"Aye. But they say that she is weakly. Sickly."

"But beautiful, Sire. The sickness may have been but some childish trouble. She is but fifteen. I am told that she is the fairest flower in France!''

James licked his lips. He was notably impressionable with regard to women, and already his adventures in that direction were the talk of the country. He did not so much tie himself to recognised mistresses as dip and taste and move on at large in the country, sampling noble and simple alike, rich and poor, young and less young. Indeed the monarch's favourite diversion was to roam his realm in disguise, often under the pseudonym of the Goodman of Ballengeich.

"Beautiful, you say? And but fifteen?"

"Talented also. I have heard that she sings like a lintie. And indites poetry."

He knew his James — who, with all his philandering experience was at heart an incurable romantic, like his father before him.

"M'mmm. Aye, well. I had not thought of marriage yet awhile, mind . . ."

"Perhaps not, Sire. Yet it might be wise to consider it, nevertheless. For so long as you have no heir, you will have trouble with the Hamiltons, my lord of Arran being next heir to the throne after the Duke of Albany who has abjured any succession. They would have you childless, I know."

"You think it? But . . . would Francis give me his daughter?"

"I believe that he could be persuaded. In especial if I was to tell him that, if I could not gain you a Princess of France, I should go on to see the Emperor Charles. Who has a young widowed sister, the Queen of Hungary. Less desirable, but possible! Francis hates the Emperor above all men, who occasioned his defeat at Pavia and lost him Milan. He would not wish an alliance between Scotland and the Empire."

"Ha! This requires thinking on. This lady of Hungary. Is she . . .? H'mm." He cleared his throat, and glanced over at Gilbert and Barclay. "But these are privy matters, not for discussion before others . . ."

"True, Your Grace. And so we shall discuss them, later. But these are my good friends, the Dean of St. Andrews and the Chamberlain. They are entirely to be trusted. Moreover, there is another reason why I should journey to France. Which concerns them, as churchmen. Francis is a good churchman also. He has given the Cardinal of Lorraine, and his brother the Duke de Guise, the fullest powers to put down the reforming heresy in his realm. With the Emperor and Spain against him, he must remain in good odour with the Pope. If I was to lay before him what Henry Tudor was doing to undermine and bring down the Church in Scotland, he could not but be incensed against Henry. And if I was going on to visit the Pope in Rome thereafter, I think that Francis would perceive that action was required of him. Holy Church united against Henry the heretic! You see?"

King James laughed. "Aye, Master David—I see! You are a canny carle! I think you must needs go to France. And, God's eyes—I think that I might go with you! It would be a notable ploy!"

David blinked. "Alas, Sire—that is scarcely possible. Not now. Not yet, I fear. With your royal self out of Scotland, who knows what your enemies would attempt. Angus. Bothwell . . ."

Chapter Eighteen

JAMES STEWART had his way—but not that year. It was in fact three years later, in 1536, before he set out on his notable ploy, his romantic quest for a bride—three years in which an uneasy balance was maintained in Scotland, not without difficulty, and Henry of England's continued threats and menaces were kept approximately at bay. David Beaton went alone to France—or at least, with fellow-envoy Sir Thomas Erskine, in keeping with the canny Scots custom of always sending two ambassadors on any mission, of different parties, to ensure if possible probity of behaviour. His visit had been, in the main, successful. He had brought home the promise of a French wife for his sovereign—not the beauteous Princess Madeleine who was pronounced too delicate to marry, but Mary de Bourbon, daughter of the Duke of Vendôme; and he had managed to drive something of a wedge between King Francis and King Henry. The Anglo-French alliance was not actually cancelled, but it had become much impaired, with mutual suspicions rampant. In consequence, the English had had to be much more discreet in their attitude to Scotland, their dread of war on two fronts being very real. War in four fronts indeed—for Henry was also, of course, at logger-heads with the Empire and with the Pope.

Nevertheless the projected royal marriage had been delayed

and delayed—to David's marked concern. Too many interests were at work against it. The Hamiltons, who were anxious that the King should remain unmarried; the pro-English party; King Henry, who still would have his daughter Queen in Scotland; even the Emperor, whose policy was to isolate France from all supporting alliances. Between them they had managed to hold up the match as months extended into years, while James fretted.

David had, in the end, had to make still another visit to France, and to Rome, endeavouring to smooth out these difficulties, and to keep King Francis, under pressure from all sides, steady to the Auld Alliance. But at least these prolonged absences abroad had their advantages. In Church matters, in that it meant that others had the unpleasant duty of putting down heresy with a strong hand; and in his private concerns, it allowed time for the uncomfortable situation with Marion Ogilvy to resolve itself somewhat, without David having to see too much of her in the interim. His love for her was as strong as ever, but he did not fail to perceive the advantages of love at a distance meantime. Young George and Elizabeth, with the new baby, Margaret, all had been through the expensive and rather humiliating process of legitimation, by Act of Parliament and royal assent—which was the first that most people had heard of their mother, the Apostolic Protonotary's mistress, or "chief lewd" as Sir James Hamilton of Finnart described her during the process.

But now, in the autumn of 1536, conditions in Scotland seemed sufficiently settled for the King safely to leave the country for a spell, to pursue his marital destiny. So, with a large and glittering retinue, in no fewer than seven vessels—largely paid for out of Church revenues and fines—King James sailed from Leith for France, the Lord Privy Seal and Apostolic Protonotary in attendance, leaving as Council of Regency the Archbishop of St. Andrews, Primate, the Archbishop of Glasgow, Chancellor, and the Earl of Moray, James's illegitimate half-brother, their hands guided by Robert Cairncross, Treasurer. Sir James Hamilton of Finnart travelled with the King—largely because David Beaton by no means dared leave him behind.

From the moment of stepping aboard his ship, James Stewart threw off all cares and worries of state, and became no more than a high-spirited young man embarked on high holiday. The royal flotilla was favoured with fair winds all the way, and the voyage developed into a carefree excursion over satin seas, with music, gaming, practical jokes and races between the vessels. James's only complaint was that they had brought no women for their sport—to which David diplomatically pointed out that not only might such have looked a little strange on this bridal quest, but that it would leave them all in much better fettle to deal with the French ladies when they reached their destination.

A sharp look-out was kept, of course, for interception by English ships—but none materialised.

They reached Dieppe ten days later, to a thunderous royal salute of cannon—which unfortunately had the effect of depressing King James somewhat, bringing back recollections of Tantallon. However, the appearance of King Francis's son, the Dauphin Henry, with the Cardinal of Lorraine, on the quay to meet him, banished his frowns.

The Dauphin was a pale and weedy youth of seventeen, uninspiring to a degree. But the Cardinal was markedly otherwise, a tall, handsome man in his mid-twenties, dark, saturnine and slender as a rapier, dressed in the height of fashion in scarlet velvet, with otherwise no hint of his clerical standing. His intelligence was obvious, his manners impeccable, his elegance extraordinary. David, who had not met him previously, was impressed by his youth—taken in conjunction with his bloody reputation.

After an exchange of courtesies and presents, a start was made on the long journey to Paris. The Frenchmen had come provided with a vast number of horses and huge baggage-train, and they made a lengthy and most splendid cavalcade. And an unhurried one. Very soon it became evident that this was to be no expeditious ride to the Capital, but a leisurely and festive progress through France.

If the Dauphin was but poor company, the same could not be said about the Cardinal, whose swift wit and mordant humour appealed to the Scots—in especial to Sir James Hamilton, with whom he seemed to find much in common. David himself could not be quite at ease with him, fellow-churchmen as they were. James was impressed—but not infrequently eyed the Cardinal askance, his romantic soul affronted by the Frenchman's cynical attitudes. All along the route he had organised entertainments for the visitors — displays, pageants, joustings, bear and bull baitings, receptions. This made for very delayed journeying, often with less than a score of miles covered in a day. Great tented camps had been erected for them at short intervals, and nothing was overlooked for their comfort and amusement — including ladies, who were much appreciated by all — save unfortunately King James and the Abbot of Arbroath, who felt, in their positions, precluded from active measures of approval, despite the Cardinal's example; a galling situation.

At the town of Gisors an especial entertainment awaited them — a huge *auto-da-fé*, a mass-burning of no less than fifty heretics, men and women, with the Cardinal applying the first brand. This was a divertissement not much to the taste of most of the Scots — and the Cardinal was perceptive enough to recognise it after a little while. Next morning he confided to David Beaton that he would cancel the mass-drowning of further reformers arranged for the following evening in the River Epte.

After five days of this, King James also came to confide in David, in his private tent.

"See you, Master Davie," he declared, "I have had a sufficiency of this! I came to France to seek a queen — not to idle around the country and watch folk burn. That ninny, the Dauphin, says now that his father is not even in Paris yet. He is somewhere in the south, apparently — but will be in Paris to greet us when we reach there after six or seven more days of this!"

David nodded. "I had heard as much, Sire. It is but the French habit. Time is less important to them . . ."

"Then I care not for it. I am no idler. I intend to gang my ain gait."

"What do you mean, Your Grace? If King Francis is not to be in Paris for a week, then what harm is there in thus idling? Better than for the King of Scots to seem to kick his heels waiting for him in Paris."

"Perhaps. But nevertheless I am going to leave this creeping progress. I am going on ahead to Vendôme. It is to see this Princess Mary of Vendôme that I am come to France, is it not? To see if she will serve me for a wife."

David drew a hand over mouth and chin. "You came, rather, to *marry* her, Sire — did you not? All was arranged, decided."

"Not by me!" James said sharply. "Only by you, if it was

so. If we were to wed, regardless of all, then she could have come to me, in Scotland. As would have been more proper. Think you I came all the way to France for nothing? I came to see *whom* I would wed. To see, and choose, Master Davie — not to be married off like some ward of the Council! I am the King."

The other moistened his lips. "This is the first that I have heard of it, Sire! The first time that you have, h'm, honoured me with this confidence! Despite the fact that I have twice come to France as your envoy in the matter!"

"*My* envoy?" James said, raising his reddish eyebrows. "Or your own, my lord?"

They stared at each other.

Then James moved over, to clap David on the shoulder, smiling suddenly. "Be not so taken aback, man. Here is nothing so ill. I hope to marry a French wife, yes — but I would choose her myself. At the least see what choice there is. I go first to Vendôme. We shall see how looks this Mary de Bourbon. If I like her — very well. If not — why, I go elsewhere."

"But . . . Your Grace — how can you do that? She is expecting you. Later. To wed her. How can you go, to . . . to inspect her?"

"Easily, my friend. I shall go undisclosed. Secretly. As I have visited full many a house, at home."

David paced about his tent. "How shall you be accepted, Sire? At Vendôme? If they do not know you for the King? How shall a mere stranger come close to the Princess? Your Grace's French is good — but you will be known as from another land . . ."

"I have thought of that, Master Davie. We shall go together. Myself as your esquire and secretary."

"I, Sire? I cannot do that."

"Yes, you can. And shall, my friend — since I command it! You have been to Vendôme before. They know you. It will not seem strange. That you should come ahead of your king, to make preparations."

David sighed. "How is it to be achieved, Sire?" he asked flatly. "How are we to win clear of the Dauphin and the Cardinal? You cannot ride away and leave them thus, like . . . like . . ."

"That I leave to you, my lord Abbot. You have the nimble wits, and know these people. They are your friends, not mine. See you to it." Smiling, and waving a kingly hand, James moved to the tent door. "Tomorrow we ride, Master Davie. Alone."

A subject cannot blankly refuse his king, and James was entirely determined. Next forenoon, the two of them rode off south-westwards, David intimating confidentially to the Dauphin and the Cardinal that King James, with himself as chaplain and confessor, desired to make a very private pilgrimage, as soon after landing in France as was possible, to Orleans, to the tomb and shrine of Saint Jeanne D'Arc. The Cardinal cocked a politely sceptical eyebrow at this, but was in no position to detain the King. The truants left a number of very wondering Frenchmen behind them.

Vendôme was quite a long way off, in the Orleannais, over a hundred miles south-west of Paris, and another fifty from their present position, requiring considerable hard riding if the expedition was not to be unduly prolonged. King James was in the best of spirits, and it was not long before David Beaton, despite himself, found his forebodings slipping from him and a more carefree, live-for-the-moment mood taking its place. For all his reputation, experience and position, David was not essentially a sober-minded man. Indeed, part of him was almost as persistently youthful as were his looks — neither any asset to his career. Now, this golden October, he found himself riding the lanes of the Ile de France and the Orleannais laughing and singing at least in some harmony with his headstrong liege lord, a happier man than he had been for many a day.

They covered a great mileage that first day, and reached the town of Chartres by darkness, putting up at a modest inn. James had changed, en route, into more inconspicuous clothing, and now insisted upon being referred to as Jacob by David, with all royal salutations forbidden.

Next day they turned some way aside to visit Orleans, and the shrine of Saint Joan, David declaring this to be essential to substantiate his story. After paying very perfunctory respect at the martyr's tomb, but leaving a bag of gold pieces with the astonished friar in charge, they pressed on, due westwards now.

By making a major effort they came to the ancient town of Vendôme, on the Loire, crouching beneath its proud, many towered castle, amongst vinyard-clad hills, before nightfall.

As was to be anticipated, with King James not expected for a couple of weeks yet, arrangements were not fully advanced for the great reception. But a large party was already assembled nevertheless, and it was to a gay company that the travellers arrived. The Duke of Vendôme himself, related to the King of Navarre, was not present – having gone to Paris to meet the royal visitors there and to conduct them hither – but his daughter and many of her friends and relatives were there, and in high spirits.

The Abbot of Arbroath's arrival occasioned much surprise but gratifying enthusiasm, and his red-headed and uninhibited secretary was welcomed freely.

Mary de Bourbon proved to be a cheerful, hearty and un-complicated young woman, by no means beautiful – indeed very slightly deformed with one shoulder lower than the other – but otherwise well-enough made, and good company. James got on well with her, from the first meeting, for she was free and frank – to David's enormous relief. It seemed as though the clouds which had formed over the strange odyssey might disperse of their own accord.

David now became anxious to get the King away from Vendôme before complications might arise – especially as James was tending to become over-familiar for a secretary with the other guests in general and with Mary de Bourbon in particular. Also it looked very odd for David himself to be lingering here, when he should have been with his master on the way to Paris and the King of France's reception. His excuse for coming to Vendôme had been to bring a royal gift, in the form of a great jewel, and to assure himself that all was suitably in train for the arrival of his monarch. This could not be spun out to occupy any great length of time.

But James would not hear of leaving. There was so much to do for the reception of the King of Scots, and it tickled him to assist thereat – decorations to be put up, triumphal arches erected, pavilions to be pitched, wine-fountains to be contrived, per-formers to be schooled.

So three days passed. Then, with a colourful party of new-comers arrived another princess, Mary de Guise, Duchess of Longueville, sister of the Cardinal of Lorraine – to the consterna-tion of David Beaton, if not his royal companion. The situation promptly took several turns for the worse.

Mary de Guise was a friend of Mary of Bourbon, of approximately the same age, rank and background, but otherwise as dissimilar as could well be imagined. Where the Vendôme daughter was artless, uncomplicated and homely, the newcomer, without being actually beautiful, was one of those women who consciously or otherwise are a challenge to all men, graceful, magnetic, captivating. She was tall, darkly handsome of feature, with a glowing eye, a deep husky voice, and supreme assurance. The impressionable James was entranced by this man-trap from the first glance, and most evidently did not mind who perceived it. Not that he was alone in this; but his lowly position as secretary made his fervour the less suitable. Not that the lady herself appeared to mind. Apparantly she had left her husband, of the blood-royal, in Paris, to take part in the welcome to the King of Scots, and had come on here to support her friend.

David was now more concerned than ever to get his charge away from Vendôme. Even though the daughter of the house was not as yet sufficiently interested in the red-haired Scots secretary to be grievously upset by the obvious transference of his allegiance to her friend, the time would come when, in retrospect, his behaviour would not lack its due significance.

But James, if he had been reluctant to go before, was now the more determined to linger. In the end, growing additionally anxious that they might keep King Francis waiting in Paris, David, grown desperate, had most unsuitably to blackmail his monarch into departing, by threatening to disclose his true identity to all concerned. The King's reaction was strange. He actually laughed.

"My friend—you are too late!" he said. "Mary of Guise, at least, already knows it."

"What!" David gasped. "You have told her?"

"She as good as guessed it. She is no dullard, that one. Last night, when we were alone, she asked me who I truly was. She said that she knew that I was no secretary. She declared that you, my lord Abbot, went in some fear of me! And she knew that the King of Scots had red hair! I could not but confess to the charge."

"God save us—then all is lost!"

"No. I swore her to secrecy. And she is a woman who can keep a secret, see you. Of that I am assured."

"You are exceeding knowledgeable as to the Duchess of Longueville!" David asserted grimly.

James smiled.

"You were alone with her? Last night."

"Aye, my holy Father-in-God! There is a most convenient pavilion in the water-garden!"

"But this is the sheerest folly, Sire! Would you ruin all? A married woman, in cousinship to the King of France! Almost worse, sister to that devil, Charles de Guise, the Cardinal!"

"Tut, man—she is safe enough. Do not cluck like an old hen!"

"Your Grace! This finishes the matter, I swear! We leave for Paris tomorrow morning—or I go to Mary de Bourbon of Vendôme and tell her all. And thereafter leave you, to win out of this coil as best you may!"

The other grinned. "Very well, Master David—I will come with you to Paris now. We must not keep King Francis waiting—although he, it seems, would have done as much to me! No doubt Mary de Guise will still be here when I come back . . .!"

It was over one hundred miles to Paris, but by hard riding the truants reached there by noon of the second day. They had no difficulty in finding their retinue, quartered in the old Castle of the Louvre, having arrived only the day before. They found a double agitation reigning there—not only anxiety over the Scots King's absence, but that of His Most Christian Majesty of France also. The Dauphin, fluttering between palaces like some twittering but mournful fowl, had to admit that his father had not yet put in an appearance either. The Cardinal seemed icily amused, but everybody else was mightily relieved when King James burst into hearty laughter over this ridiculous situation, and declared that he was going to bed for some major sleeping.

Fortunately King Francis reached the Palais Royal that evening, and sighs of relief were emitted all round. The meeting of the two monarchs would take place next day, as planned.

That night an unobtrusive messenger came to David Beaton's quarters to convey him secretly to the French King's presence. Not entirely surprised by this summons, he followed his escort.

Francis awaited him in a small private room off an ornate salon. When they were alone, he came and clasped David round the shoulders.

"Well, my old friend," he said. "It is good to see you. How do you always contrive to look so young? You seem but little

242

older than when first I knew you, twenty years ago. Yet you must be near to forty. Or more? As for me — *helas*, just look at me! Only a few years older." And he spread his arms ruefully.

Francis had certainly changed from the slender, elegant young Count of Anjoulême of former days. He had thickened, grown a belly and become florid of face. Nevertheless he was still an impressive-looking man, and every inch a king.

"Your Majesty is too critical of yourself. And too kind to me!" David assured, touched. "I hope that I see you well? Not over-borne by the cares of state?"

"At least you see me, you mean! And feared that you might not? In time, and, *ma foi*, you were almost right! I have had the Devil's own task to reach Paris in time not to insult your James. I have ridden the length of France in six days!"

"The length of France? Then you were not hunting at Fontain-bleau, Sire?"

"Did you think it? No, I have been down in the Pyrenees. In Navarre. On sorer business."

"Navarre? Into Spain, Sire?"

"Not into Spain. Navarre is not yet Spanish, whatever the Emperor claims. That is why I, the King of France, must needs go running to reason and plead with Henry of Navarre. Henry, you see — a curse on his thick head — has become sadly infected with the doctrines of Luther — or with those of that Picardy lawyer, Jean Calvin, which is the same thing, or worse. He cherishes heretics and reforming zealots. To the grievous danger of France."

"Danger, Your Majesty? Can little Navarre endanger great France?"

"Aye, David, she can. The State of Navarre, in that it straddles the Pyrenees on both sides, is in effect in both France and Spain, a small part carved out of each. Spain has been claiming its overlordship — therefore King Henry of Navarre has turned to France to maintain his independence. I have supported him — for we do not want the Spaniards across the Pyrenees and into France. But now, this flirting with the so-called protestants endangers all. Charles, who is the Most Catholic King of Spain on the one hand, is Emperor on the other, and it is in the Empire that this reforming heresy has made greatest headway. Many of his German states have already thrown off allegiance to Rome.

243

The Emperor Charles, outside Spain, has become the protector of the protestants. Henry of Navarre now veers towards him. *I* support Holy Church. Hence the danger to France. If Navarre accepts the protection of the Emperor, the Spaniards will move over the mountains and in at my backdoor!"

David rubbed his chin. "The King of Navarre is a fool if he believes that the Spaniards will sustain him against the Holy See."

"My kinsman of Navarre *is* a fool. A well-meaning, amiable fool. For two weeks I have been trying to make him see it. Without avail. He will hear naught of ill against Charles. It is madness."

"Madness, yes, Sire. Madness that a weak fool should endanger Holy Church. As well as France. And even greater madness, I think, that at this sore pass in the Church's history, the two great Catholic powers of France and Spain should be at each other's throats! And tiny Navarre able to use them against each other thus."

"M'mmm." The King looked at his visitor thoughtfully. "But that is the way of affairs. France and Spain have seldom been friends."

"But they could, and should, be, Sire. And if they were, all Christendom would be the richer. And the safer."

"This is strange counsel from David Beaton! Once, I recollect, you advised otherwise!"

"Times have changed, Your Majesty. Few could have foreseen how this reforming heresy would endanger the whole fabric of Christ's Church. For long I have looked on this warfare with sorrow. And here, I think, is opportunity to heal it."

"What do you mean?"

"This of Navarre. Use King Henry not as a force to divide you, but bridge. To bring you together. Make this heretical prince to save Holy Church. The Emperor Charles cannot be happy over the position of Navarre and his reforming zeal. Nor of his own divided position. At heart he is a Spaniard, His Most Catholic Majesty of Spain. I believe that he might welcome a move to end this hostility. To keep Navarre from being a heretical canker between your two realms. Let Henry of Navarre be your pretext, warrant . . . and ambassador!"

Francis was silent for a little.

"It would greatly please the Pope," David went on. "Who knows — he might even give you back Milan!"

"Ah, yes — the Pope! Undoubtedly it would please His Holiness. And only two hours ago, somebody told me that you and your young King James, since landing in France, had made a most hurried and secret journey to meet the said Holy Father, somewhere on my borders! Could it be that you act on his behalf, rather than on mine, my friend?"

"Your Majesty has been misinformed. There was no meeting with the Pope. But none can doubt the effect of this on His Holiness."

"Nor, I think, on the King of England!"

"True, Sire. Henry Tudor — who still signs himself King of France as well as of England — would be isolated. Alone. If the Emperor could be swung against heresy."

"And Scotland advantaged!"

"Precisely, Sire. Scotland advantaged. With France. With Christendom."

"You were ever a notable plotter, David! I will have to consider this. Consider deeply. But . . . that is not why I summoned you here. Privily. It was to seek information about your King. I am told that he is a young man of independent mind? Tell me . . ."

When David had answered the other's questions as best he might, and an attendant had been sent for to escort him back to the Louvre, Francis touched his arm.

"And now, old friend — where were you and our royal guest for the eight days between leaving Gisors and reaching here? I have told you where *I* was! My information is that you devoted less than one hour to the good Jeanne D'Arc at Orleans. Which leaves some time unaccounted for does it not?"

David, smiling, took a chance. "King James's independent mind took us to Vendôme, Your Majesty. He masquerading as my secretary. To cast an eye over Mary de Bourbon. Before deciding whether to wed her!"

"Ha! Did he, by God! Despite our compact, And with what result?"

"I think he decided, Your Majesty, that there might well be other young women in France who might repay some further consideration."

"You say so? *Parbleu!*" Francis slapped his thigh. "And who says that he is not right? Not I! Mother of God — I say James Stewart may have the right of it! I admire him the more. We must see what we can do for him in the matter! Never fear — I will keep your secret. And I will consider what you have said about the Emperor . . ."

The meeting of the monarchs, next morning, was a magnificent occasion, all glitter, ceremony, pomp and protocol, with only formalities, speeches, gifts and compliments exchanged. But even so, impressions were made. One in especial.

In the Throne-room of the Palais Royal, King Francis received his guest, to a great fanfare of trumpets, leaving the chair-of-state to come down from the dais, to grasp both King James's hands, kiss him on both cheeks, and turning, lead him up to present him to his Queen, and seat him on another throne alongside his own. But even as they went through all the formal motions, even the investing of the Scots monarch with the insignia of a Knight of St. Michael, David, from further back, could see that James Stewart's glance kept turning in a certain direction, to where, a little to one side, a young woman stood, beside Henry the Dauphin. It was the Princess Madeleine, the King's daughter, she of the delicate health.

Well might he look, of course. The girl was of the most exquisite and ethereal beauty. Great-eyed, fair, with the hectic flush of her trouble, of slight figure and slender build, she managed to combine an appearance of great vivacity with a wistful gravity, infinitely appealing. Intelligence, grace and a quiet serenity allied to a sort of inner electric urgency, made a potent and inevitable demand on a romantic young man.

It was the same during the less formal and more relaxed banquet, ball and masque which followed in the evening. James's attention was never for long directed elsewhere than upon the Princess Madeleine, and for the latter part of the proceedings he seldom left her side. A large proportion of the grace, wit, beauty and pulchritude of fair France was there for his admiration that night, but it was all too patent that he had only eyes for Madeleine de Valois. That she, for her part, was far from impervious to the attentions of the vehement, gallant and exalted guest, was equally clear.

King Francis was, at first, not a little amused by his daughter's rapid conquest. But as James's admiration became ever more emphatic and exclusive, he began to look a little concerned. He mentioned the matter to David, only part-humorously, after a while, pointing out that it would be a pity if Madeleine was to be courted sufficiently to involve her own affections in any serious degree. His physicians were united in declaring that the state of her health precluded any thought of marriage. If her life was not to be a long one, at least there must be no heartbreaks in it.

David assured the anxious father that King James's sudden involvements were frequent and apt to be of short duration. For himself, he was only a very little apprehensive, being thankful that at least his susceptible monarch's mind no longer seemed to dwell upon the Duchess of Longueville.

However, after a week wherein festivities, tournaments, pageants, play-actings, feastings and every sort of entertainment followed each other in bewildering profusion, and James Stewart in whose honour all was contrived, seemed only half aware of it, so greatly was his attention centred on Madeleine de Valois, David Beaton ventured a warning.

"Your Grace," he said, during an interval at a rout, with the ladies temporarily retired. "The Princess Madeleine is very beautiful, and worthy of all your so evident admiration. But it would be wise, would it not, to, h'mm, limit your royal attentions? Since she is not the lady you are going to marry, it would be unfortunate if . . ."

"Who says that I am not going to marry her, my lord Abbot?"

David's brows puckered. "Who? Why, Sire—there is no question of it. Can be none. You know that. It is impossible."

"Nothing is impossible, sir, from a subject to a king! In especial your king's choice of a wife."

" 'Fore God—you cannot mean this? Your Grace is not contemplating marriage with the Princess Madeleine?"

"I am not contemplating it, no. I intend it. We shall marry."

David shook his head, helplessly. "Sire—consider! For what do you marry? Not just to bed with a fair woman. That you may do with almost any you choose. Not for wit and talents, however notable. These you can enjoy without marriage. No—you wed to produce children. An heir to your throne. Can this lady give you that?"

"That is in God's will. But I have no reason to believe that she cannot. Is that all that marriage means to you, Master Davie? Child-making? Have you no thought beyond the bed? No notion of true love? Of the marriage of souls, as well as bodies? Of the great passion . . .?"

"I am not wholly ignorant of these, Sire. If they can be found in your royal marriage, none will be happier than I. But . . . your first requirement, I venture to assert, is a consort who can act the Queen in Scotland, and bear you an heir. This lady, fair as she is, suffers from the wasting sickness. Her physicians declare her unfit for marriage. As does her father, the King. If she *could* bear you a child, what sort would he be? Would you give Scotland a prince diseased from birth, lacking health and vigour? Possibly wits?"

"Sir—you presume! You go too far. You will speak more respectfully of my future wife. Your Queen to be. My mind is made up. Such talk, of children, is idle, of no certainty. The Princess's delicacy of health may be but passing, a matter of youth. Marriage could well be to her true weal. Happiness can be a great healer. I will give her that happiness. And she would have it so."

"My lord James—if that could be the outcome of your union, I would rejoice. But is it a sure base on which to build a royal match? Will this keep the Hamiltons out of your Stewart throne?"

"Enough, my lord! I will not barter more words with you on so sacred a matter. The issue is decided."

"Your Grace may command me. But you cannot command King Francis . . ."

"Leave King Francis to me, sir. He will not deny his daughter's happiness. And my most assured desire. Moreover, it is my royal command that you do not discuss this matter with him. I know well your abilities as a persuader. In this you shall not interfere— save at your peril! You understand, my lord?"

David bowed. "And Vendôme, Your Highness? Your visit to Vendôme?"

"That shall take place, as arranged. But my betrothal to the Princess Madeleine will be announced *before* we go."

"King Francis permitting!"

"King Francis will not refuse. Or I leave for Scotland forthwith . . ."

James Stewart had his way, King Francis being too fond of his daughter to forbid what her heart was so evidently set upon; nor, of course, was he wishful to antagonise the King of Scots. No one else was in a position to object. The bethrothal was announced, and intimation made that the royal marriage would be celebrated there in Paris on the first day of the New Year, 1537.

Thereafter, the projected and now somewhat embarrassing journey to Vendôme was embarked upon — although it was made only the first of a series of visits round other princely houses, to demonstrate the felicity of the royal lovers, and so made the Vendôme affair somewhat less pointedly an awkward anticlimax.

In the event, Mary of Bourbon took it all very well, both the revelation of the earlier subterfuge and the marital rebuff. Perhaps, in the presence of two kings and all the Court, she could do no other — but David Beaton, for one, gained a shrewd impression that she was in fact not a little relieved. King James indeed later informed him that the Duchess of Longueville had assured him, in confidence, that her friend was secretly in love with the young Count d'Auvars. As for Mary of Guise herself, James was evidently still in a mood to see her privately, to obtain such confidences, her husband's presence or none, and no unpleasantness developed in that quarter.

With the November weather deteriorating, a return was made to Paris, to prepare for the great wedding planned for six weeks ahead. This did not apply to David, however. After much closeting with King Francis, in various houses, he set off on business of his own, King James no longer, as was most evident, requiring his immediate services. He went north-east, first, to Brussels, to the Court of the Emperor Charles the Fifth. From thence he travelled south, to Rome, by a round-about route to avoid the winter Alps. He was back in Paris just in time for the Yuletide celebrations and his monarch's marriage.

Paris was full, that Yule. Half of Europe seemed to have assembled there — and most notably, the Emperor was represented at the wedding by an illustrious embassage, which certainly set tongues a-wagging. The Pope, with a like significance sent a resounding company including no fewer than six Cardinals other than Charles de Guise, who conducted the ceremony. The King of Navarre was there in person.

Whatever he though of the suitability of the bride, David was content with the wedding itself, and what it meant. It represented the harvest of so much that he had laboriously sown — and the sowing of so much more. His travels and discomforts, his secret conclaves, his importunings, manœuvrings and pulling of strings — these were beginning to show results.

The wedding itself was suitably magnificent, in the vast cathedral of Notre Dame — which was so crowded with the cream of the princes, nobility and clergy of all Christendom that there was no room for many of the celebrities. Only the representatives of Henry of England were absent — although undoubtedly his spies were present and by no means unmoved by all that went on. It was the most splendid nuptuals of any of the long line of Kings of Scots — and a most resounding demonstration of the persisting power and solidarity of Holy Church.

From an inconspicuous spot, David Beaton watched it all, and was satisfied.

James and Madeleine looked radiant, a thing seldom seen at royal weddings.

Chapter Nineteen

KING JAMES stalked the wet deck of his ship, frowning blackly at the long-awaited sight of his own realm and homeland, after nine months of absence. It was not reluctance to be back, or to face the problems of rule inevitably awaiting him — for he had been fretting to reach Scotland, and to show his beloved her new country, for days. It was the weather that infuriated him. For although it was late May, and the sun had shone throughout the voyage from Dieppe — indeed was still shining as they passed Dunbar and the East Neuk of Fife — the moment that their fleet had entered the wide mouth of the Firth of Forth, the grey clouds had come down to blanket all, and the chill rain had enveloped them. Now, approaching Leith harbour, the great bulk of Arthur's Seat that rose above Holyroodhouse, and the jagged outline of Edinburgh Castle, showed merely as misty vague shadows, with not a spot of colour or animation to the entire scene. It was maddening.

James, solicitous for his young wife's health, had deliberately delayed their journey north until now, so that the seas should be gentle and her arrival in Scotland congenial. She had been coughing a lot during the voyage, and the two French physicians who accompanied her had been shaking their heads and making gloomy prognostications. Now, they were gesticulating at the rain and greyness with Gallic dramatics and forebodings.

When presently, however, the young Queen herself appeared on deck, it was with no signs of gloom or dismay. She ran, smiling, to her husband's side, to take his arm and look shorewards, exclaiming eagerly, in typically appealing fashion. She was looking pale and perhaps a little thinner, her three months' pregnancy not yet showing; but her vivacity seemed if anything enhanced, and her great and lovely eyes even larger than ever.

At her back, David Beaton came hurrying with his cloak to throw over her shoulders.

To the distant rumble of cannon-fire from Edinburgh Castle, the vessels drew in to the quay at Leith, where great crowds were assembled in the rain.

"I am sorry, my love," James declared, holding her close. "This rain. You will esteem Scotland even worse than you have been told! But it does not always rain. And when the sun shines, it is a land of colour and light not to be matched. As you will discover."

"Never care, heart of my heart!" the girl cried. "I love the rain, this soft rain which kisses me welcome to your dear land!"

"May Your Grace say as much after weeks of it, at Holyrood!" Sir James Hamilton commented grimly, from behind them.

As the King turned hotly on the speaker, David intervened. "Sire — if you would have Her Grace dwell in sunshine, you should find her a house on the very eastmost point of your domains. At St. Andrews, for instance. I have found that there, and at the tip of Lothian, the sky is frequently clear when all the rest of the land is grey with cloud. You saw how it was as we passed Dunbar. Yet here . . ."

"That is an excellent notion, Master Davie. St. Andrews, yes. Near to Falkland, my love, where I hunt the deer. And from which the good Abbot here aided my escape from the evil Douglases. Aye, it shall be so. But no ordinary house, see you. A new house, a little palace for my heart's darling. That is it. See you to it, my lord. New-built, especially for Her Grace. A wedding-gift from Scotland for her Queen! A palace in the sun, for this fairest Lily of France. Where our child shall be born . . ."

"Oh, James, my adored!"

"It shall be done, Sire . . ."

As the royal vessel was warped in to the quay, and a gangway was run out, to the cheering of the crowds, musicians started up glad music and the official welcoming party, headed by the Archbishops of St. Andrews and Glasgow, moved forward. The Primate was looking very old and dissipated, and hobbling with gout. King James suddenly stopped to sweep up his Queen in his arms. Tall and muscular, with his bride all too light, he strode across the narrow gangway and over the wet slippery timbers of the quay, red head thrown back, in laughing pride, while the girl looked radiantly from her gallant husband to his wildly-applauding subjects. Reaching the firm ground of his ancient realm, he set her down, kissing her lustily on her parted lips, there before all.

"The threshold of my kingdom!" he cried. "Yours, now. All yours."

Madeleine stood, tears in her eyes, her slight figure made even more so by David Beaton's cloak, blinking a little. Then swiftly but gracefully she knelt there in the rain, and reached out to pick up a handful of the wet sandy soil and convey it to her lips. Kissing it, she exclaimed,

"The blessing of the good God be upon this dear earth, that shall henceforth be mine! And upon my beloved lord and husband! And upon all who walk it with us!"

Even the Hamiltons, thereafter, who saw no cause to rejoice in the arrival of a queen, could not withhold a welcome.

Scotland was all welcome, indeed, those next weeks. The Capital's own reception was delayed for a day or two until all was in readiness — the royal voyage home having been slightly more expeditious than anticipated — but when it was staged, it surpassed all that had ever been attempted heretofore, in pageantry, spectacle, parade and allegory, in fantasy and poetic declamation — and unfortunately in the somewhat long-winded speechifying, especially in Latin, beloved of the Scots. Other towns vied with Edinburgh to do homage to their new and beautiful queen, so different from the plain, embittered and ageing woman who had hitherto served them in that capacity. A romantic race at heart, despite their protective pose of stern dourness, the Scots, when they let themselves go, can be outdone by none in spirited celebration.

It was all most heartening, reassuring — and very tiring.

It might indeed be said that Queen Madeleine's life in Scotland was all welcome — for within six weeks of landing at Leith she was dead. Whether it was the climate, as the French physicians averred, or the effect of pregnancy on her consumptive condition, or exhaustion caused by the over-enthusiastic reception and constant emotional strain — who can tell? Perhaps she would have lived no longer in her own France. The blow fell suddenly, abruptly, in a flux of blood, and in her husband's arms. A stunned land turned from gay rejoicing to appalled mourning. Indeed mourning clothing was worn in Scotland, then for the first time — a French custom to bewail the fragile Lily of France.

Madeleine de Valois never saw her little palace in St. Andrews of the sun and sea — although David Beaton did just manage to have it finished in time, a day or two over the month his king had allowed him. The royal couple were indeed on the point of leaving to inspect it when the girl was stricken down.

If the nation was stunned, James was utterly prostrate in horror and grief, silent, appalled, overwhelmed. He shut himself away in a tower-room of Holyroodhouse, revealing as the days passed a new side to his nature, in utter surrender. He would neither eat nor drink, would speak to none, see none. To get him to attend the funeral, when Madeleine was laid to rest in the Abbey adjoining, taxed even David Beaton's powers of persuasion.

Thereafter David, in common with others, tried everything that he knew to arouse, at least, his heart-stricken prince, even though to allay his sorrow was impossible. But with little avail. James appeared entirely to have let go, to have abandoned the business of living as completely as hitherto he had embraced it. With accumulated matters of state requiring decision, and new problems coming up almost daily — not the least of which were inevitably concerning the French alliance thus tragically impaired — a firm hand on the rudder of the realm was imperative. Others might plot the course and hoist the sails, but for much the monarch's personal decision was indispensable.

David thought long and deeply about James's nature, to

discover, if he might, how he could arouse him. Wholeheartedness was the key to the King's character, obviously — wholeheartedness in attack, in enjoyment or in surrender and declension. If he was to be reached, it must surely be through playing on this pre-disposition. Within this framework his impatient delight to do battle, and his weakness for women, all women, stood out in especial. Since the second was a string over taut to play on now, perhaps, David tried the first.

During the absence in France the Douglases had not been entirely inactive, either in Border raiding or in plots within the kingdom. Two alleged conspiracies had been communicated to David, on his return neither seeming pressing or important enough to trouble the King with in his felicity. Now, in his despair, their revelation might stir him. He announced them now — and noted that James's lack-lustre eyes sharpened distinctly when he mentioned that they both concerned sisters of the Earl of Angus. One had married the Master of Forbes, and he, Huntly declared, was involved in a plot to bring back the Douglases secretly, and if necessary to murder the King. The other conspiracy, although probably both were linked, concerned her sister, Janet, the Lady Glamis, who was accused of a machination to effect the King's death by poison. How much truth there was in these charges, David did not know — but it surely behoved His Grace to investigate them?

He had judged aright. While James, for the moment, cared little for his own life, the suggestion that the odious Douglases might be actively seeking to deprive him of it, at last stirred the young man to violent resentment. Apparently he had not forgotten how to hate.

David now took a deep breath, a chance, and a major decision. "Sire," he said, "I have had other news this day, likewise. Notable news. From France, and from London. The Duke of Longueville has died. Husband to Mary De Guise."

James looked at him with a slight widening of the eyes, but said nothing.

"And King Henry Tudor, I am reliably informed, has besought the lady's hand in marriage! Already!"

"Damnation! No!" That was wrung out of his hearer. It was the first such outburst that he had produced in weeks.

"But yes, Sire. Henry, having gone through three wives,

would outwit you, out-play-you, with a French match. To win France back to his side. And Mary of Guise to his bed!"

"Fiend seize him! It shall not be, I say!"

David bowed. "As you say, Sire. But, if it is not to be, we must act fast. I believe that there is still time. Indeed, my message, from the Cardinal of Lorraine, hints as much. That he, a Prince of the Church, would have no heretic for a good-brother — especially one so sore on wives! And King Francis would spite Henry if he could. Short of outright challenge. They will hold up the match so long as they may. The Cardinal adds that his sister, with himself, sends Your Grace warmest greetings with humble reverence."

"She does?" King James, haggard but with life again about him, bit his lip. "A courier," he jerked. "Send a trusted courier to Francis. To Mary. Forthwith. Henry not to have her. You hear? There must be no English-French match."

"Why send a courier, Your Grace? Send me. I can do the business more expeditiously. Months will be saved. A French match for *Scotland* is as important as ever it was. As is an heir to your throne."

Long the younger man stared at him. Then, sighing, he nodded. "Aye. Go, and do as is required. If I must wed again, Mary of Guise will serve well enough. Mind, it will be no true marriage. But an empty shell. Tell her so. My only true wife lies in yon tomb. But . . . so be it."

"Yes, Your Grace. To be sure. That is understood. So, while you deal with Henry Tudor through the Douglases here, I will deal with him in France! I suggest a proxy wedding, if the lady will agree. Thus publicly to flout Henry, before all."

"Aye — that would flay my brutish uncle! Who could I send, to stand proxy . . .?"

"Your half-brother, Sire. The Earl of Moray. Of the blood-royal, though in bastardy. A man you may trust."

James nodded. "As you will. Take Moray . . ."

So David sailed once again the familiar road to France, only five months after leaving there, this time in the company of the astonishingly sober love-child of the ebullient James the Fourth and Flaming Janet Kennedy.

All along, everything went like clockwork, an uneventful

voyage, a quick journey from Dieppe, and satisfactory interviews with King Francis and the Cardinal, in Paris. David had been somewhat dreading giving details to her father of Queen Madeleine's stay in Scotland, and death, but in the event Francis was not difficult, having long been reconciled to his daughter's early end. He expressed himself as happy that at least she had gained her heart's desire before her passing, something denied to many. He made no difficulty, either, in the matter of Mary of Guise, agreeing that a Scottish-French match was more to be desired than ever, now that he had come to an agreement with the Emperor Charles. England was quietly to be isolated, and apostate Henry's demand for the lady's hand had been a major embarrassment.

Francis had a further acknowledgement to make. A ten-years peace with the Empire was to be signed, the Navarre danger had been quenched, and its King's heretical tendencies made harmless. France stood in better odour, therefore, with the Holy See, than for a century. And everywhere the Church stood strengthened. For all that, he had to thank his old friend David Beaton. In token of his gratitude, therefore, and under the authority of the Pragmatic Sanction which made him head of the Church in France, he herewith nominated and appointed the said David to the rich and vacant bishopric of Mirepoix, in the Languedoc, with French citizenship to hold it, and its annual revenue of ten thousand gold crowns. It was high time, he asserted, that Scotland's Apostolic Notary was something loftier than an abbot. The Holy Father had concurred in this, and wished to see the new bishop, in due course, in Rome.

David was much affected by this unexpected gesture. A French bishopric was bound to be more of an honour than anything else — but the ten thousand crowns that went with it each year was a magnificent gift, and the more welcome in that his uncle's fortune was by no means what it had been, thanks to his own open-handed spending in the cause of Church and realm. This was a princely income, for Scotland, and should banish not a few problems.

In company then with Charles de Guise and the Earl of Moray, David journeyed on to the province of Languedoc in the very south of France, to the city of Foix, in his see of Mirepoix, where, in the venerable cathedral, the Cardinal installed and consecrated him Bishop. Then they returned to Paris, where the Duchess of Longueville had been summoned.

David's interview with the tall, magnetic and assured Mary of Guise could scarcely have been more favourable. Here were two people of clear decision, who knew their own minds. Although the official intimation of the King of Scots' suit was to be an affair of ceremony, with the King of France and the Duchess's four distinguished brothers present, David contrived a private meeting first, in the Palais de Guise. After the first brief exchange, he knew just where he stood with this young woman, knew that they could work together.

"I regret, Madame, to come thus troubling you, so soon after your husband's sad death," he began. "Only untimely importunacy from another quarter would have forced me, and my prince to intrude so early on your grief."

"You are kind, my lord Bishop," she acknowledged, with the faintest smile. "My husband, however, was great deal older than am I. Nor was he ever of robust health. In consequence, the parting was less bitter than it might have been! I recognise the causes of your urgency. And respect them."

"You make my task a pleasure rather than a duty, Princess!"

Her fine eyes gleamed. "You did not expect it to be, my lord?"

"I had my hopes!" he admitted, mildly.

The gentle but throaty laugh which answered that set the seal on the matter, thus swiftly, and was the token of their co-operation – their enduring co-operation. From then on, Mary of Guise and David Beaton were partners. The talk of King James, and Scotland, of France and England, of dowries and jointures and revenues and the situation of the Duchess's nine-year-old son, the new Duke of Longueville – all these were in fact only words. Personalities spoke a deal louder – and these two were out of a like mould.

Even though all of importance was thus promptly and satisfactorily settled, there remained a great deal to see to, and some decent interval to elapse, before the proxy marriage could take place. David occupied the time by obeying summons to Rome, leaving Moray to the delights of Paris.

He was surprised at the warmth and scale of his reception at the Vatican. Evidently his efforts on Holy Church's behalf did not go unnoticed. His Holiness Pope Paul the Third was particularly impressed, it appeared, by his initiative in bringing together King Francis and the Emperor Charles, and the consequent easing of the Navarre situation, and expressed his gratitude — as well he might, for the rupture between these two giants of Christendom threatened the whole Church Catholic. He was positively gleeful over the opposition offered, on various fronts, to his *bête noire*, Henry of England, and urged continuance of the good work. And the Pontiff was greatly concerned over the state of the Church in far-away Scotland, conceiving it to be a remote but essential, and very vulnerable, bastion against the tide of heresy, which must be held at all costs. Weaklings must be weeded out of high places. Beaton's attempts at reform within the Church were necessary and commendable — but such would never win the battle. It was a time for putting on the whole armour of God, not only to quench the fiery darts of the Devil but to turn them back upon their launchers! Let him see to it, and so save his immortal soul, and the souls of countless others — for it seemed that the Church's other servants in Scotland were but broken reeds.

David was still bemused a little by this strange admixture of gratitude and glee with stern warning and implied reproof, when any previous wonderment was completely lost and submerged in a flood of astonishment at the Pontiff's next statement.

"And so, my son, in order to strengthen your hand, and sustain the arm of my beloved brother James Beaton, your uncle, and to declare my confidence in your continuing great services to the body of Christ on earth, as in the past, I have decided to elevate you to be a Prince of the Church, with the title of Cardinal of St. Stephen in Monte Coelo. And since to be Cardinal and no more than a bishop would be unsuitable and cause difficulties of precedence and authority with your fellow-bishops in Scotland, I hereby appoint you Coadjutor-Archbishop of St. Andrews, to aid your uncle in life and succeed him in death. And may Almighty God confirm and strengthen you therein, my son."

David Beaton was rendered speechless.

"Come, my son. It is customary to kiss the Holy Father's foot, on such appointment . . .!"

And so, at the age of forty-three, David Beaton suddenly and without warning, as much to himself as to others, donned the scarlet. With one giant stride he stepped up to the highest rank and influence in Holy Church, under the Papacy itself, a unique situation as far as Scotland was concerned – for the only previous Cardinalship granted in that country was disputed by Rome, having been a nomination from Avignon, and so was purely titular.

Still scarcely believing it all, David returned to Paris, whither the news had preceded him, and was received with the most gratifying pomp and respect. Three Cardinals thereafter officiated at the proxy wedding, held in the Cathedral of Notre Dame exactly a year after the other – for the Duchess's third brother, Louis, had also recently been elevated to the Sacred College, as Cardinal de Guise.

It was not until after the glittering ceremony, at which also King Francis conferred on her the title of Daughter of France, that David saw Mary de Guise alone again. He came to her in her new suite in the Palais Royal, and bowing low, took her hand to kiss it.

"Your Grace," he said. "I greet you as Queen! And declare myself to be your most loyal, devoted and delighted servant. This day is Scotland much enriched. You will do much for my country of that I am assured.

"*We* shall do it, my lord Cardinal – not I!" she answered, taking his hands and raising him up. She continued to hold both hands, as she looked into his eyes – and did not have to glance up to do so, for she was a tall and well-made woman, as tall as he was.

"You are kind, Madame," he murmured.

She nodded. "I can be," she agreed, both simply and far from simply.

They both smiled a little, and he pressed her slender but strong fingers only just perceptibly. He turned away. "This will be a strange wedding-night for you, Your Grace!"

"I shall survive it! There are times for all things. My lord – tell me of King James. My husband. Does he grieve sorely for poor Madeleine?"

"Aye. He was hard stricken. He believes his heart clean broke. But . . . hearts mend again. Especially under skilful and sure fingers, Your Grace. Moreover, His Grace is of a lusty and hearty disposition, at root."

"So I concluded! At Vendôme. But you, my friend – you

speak as though you knew much of hearts? From closer than the confessional!"

He inclined his head, and spoke slowly. "That is true. I have a lady. By the silver northern sea. Whose heart I held once. And who holds mine yet."

Shrewdly she considered him. "Held . . . and holds, my lord! In these two words is all life encompassed! Joy and sorrow. Is it not so? It could explain much."

"Does much require explaining?" That was slightly harsh.

"I think so. There is warfare in those clever eyes of yours, Monsieur David. Sore stress — for one so celebrated, successful. So sure of one self — yet so doubting of another! You should never have been a priest, I think, my lord Cardinal!"

He shrugged one shoulder. "It may be so. I perceive that you are a wise woman, as well as beautiful and able. And my Queen."

"Say that I have had much opportunity for learning! Not truly wise, God knows. Only wise enough to know and choose my friends. And my enemies!"

"I said that you were kind, also."

"And shall be kinder, perhaps, my lord. One day." She produced that little throaty laugh. "After all, you saved me from a great hurt. Henry of England!"

"Aye — that royal boar! I thank God that you were spared that!"

"God — and David Beaton! Though, mark you, I sought to save myself also. When he sent his envoy, saying that he was a big man who needed a big woman such as Mary de Guise, I sent word back that I might be big enough for Henry Tudor but that I feared my neck to be too slender!"

David smiled. "Well said! Although, I think, Henry will not forgive you that."

"Such is my hope — for the man is a monster. You . . . you must never let me fall into his hands, Monsieur David!"

"That I promise you!" he agreed, grimly.

"I thank you." She smiled again. "When do we set out for Scotland? You will be wearying, I think — for a place by your silvery northern sea . . .?"

So David Beaton conveyed back another queen for Scotland — and this time, James, taking no chances with the weather, sent a courier to tell them to come straight to St. Andrews. Ironically, they had stormy weather all the way from France until, in bright sunshine, they sighted the Scots coast, the Bass Rock and the May Island. Thereafter it was sun all the way.

They reached Fife Ness, but the seas, whipped up by the strong north-easterly winds, were rough enough to make hazardous any landing at St. Andrews' rockbound haven. So they put in under the lee of Fife Ness itself, and landed by small boats on the golden sandy shore, near Sir James Learmonth's castle of Balcomie. There, in the tall, grey stone tower, around which the seabirds wheeled unendingly, David found Queen Mary and sundry of her French retinue shelter, while the Earl of Moray borrowed horse to spur on the ten miles to St. Andrews to inform the King.

James came in haste to Balcomie, with a gallant train, and whatever his memories might be of a year before, now greeted his new bride with suitable fervour and display. Mary, for her part, was quietly warm, gracious, tactful. All went entirely well, without hitch or embarrassment.

King James was lodging in the archiepiscopal castle of St. Andrews, with James Beaton, but he conveyed his bride to the tiny new palace built for her predecessor, unoccupied hitherto. The city was as full and as busy as a hive of bees.

James Beaton's reception of his nephew was a little strange. Indeed, by and large, that could be said of David's reception by most others, in Scotland, that early summer. There was offence in it, somewhere—respect, esteem, but offence also; a kind of grudging resentment. David Beaton—a Cardinal! To go away an abbot, and come back a bishop—indeed an archbishop, since he was now full coadjutor—and a Prince of the Church, was not only scarcely believable, but unsuitable, somehow unacceptable. Not in a man they all knew. James Beaton, who had himself once aspired to be a Cardinal, could not find it in himself to be pleased. And he had not asked for a coadjutor.

Of all, only Gilbert Ogilvy, Dean of St. Andrews, seemed to be genuinely pleased.

King James himself appeared to be just a little put out, as though his Master Davie was seeking to put himself in a position of too much authority *vis-a-vis* his monarch. But otherwise the King was almost himself again. His activities against Douglas plotters seemed to have done him a power of good. The Master of Forbes had been tried, condemned and executed all in the same day; and Janet Douglas, Lady Glamis, had been convicted both of treason and witchcraft, and duly burned. James reckoned that plots against his life would be less popular.

David officiated at the true wedding of the royal couple in the Cathedral of St. Andrews, amid scenes of great splendour, during which he handed to the King a Papal sword and invested him in the dignity of Defender of the Faith, which Henry Tudor had forfeited. At a certain stage in this ceremony David's glance was caught and held by that of the new Queen, and for timeless moments they considered each other. Mary made a tall, graceful and handsome bride, decked with jewellery of a magnificence never seen before in Scotland; but the folk did not take to her as they had done to the frail Madeleine de Valois.

The celebrations thereafter were on a lavish and prolonged scale, but David excused himself just as soon as he decently might. James scarcely noticed his going — but the Queen questioned him gently.

"You go north, my friend? To the place by a still more silver sea?" And when he bowed, "Then, I wish you very well. May you change again held to hold! And tell the lady that Mary de Guise conceives her . . . fortunate!"

Chapter Twenty

It may not have been discreet or suitable for a Prince of the Church, and the Lord Privy Seal of the realm, to ride by himself and unescorted through the land; but that is how David Beaton felt, and what he did. Alone and fast he rode north, was ferried across Tay, and took the road for The Mearns.

The Abbey of Arbroath saw nothing of its lord as he passed it in the late afternoon.

The sun had set in pearly-grey calm and the plain of the sea was burnished silver indeed when David came to Ethie Castle, dusty, tired, but notably excited. No lights gleamed from the tall keep, but a faint plume of blue wood-smoke drifted above the high chimneys.

His approach had been observed, and he had barely dismounted in the little courtyard before the door was opened and Will Fiddes stood there, jerking his grizzled head in what was meant for a bow.

David waited beside his panting horse, listening—listening for a loved voice crying out welcome; or at least for the shouts of the children—though these might be in bed. But no such sounds reached him. Only the old servant's mumblings.

"So, Will!" he called, then. "Home again. After long. I see you well? Older—but we all are that."

"Aye—Master David—my lord. It's good to see you. But . . ."

"Well, man—do not just stand there blinking! Go tell your mistress that I am here. Or—stay. I will do it myself. Your bones grow stiff for the long stairs, eh?"

The other wagged his head. "My lord—it's no' . . . it's no' that way. No' that way, at all,' he said thickly. "The Lady Marion's no' here."

"What! Not here? You mean, she is from home? Gone visiting . . .?"

"No. No' visiting, Master David. She . . . she doesna bide here, any mair."

"Dear God—what are you saying? Out with it, man! What folly is this?"

"She hasna bided here at Ethie for months," the servitor declared, miserably. "For near on a year. She comes, whiles, to see to all. To see all's in order. She was here three days back . . ."

"Damnation, man! What's this? Where is she, of a mercy?"

"I dinna rightly ken. Any messages, I maun send to Airlie. Airlie Castle, my lord Abbot . . ."

"Airlie! She has gone . . . home!"

The other looked down at his boots, and nodded, wordless.

"A year! She left Ethie . . . and I knew naught of it!"

"All is in order, my lord. All ready for your use. Aye. The Lady Marion was right strong on that. All kept for you, in order. Fires each day. Your bed aired . . ."

"A plague on aired beds and fires!" David cried. "What are these when she is gone?" He pulled himself together. "Fetch me a flagon of ale, Will. And a bannock. No—that will serve me sufficiently well. And get me a fresh horse. I must be off."

It was nearly twenty-five miles from Ethie to Airlie, and it was in the wan gloaming that David at last climbed the steep winding track up to the proud fortalice above the sheer twin ravines, to clang the bell that hung at the edge of the great ditch.

His summons at length produced a sleepy voice from the porters' lodge in the gatehouse, making querulous demands in the Gaelic. Insistence on English speech, and intimation that it was the Abbot of Arbroath who called, elicited astonished and halting assertions that, as the saints bore witness, the Lord Ogilvy was a-bed with his new wife, and the Lady Marion was not there at all. Futher shouted questions effected the information that the Lady Marion now dwelt in the small Ogilvy castle of Balfour, in Kingoldrum, near to Kirriemuir.

David turned away, frowning, He knew this Balfour — for he had been brought up in another Balfour Castle, in Fife.

Through the shadowy foothills, disturbing sleeping cattle that lumbered off in fright on every slope and hillock, David rode wearily, a black depression upon him, following mainly the twisting little valley of the Cromie Burn. It was an hour past midnight when he came to Balfour, a small and dilapidated, indeed half-ruinous, stronghold of four round towers linked by a crumbling curtain-wall, set on the long, open, south-facing slope of the Kirkton of Kingoldrum Hill. Even in the vague half-light the decayed meanness of the place was evident, the little gatehouse broken down, windows gapped, one of the towers roofless. To have left Ethie for this!

David's rapping on the great oaken door — stout enough, certainly — boomed hollowly, in keeping with the hooting of the owls. The single cry of a sleeping child sounded in brief alarm — then silence. He knocked again.

At length the peep-hole in the door creaked open, and a distinctly frightened old man's voice quavered to demand who came to disturb honest folk at this hour?

"The Abbot of Arbroath. Seeking the Lady Marion Ogilvy. And . . . and his children!" David jerked. He swallowed. "I crave admittance to Balfour Castle."

There was a gasp, a muttering, and then the peep-hole shutter slammed, and footsteps shuffled away beyond.

He waited, a prey to conflicting emotions.

Presently there sounded different footsteps, light and running. Chains and bolts rattled, and then the slithering sound of the great greased draw-bar being run back into its socket in the walling. The heavy door was thrown open. Wrapped in a long furred bed-robe, Marion stood there, wide-eyed, in the light of a lamp held up by an ancient bent man close by. Her lips were moving – but no words came forth.

"My dear! he said, simply, sadly, and held out his arms.

"I . . . I . . . greeting, my lord!" she panted. "Here is . . . surprise. No warning. You should . . . have warned me. I would have shown you better welcome. Than this. I . . ." Her voice broke, and suddenly running forward, she threw herself upon him. "Oh, Davie! Davie!"

"Marion – my heart's heart!" He held her to him, clutching her fiercely. "Thank God! Thank God!"

For long they clung to each other, gulping incoherences, aware only that they were together again. Then, remembering the servant, now joined by a toothless crone, equally aged, they drew apart.

Marion took the lamp, instructed the half-clad old man to see to the Lord Abbot's horse and then lock up again, and told the beldam to fetch washing water and food and drink to the Hall above. Then she beckoned to David.

"Come," she said, and led the way up the worn treads of the narrow damp-smelling turnpike stair.

In the Hall, a bare place of stone walls and stone-flagged floor, brightened by many jugs of flowers and fronds of greenery, she set down the lamp on the table, and moved over to use the bellows on the dark peats that still smouldered in their own ash in the wide fireplace.

David came behind her, to raise her up. He was very much aware by the feel of her that beneath the loose robe she was naked from her bed. "Leave that," he ordered. "I did not come here for fires and food. I came for you, my love!"

Rising, she turned to him, but held him away a little, "Perhaps, Davie – but that resolves nothing. This is not how I intended to greet you. I am weak and foolish – but naught is changed between us . . ."

"Naught changed, no. Still we love one the other. That is the truth of it. What is important. That you cannot deny, my dear."

"Deny, no. Yet that changes nothing. That we knew already . . ."

"Why did you leave Ethie?" he demanded, abruptly interrupting her. "Why, Marion? Ethie, our home. *Your* house. All yours. For this!"

"Your wife's house, Davie—not mine! Not mine, any more. I am sorry my dear—but I could not stay."

"Why? You were happy there. All was as you would have it . . ."

"I *was* happy. Until . . . until all changed. When all that I loved and cherished there became . . . otherwise. Turned sour for me, like curdled milk. Oh, I know that the fault is my own. That I am a wicked proud woman. The devil of pride is strong in me—gives me no rest. Can you not understand, Davie? I *had* to come away. Everything, every place there, everywhere I looked, spoke to me of what had been—and which was no longer. I thought that I had come to terms with . . . with my fate. But it was not so. It could not be—not at Ethie. Here it is different. Here I can just be Marion Ogilvy, David Beaton's mistress. Mother of the children by him. At Ethie I was the woman who had been David Beaton's wife—and was no longer. Can you not see it?"

He emitted something near a groan. "I see that I am the most accursed of men! That I have taken your life in my hands, and broken it! That, I see. That I have ruined what I hold most dear. In order to save a tottering, decadent Church, and a broken, treacherous realm! God forgive me!"

She mustered a smile. "How like a man, to turn it so, to himself! It is not so bad as that, Davie! I am less than ruined, I think. Nor wholly broken, yet! And what is one weak and foolish woman, to the Church? To the realm of Scotland? Have you saved them, Davie?"

He stared at her, shaking his head. "I am sorry, Marion. Sorry."

"Sorry, yes, Davie. But you would do the same again, would you not? Because you must. And who am I to say that you would be wrong?"

The old woman came in with a tray bearing warm water, cold meats and ale, and another lamp.

"This is poor fare, Davie," Marion said, biting her lip. "I fear I can offer you no better. We do not keep any great store. Live simply, the children and I. If I had known . . ."

"Aye—the children? Are they well? How do they here? In this . . . this rickle of stones!"

"They do very well, I think. They grow. And learn. And laugh. Even they make their mother laugh! Which is well, is it not? George is very like you, I think. He reasons with me—and despairs of me also! And it is none so bad a house this, Davie. We look out over a fair prospect—yet do not see the sea . . ."

"It is a barren, broken shell! When Ethie was . . ." He wagged his head. "Why *here*? If you had to leave Ethie, why here? Why not at Airlie? Or in one of the Abbey houses? Gibbie would have found you one . . ."

"Because here I am beholden to none. I would not have the children grow up in another's house. This Balfour was my brother's house." She shrugged. "But—enough of this. Draw in to the table, Davie. Standing there! You must be weary. Hungry. Here is water to wash. Where have you ridden from . . .?"

"From St. Andrews. Where two days ago I married the new Queen to King James!"

"*You* married them?"

"Aye. Another step towards the saving of this realm! A large step, I believe." He threw off his dusty travelling cloak, and stood revealed as wholly clad in fine broadcloth of scarlet—scarlet doublet, trunks and silken hose, relieved only by a gold belt studded with rubies, and a tiny gold cross on a slender chain. Even his sword was sheathed in scarlet. It all made a blazing elegance which went but strangely with his heavy thigh-length riding-boots. "Mary of Guise will be a notable friend to Scotland. And the Church. Of that I am convinced . . ."

"Davie!" Marion interrupted. "Your . . . your clothing! Why are you dressed so? All in red. I have never seen you thus. Is this some new French fashion . . .?"

"It was a gift. From the Cardinal of Lorraine. Charles de Guise—the Queen's brother. Though a man I do not like. Made for me by his personal tailor. Three sets—one satin, one velvet, and this broadcloth. All scarlet. Suitable for Cardinals . . . who do not wish to look like Cardinals!"

"But why? To you . . .?"

"You have not heard? Of course, you would not. Then, my

267

dear Marion—look well! For you see before you none other than David Beaton, Cardinal of St. Stephen in Monte Coelio, Archbishop-Coadjutor of St. Andrews, and Bishop of Mirepoix, in France—God help him!"

She stared. "Cardinal . . .? You!"

"Aye. Cardinal David Beaton, Prince of Holy Church. One step only below the Supreme Pontiff and the Throne of St. Peter! You see, my beloved—when I put away my wife, I did so to good effect!" Abruptly he turned away from her, and sat down at the table, slender scarlet back stiff, rigid.

Presently she came behind his chair, and put her hands on his shoulders. "Oh, Davie—dear Davie! What can I say?" she asked.

"Say nothing," he told her. "For there is nothing to say. Nothing that I have not said to myself, full eloquently, a thousand times! And yet . . ."

"Aye. And yet! And yet—does it seem to you folly, Davie, when I say that I am proud of you? I am, I swear."

"Then we are apart in this also, Marion," he declared levelly. "For I am not!"

"Are you not, my dear? Just a little? I think that you must be—else why come to me in this scarlet? You should be, indeed. To have risen so high. The youth who came to me, at the stables of Lunan Priory. And said that God demanded of a man, in worship, that he used all his wits and abilities. Not to let them lie, but to use them. You have used them, to some effect, Davie! You cannot but be proud. Has there ever been a Scots Cardinal? But . . . eat, Davie. If I may so address a Cardinal! It sounds improper. Should not I name you Holiness? Or Beatitude? Or something such?"

He smiled, then, for the first time that night. "I will think about that."

As he ate and she watched him, his gaze kept dropping to her chest, where her loose robe, opening, revealed something of her splendid bosom. Noting it, she shook her head reprovingly, and drew the robe close.

"My lord Cardinal!" she said.

Presently Marion questioned him. "So that is why it was you who married the King? You are now higher in rank than your uncle? Or the Archbishop Dunbar?"

"In rank. But not in position. My uncle is still Primate of Scotland. And Dunbar is Chancellor. I officiated because the

Queen would have it so. She is an able and wise woman, with whom I can work."

"And beautiful?"

"Not beautiful, no—as you are beautiful. But handsome. Taking. And clever. Knowing her own mind. She will be good for King James—who is headstrong and blows hot and cold. A good Queen for Scotland. Better than poor pretty Madeleine de Valois."

"So! She was *your* choice? Not King James's?"

"James saw her in France. And was . . . impressed. Indeed he caused me some anxiety concerning her. When her husband was alive."

"I do not think that I like the sound of Queen Mary de Guise!"

"Then you are mistaken, Marion. Not knowing her. For she is a woman of great parts."

"So you make clear!"

"Moreover, she thinks well of *you*. Kindly."

"You have told her of me?"

"Why, yes. She perceived that my heart was somewhere afar off. And enquired . . ."

"And how, pray, did she perceive that?"

"By using her wits, lass. Should it be so hard to perceive? She sent you a message, indeed—although, in this, I think she errs. She said to tell my lady by the northern sea that Mary de Guise considers her . . . fortunate!"

"Does she, indeed!" Marion rose and walked over to the fireplace. "Her Grace, since she is so able and clever, would be wise to speak of what she knows, I think!" She bellowed the peats lustily, raising white clouds of ash.

At her back, David Beaton smiled a small secret smile. Presently, finished his meal, he went over to stand behind her, taking something from his doublet pocket. Then he stooped, and slipped over her bent head a looped chain and pendant.

"A small gift," he said.

"What . . . what is this?" she demanded, clutching something that blazed with a vivid red fire. "Davie . . .!"

"Something with which you may remember the Cardinal, when he is absent," he told her lightly. "I gained a red hat. You must gain something red, surely?"

It was an enormous ruby, set simply in gold, larger than any she had seen or thought of – the largest indeed that the man had ever known, likewise. It seemed to glow and flame as with a fierce inner fire of its own, so that she dropped it from her fingers as though it had burned her.

"Davie!" she all but wailed. "What have you done? I cannot take this. It is not for such as I. This must have cost a ransom! Such a great jewel. You should not have done it."

"No? You do not like it?"

"It is wonderful, Magnificent! But . . . too much. What can I do with it? What use have I for such splendour? Who will ever see it?"

"Jewels are never of use. Save as a token for something other. This, of my true love. Whatever I have done. Is that not use enough? What matters if none see it, but you? Wear it, my heart – wear it somewhere *close* to your heart. At times. To bring to mind the man who wronged you. And loves you. And needs you."

Biting her lip, she clutched the jewel again, head down.

"Come, Marion – I would see the children," he said, in a different voice. "I have brought them small tokens also. Not to waken them, now. Just to see them . . ."

They passed the open door of the room on the next floor, and ascended higher to the garret chamber within the parapet-walk. All three children slept here, in cots, in an apartment bare of all else save wooden chests for their clothes. George, a slight boy of nine, with delicate features and long sweeping eyelashes but a good firm chin, slept curled up in a tangle of bed-clothes. Elizabeth, seven, dark hair spread over pillow, was going to be beautiful; her lips were parted now in a half-smile. Margaret, the baby whom David hardly knew, lay on her back, covers thrown off, a naked chubby cherub, clutching a piece of wood whittled approximately into the shape of a doll.

Father's and mother's eyes met, over the last cot, and David spread his hands in a gesture strangely helpless, but eloquent. Churchman though he was, he made no conventional signs over them – and his lips were too tightly closed to mutter benedictions.

Outside again, he stood on the landing, staring out of the open door to the parapet-walk, silent. At length he spoke.

"How does God judge a man?" he demanded.

"Do not ask me that," she told him quietly. "*I* am not the priest."

"Nor am I! God knows! You know. I know. That I am no priest, in truth. I am but a hollow mockery of a priest. I but use the office. To gain the power I need. Since that is the way this world's war is waged. For power, one must be a prince, a great noble — or a successful priest! I am no more a true priest than . . . than is that devil Charles de Guise! I use the words, make the motions — that is all."

"And . . . and deny yourself a wife?"

"Aye. Deny! But, God knows too, *need* one as much as ever! Need *you*. What folly decreed that priests cannot marry? Against all the laws of God's creation? Priests are men, are they not?"

"Who made this rule?"

"Who knows. Some long-dead Pope, in Council. Epiphanius. Siricius. Founding on Paul, no doubt. But what of the others? Paul was not alone in building the Church. We know little of the views of others, on this. Or Christ's own. On my soul — it would be worth my reaching for the Papacy, to put this to rights! If nothing else . . ."

"Davie! The Papacy! You . . . you would not, could not . . .?"

He shrugged, and shook his head. "Heed me not, my love. I was carried away. But blethering." He turned back. "Come, woman — enough of profitless bemoanings. Here is no time for that."

They went downstairs.

At the landing beneath, Marion paused, hesitant, putting the lamp in a niche in the walling. "You will be weary," she said. "It is late. You have ridden far . . ."

"I have never felt less weary in my life!" he assured her.

"Oh. Then . . . then, what now? What is your wish . . .?"

He barked a laugh. "Save us — there is no doubing what is *my* wish, my heart! But that is not the prime concern. This is your house. I have descended upon you without warning. All shall be as *you* wish."

"I but wish to, to serve you, David."

"And I will have none of your service! Think you that is what I want? I came hoping . . ."

"Yes, Davie?" she said, when he paused.

"Oh, Marion—you are lovely! Maddeningly lovely. Desirable. I want you, need you, every inch of you." He reached out, to grasp her, vehemently, almost roughly.

Under her robe his hands could feel all the silken, firm fullness of her, and his fingers went wild with the urge of it. The robe, wrenched aside, fell away from her, and she was all trembling, smooth, warm delight in his arms. She did not thrust him from her.

He it was, indeed, who presently pushed her away a little, to gaze at her.

"Woman! Oh, woman!" he gasped in a strangled voice. "You are glorious! I ache and burn for you!"

At first she had stood with her hands clasped before her, in a sort of elementary modesty. Now she dropped them to her sides, in frankest compliance.

"Then take me, Davie," she said. "I am your mistress yet, am I not? Have I ever denied you this body . . .?"

It was in him to shout that he did not want a mistress's body, magnificent as it was. But his own body and passions were too strong for such niceties. Striding forward, in an access of impetuous strength, he swept her up in his arms and carried her into the bedchamber, to throw her on to the rumpled bed and himself after her, cursing his cloying Cardinal's clothing.

When the hot tide, ebbing, left them in a warm languorous pool of content, David spoke gently,

"You are very kind," he said. "But more than kind. Very . . . able. And requiring. You are all woman—and demand all a man's manhood."

"More so than do other women, Davie?"

"Aye, lass. I have never deceived you in that, at least. That I have taken other women. Used them—you understand? Used is the word for it. *You* have all my love. And this. This is only yours, and mine. The other is but dross to this fine gold. Can you understand?"

"I hear it, at least. As I have heard it before. And must believe. Believe that you would not deceive me in this, either."

"No." He paused. "And yet, *you* deceived me, Marion of my heart. Just now."

"Me . . .?"

"Back yonder. This was no mistress's loving, woman! No

272

dutiful surrender of your body. Indeed, no surrender of any sort! That was *you* — all you!"

"Was it?"

"Aye. In such a matter I am not to be deceived."

"The man of experience!" She sighed. "It is true, yes. It was just . . . myself. What I wanted."

Presently her hand came over to stroke his. "Davie — what is to happen to us?" she asked. "You are a notable planner and schemer. Where do we — you and I — come in your planning?"

"Need you ask, Marion? Now, and here? This is what I plan, always have planned, for us. That we should be together. With our children. When I am not doing the business of the state, or the Church. To me, you are my wife still. Always will be. To share my bed and home. But not this house . . ."

"I will not go back to Ethie," she interrupted him quickly. "I would keep Ethie as a dear memory. Not as a sore reminder."

He sighed. "As you will. Some other house, then. Where we may be together again. As a family. We are that in truth, Marion. Only in name is it otherwise. And, who knows — in time it may be possible to be together in name again, also."

"What do you mean?"

"Marion — it may be that I can see an end to my work. A few more years, and it may be possible for me to leave it all. With Scotland and the Church saved. I am more hopeful than I have ever been. I shall soon have supreme power in this land. My uncle is very frail. He cannot live much longer. I am to succeed him as Primate. So the Pope desires — and King James will not refuse. Whether I take the Chancellorship from Gavin Dunbar matters nothing. Already he does as I tell him. Then there is the Queen . . ."

"Yes — this Queen! You build much on her, it is clear."

"And with reason. She is a woman to build upon. She is none the less a woman for having something of a man's mind! Mary of Guise will work with me — that I do not doubt. She is stronger than James will ever be. She hates Henry Tudor, and will maintain the French alliance. Sister to two Cardinals, she will cherish the Church. She has already had a son — so it is likely she will produce an heir to James's throne. Give me but a few years, and I think that I may be able to lay down my task."

"You would never do it. Give up your power."

"Why not? I never sought power for its own sake. Only for what might be done with it. To save Scotland. When that is done, think you I must cling to the power?"

"Can a Cardinal give up being a Cardinal? I have never heard of such."

"A man, if he is of sufficient decision, can lay down anything that he has taken up."

"I think that you delude yourself, Davie. You even spoke, back there, of the Papacy . . .!"

"That was idle dreaming. A phantasy."

"Are you sure?"

"Aye. Give me but a few years more, my love, and I will prove it."

"I cannot withhold them, David. As I cannot withhold much else!"

He rolled over. "My heart . . .!"

PART FOUR

Chapter Twenty-one

"THE situation is delicate, Your Grace. Otherwise I would not trouble you. I require Your Grace's aid . . ."

"What is this, Monsieur Davie? You have needed my help a hundred times in these eighteen months. And I yours. But never come to me thus hesitantly." The Queen smiled. "What have you done, my friend?"

"It is not what I have done, but what I must do," David told her. "I come to you in some doubt, because this concerns His Grace."

"Ah!"

"As you know, I am about to launch this drive against heresy. At St. Andrews. To mark my assumption of the Primacy. But I am hindered and constrained. Because it is believed that King James is insufficiently concerned against the heresy. That he will do little to halt it."

"With some truth," Mary de Guise admitted. "James is scarcely a man of religious mind."

"Nor am I!" David returned dryly. "But I can perceive the danger to his throne and realm if the Church is undermined." He paused. "As can Sir Ralph Sadler, the new English envoy!"

"You believe Sir Ralph to be a danger? James treats him kindly — for he does not dislike the man. But he firmly rejects his submissions."

"Aye. That is well. But Sadler is subtle — a man to be watched. Henry has sent him with special intent. He is to weaken the Scottish-French alliance by all and every means, but especially by seeking to set the King against the Church. His Grace is ever short of money — it is a grave failure in our Scottish system. Sadler is to keep pointing to King Henry's success in this respect, the enormous wealth of the Church which he could take for his own coffers. Sadler reminds that his master has suppressed six hundred religious houses and two thousand chapels and hospitals, thereby enriching his own pocket by no less than one hundred and sixty thousand pounds each year. It is notable pleading, for a prince with an empty treasury. You know, too, that Henry accuses me, to the King, of plotting to destroy him and make Scotland a Papal State? That Sadler has brought a letter of mine to the Pope, intercepted by English pirates, purporting to set this forth? Cleverly done — a true letter, cunningly forged, cut and added to . . ."

"I know of it, my friend. James laughed at it, and handed it back to Sir Ralph, declaring that you were more like to take over the Papacy than to let the Pope take over Scotland! Do not doubt His Grace's faith in you."

"*I* do not — in especial, while he has Your Grace at his elbow. But others are less sure. Others perceive that he has many heretics amongst his close associates and friends. And assume that I dare not take the steps necessary to cleanse the Church, in consequence. Either in putting down the heresies, or in rooting out corruption."

"I see that, Monsieur Davie. It is unfortunate. But not new. What am I to do?"

"I require to destroy this assumption. But . . . without giving offence to His Grace. Delicate, as I say."

"Proceed."

"I require to make an example. That others may note the power of Holy Church, and mend their ways. Sir John Borthwick, Captain of His Grace's castle and palace of Linlithgow, has become much tainted with the doctrines of Luther. I have warned him, reasoned with him — but to no effect. He is a man of some parts, kin to Lord Borthwick — and the King esteems him well."

"You cannot lay hands on Sir John, my friend, without embroiling James."

"Aye. You know that, Madame. As do I. But . . . does Sir John?"

"You mean . . .?"

"If Borthwick was to learn that the Church was to summon and try him, on a charge of heresy, at the forthcoming assembly at St. Andrews — would he believe that King James could and would save him?"

"That I do not know. Who can tell?"

"If your Grace, who is known to honour me with your confidence, was to warn him. Quietly. To urge him to escape to

England, while there was yet time. Think you he would take no heed?"

"I see," the Queen murmured. "I see. Clever. But then, you were always that. You wish him away? Fled? Will that be enough to serve your purpose?"

"Try him, *in absentia*. His guilt proclaimed and admitted, by his flight. Sentenced – and burned in effigy! The example made, the warning given – and no one hurt."

"Better and better! I congratulate you!"

"What, think you, will King James say?"

"What can he say? Who may he blame? Save only Sir John, for indiscretion and cowardice."

"Aye. Then you will do it, Madame? And further earn my gratitude. Moreover, I will seek sweeten the dose for His Grace by demanding from the assembly a large levy for the treasury from Church moneys."

She nodded. "Very wise."

"King James is hunting at Falkland. Your Grace could, perhaps, journey to join him sooner than you intended. Tomorrow? Calling in at Linlithgow on the way."

"You leave little to chance, my lord Cardinal!"

"I worship at the shrine of truer, more reliable goddesses than she, Highness."

"Go tell that to the Lady Marion – who, no doubt, knowing you, will believe it as little as do I!" The Queen smiled. "Now come with me and pay court to your godson. He is better today, I think." She sighed and grimaced comically at the same time, in typically French fashion. "That my potent prince should have so great a host of brave and healthy bastards – and only this frail mite as lawful heir! He holds it against me, you know."

"Not so, Madame. His Grace esteems you in all things. As well he may. Besides, you already have one stout son, in the Duke of Longueville . . ."

"Which is scant consolation for James, I fear! However, I am pregnant again. Did you know? Though that is a foolish question to ask? Monsieur Davie knows everything that happens in Scotland!"

David blinked. "I congratulate you both . . ."

"No doubt. Well – come and say a Cardinal's prayer over my

little bantling, James Duke of Rothesay. For I fear he needs it."

David Beaton was not, in truth, a great one for pomp and ceremony. But he knew how to use it if the occasion warranted. He had been in St. Andrews since his uncle had died, of course; but that was late in the year and no time for display. This, his first official entry into the archiepiscopal capital since his elevation to the Primacy and full archbishopric, was to be a very special occasion.

With still vivid memories of his uncle's first progress into the city, twenty-seven years before, and of the threadbare student who had watched and jeered – and yet that day made up his mind to the future which led to this – David had spared neither cost, forethought nor trouble. The procession which wound its attenuated way through the narrow gateway of the West Port, was the best part of a mile long, and of a splendour and brilliance never before seen in the train of a man who was not king. Indeed, it far outshone either of James's bridal processions. No fewer than six earls, eleven lords of parliament, and over seventy knights rode there, led by the Chancellor, Archbishop Dunbar of Glasgow, with most of the members of the King's government. As for other churchmen, only one of all the bishops was absent, a man so gone in drink that he would have been a liability. Even Bishop Hepburn of Moray was present. Practically every abbot and prior likewise graced the occasion, however much many of them would have preferred to be elsewhere – for even though they had dared absent themselves from this entry, they could by no means ignore the summons to the great assembly and solemn conclave of the Church to be held immediately afterwards.

Even the English envoy, Sir Ralph Sadler, rode in the procession, by special invitation – for his master in London's better information.

David himself, well towards the rear, moved between massed choirs of sweet singers. Where everyone else rode or walked, he was carried in a great canopied litter of scarlet, borne by a score of brawny fellows, also in scarlet. His own herald, trumpeter, secretary and chaplain preceded him, and double rows of the Cardinal's French Guard, gorgeous in scarlet and gold, flanked his litter. David for once was dressed in full Car-

279

dinal's red robes and hat, but simple and plain, without any sort of adornment.

Half of Scotland seemed to throng the narrow streets as the Prince of the Church entered his inheritance. The said prince, who eschewed any cross-signings and wholesale benedictions, wondered whether Chrissie — or was it Katie — the scullion-maid, was there watching, repository of his early confidences — and more than that.

Amidst chanted psalms and clashing cymbals, the long cavalcade wound its way to the Cathedral, where Gilbert Ogilvy, as Dean, conducted a service of dedication and praise, and David was forced to do one of the things he found most distasteful, to pronounce an elaborate benediction, knowing himself hypocrite.

Thereafter followed a banquet in the Great Hall of the new College of St. Mary. It was during this prolonged and noisy repast that a courier, pushed in behind the Cardinal's chair and handed him a close letter bearing the royal seal. Opening it, David scanned the few words in the clear, firm feminine handwriting of Mary of Guise, and nodded, satisfied.

Later, with all traces of the banquet cleared away, unauthorised persons banished and the seating re-arranged, David summoned the hundreds of senior churchmen to solemn conclave. Not a few were drunk, and many more would quickly be asleep — but in some cases that would be all to the good. He had a surplus of enemies in this hall already; the fewer who were coherently vocal, the better. But it meant an unseemly noise, and considerable beating upon his table, before he could make himself heard.

"My lords, colleagues and friends," he began, "I greet you all in love and affection. I come before you humbly, modestly, only too well aware of my shortcomings and my inadequacies for the high office to which it has pleased Almighty God, and His Holiness the Pope, to call me. We meet together in a time of great stress and decision. The Church is under assault as never before in her long history — assault from within. This assault has two sources, as we all know; heretical doctrine, and corruption amongst the Church's servants. Assault intellectual and moral. Both must be fought, and conquered."

There was a certain amount of cautious assent.

"I have a message for you from the Holy Father himself. His Holiness's letter is long, and I shall not read it all. He says, in sending you his heartfelt greetings, that he looks upon you as in the vanguard of the Church's warfare. That Scotland is an essential bastion of Christendom, and that it must not, shall not, fall to the attacks of the Evil One. All too much has fallen already, and wicked men everywhere would rejoice exceedingly if Scotland could be overthrown. In especial, the apostate and foresworn Henry Tudor, King of England, who is doing all in his power to bring down the Church in Scotland. For his own purposes. That he might conquer you by disruption, since he may not do it by arms. His Holiness commends you to God's protection, and, h'm, lays upon you the injunction to support his legate and emissary — myself — under pain of his sternest displeasure."

Another significant pause, and David smiled his sweetest smile. "Now, my friends — we are here to discuss and decide upon how the Holy Father's edicts may best be carried out."

All things considered, the great company listened to him as well as he could have hoped. But it was obvious from the first that he could not expect to have things all his own way. It was, in the main, not the matter of heresy that disturbed the majority; he could do as he liked in that respect. It was his attempt to interfere in the corporate and private lives of the clergy, that aroused the opposition. One after another bishops, abbots and priors rose to protest against unwarrantable aspersions and intrusions in their personal affairs, arising out of the impudent visitations of Dean Gilbert Ogilvy and his fellow spies, and the fines and mulctings of Abbot Cairncross's courts.

David was patient, moderate, civil. While supporting his lieutenants to the hilt, he sought to soothe tempers, lower the temperature, emphasise points of agreement. But it was not to be blinked that there was a large element of those present who were not to be appeased or placated — who were, indeed, out for trouble.

It was equally recognisable that these recalcitrants represented a distinct and very influential group of the prelates — those of noble blood. For long it had been the custom in Scotland for the powerful lords and lairds to insert their younger sons and bastards into the best offices and richest charges of the Church, to its great detriment. Sometimes these nominees proved good churchmen, but much more often they were the reverse — lazy, tyrannical and ignorant. Not a few of the loftiest present, for instance, could not even sign their names, much less read Holy Writ. It was these in the main who now made evident their opposition to the Cardinal.

Prior Patrick Hepburn of St. Andrews was the acknowledged spokesman of this solid and influential party—with frequent glances at his father, the Bishop of Moray, who was uncle to the Earl of Bothwell—for unspoken but evident support.

At David's side, Gavin Dunbar muttered that this assembly was a mistake, that it had been folly to thus bring together the forces of reaction, to demonstrate the divided state of the Church.

The other shook his head. "Wait," he said. "The honest men are not talking."

When, after a fiery tirade, in which Patrick Hepburn shouted about up-jumped clerks and bookish pedants, as scornful as any great lord, and paused for necessary breath, David rose—and smashed down his hand on his table when Hepburn did not resume his seat. Nevertheless, when he spoke, his voice was still mild.

"My lords," he said, "Here is much heat and emotion. Worthy of a moonlight evening in the Borders!" This allusion to the cattle-lifting propensities of the Hepburns drew a laugh from the majority of those present. "Let *me* appeal to your reason, my friends. The Church, mother of us all, faces disaster. If it goes down before the onslaught of the so-called reformers, how many rich benefices will survive? Not one. All will be lost in the flood. As has been the case in England. And in the German states. Think you it will be any different in Scotland? Now, the sharpest weapon in the armoury of these reformers is the *need* for reform in the Church. Not in the doctrine so much as in the lives of churchmen. So long as they can point to corruption, evil-living and sinful extravagance amongst the clergy, our strength is grievously weakened. We must set our house in order, my lords."

"Where shall we begin, my lord Cardinal?" Hepburn cried loudly. "At the house of Ethie, in the abbacy of Arbroath? I have heard that there is a lady there, and two bairns. In great splendour. Not ten miles from the Abbey. If there is truth in this, might there not here be cause for reform?"

There was shocked silence in the great hall—save for snores; shock not at the charge, which many had known about for long,

282

but that it should have been voiced thus, before all, in defiance of all custom, courtesy and authority.

David Beaton alone appeared to be unperturbed. After all, he had been anticipating something like this for years. He looked around him, smiling.

"My lord Prior," he said easily, unhurriedly. "Your researches would do you credit, I vow — were they more accurate! Ethie Castle was never part of the Abbey of Arbroath. I bought it, many years ago, of my own money. It is not resplendent, but a simple stone tower by the sea. And, alas — it stands empty. The lady to whom you refer no longer dwells there. That lady, were priests permitted openly to be married, as some of us advocate, would be my wife. The children are my pride — and there are three of them!"

It was simply but skilfully done. None desired to pursue the matter further, not even Hepburn. He changed direction.

"As to benefices and extravagance, my lord Cardinal, we hear that your bishopric of Mirepoix in France is a wealthy one."

David nodded. "Here the good Prior is on surer ground. It is notably so. Surpassing any benefice in all Scotland. It brings me ten thousand gold crowns each year, no less. A token of esteem from the Church in France. For services I was privileged to render. Ten thousand crowns which are serving Scotland well. For without it I must needs draw more heavily on revenues nearer home, for the direction of the Church's work. Your own, my lords! To pay for many things. This assembly, and what is to follow. Even the repast you have just enjoyed!"

Men smiled, and Patrick Hepburn held his peace.

Quite suddenly David Beaton changed. From mildness and patience and reason, he switched to stern vehemence, crisp and assured — and just when he seemed to have silenced the opposition. One moment he was smiling upon the company, bearing with it, accommodating — the next he was all Cardinal, master, hand out, finger pointing.

"Hear me now," he cried. "The Church in Scotland will *not* fall. Not so long as *I* live! That I pledge you. That I *warn* you! What steps are necessary to save her, to protect her, will be taken. However unsavoury to your palates, or to mine. I remind you that never before has the Primate of Scotland been also Legatus Natus, Apostolic Protonotary and of the Sacred College. No

Churchman in this land has ever held the powers I hold. I can banish from holy orders. I can promote and reduce, without reference to Rome. I can command absolute obedience on any matter concerning the Church. I can expel from any benefice or appointment, from the lowest to the highest. I can pronounce anathema and excommunication at my sole will and discretion. And I can burn, my lords — burn! Any that I will." He paused. "Let he now raise his voice who presumes to say otherwise!"

In the quivering electric quiet only a drunk mumbling thickly to himself and some steady snoring, greeted his challenge. No other man, it seemed, so much as moved a muscle. The slight boyish figure in red — in appearance so at variance with the harsh and terrible words spoken — held all eyes, almost all breaths.

David stood silent for a full minute, looking around him. Then he sat down, gesturing to Patrick Barclay of Collairnie to continue.

Barclay, in businesslike and unemotional tone, read out the list of proposals, measures and enactments put forward to deal with the crisis. These were drastic, and made earlier edicts seem mild, almost petty. They were almost entirely directed at the clergy, the laity and common people being barely mentioned. All private religious meetings and conventicles were to be forbidden; to question the spiritual infallibility of the Pope to be a capital offence; no person suspected of heretical opinions to be admitted to any office in Church or State; no churchman to be permitted so much as to converse with known heretics. At the same time measures against the misrule and dishonesty of the clergy, the re-institution of lapsed services and worship, and the dissemination of religious knowledge amongst the ministry, to be given first priority. Penalties were stepped up almost to the point of savagery — and the proceedings of such findings to be handed over to the King for the better governance and defence of his realm. Church and State, clearly, were to be integrated as never before. Yet any prelate or incumbent, bringing in his noble or lairdly supporters to enforce his interests in matters ecclesiastical, was to be dismissed his benefice forthwith.

When it was finished, there was much muttering, head-shaking and colloguing. Then William Chisholm, the brash, crude but popular Bishop of Dunblane, rose to somewhat unsteady feet. On the whole he was a supporter of David's, not so much out of conviction probably as because he perceived that any other course would be apt to involve him in more trouble than it would be worth.

"Our maist venerable Father in Christ, Cardinal Davie—whom God preserve—has let loose a sair blast upon us this day!" he observed, in his rich Doric. "We'll just need to thole it, nae doubt—for he kens best, to be sure. Mysel', I'm no' a man for postulations and dispute—nor yet ower strong on doctrines and the like! But I'm thinking that our good Davie has maybe no' just looked sufficient far *outside* the Church! Heretics within the Church he can deal with. But what o' those outside? Those in high places? Aye—and those protected in the highest places of all?"

There were some quick-drawn breaths at this bold bringing into the open of the ticklish problem of which they were all aware—that the King's unconcern with matters of religion, allied to his erratic judgement of character, was causing him to surround his person with unorthodox friends.

"His Grace will not hinder Holy Church in the carrying out of its duties," David said. "Of that I am assured."

"Och, aye." the other observed, doubtfully. "Maybe. But His Grace has some right strange friends. Yon man Lindsay, the Lord Lyon King o' Arms, had the effrontery to perform before the King and Court at Linlithgow, yon devilish play-acting that they ca' The Satire o' the Three Estates. A bold mockery o' the Church. I saw plenty, there, fair bursting themsel's wi' ill merriment, at his lewd sallies . . ."

"No doubt, my lord. Perhaps you even saw myself! I admit it, I laughed as much as any. For there was much truth in it all, amongst the mockery. We have to learn from such. Give less cause for such entertainments. The fact that His Grace permitted such performance does not mean that he is not a good son of Holy Church. I said that I was assured that he would not hinder us." David glanced along at Patrick Barclay. "In token whereof I deem this a suitable moment to transform this assembly into its second aspect—that of supreme court and tribunal of Holy Church in this land. And in my capacity as preses of that court, I have summoned to appear before it, on a charge of heresy, the first layman so arraigned and accused in this land. Five priests were tried, condemned and burned, two years ago, by special tribunal. Today, in witness of the Church's determination to stamp out the noxious weed of heresy, as well as the evils of corruption, we make trial of another. I summon before this court Sir John Borthwick, Knight, Captain of the castle and palace of Linlithgow."

If it had been David's intention to create a sensation, he could hardly have been more successful. Here was challenge enough for anyone — the keeper of the King's favourite palace, a noted jouster and player at the ball, and a crony of the monarch. Cardinal Davie was playing for high stakes.

Barclay was on his feet. "My lord Cardinal," he called out. "He is not here. I fear the panel is not present . . ."

"Not present, sir!" David half-rose in his chair. "What do you mean — not present? He was summoned to appear. With due warning. Before this solemn tribunal. How dare he . . .?"

"My lord — my information is that he has fled. Sure information. Fled to England. With two companions. Yesterday. To England . . ."

"A-a-ah!" David's long sigh was echoed all round the hall, as everywhere men perceived the writing on the wall. The King had not saved his friend from the Cardinal — had not chosen to or had not been able. The gauntlet had not been picked up. The tide was flowing David Beaton's way.

David, after deliberation with Archbishop Dunbar, declared that the trial would go on, *in absentia*. Let none think that they could flout the Church's solemn summons. He called for Barclay to read out the indictment.

The trial was not scamped for lack of the accused. Witnesses were called to testify that on many occasions Borthwick had made public heretical statements, had advocated the overthrow of the Papacy and the adoption of Jean Calvin's doctrines. There being no denials or pleas, the court could do no other than find the accused guilty of heresy in the first degree.

David pronounced automatic sentence of burning — but since the heretic was not available for the stake, he ordered that he be burned in effigy, that night in St. Andrews and the following night at the Cross of Edinburgh. Moreover, according to canon law all a heretic's goods were forfeit; but the Church, wishing to gain no benefit from such as he, all Borthwick's lands and properties were hereby confiscated and handed over to the Crown. Let all observe and take note.

There were some chuckles at this final thrust, the gifts to the

King of the estate of his condemned friend. All agreed that it was featly done. King Henry would no doubt now cherish the exile, along with all the others – but notice had been served on all that in Scotland, at least, the Church was still master in its own house.

Discerning an end to the proceedings, many were beginning to stir, eager to discuss all this drama, when David raised his, hand with a final morsel with which to regale a memorable assembly.

"One more matter for your ears, my lords, before you disperse to carry out our decisions – although strictly, it is not a matter for this court, but for another. It concerns us all, however, as upholders of the right, and good subjects of His Grace. The right royal burgh of Linlithgow has been much to the fore these last days, for good or ill. The Sheriff thereof, Hamilton of Kincavil, has disclosed to the Privy Council that some years ago a plot was laid to murder the King's Grace. In his own bedchamber. It was during the régime of the evil Douglases. Sir George and James Douglas of Parkhead, Captain of the Royal Guard, were privy to it. But the instigator of the plot, and the miscreant whose hand was to assassinate the young monarch was Sir James Hamilton, the Bastard of Arran!"

The corporate gasp of the assembled churchmen was perhaps occasioned more by the public proclaiming of that name than by the man's identity or even the enormity of the accusation.

"The plot was to put the Bastard's father, the Earl of Arran – now deceased – upon the throne. It was not carried out, not because of any relenting by wicked men but because timely arrangements were made for the rescue of our liege lord from the Douglas hands, which some may remember. Sheriff Hamilton – who is brother to the late Patrick, Abbot of Fearn, who suffered for heresy here in St. Andrews – has revealed the secret now, on a matter of conscience, being in fear of his life from his kinsman Sir James, and consequently being desirous of being at peace with Holy Church! The said Sir James has been arrested and will be tried forthwith. I pray that he will receive the fate he so justly deserves. Before my own eyes he stabbed to death the unarmed and wounded Earl of Lennox after the battle of Linlithgow Bridge. It is perhaps apt and just that his downfall should proceed from the same Linlithgow! My lords, I thank you for your attention and call upon the Archbishop of Glasgow to pronounce the benediction. This assembly and conclave stands adjourned."

David Beaton, then, had thrown down the gauntlet, not only to his recalcitrant churchmen, to the nobles, to his monarch, but to the powerful House of Hamilton as well. He left the assembly with no more friends than when he entered it — but not a few, who would never have admitted it, thanked God in their hearts that a strong man had arisen in Scotland, at last.

Chapter Twenty-two

DAVID could not sit, although he was very tired, so long as his monarch was on his feet; and James Stewart's dogged pacing seemed to have been going on for hours. They both had been up all night, and both had spent most of the previous day in the saddle, James summoned to Stirling from the west country, David from St. Andrews. The infant Prince Arthur, second son of the King, had however died before either of them reached Stirling; and his brother, James, Duke of Rothesay, heir to the throne, was stricken with the same dread infantile illness.

It was now almost mid-forenoon, and in the bright sunlight both men looked grey, haggard. James had been looking thus a lot, of late, although he was only twenty-eight. Some said that he was wearing himself out with his strange roamings of the land, in disguise, bedding night after night with different women; some said that Sir James Hamilton, the Bastard, at his execution, had put a curse upon his King, declaring that he would be with him in hell, and David Beaton also, in two-score months — and that the monarch had scarcely slept soundly since. Whatever the cause, James was not the man he had been. As for the Cardinal, he still did not look his forty-seven years — but he too had aged this past year. He was overworking, bearing too much of the burden of state — the more so as James's moral fibre seemed to disintegrate; moreover the smell of burning flesh was seldom out of his nostrils these days — for it was considered essential that the leader of the Church himself should preside over the execution of the Church's heretics, sick as the ghastly process made him.

James, in his pacing of the little gallery beneath the tower room

288

where the feverish princeling lay, tripped over a stool on which were set untouched wine and meats. Violently he kicked all across the room.

"God's wounds—must you stand there and stare at me, man!" he shouted. "Can you do nothing but stand? Is nothing to be done?"

"Sire—all is being done that can be done," David assured, not for the first time. "The best physicians in the land are with the prince. Prayers are being said before a score of altars. His lady-mother is with him. We can do no more, Your Grace."

"It is poison, I tell you!" James cried. "First the bairn—and now this! My enemies, who would have my throne! The Hamiltons. They hate me. Scheme my hurt, always. Since James Hamilton's death I have had no peace. That was your doing. You compassed his execution . . ."

"Sire—there is no trace of poison. I told you. Both children have been examined. None of the signs are there . . ."

The other was not listening. "Bastards!" he muttered, staring out of the window over the fair carse towards the towering purple ramparts of the Highland Line. "How many bastards have I spawned? God only knows. But all stout. Strong. Is a curse indeed on me, that only my true sons, heirs, must dwindle and die? Sickly from birth. It is too much. More than I can bear, I tell you . . .!"

"It is grievously hard, Sire. All your realm, all Christendom, sorrows with you. But all is not yet lost. Prince James may live. And your Queen is young. She will bear you other children."

"More weaklings!"

"The Duke of Longueville is no weakling, Highness. Do not despair." To distract the other's mind, if possible, David returned to an earlier theme. "The Irish princes wait below, Sire. Even if you cannot grant them audience at such a time, a decision must be made on their proposals. They are offering Your Grace another crown—even though it is one you scarcely want . . ."

"What care I for their crown? An empty title, no more. Only offered me because Henry has decided to call himself King of Ireland!"

"To be sure. But it could be another weapon with which to strike at King Henry. Once, they say, a Scots prince was crowned King of All Ireland. Do not then reject this offer out of hand,

Sire, I say. Nor wholly accept it either. Graciously acknowledge their offer. Say that you will investigate and consider your ancient claim. That at least will confound Henry's arrogant assumption of it."

"To what end, man? How will that either help me, or hurt my precious uncle?"

"Thus, Sire. It will enable you to send troops to Ireland. To help guard your possible throne. And protect your possible Catholic subjects against the protestant fury of the heretical King of England."

"God's sake, man — talk sense! What men have I to send to Ireland? You know that I need every man that I can find to protect my own Borders from English raiders."

"There are some you can spare — and notably well! The Islesmen. The Clan Donald federation. They are ever a thorn in your flesh, revolting against you. A danger at your back, with the English in front. But they have many ties with their O'Donnell cousins in Ireland. Always they are spoiling for an expedition thither. Send them to Ireland, with your blessing. Let them make trouble for Henry, not you!"

James groaned. "How can you talk of such things now . . .?"

"The business of the realm must go on, Sire."

The door opened. The Queen walked in, alone. She was calm, clear-eyed, upright, although there was weariness in her carriage.

"It is all over, James," she said quietly. "The child is dead."

Her husband raised his clenched fists high, and a long shuddering cry escaped him. He found no words, only the wail of a broken spirit.

"I am sorry," Mary of Guise said simply. "In the end there was no pain, at least."

Unspeaking still, the King turned to the wall, to beat his hands against the panelling, on and on.

The Queen raised her tired eyes to meet those of David Beaton. That man spread open eloquent hands in a silent gesture, shook his head, and bowing, left them alone.

The death of both sons of the King of Scots was not only a personal and dynastic tragedy, it was a political disaster of the first magnitude. With James obviously a man both unlucky and of failing health, the succession was clearly open. The ambitious in that respect, therefore, were encouraged to redouble their efforts. For practical purposes these were reduced to two — although various outlying branches of the great House of Stewart made far-fetched overtures, as a matter of prestige. Albany had died in France, childless. So that only the King of England and the Hamiltons were left to make serious claims. Henry, of course, had no conceivable right, save that of might and a fierce lifelong desire. Old Arran was dead — but he had left a legitimate brood, as well as otherwise, and the new Earl, his son, a weak and haughty young man, was a great-grandson of James the Second, and no-wise lacking in ambition.

The Hamiltons, then, seeing the crown nearer to their grasp than they could have hoped, began to intrigue vigorously, seeking supporters amongst the nobles angry with the King, and pro-mising the plums of office to all who aided them to the throne. Arran even approached David Beaton, intimating that if he could count on his favour, the Hamiltons could be relied upon to be good sons of Holy Church; on the other hand, if not, he could hardly fail to discern undoubted advantages in the tenets of the new religion.

Henry Tudor was even less subtle. He issued a proclamation declaring himself to be Overlord of Scotland, announced that the Popish churchmen in the northern kingdom were tyrannical imposters, since ecclesiastically all Scotland came under the authority of his reformed Archbishop of York, and ordered his Wardens of the Marches to cross the Border with all possible force and fury, while his Earl Marshall, the Duke of Norfolk, was to gather an army for full-scale invasion. Undoubtedly Henry was encouraged to this course by reports of quarrelling between the King of France and the Emperor Charles. All-out war abruptly loomed closer than at any time since Flodden.

King James was as a man felled, stunned by the weight of woes descended upon him. It seemed scarcely credible that so vigorous and lusty a young man could so suddenly have altered. The Queen declared to David that she was sure that his sickness was not all of the heart and head; she feared some wasting ail-ment.

A Parliament was hastily called to deal with the crisis, the King attending in listless lethargy. Even the word that the Douglases were assembling again in force all along the Border failed to rouse him. The raising of armed forces was obviously the first priority – but as usual the Treasury was all but empty. A special levy was agreed to, with marked reluctance, stimulated by the Cardinal's promised 30,000 gold crowns from the Church – as by a still more telling pronouncement David almost casually intimated that he had had drawn up a list of important men suspected of heresy, to the number of 360, and it was to be hoped that, at this time of national danger, these would not have to be proceeded against. The inference was evident – and effective. It was sheer blackmail, of course – but the money flowed in.

The Earl of Huntly, chief of the Gordons and Lieutenant of the North, was appointed to command the new army, and ordered to the Borders forthwith. Fortunately the cream of the Clan Donald warriors were already on their way to Ireland.

With the fever of war in the air, Scotland closed her ranks, as always. The Hamiltons, who whatever leanings they might have to Protestantism – and the new Earl of Arran claimed to be the first name on the Cardinal's black list – would have seen an end to all their hopes in a victory by Henry, threw their weight into the struggle.

In the midst of it all, the Queen-Mother, Margaret Tudor, died suddenly at Methven, even as she agitated for another divorce. Her brother in London, cordially as he loathed her, immediately found a new stick with which to beat his nephew – she had been poisoned by her most unnatural son. Henry announced that he was coming north in person to take order with the unsatisfactory James.

David was presiding at an Inquisitorial court in Aberdeenshire when the tidings of Henry's latest move arrived at Linlithgow, and James was in a quandary. The armed forces that he needed were as yet far from assembled and equipped, and he was in no state for any major trial of strength. On the advice of Chancellor Dunbar he sent a temporising note to his uncle, declaring that he would meet him on their mutual Border, to discuss their differences in peaceable and amicable fashion as became kinsmen. Henry sent back word that he was on his way, and would interview his nephew at the Tweed.

David, summoned south urgently by the Queen, was much perturbed. He said that the King should on no account meet Henry. The Tudor would arrive at the head of a great army, and

James would be in a position of hopeless inferiority from the first. The English king would bluster and threaten, and his nephew could not hope to prevail. David could hardly declare that his liege lord would be wholly outwitted, as well as outmanned – but that was his belief.

James might have held stubbornly to his decision once; but he was not the man he had been. A courier was sent, cancelling the meeting.

Couriers crossed, actually. Henry also had changed his mind. Now he announced that York was as far north as he could afford time to travel. James was summoned to meet him there.

David's attitude was notably vindicated by this autocratic demand. Deep in England, at York, James would be as good as a prisoner. The Tudor's tactics were nothing if not plain and unvarnished.

Henry's reaction to the King of Scots' decision to decline the meeting was typical. He ordered Sir James Bowes, his Warden of the East March, to collect all available forces and march on Edinburgh forthwith to capture James Stewart and bring him into his presence at York. With Angus, and a large contingent of Douglas supporters, Bowes crossed Tweed.

Huntly, based at Kelso, had been dealing with scores of sporadic small-scale raids for weeks. Now, though much of his force was dispersed, he sallied out to meet the invaders, and encountered them at Haddon Rigg.

The sides were fairly evenly matched, although Bowes and Angus had the preponderance. For a while the battle swayed this way and that. Strangely enough, at the last major conflict on a national scale, that of Flodden Field, twenty-five years before, the issue had been largely decided by the Lord Home defeating the English right wing and then pursuing them off the field and into the hills, thus leaving his own Scots left wing unprotected. Today the reverse eventuated. That Lord Home was dead, but his son and successor, hurriedly summoned from Home Castle across the Merse, arrived at a critical moment with four hundred moss-troopers and bore down on the English right. Probably the invaders believed that this was only the advance-guard of a larger host – and certainly they had reason to dread the ominous slogan of "A Home! A Home!" At anyrate, their right broke in panic, and with Huntly redoubling his efforts, the entire English front collapsed. Great was the slaughter, and great the numbers of ransomable prisoners taken. Bowes himself, with his brother, had the humiliation of being captured, as well as most of his captains. Indeed Angus also was taken – but after yielding his sword, by quick dagger-work slew his captors and escaped.

It was a notable victory, and Scotland rejoiced and breathed more freely. But Henry's fury knew no bounds, and though he turned for the south himself, he ordered Norfolk to make all haste with a major invasion, despite the onset of early winter weather.

So there was only a brief breathing-space for the Scots. The royal army assembled on the Boroughmuir of Edinburgh.

David Beaton, who saw war not only as major folly but as the failure of statecraft and all that he stood for, never ceased to work for a negotiated peace – even while he poured his own and the Church's money into the royal coffers to buy arms, ammunition and mercenaries. His busy emissaries hurried to London, Paris, Brussels and Rome, and, nearer at hand, to Norfolk's host, temporising, tempting, threatening. James allowed him to do as he liked; indeed he seemed scarcely interested. More and more David went to the Queen for decisions. She was pregnant again – so James had not wholly lost his manhood.

Norfolk crossed the Border with forty thousand men, and the Earls of Southampton, Shrewsbury, Derby, Cumberland, Rutland and Hertford, as well as the insatiable Angus, and the lovely dales of Tweed and Teviot, Esk and Liddel, blazed again. Although it was a hard November, and no campaigning weather, King James and his host, of nearly thirty thousand, moved south. David Beaton, engaged in raising and equipping more men, was to bring them on as soon as might be.

The reinforcements, mainly hired by Church money, never got beyond the Boroughmuir of Edinburgh. King James himself arrived back in the capital, alone save for one or two close companions, a dejected, almost broken man. The royal army had got as far as Fala Muir, at the north end of the Lammermuir pass over into the Borderland, when word reached them that Norfolk was in full retreat. Or, at least, retiral. The English were the victims of their own tactics. The Borders had been raided and burned so often that the land was now a blackened desert. There was no sustenance here for a great army. Norfolk's lines of communication stretched all the way from York, and the severe winter conditions made provisioning almost impossible. His father, the old crooked carle Surrey, victor at Flodden, would never have allowed himself to get into this fix, whatever Henry's orders. With nobody to fight, save small raiding parties of Borderers from the hills, the English commander had bowed to the inevitable and started back on the long road to York.

James had seen his opportunity – pursuit, annihilation, revenge. Northern England lay wide open to his army. He would teach Henry a lesson that he would never forget. But the Scots nobles, whose levies formed the bulk of his army, had blankly refused. As it happened to his grandfather, James the Third, at Lauder, so it was repeated at Fala Muir. The lords utterly rejected the King's command to advance. Now that the threat of invasion of their lands was lifted, they were going home with their men. Their prolonged resentment at their monarch for his reliance on the churchmen boiled over. They wanted no bad-weather adventures in England – where the very conditions that had assailed Norfolk would strike them. Had James been his father – or even himself a few years earlier – he might have dominated them. As it was, his pleas and entreaties, like his commands, were roughly repelled.

The invasion threat was lifted meantime – but the King was as a man prostrated. And since so much in Scotland depended upon the monarch, the kingdom's state was parlous in the extreme.

During that grim winter David, in co-operation with the Queen, did everything in his power to bolster the King's morale. Somehow he kept together the army of about eight thousand, assembled to reinforce that of the King. He urged James to a number of knightings, which only the King might perform and which gave an impression of power. He prevailed upon the monarch to involve himself in an extension of the powers of the new College of Justice, which David himself had been instrumental in instituting a few years before, to counter the biassed hereditary jurisdictions of the barons. In all, Mary of Guise aided and encouraged – although her own greatest hopes for her husband's betterment centred on the child growing in her womb.

Henry proved that he, at least, was not a man to be discouraged, by sending yet another expedition against the Scots. This one, under the command of Lord Dacre, made its assault on the West

March, for a change. Lord Maxwell, Scots Warden of that March, made urgent demands for aid. David's waiting host, now sadly depleted in numbers, was despatched south by west.

Believing it to be to James's advantage to be actively involved, David prevailed on him to accompany the troops, at least as far as Lochmaben Castle. He himself went on a hurried tour of the West Country, to whip up more men from lords who might still be considered loyal.

He arrived at Lochmaben a few days later — just in time to witness the shocking panic of an army in hopeless rout. James was already gone, fleeing north again, a man scarcely possessed of his wits.

David got the shameful story from Lord Maxwell's son, apparently one of the few men of note who had escaped capture in the most disgraceful military disaster in all Scots history. King James had remained at Lochmaben while his host had moved on to a strong position on the River Esk, in the levels of the Solway Moss, to prevent the English force from crossing into Scotland. There an unseemly altercation had broken out as to who was to command. Maxwell, as Lord Warden, had assumed the lead to be his — but certain of the lords from the north would have none of it, declaring that his was only a local command. Cassillis and Glencairn, in particular pointed out that they were earls, and senior. Matters had almost come to blows when the churchmen, whose forces composed the greater part of the army, declared that the King must decide. So, with the enemy not far off, couriers had been sent back to Lochmaben. They had returned, presently, not with the King but with a young man, newly knighted, named Sir Oliver Sinclair. He was almost unknown to the others, one of the new and strange favourites that James had gathered round him. This was to be the commander.

The Scots camp degenerated into chaotic tumult at the news. Scarcely a single leader or captain would serve under this nonentity, nor allow his men to serve. Sinclair's very life was in danger, and the Warden found himself in the astonishing position of having to use his best men to protect the usurping commander-in-chief. It was during this heartbreaking folly that the English attacked — as well they might. A vastly smaller invading contingent, under Sir Thomas Wharton, drove in upon the disorganised and arguing Scots; but there was no fight, no battle —

only a rout, a massacre, and panic-stricken headlong flight back across the Esk, where hundreds drowned, and into the quaking marshes of the Solway Moss. Over a thousand were captured, including Sinclair and the Warden, the Earls of Cassillis and Glencairn, the Lords Somerville, Oliphant, Gray, Fleming and the Masters of Erskine and Rothes.

The Battle of Haddon Rigg was avenged indeed.

Next day David caught up with the fleeing King and a few companions at Shotts, near where Lanarkshire runs into Stirlingshire. He was barely to be recognised as the swack and vigorous young monarch who had cut so fine a dash in France not so long before. Bent, shrunken, gaunt, eyes wild, mouth slack, he seemed a totally different person. He did not appear to recognise David as he joined them; indeed he spoke to none, lost in an unhappy world of his own.

It was only as they came down from the high ground to the valley of the Forth, near Falkirk, that David realised that the King was not making for Linlithgow, but heading northwards for Stirling Bridge. Queen Mary lay at Linlithgow, awaiting the birth of her child. But James, despite the Cardinal's pleas and urgings, would not hear of riding to his anxious wife. He only muttered the word Falkland again and again. In the end, David requested permission to leave His Grace's presence meantime to go to the Queen. Permission was neither granted nor withheld, James scarcely seeming to hear.

It was three days later before David came to Falkland, in the forest, bearing his news. An aura of deep gloom enveloped the palace. Balfour of Fernie, the Keeper, told him that the King was grievously ill, in body as in mind. Since his arrival he had shut himself in his own room and would see none — least of all the physicians they had summoned. He neither ate nor drank — but they could hear him talking to himself, sobbing and beating the walling. Sometimes he cried out, as though in mortal pain. All at Falkland were profoundly thankful that the Cardinal had come.

James was lying on an untidy bed, half-clothed, staring up at the ceiling. He did not even turn his head as David entered. The room smelt stale.

Bowing briefly, David want straight to the bedside. "Your Grace," he said, quite sharply. "I have tidings for you. Good tidings. From your lady. The Queen sends you greetings and loving care. She is well, thank God — and delivered of a child!"

The man on the bed still stared straight upwards. His voice seemed to come from a long way off. "Dead?" he asked, "Like the others?"

"No, Sire. Alive, sound, and in good health."

"But . . . not a son!"

David swallowed. "No, Sire. A daughter. But a fine girl, fair and strong."

James said nothing.

"Your Grace — here is joy! You have a child again. A Princess of Scotland. Hale and bonnie. The Queen also is well. You must be up and doing, Sire — as soon as you are able. To ride to see them . . ."

He gained no sort of response.

"My lord James — do you not understand? You have an heir. To your throne. There is naught that says that a woman shall not succeed to the crown of Scotland. There has never been a Queen of Scots — but what of that?"

The King had not once glanced at him.

Shaking his head, David turned to try another subject. "The word from the south-west is that Dacre has turned back. With his prisoners. He has burned a few towns and peel-towers — but that is largely Douglas country, and Dacre will not offend Angus."

This deliberate bringing in of the offensive name aroused no answering spark of hatred.

"He has a thousand prisoners, including many of Your Grace's lords. And Oliver Sinclair. Is it your wish that ransom negotiations be set in train?"

Shame no more aroused the King than did hate.

"Sire — you are ill. Sick. Have you any great pain . . .?"

James raised himself on the bed, and though he now looked at David his eyes were strangely out-of-focus. "Fiend . . . take it!" he gasped. "It came with a lass. And . . . and it will gang with a lass! Fiend take it! And me!" And sinking back, he turned his face to the wall, and so lay.

David knew what these strange words meant, of course. The crown had come to the House of Stewart two blood-stained centuries before through the marriage of Marjory Bruce, only surviving child of the hero King Robert, with Walter the High

Steward. King James now visualised its passing, in the same fashion. He shrugged.

"Your Grace may yet have sons," he said. "And are there not a sufficiency of members of the House of Stewart whom your daughter might wed, to keep the name?"

But James paid no heed. Indeed there was nothing that David could do thereafter, try as he would, to persuade the stricken monarch so much as to turn his back from him. Silent, motionless, he lay, the inert husk of a man. Eventually, sighing, David left him alone, if not in peace.

In the days that followed, King James quite literally and visibly, before the eyes of such as penetrated to the royal bedchamber, wore away. He was clearly dying, presumably of some wasting disease — although, on the face of it, the cause seemed rather a complete lack of any desire to live. He vomited painfully at times — but only brought up a colourless fluid, and this might well have been the result of starvation, for he would eat nothing.

On the sixth day after the birth of the princess, David Beaton was desperate. Summoning Henry Balfour, a notary, and kinsman of the Keeper of Falkland, he set him to write in an ante-room off the King's chamber. Taking only the Earl of Moray, the King's illegitimate half-brother, and shutting all others out, he approached the royal bed determinedly.

"Your Grace," he said loudly. "You must heed me now. The time may be short — and there is the realm to think of. You hear? Understand?"

He received no least acknowledgement.

With a glance at Moray, he did the forbidden thing. He reached out, and laid hands of the King's person, turning him over, towards him.

James's limp body offered no resistance. The blank and clouded eyes registered no emotion.

"Sire — your daughter," David went on, close to the royal ear." The realm must be governed. When you are gone. She will be Queen. An infant. She must have governors. Regents. Who is to be Regent?"

There was still no sign. Moray shook his head.

"Your Grace — you must give your decision. It is your bounden duty." David paused, frowning. "Will you hear *my* advice? I say, a Regency of four. Four governors, to aid her mother in the upbringing and rule of the Queen. These four — James, my lord of Moray here, your brother; George Gordon, Earl of Huntly, your Lieutenant of the North; Archibald Campbell, Earl of Argyll, the Justiciar. Honest lords and sound churchmen. And myself, David Beaton. Will you have it so, Sire?"

Silence.

"Speak, Sire — in the name of God! Or show some sign."

The lack-lustre eyes blinked, once. That was all.

"You saw?" David demanded of Moray. "Is it enough? It is all we will get, I swear!" And at Moray's nod. "Balfour man, here! Your paper . . ."

He took the unfinished parchment from the notary, which began '*I, James, by the Grace of God, King of Scots, Defender of the Faith* . . .' Also the pen. "Sire," he said, "This must be signed. Your royal will and declaration. Here is the pen . . ."

He turned to the Earl. "My lord — will you hold him?"

As Moray held his half-brother approximately upright, David took the limp hand, put the pen between the fingers, and guiding them firmly, wrote at the foot of the paper, *James R.*

"It is done," he said, letting the hand fall. "And God forgive me!"

The taciturn Moray shrugged. "It was necessary," he said.

Some time that night James Stewart died, without a word spoken, an old done man of thirty, leaving behind him chaos — and more royal bastards than any other monarch on record. And Mary, Queen of Scots, one week old, reigned in his stead.

Chapter Twenty-three

DAVID the Cardinal stared out of the iron-bound window of the royal fortress of Blackness Castle, at the slate-grey winter waters of the Firth of Forth surging sullenly on the rocks a mere twenty feet below, an angry and frustrated man. Two weeks after the King's death, with a thousand matters demanding skilled guidance in the rudderless ship-of-state — yet here he was trapped, imprisoned like a felon on this rock in the Forth, helpless while all went to ruin around him.

David Beaton had not been the only one to take precautionary action while King James had hovered on the brink of eternity. The Hamiltons had seen their opportunity, and taken it. They secretly gathered their strength, and with the support of the anti-Church nobles, seized the capital the moment the King's death was announced. David had had much to see to, those first days, on the business of the realm. After a conference with Mary of Guise, riding from Linlithgow to have the Regency of himself, Moray, Huntly and Argyll officially proclaimed, he had been set upon by a large armed force of Hamiltons, and brought here to prison at Blackness. Arran, who claimed that as next heir to the throne he was entitled to be Regent, had himself proclaimed instead.

If David's mood was almost as stormy as the waves which beat upon the rocks below, he had nothing of their sullen acceptance. Whatever his anxiety and physical constriction, his mind was busy. The situation was not hopeless, he told himself. He still had enormous powers – if he could but bring them to bear. And he had one great advantage, if he could but exploit it. He was dealing with a weakling, whatever his armed strength.

There must be a way of outwitting Arran, even from a prison cell. Would a threat of excommunication serve? Probably not, since the man was obviously much infected with heresy. Also, it had to be remembered that if the infant Queen Mary died, as her two brothers had died, Arran would be the legitimate King of Scots – and it would be no advantage to have previously excommunicated the King! This was Arran's strength, in so many aspects of the situation. What then were his weaknesses, apart from those of character?

The wits of his advisers – that was where to concentrate. It would have been different if Sir James the Bastard, his half-brother, had been alive – for, whatever else, *his* wits were shrewd enough. Indeed, had he been alive, it is probable that by now David himself would not be so; Primate and Archbishop though he might be, he would have been slain out-of-hand. But Arran's principal adviser now was another illegitimate half-brother, John Hamilton, Abbot of Paisley. He was a clever man – but vastly different from Sir James. He lacked ruthlessness and swift decision. He was not much of a churchman, but was not thought to be tinged with the heretical trouble – naturally, since through the Church he had gained great riches. Probably he was enough of a cleric to be somewhat in awe of a Cardinal — and, better, to realise what a Cardinal might see fit to do. John Hamilton was the man to work on.

Promptly David rang a bell, for paper and pens. At least he could write letters from here. Indeed he had no complaints on the score of comfort and conditions in his imprisonment. Patrick Barclay and his servants had been captured with him, and now waited upon him. But he would write this letter to the Abbot of Paisley privately.

He was half-way through a communication which ought to leave John Hamilton in no doubts as to his ecclesiastical future should his superior in Christ not be transferred, for a start, to his own castle of St. Andrews, when Barclay knocked at the door to announce a visitor for the Cardinal — none other than the Earl of Arran himself.

David hid his surprise as best he could, and schooled his mind to deal with a totally unexpected situation.

When the Earl was ushered in, David was over at the window again. He did not turn. His back looked very stiff.

"Greetings, my lord Cardinal and cousin. I hope I see you well? And lacking nothing for your comfort? "Arran said. He had a slight lisp.

"I lack the principal ingredient of my well-being *and* comfort, sir. My freedom!" That was crisp, and addressed to the waves.

"Aye, well . . . let us hope that will be of short duration."

"Hope, my lord? I require more than hope from you. Since I understand that it is on your orders that I am here. You have presumed to interfere with a Prince of the Church and a Regent of this kingdom . . ."

"*I* am the Regent," the other said shortly. "I only."

"Lacking the royal nomination, not until Parliament so appoints you, my lord!" David turned round.

The Earl said nothing. He was a tall, lanky young man of twenty-five with a foxy face which yet lacked a fox's cunning. There was a certain intelligence about the features, but it was marred by indecision.

They considered each other. "Well, my lord?" David said, at length.

Arran spoke jerkily. "I regret that we are at odds. It need not be so. Together, you and I might do great things, my lord Cardinal. After all, we are cousins."

Strangely enough, that was the truth. The old Earl of Arran had married a second time late in life, Janet Beaton, daughter of David's uncle, and left this legitimate son, as well as seventeen bastards.

"Great things for whom? I serve the infant Queen and her realm. And Holy Church."

"As do I, of course. And . . . I could offer you much."

"Could you, my lord? As instance?"

"I could permit you to return to St. Andrews."

"Permit? I *require* you to do so, as a son of the Church. In simple duty. Nor to seek to restrict me further, in St. Andrews or elsewhere."

The other scowled. "I think you misunderstand the position, my lord. By holding you safe here, I am protecting you. Sheltering the Church's head. From those who seek your blood. From the reforming party. And the English party. King Henry has ordered that you be slain."

"Ha! So that is your excuse? And do Henry Tudor's commands now rule in Scotland?"

"No. But not a few would be glad to obey them. And receive his rewards. Especially the Douglases. They are scarce friends of yours — are they, my lord Cardinal?"

"They are my enemies, yes. But scarce close enough to endanger my person . . ."

"Close enough, I think! My lord of Angus, and Sir George, reached Edinburgh yesterday! King Henry has sent them back. With letters to myself."

"Precious soul of God! Angus! Back!" For once, David Beaton was shocked.

"Aye. And not loving you. So now you see why you are safer in this stronghold. And, if I allow you, in St. Andrews Castle. Biding there, secure."

David pulled himself together, forcing his trained and disciplined mind to cope with this situation. It was only an excuse, of course, since Arran had imprisoned him before Angus returned — but it did explain Arran's presence here now. He needed help, with the Douglases back. How long could he retain power in Scotland with Angus there?

Even as he asked himself that question, its corollary came equally clearly to his busy mind. How long could *he* survive, against Arran and Angus both? If Arran joined forces with Angus now, he and the Church both must fall, and the child Queen become a mere puppet in their hands. If Arran needed help, so did he. And the fact that Arran had come here, to see him, showed not only that he knew it, but that it was Beaton's help he would have, if he could. He feared Angus — as well he might. There was nothing for it, then. He must work with this foolish cousin of his, little as he liked it. But . . . on the best terms he could gain.

None of all this was allowed to be apparent when he spoke. Cool again, he said, "You would have me secure in St. Andrews, my lord — well away from Edinburgh. Until your Parliament is over! That I may not oppose you there. In case it is I whom Parliament appoints as Regent — not you!"

The younger man flushed. "You are too sure of yourself, my lord Cardinal!" he exclaimed.

"Say that I can see the nose before my face! What else have you to offer me, my lord?"

"I came to offer you the hand of friendship, sir — not to be mocked! And your Church requires my friendship, I think!"

"My Church — and yours, I hope?" David paused significantly. "In what does Holy Church require your aid? Has Angus brought King Henry's commands to you to assail the Church?"

"Well you know that the Church requires my aid. As Regent. Angus is against it, yes — but that is not my meaning. The Church totters. You know it. You alone sustain it. But for you it would have fallen, here in Scotland, ere this."

"You flatter me, my lord!"

"Wait and see if I flatter you! How shall your Church stand if it learns that its support has feet of clay? Suppose it is declared at the Parliament that you forged the late King's testament appointing you to the Regency?"

David drew a long breath, before speaking very carefully. "I counsel you, my lord, to take heed to your words!" he said softly. Who had babbled — Moray or Balfour?

"I do — and take heed to the words of some others, likewise! As should you. For your own weal, my lord Cardinal. And other sorer words still."

"You have an ear for slanders, it seems?"

"Many are saying that His Grace died of poison! And all know how close you cherished and kept him! Keeping others away."

"God's mercy! Are you crazed?"

"I do not say it. But some do."

"None would truly believe that!"

"Do not be so sure, my lord. In especial, when it is linked with the other story. Of the princess. The infant Queen. Some doubt that His Grace was her father. Preferring yourself!"

"Holy Mother of Christ! This is beyond all! What kennels have you been scraping, man, to glean such foul slanders?"

"It is in the Court itself that such things are said. The English envoy writes them to his King . . ."

"Aye — there you have it! This smacks of Henry Tudor! It is in his polluted den, I swear, that these lies were conceived!"

"Perhaps." Arran shrugged. "But all know how near you are to the Frenchwoman. That she smiles on you — and you are deemed to be a man partial to women, are you not, my lord Cardinal? Moreover, many of the Court hold that His Grace, sick man as he was, could scarce have conceived this child!"

"I' faith — he was *not* sick! I poisoned him — do you not recollect?" David drew himself up. "My lord of Arran — enough of this. If you came here to chaffer scandalous tales, like any fishwife, I fear your journey wasted."

The younger man flushed again. He seemed to be troubled that way. "Sir," he said stiffly. "I came to offer you my hand. In goodwill. That we might work together. Not to be insulted! I am Regent of this realm, and heir to its throne . . ."

David wondered if he had it all now, knew the best and the worst of it, the weaknesses and strengths of the situation? Arran indeed wanted his help — and would use such means to gain it. He must require it greatly, then. On the other hand, he himself had to get out of this prison before he could improve his own case, as well as Scotland's. He could afford no tantrums in this pass, at anyrate. There might be something more. Arran was a proud and arrogant young man. It must have been something of great urgency that brought him thus personally to Blackness. It had been sufficient to imprison the Cardinal, a few days before; now it was not. He must want something that he could not get from Gavin Dunbar and the others. Was Angus's arrival sufficient reason?

"No insult intended, my lord," he said, less severely. "I but questioned the need for you to repeat these lying tales."

"I inform you of them. That you may perceive the danger. Not only to yourself but to your Church. If they were sufficiently noised abroad. And given credence – in a Parliament. Much hurt could follow."

"And you could prevent that, my lord? At a price?"

"I could prevent much, yes. Command my supporters at the Parliament not to speak of it."

"Since it seems that I am not to be there to give such charges a true answer, I take your point!"

"You dare not be there! Or Angus will have you."

"M'mmm. Then . . . what is your price?"

"First – that you will keep your churchmen away from this Parliament."

"Ha! I see. And second?"

"The Frenchwoman. Her Grace the Queen-Mother is proving . . . difficult."

"So-o-o! I understand. And she holds the infant Queen – without whom you can do little?"

The Earl nibbled his lip. "She holds herself, and the child, close. In Linlithgow Palace. None may come to her. Therefore, until I am confirmed by Parliament in the Regency, the daily business of the realm is sorely hampered. It is insupportable."

"Her Grace is a woman of parts, my lord. After all, she is a daughter of Charlemagne. You should have known that."

"She entirely refuses King Henry's demand. She will not so much as discuss it . . ."

"Henry? What does he demand now, other than my death?"

"Why – that the infant Queen should be affianced forthwith to his son, Edward, the Prince of Wales. That is the word Angus brought."

"God be good! This, now! So soon! Aye – that is Henry. The bairn is but three weeks old. Do you wonder that her mother will have none of it? You – you would not agree to this, my lord?"

306

"How can I say otherwise? Scotland is in no state to withstand him. Especially with the Douglases back, as good as an English army in the land! Indeed, I fear that Angus may at any time descend in force on Linlithgow, to seize the child Queen. Hence it is the more necessary that the Frenchwoman works with me. And quickly. You could persuade her."

"You have chosen an ill moment to seek the rule of this land, my lord! But this of Henry—it is not to be considered. Allow the betrothal, and Henry would immediately demand the care and keeping of his son's affianced bride. Then, he would have Scotland in his grasp indeed. It must not be . . ."

"But what can we do, man? We dare not refuse him."

"Not outright. Not flat rebuff—more's the pity!" David took a turn or two back and forth. "We must use our wits, my lord. Play Henry at his own game. Temporise. Tell him . . . tell him . . . ha—I have it! Tell him that it is difficult. Your own son! You see it? Your own son, my lord, is already selected as husband for the little Queen!"

"Eh . . .? Christ-God—my son!"

"Does the notion not appeal to you? You are next heir. To bring together the two lines would be a notable move. An understandable one. To ensure unity and peace in Scotland. Henry could not claim to be slighted, in such family matter . . ."

"But he is not going to accept that! Henry will have his own way."

"To be sure. But it gives us time. Time is the essence of statecraft. Time to send ambassadors to discuss the matter. Negotiations. Time for Scotland to set her house in order. Aye—and time, for Henry, may be short. He is now past fifty, and gross of body. For long he has misused his person. He will not live to old age. Long before our small Mary comes to marriage, he will be dead. So long as we can keep the child out of his blood-stained hands . . .! All we need is an excuse for temporising, meantime. We do not reject his proposal. Parliament will debate it. Possibly even agree on conditions. So long as we do not determine the matter. All we need is an excuse, difficulties. Your son's prior nomination will serve as well as any. And, my lord—is it so ill a notion, in itself?"

Arran cleared his throat. Obviously he had never contemplated any such thing—nor, of course, had David Beaton until this

307

moment. But he could not fail to see the possibility as greatly strengthening his own position in the land. David saw it rather differently; apart from its immediate value regarding Henry, it would give him a major hold over Arran, bring the Earl into a position of dependence upon himself. It seemed that he was going to have to work with Arran; therefore all such would be valuable.

"This requires thinking on," the younger man said, biting at his nails. "How . . . how would the Queen-Mother take it, think you?"

"I would require to put it to her. Discreetly. Sound her gently. But I think I could persuade her, my lord."

"Aye. But . . . there is Angus. Angus will not smile on this. What am I to do about Angus?"

David smiled to himself. Already this young man was leaning on him, requiring his advice. He must be made to require it much more, above all. And pay for it. "Angus is a burden . . . which we must lessen as best we can. Until we are strong enough to deal with him. That strength we shall gain, here at home, and from France. And Rome. But, this also takes time. And, meantime Angus must not be permitted to raven the land like a wolf at loose. Send him where he can do least harm, my lord. Seem to welcome him — but send him to the Borders again. Make him Warden of the Marches once more. It will please him, to be so accepted. And please Henry. Yet there is little harm left that he may do there. And much to occupy his time. The place is a wilderness, full of thieves and broken men. Aye — buy time with the Marches, for Angus!"

The other eyed him with something like wonderment. "You . . . you have a nimble mind, my lord Cardinal," he admitted reluctantly. "And you said gain strength. From France. Can that be done? Men? Arms? Money?"

"I can do it," David told him briefly. "King Francis is my friend." He paused. "But . . . he is not going to send these to a prisoner in St. Andrews Castle!"

"M'mmm." Askance, Arran eyed the other, become aware that he had been outmanœuvred, that their roles had been largely reversed, that he, not Beaton, was now in the position of suppliant. He drew himself up, in an attempt at least to sound authoritative still. "Well, cousin," he said, "I came here in the belief that we might find means to serve each other. It seems that I was right. I shall have you escorted forthwith to St. Andrews — if you will undertake not to interfere in the forthcoming Parliament. And to use your influence with the Queen-Mother. And to urge the King of France to send me aid . . ."

David smiled. "You are generous, my lord! I require a little more, for my aid."

"What do you require?"

"The Chancellorship."

The Earl's mouth opened, and stayed so for seconds, as he blinked.

"It is the obvious move," David went on smoothly. "Saving you much care and anxiety. And . . . many visits to seek my advice! Together we may do great things — you as Regent and myself as Chancellor."

"But . . . but . . . it is inconceivable! Not to be thought of. None would accept it. Henry. Angus. The lords. My party. Parliament . . ."

David inclined his head. "Not now, no. To announce it now might be too . . . precipitate! Time again, my lord. Let it be but a compact between us, for the moment. A secret. But I in fact will be Chancellor. Lest Angus demand it!"

"You think . . .?"

"It will not be long before he demands the office, I swear. Either for himself or one of his brothers. And how will that serve you?"

"But . . . but . . ." Arran shook his head helplessly.

"You are going to need me as Chancellor, my friend. You cannot do what must be done, without me. Have yourself appointed Regent by this Parliament. I shall hold aloof. Then, when you are Regent, in truth, have Gavin Dunbar make way for me. He will not make objection — that I can assure you. But, that there be no doubts about all this, have him deliver the Great Seal of Scotland to me at St. Andrews, in token! It will be safe there from Angus, moreover! As it was before, for twenty years. Is it agreed?"

The other moistened his lips, and after a long pause, inclined his head without speaking.

"Good, my lord .. ."

Chapter Twenty-four

DAVID rode through the sparkling May morning, and sang, actually sang aloud in the saddle — and it was a long time since he had done anything of the sort. At his side, Marion Ogilvy shook her lovely head although she smiled.

"You are too gay, this morning, for my ease of mind, Davie," she objected. "This presages some devilment, I swear!"

"You would have me gloom and mope, my dear?"

"No. I would but safeguard myself from your designs! Besides, it is not suitable, this carolling! For a man of middle years, out with the mother of his five children! For a Prince of the Church, moreover — Cardinal, Archbishop, Primate, Lord Privy Seal . . ."

"And Chancellor. Let us have the roll complete, my heart!"

Marion turned to stare at him. "You said . . . Chancellor?" she got out, moistening her lips.

"Aye — no less. First minister of the realm. In proof whereof the Great Seal of Scotland lies again in my deepest vault at St. Andrews."

"But . . . Davie! How can this be? What madness is this? You said, when you came last night to Balfour, that you were fleeing. From your enemies. A hunted man . . ."

"All true, lass. Henry and the Douglases seek my life, actively. For the moment I am no longer safe, even in St. Andrews Castle. Henry has indeed sent the Lord Lisle, his Lord Warden, with an army, across the Border, with orders to take or slay me — it matters not which! Also to capture the young Queen and carry her south to him at London. And since my lord of Angus is now Scottish Warden of the March I cannot conceive of the English suffering any grievous delay in their project! Steps are taken to hide the young Queen — and thus I am permitted this pleasant sojourn in the North!"

"I do not understand. How then may you be Chancellor?"

"It is something of a long story, my dear — and consequent on the ambitions, frailties and doubts of James Hamilton, Earl of Arran, heir to this unhappy throne. Still something of a secret, see you. Few know it, as yet. It has not been confirmed by a Parliament. My good brother in Christ, Gavin Dunbar, was glad indeed to hand over the seals to me. I fear he never greatly loved nor adorned the office. With the kingdom in chaos, he is glad to be done with it."

"With the kingdom in chaos!" she repeated. "And you, who it now seems have the prime responsibility for controlling that kingdom, in Church and State, in flight from your enemies — you sing, like, like one of these larks!"

He grimaced, and spread his hands. "Better to sing than to weep!"

They were alone, walking their mounts up the long ascent of the Aberlemno ridge that gave on to a great and broad hogsback of land rising out of the northern end of the Vale of Strathmore, some five miles south of Brechin. They had already ridden fifteen miles that morning, east from Balfour. David turned in his saddle, and looking back across all the coloured distance to the unbroken barrier of the far mountains, hazy-blue in the forenoon sun, he stretched out his arms.

"I' faith — this is good!" he cried. "All this. The sweep of it. The freedom. These larks shouting joy to their Maker. I needed it. As I needed you, Marion."

"You were sore confined? Imprisoned again? And by the same Arran! You would suffer that ill, David."

"Aye. Two weeks and more in Blackness, close held. Then two months in my own castle of St. Andrews. Not close, but trammelled, restricted. While Arran held his Parliament. Dunbar's last as Chancellor. And while Angus waited for me! He waits still — a cat at the mouse-hole. Bell-the-Cat's grandson! But this mouse has bolted! And now climbs Aberlemno Hill under the May sun. And sings!"

Marion shook her head. "I do not understand it. Any of it. But I rejoice at least that you are here. Even that you sing!" And, as he urged his beast on. "Where are you taking me, Davie?"

" I told you — it is a secret. You will find out."

"It is a long ride . . ."

Surmounting the ridge, they found themselves on a broad and rolling plateau of wide vistas and great skies, carpeted with wild flowers. No cattle or sheep grazed here, strangely, although the pasture was knee-deep. Seaming this grassy tableland were sudden steep valleys, almost ravines, leafy with trees which grew only there, and loud with spouting burns. The breeze and the wild flowers and the larks had all the rest to themselves.

"I have never been here," Marion said. "It is a good place. A place by itself, apart, yet secure. What is it called?"

"Melgund," he told her. "A land forgotten. Left high by the tide of men. I believed that you would like it. That is why I brought you.

"One day, hawking with my lord of Crawford, from Finavon, two years back, his favourite hawk was lost, and we followed it up here, searching. It was his land, but he scarce knew it."

Cantering over the high meadowland, where the bees humming in the deep clover was as a pulsing of the scented air, abruptly they came to the lip of another of the hidden valleys, somewhat wider than the others. Marion's cry of sheer pleasure was drawn from her involuntarily. At the far side, in a crease of the green land, graced but not embowered by trees, sat a rose-red castle glowing warm in the sunshine.

Never had she seen so lovely a house. Strong but lightsome of line, with two tall towers, squared and circular, linked by a long lower range that was enhanced by many large windows and delicate with corbelling, stringcourses, dormers, turrets and crowstepping, in the French style, it was large but not sprawling, and there was not an ungainly or clumsy line to its entirety.

"It is beautiful!" she exclaimed. "Truly beautiful. What house is that, Davie?"

"Call it Melgund Castle. Or any other name you would wish," he told her, riding down into the valley, spurring quickly now.

When next he drew up, it was before a gatehouse set amidst a trim laid-out garden that enclosed a little formal pond where waterfowl swam. Here was no moat and ditch, drawbridge and portcullis; only this little gatehouse and flanking walls decorated with stone medallions and inscribed panels. David was looking up, above the gatehouse arch, where a splendid heraldic achievement was displayed in the rose-red stone.

"They have fashioned it none so ill, I think," he commented.

It was handsomely wrought indeed, a flourish of the stone-carver's art. The great shield was divided down the centre. On the left was emblazoned the chevron and three otters' heads of Beaton; on the right the crowned lion passant-gardant of Ogilvy.

Beneath was the date 1543 flanked by the initials D. B. and M.O.

"Oh, Davie!" Marion said, blinking rapidly, and biting her lip.

Dismounting, he aided her down, and opening the heavy oaken door, led her in through the gatehouse pend, past the porter's lodge. No guard waited there, no sign of life showed, save for two peacocks which strutted amongst the flag-stones and flower-beds of the forecourt.

Gazing up at that lovely house, close to, Marion perceived that it was all new. The stonework itself, although of a most mellow warmth, was fresh-cut, not worn by time and weather. Everywhere the glowing masonry was lovingly fashioned by cunning hands and man's artifice, in heraldic decoration, ornamental gunloops, canopied niches, embellished window-surrounds — yet chastely, with nothing of fuss or clutter. And all the heraldry showed only the devices of Beaton and Ogilvy; and every decoration was somewhere adorned with the initials D. B. and M. O., lovingly intertwined.

Marion turned and threw herself upon the man, face against his shoulder, sobbing.

He smiled down at her. "Come my dear," he chided gently "This was not fashioned for your tears but for your pleasure."

Still she could not find words, as he led her around the great house. It was built to represent an ancient castle that had grown through the centuries — as had so many — starting from the tall, squared keep, and added to in towers and halls and wings, generation by generation. It was skilfully done, so that, had it not been that all the stonework was equally new, none would have known that this was not a house that had been hundreds of years a-growing. And that all its many owners had had for initials D. B. and M. O.

In all the wonder of it, those proliferating initials were what most affected the woman. For, of course, it was the age-old tradition in Scotland that when initials were carved in stone on any part of a house they must be those of husband and wife.

"What can I say?" she blurted, when at last she recovered her voice. "It is all . . . beyond words. So fair. So much of thought and care. So noble a house. A palace. Oh, Davie — you should not have done it! But — I love you for it! For every stone of it. In especial, every linking of our names. That was kindly done."

"I am glad," he said simply. "I came here yesterday, on my way to you at Balfour. And saw it complete, after many months. I lost my fear then. I knew that you must like it. That it was indeed *your* house. More than mine. That it would stand, as our monument. Down the centuries . . ."

"Davie! Monument! What do you say? What do you mean?"

"I sometimes have another fear, my heart. But . . . not now, Marion. Not today. Today is for joy. Come. Indoors. It is not finished there yet. Not quite. Yesterday it was all a-clang with hammer and chisel . . ."

"And today—nothing? I have not seen a soul."

"There is no one within two miles of us. Or so I gave order. This was to be your day. Tomorrow they will be back again."

For an hour thereafter, Marion ran, exclaiming, about the great empty, finely proportioned house, that smelled of new woodwork and the strange astringent scent of tempera painting— for the walls, where not panelled in pine and oak, were ablaze with colour. In an age when windows were kept small and to a minimum, for security, this house was lit profusely, with light streaming in. The Great Hall, occupying all the first floor of the lower wing between the towers, was the most brilliant room Marion had ever seen—which was not strange, for there was indeed not another like it in all Scotland. The walls here were actually white, with only a delicate and chaste design in colour; and the ceiling was neither the usual stone vaulting nor painted beams, but covered with a magnificent decorative plasterwork, unknown outside Italy and France, gleaming with gold-leaf and all the tinctures of heraldic art.

"It is . . . it is beautiful beyond all telling!" the woman cried, again and again. "A house out of a dream!"

"Better than Balfour, at least!"

"How did you do it, Davie? How was it possible?"

"I brought masons from France. Plasterers from Italy. Painters from the Low Countries. I have long looked at houses in those lands. Esteemed the best in them. Planned to wed them to our own sturdy Scots style. Many have aided me to build this house for you—the King of France, the Emperor Charles, the Pope himself. All for Marion Ogilvy and her brats!" He laughed. "My difficulty was not in the contriving of it, but the keeping of it secret. You would not believe the task it has been, the straits I have been put to. Lest you should hear of it. I had to come here disguised. Few must know that a house was building here – and none that it was the Cardinal's doing! You heard no word of it? No? The place is remote, of course. And I swore all I could to secrecy . . ."

Presently, after allocating rooms for George and Elizabeth and Margaret, now fourteen, thirteen and ten respectively, and for the year-old twins James and Alexander, they stood out on the parapet walk of the keep, which rose high enough to allow them to see out of the valley and over the sweep of the rolling grasslands. Because of its slightly curving formation, this strange verdant plateau looked to be a world all of it's own, no other land showing beyond, neither the long bastions of the mountains on one side, or first, Montreathmont Muir, and then the endless plain of the sea, on the other.

David waved his arm around. "All that you see is yours, my love," he told her. "I bought it from Crawford, who cared nothing for it. From Flemington to Aldbar. A thousand acres. Your kingdom . . ."

"Ours," she amended.

"Perhaps. But all is chartered in your name. As at Ethie. It is yours, whatever may befall me. I would have it so . . ."

"David! That is the second time you have said the like." Marion clutched his arm. "Why? What ails you? Is something on your mind? You who were singing so blithely! Is it King Henry? For fear he may get you?"

"No, no – never think it! But . . . I have enemies a-plenty. And not all would scruple, any more than Henry, as to how they got rid of me. Only a few weeks ago I had word, from a spy in London, that a man Wishart, a renegade Scot, had been sent north to encompass my death. By poison, it was thought. The Douglases have sworn to have me. And Sir James the Bastard's son is said to scheme my end! Certain of the reforming party, also. So, you see, I am wise to take precautions."

"Dear God! Has it come to this? All your power and splendour! You live in dread of the assassin's knife and the poisoned cup? Oh Davie . . ."

"Not dread, Marion. After all, I have lived with such shadows for a score of years. And avoided them with little difficulty. It is the price a man must pay for the rule over other men. My uncle

315

paid it — and wore armour below his clothing all his days. I do not do that, at least!"

She looked away and away. "When, oh when, will you have done with it, David Beaton? Will you ever, indeed, give it up? This evil game of power. Will you ever come here to this Melgund, to me, done with it all? Or must I always sit and wait and dread?"

At the level tone of her voice, so unlike her usual, he turned to touch her blown hair lightly. "That was, in part, the notion behind this house, Marion. This little world of Melgund to be our refuge from that other great world which I plan to leave. For plan it I do. I have had sufficient. But . . . this death of the King, and the disasters of late, have thrown all awry. My task, the saving of Scotland from Henry, has been set back. It will all take a little longer now . . ."

"Davie — do not delude yourself, my dear. You alone cannot save Scotland. In any other, it would be sheerest presumption to consider it. I know it is not so with you. And you have done so much. But — you pursue a dream, Davie. The tide is against you. Do not expend *all* your life on a dream that may not be!"

He smiled thinly. "Some would not call my activities a dream! Half the prelates of this realm, I swear, would question your word for it! And others I can think of."

"Others, yes." She faltered a little, and then went on. "Others might call them a nightmare! Others who die horribly. Bound to stakes!"

He nodded. "A barbarous custom. Offensive to every sense. Would that it could be otherwise. But, unhappily, it is the Church's irreducible and irrevocable penalty for heresy in the first degree. Burning. The reward for the crime of treason to the Church. I cannot alter that. I must stamp out heresy . . . Seven men have been burned, since Patrick Hamilton, yes. Would God that it might have been fewer — for the business stinks in my mind, as well as my nostrils! But — what is that compared with other lands? Henry burns and disembowels hundreds, of the Old Faith, for every one who suffers here. In France and Spain and the Low Countries, men die by the thousand, in this fight to the death. For that is what it is. Here in Scotland seven have been slain. Yet men talk as though it was a multitude. Henry sees to that . . ."

"Henry! David—all the ills of Scotland are not King Henry's doing! Has Henry not become for you a monster, an ogre. You see him always . . ."

"Always, or nearly!" he agreed sombrely. "My dear—for thirty years Henry Tudor has been trying to grasp Scotland. Now he is an ageing man, corpulent of body, vicious of temper, his mind but little short of madness. His ministers and captains, like his wives, go to the block. His own children quail before him, dispossessed. He knows his time is short—and he will have Scotland, if he can, before he goes. His armies lay waste our Borders and southern shires—but cannot gain him what he would have. So he uses every other method he may—bribery, poison, the dagger, calumny. Above all, religion. A man of no religion himself, he yet perceives that religious strife may do what armies cannot. Especially against the Scots, who love argument and dispute on all matters of the mind. So he pours gold into Scotland, with his agitators in the guise of reforming preachers. Civil war is their aim—not reform. And so many here cannot see it, and play his game for him."

She was silent.

"Only a month past he sent Arran offer to make him King of Scotland beyond the Forth. Under Henry's overlordship. With an English army to maintain him. And his first duties—to hand over myself and the infant Queen; to throw off all allegiance to the Pope; and to accept him, Henry—Henry Tudor, mark you—as head of the Church in these islands!"

"The man is crazed . . ."

"Crazed, yes. But cunning. And greatly powerful. To prepare the ground, he diligently spreads lies, tales, slanders. And they bear fruit. You, my dear, have just proved something of his harvest! Even at Balfour you have heard that this land reeks of persecution and burning flesh. On account of seven heretics in fifteen years!"

She swallowed. "They say that you forged the King's will, Davie. Appointing yourself Regent and Governor of the kingdom!"

Set-faced, the man inclined his head. "That one is true," he said.

She did not speak.

"It was necessary. Or so I believed. The King lay like a log

Unspeaking. Unthinking. Dying. Someone had to act. Make provision for his realm. And the infant he had not seen. Spurned. And for his wife. I esteemed it for the best. I guided his hand to sign a testament appointing Moray, Huntly and Argyll as Regents. With myself — since none of these have any knowledge of government. Moray, the King's natural brother. Huntly, son of Margaret Drummond, James the Fourth's natural daughter. Argyll, Moray's goodbrother. These were close enough kin to the child Queen to cherish her — but all with the stain of illegitimacy, so that they could not covet the crown for themselves. As might Arran. I should have included Arran — and watched him like a hawk! That was my mistake . . ."

"Mistake! Dear God, Davie — is that all you see? You did this thing — and see it as no sin! Only a mistake to have left out Arran!"

"I believed it necessary, for the realm's good, I tell you."

"Belief! Necessary!" the woman whispered. "Necessity! That is your true and only belief, David, is it not? Have you any other besides? Sometimes I ask myself! I think you do not truly believe in the Church for which you fight so hard. You say yourself that you are no priest. You burn men, even though you mislike it. You raise men up, and cast them down. Oh, God — do you indeed believe in anything, Davie?"

At the anguish of her cry, the cold, hard look softened on his face, and he spoke slowly. "I believe in God, Marion. And Scotland — aye, I believe in Scotland! And — why, in David Beaton! And you, my dear. That is enough belief for me, I think."

There was a long silence between them.

"So, you hold me guilty," he said, at length. "In this of the forgery. Perhaps, then, you credit the other tales, also? That I poisoned the King? And fathered the infant Queen on Mary of Guise?"

She turned away, as though she had been struck.

After a little, the man sighed. "I am sorry," he said, to her back. "Forgive me, my dear. That was an ill thing to say. In especial here, in this house."

She turned, and threw her arms around him. "Davie, Davie! God pity us that we should hurt each other! Oh, do you not see? This life of power and rule and intrigue has nothing to offer you now. Only fear and hurt and sorrow. And hatred. Leave it all, Davie. And come here, to this peaceful place, to live with me and your children. Leave the fight and the struggle to others. To this Arran. And those lords you named. You have done enough."

"That I will, yes. That is my intention. But I cannot just leave all, of a sudden. Drop from the rule of the land and the Church like a stone into a pool!"

"You could — were you stricken ill. Or caught by Henry!"

"A man may not abandon a life's work so easily, lass. Besides, I have sent to King Francis and the Pope for help. Men, ships, arms. I cannot fail all, now. Give me but a little time. Then I shall drop my burden."

"I wish . . . oh, I wish I could believe even that!" she cried.

They clung together, there on the airy parapet-walk, and at length something of the peace of the great quiet house and all the rippling table-land returned to them.

"I was singing but two hours ago!" David observed presently, ruefully.

"And will sing again," she promised him, bravely. "This is a house for singing. And you are here for longer than is your wont? That I have, at least. When shall we bring the children?"

"Any day. But quickly. The sooner you leave Balfour for Melgund the better."

Chapter Twenty-five

THE little company clattered up the steep climbing streets of Stirling towards the castle on its proud rock, and the townsfolk, used to much more spectacular comings and goings, scarcely spared it a glance. Save for the quality of the horseflesh they rode, they might have been the servants of some small laird or minor churchman, unimportant enough not to be decked in the colours of their lord — for the five men and three women, despite the bright July sunshine, were clad in nondescript clothing and shrouded in grey or black homespun travelling cloaks. Yet the party was as distinguished in composition as any that had ever climbed those cobbled streets — for it included two queens, the bastard son and grandson of a king, and the Primate and Chancellor of the realm.

There had been a great and successful coup — although in

319

essence one of the simplest and least ambitious conceivable. No large forces had been involved, no dramatic gestures. Indeed, it had been an affair after its inceptor's own heart — for however soaring his projects and ambitions, David Beaton always preferred the quiet, carefully-thought-out manoeuvre to the striking and flamboyant action. All had been meticulously planned, and, contrary perhaps to normal, all had fallen out as such planning deserved.

Mary of Guise and her baby daughter had been as good as prisoners in Linlithgow Palace for seven months, suffering a curious double encirclement. Her own French Guard, plus that of the Cardinal, had held the palace-fortress itself secure, allowing in only whom the Queen-Mother would — which latterly, although without enthusiasm, included the Earl of Arran, now accepted by Parliament as the lawful Regent. All around sat the Hamiltons, this of course being Hamilton country. And outside the ring sat another — the Douglases, watching their chance. The Hamiltons had been protecting the young Queen from the Douglases, and Mary of Guise protecting her daughter from the Hamiltons.

Today's work had drastically changed the entire pattern. With the seven-month-old Queen of Scots wrapped in a bundle beneath her nurse's cloak, Mary of Guise and the Countess of Moray, lady-in-waiting, had slipped out of the palace by a postern before dawn, and quietly rowed in a small boat across the dark waters of Linlithgow Loch, to the north shore. There David Beaton and Patrick Barclay were waiting for them. On foot, not risking the noise of horses, they had made their devious and secret way, led by a servant of the Laird of Bonhard, to no less than Blackness Castle, scene of David's late confinement, three miles away. There, using his authority as Chancellor, David had demanded of the royal castle's Keeper a stout boat to take them across Forth, without disclosing further identifications. Moray and Huntly awaited them, with horses, at Limekilns, in Fife. And so they had ridden into Stirling, from the north, not the south, at noonday.

The Lord Erskine, Keeper, now waited for them at the drawbridge of Stirling Castle, and louted low in salutation to the tiny bundle in the nurse's arms.

It might seem to be no more than exchanging one prison for

another; but in fact all was changed. Stirling was the mightiest fortress in the kingdom, and in the middle of a loyal town. Moreover the southern Highlands were near by, where the Douglases were powerless and the Stewarts strong.

Safely installed in the royal quarters, Mary of Guise herself came to David Beaton. "I bring my thanks, old friend," she said. "It has been a long time. Much sorrow, pain and fear have come upon us since last we foregathered. But I never doubted that you would find a way to succour me and my child."

"*My* sorrow that it took so long, Your Grace. But it was necessary to lull Angus and Arran both. To slacken their watch. And to outwit Henry's minions."

She took both his hands. "All, no doubt, is not yet well," she said. "But perhaps we have turned that corner? At anyrate, I feel a different woman for having Davie Beaton by my side again!"

"You are kind," he murmured.

She gave a little laugh. "Less kind, I think, than some name me!"

"Ha! You have heard that evil tale, then? I am sorry. They might have spared you!"

"Do not concern yourself, my friend. In my country such canards are common." She shrugged — "Perhaps I should have been a man — seeking a part to play . . .?"

"God forbid!"

She smiled. "Yet, I think, my mind works as does a man's, in some measure."

"You must tell that to my lord of Lennox!" he murmured.

"Lennox? What of him? He is in France, is he not?"

"No longer, Your Grace. He has just returned, after long. You have not heard? Declaring that he intends to marry you!"

"Name of a name! The good infant! Only once I saw him, I think. In Paris. A pimpled youth . . ."

"Aye — pimpled but ambitious. And vengeful. A very different man from his father, who died before my eyes at Linlithgow Bridge of a Hamilton dagger! He has come home seeking revenge and advancement both. Since he cannot have Sir James the Bastard, he would have Arran the brother. He would displace him, both as heir to the throne and as Regent, the cockerel! He also has a modicum of the royal blood in his veins, you understand? From the same source as Arran. The princess who married the Hamilton had a daughter who married Lennox's grandfather.

It is a far cry — but he would wed Your Grace, to strengthen his position!"

"Sweet Mary! So that is it. Here is a noble youth!"

"He will be here to woo you, I warrant, before long. And without a doubt, Arran will not be far behind, in that case!"

"Arran, too! Oh, no! Arran has a wife and family, has he not?"

"To be sure. But . . . such obstacles have been overcome ere this! Hitherto he has been content with the notion that his son might wed the little Queen, your daughter, one day, instead of Henry's son. But he could not allow Lennox to wed *you*. So he must do something to prevent it!"

"*Parbleu!* The saints preserve me from your lusty Scots lords! They overwhelm me."

"They serve to put us in a very strong position, I think, nevertheless — Your Grace, and even possibly myself!"

Thoughtfully she looked at him. "I see."

"Other lords will also come knocking at your Highness's door, now," David went on. "Seeking not only your hand but your favour, your interest. You will find all changed, I think, before long. You will be able to effect much."

"Only and always with your aid and guidance, Monsieur Davie. But . . . what of the Regent?"

"Leave you the Regent to me," he told her. "We shall use him — to good effect! Meanwhile, I urge Your Grace, not to dash your various suitors' hopes too swiftly and sorely! Keep them dancing attendance. At least until aid from France arrives . . ."

"From France . . .?"

"Aye. I sent for aid to Paris and Rome. King Francis has replied to me. He is sending ships, with arms, money and envoys. I believe our days in the wilderness are nearly over, Madam."

"And Henry? And Angus?"

"Neither may come at you here in Stirling. They are Arran's problem — not yours. You have but to sit close here, keeping the child Queen and gaining strength and support. And let time work against your enemies . . ."

"Time — and Davie Beaton!"

He inclined his head.

David was right. It was not long before the lords began to appear before Stirling Castle, not to besiege it but to plead permission to pay their duty to the infant Queen and their respects to her lady-mother. The Earl of Montrose and the Lord Livingstone were the first to present themselves, living near by. Then a surprise, the sometime renegade Hepburn Earl of Bothwell, who had fallen out with Angus in England on some personal issue, and now elected to throw in his lot, at least temporarily, with the Queen's party. Then came Lord Lindsay of the Byres, who with Montrose, Livingstone and Erskine had been appointed by the Parliament in March to look to the young Queen's upbringing – but had hitherto been unable to take up their duties; his accession was a source of strength, because he brought with him the salutations and support of his kinsman and chief, the Earl of Crawford, David Beaton's new neighbour in Strathmore – which meant that the powerful clan of Lindsay was at least prepared to consider committing itself. Added to these, of course, were the Stewart lords of Innermeath, Avondale, and presently the Earl of Atholl.

In due course, as prophesied, Matthew Stewart, fourth Earl of Lennox put in an appearance, a narrow-faced, weak-chinned but strutting young man, who had been sent to France for safety from the Douglas-Hamilton faction on his father's murder, and who, on the strength of some slight involvement in the Italian wars now looked on himself as an international warrior. Something of a dandy, he affected the French mode in all things, to the extent of speaking little else – and obviously considered this, with his headship of the senior cadet stem of Stewart, his trace of royal blood and his personal excellence, would sweep the widowed Queen straight into his arms. That it failed to do so forthwith greatly disconcerted him. Mary of Guise was more kind to him than she would have been but for David Beaton's prompting, very patient and forbearing; nevertheless, Lennox was offended and disgruntled. David did his winning best with the obnoxious young man – with an eye on Arran, absent in person but seldom out of mind.

That other ambitious young nobleman at first scarcely behaved according to David's predicted pattern. He issued a proclamation, as Regent declaring that the removal of the young Queen from Linlithgow to Stirling, without his agreement, and the holding of her there, was an illegal and treasonable act – without however actually naming these responsible. When Mary of Guise questioned David on this matter, he advised her to wait, and suspend judgement. This was almost certainly a sop to King Henry, lest that angry monarch would believe Arran to have had a hand in the business and take typical Tudor steps in retaliation. Sure enough, a week or two later word reached them that Henry peremptorily required Arran to remove the child from Stirling at once, to Angus's castle of Tantallon, promising £5,000 in gold and his benevolence when this was accomplished, and announcing that the Duke of Suffolk was hastening north, with eight thousand picked horsemen, to aid in the matter. The Cardinal was to be seized at the same time.

The Queen-Mother was alarmed, but David soothed her. Horsemen, in however many thousand, could not take Stirling Castle; and not even Angus, much less Arran, would turn cannon on the fortress that contained their sovereign Queen. Besides, Henry had despatched north many of these special forces, and none had ever got further than Edinburgh. Arran might covet those 5,000 English pounds – but the last thing he would do would be to try to put the precious babe in the hands of Angus – which would be as good as deposing himself from the Regency. Wait, David insisted. Sit close on this tall rock, and let the tide ebb, as he assured her it would.

It did. With Suffolk's force laying waste the Borders, but held at the hill passes of the Lammermuirs, at the beginning of September David Beaton, still at Stirling, received a secret courier – the son of Hamilton of Kincavil, Sheriff of Linlithgow. As a consequence, the next day, with a small escort of the French Guard, he rode to Callendar House at Falkirk, the seat of the Lord Livingstone, some ten miles to the south – the furthest he had been for a couple of months.

At Callendar, another small but select party awaited him – all Hamiltons, but for once, not wearing Hamilton colours. The Regent himself was at their head.

The cousins considered each other, David smiling, at ease, Arran nervously plucking at his lip. After formal but brief salutation, the Earl drew the Cardinal aside, lowering his voice.

He beat about no bushes. "You have Lennox at Stirling, my lord?" he said abruptly. "A simpering Frenchman! Who would have the Frenchwoman to wife, I am told!"

"That I understand to be his desire, my lord," David agreed

gravely. "If by Frenchwoman you refer to Her Grace? She is a good-looking woman, of hale body, and not yet old, my lord — as you know well."

"M'mmm — this is a ticklish matter. If the . . . if Her Grace contemplates another marriage, it is of vital importance to this realm whom she weds."

"Undoubtedly," David conceded.

"In especial, when she holds the child Queen."

"I do not deny it, Cousin."

"Aye. Well . . . I . . . I . . . damn it, man — I might marry her myself!"

The Cardinal inclined his head. Despite the sudden violence of this declaration, Arran was undoubtedly watching closely to see how he took it.

When he did not speak, the other went on. "It would be a convenient match, would it not? I am the next heir. Closer than Lennox. And Regent. I am nearer her age."

"All true," David admitted. "The pity that there are . . . obstructions in the way!"

"Aye. Obstructions. But . . . they are of the sort that can be won round, I think! You, a churchman, know that full well."

"Perhaps. Won round — at a price!"

"That price, may be, I am prepared to pay."

"Indeed? But — there are still obstacles. It strikes in my mind that your wife is a Douglas, Cousin! Daughter to the Earl of Morton. That could mean . . . inconvenience!"

"God's death — I have had sufficient of the Douglases! A bellyful! They are ill folk to sup with. I can scarce be at worse order with Angus than I am! Moreover, he is not the man he was . . ."

"Ha!" David Beaton was suddenly intent.

"He has a sickness. Three times he has had it, of late. He holds to his house of Tantallon, and leaves his Wardenship of the Marches to his kin. He is growing old, praises be!"

"So-o-o! This is interesting. I have not seen him for years — I fear I have tended to avoid the man! But he must be nearing sixty. So, you feel that he is weak enough for you to defy him, eh?"

"A plague! I do not like your choice of words, my lord!"

"Perhaps not. But it occurs to me, Cousin, that you will have to accept not a few chosen forms of words from my lips, if you would follow the course you seem to steer! Is it not so?"

The Earl was silent.

"For one matter, I fear that you have not been the truest son of Holy Church, in the past. And your reforming Calvinist friends do not smile on divorcements! To divorce your wife and marry the Queen-Mother you would require Papal dispensation. I could not gain you that were you not received back to the fullest embrace of Mother Church!"

Scowling, Arran jerked a nod. "That I would be prepared to accept. My anxiety is as to the woman herself. Mary of Guise," he said shortly. "How will she take it?"

"Your suit? Why, my lord, that I cannot say. It will have to be tactfully put – since you are still married . . ."

"Aye – that is it. You will aid me in this, Cousin? It is difficult. And must be kept close, For – God's wounds! If she will not wed me, then I want no talk of divorce! You understand? I seek divorcement only to wed the Queen-Dowager. If it is not to be, then there must be no offending of my wife's family and the Douglases."

"Delicate, my lord – but understandable! I think that we may keep the matter privy. When do you intend to honour us at Stirling?"

"Now. Forthwith. The sooner the matter is put to the test, the better. And before my enemies get wind of it . . ."

"Excellent, my lord Regent! The fervid lover! Come – we shall turn a new page in Scotland's history!"

"That is as I see it my own self," Arran admitted modestly.

While undoubtedly Cardinal and Regent meant very different things by the phrase, a new page was indeed turned that day. Once Arran was in Stirling Castle, the entire political situation was changed. He was not exactly a prisoner – but he might have found it quite difficult to get out. Not that he sought to do so, being only concerned to make headway with Mary of Guise. With Queen, Regent and Chancellor together, all the constitutional authority of the kingdom, short of Parliament, was concentrated in the castle – and quickly the realm perceived it. The flow to Stirling became a flood. Even Sir Ralph Sadler, the English ambassador, had to come knocking. Only Angus and the

Douglases kept their distance, while Henry roared ferocious threats from London.

Mary of Guise played her part skilfully, and as kindly as she might. Without actually encouraging Arran she paid him especial attention, even seemed to enjoy his company. That she managed to keep him at arm's length, without forcing matters to a break, was the tribute to her wits, abilities, and possibly French up-bringing—for Arran was anxious not to waste time. She was aided, of course, by the fact that the word divorce was not to be mentioned—and so could take refuge in failing to understand his intentions.

If Arran was concerned not to waste time, David Beaton was no less so. Indeed, it might fairly be said that he hustled. He insisted that, as an earnest of his good faith, Arran must be received back into the Church with due ceremony. The very next day, therefore, the extraordinary scene was enacted, in the Franciscan nunnery at Stirling, wherein James Hamilton, Earl of Arran and Regent of the kingdom, kneeling before the high altar, made full and public confession of his back-sliding and pre-sumptuous sins, renounced the reformed Evangel, declared his penitence and acceptance of the authority of Holy Church, was given absolution and received Mass, Argyll and Bothwell holding the towel over his head as he received the sacrament, the Cardinal-Archbishop officiating, before an illustrious congregation of lords spiritual and temporal.

After that, James Hamilton would have some difficulty in using reformers and heretics for his purposes.

That was not the only example of the Cardinal's haste. The little Queen's position had to be made secure, swiftly, in more than things physical. Five days later, on the thirtieth anniversary of Flodden, he organised the most hasty coronation in Scots history since that of King Robert the Bruce. In the Kirk of the Haly Rude at Stirling the abbreviated ceremony took place, himself performing the anointing, Arran bearing the crown, Lennox the sceptre and Argyll the sword. Mary, at nine months old, was now Queen of Scots indeed.

The long-suffering people of Scotland crossed themselves, and looked at long last to see light ahead.

One set-back there was, however. Young Lennox, who had been much put out by the arrival of Arran at Stirling, outraged by his elaborate return to Holy Church, and only allowed himself to be involved in the coronation because of personal pride, now staged a violent scene before Mary of Guise and the Cardinal, accusing the former of playing with his affections, insulting him and behaving shamefully with Arran, a married man. Unforgivable things poured from him, whereafter he took abrupt departure from Stirling for the castle of Dumbarton—of which he was hereditary Keeper—mouthing threats and all but weeping with fury and mortification.

This was unfortunate but probably inevitable in the long run—for the Queen-Mother had no intention of marrying either of her suitors, and it was almost impossible that the rivals could both remain in the same party. But David had not foreseen the lengths to which Lennox, in his spleen, would go. He immediately threw himself into the arms of the English party, wrote to Henry naming himself his true man—indeed thereafter accepting a pension of 6,800 merks a year—and solicited the hand of Angus's distinctly mature daughter in marriage. Presumably he stopped speaking French abruptly.

It was bad—but not nearly so bad as what followed. The long-awaited French aid arrived at last, not sailing up the Forth to Stirling as expected, but up the Clyde. It came in a squadron of ships, which unfortunately but not unnaturally came to anchor under the walls of the royal castle of Dumbarton. The ships brought men, military stores, fifty pieces of artillery and ten thousand crowns in gold. Lennox grabbed the artillery, the money and much of the arms, although he could not hold the men. The French envoy, the Sieur de la Brosse, and the Patriarch Grimani of Aquileia, Papal Legate, arrived at Stirling shorn and in voluble protest.

It was a blow, but not disastrous. They were no worse off than they had been. And Lennox's defection at least had the effect of relieving Arran's assault of Mary of Guise of its urgency.

What the Holy Father's contribution to the struggle lacked in physical things—it consisted of only the one man, the Patriarch Grimani—it made up for in spiritual potency. For the Italian brought with him not only the Pontiff's orders to stamp out every vestige of revolt in the Church in Scotland, but the appointment of Cardinal David Beaton as *Legate a Latere*. This was the very highest delegation of power known to the Church, and it gave to David authority not only to act in the name of the Pope, in Scotland, but *as* the Pope. His ecclesiastical prerogative was now absolute, a concentration of power never before known in the land. His Chancellorship was now declared to all. David Beaton, with the infant Queen in his keeping, the Queen-Mother his closest associate, and the Regent daily coming more under his sway — partly thanks to the efforts of his illegitimate brother the Abbot of Paisley — was not only the master of the realm and uncrowned king, but infinitely more comprehensively powerful than any king Scotland had known.

Winter snows sent Henry's savage armies back to quarters in England from the smoking, ravaged Borders and southern shires, and gave the hard-pressed Scots defensive forces a breathing-space. The Lord Home, the Lairds of Buccleuch, Ferniehurst, Cessford and other battle-worn veterans who had held the passes for so long, were able at last to come to Stirling to pay their rough duties to the baby Queen. In December, David Beaton presided, as Lord High Chancellor, at his first Parliament.

That Parliament, amongst other things, countermanded the proposed bethrothal of the Queen and the Prince of Wales — to which the previous Parliament had reluctantly agreed, under threat, might take place when the infant reached the age of ten. It denounced the tentative treaty with England linked to the bethrothal. It withdrew the proclamation of treason passed on those who had removed the royal child from Linlithgow to Stirling. Instead it pronounced summons of treason against Angus, Sir George Douglas, Lennox and others known to be in constant correspondence with England. It revoked the permission for the Bible to be read in English instead of Latin, and declared the possession of any of the English Bibles Henry had been flooding into Scotland a punishable offence. Sir Ralph Sadler, convicted of instigating rebellion and treachery against the Queen's Majesty was denounced as unacceptable as English ambassador.

Lennox remained at Dumbarton, having bound himself to hand over that fortress and the island of Bute to Henry. Angus and the Douglases sulked in their strongholds. Sir Ralph Sadler fled to the security of Tantallon Castle, and Henry Tudor prepared grimly for full-scale war – and, in a madness of fury, declared war once again on France also.

Despite the evil weather, David Beaton slipped off thereafter to pass Yuletide at Melgund in Strathmore.

Chapter Twenty-six

THE company that rode hastily to war over the fair West Lothian ploughlands was illustrious enough – but seldom had a less adequate force raced to the saving of a country. Behind the resounding leadership from Stirling Castle rode a bare twelve hundred men, half of them Hamiltons, the rest mainly Frenchmen, the royal and Cardinal's guards, and the personal men-at-arms of various lords. As an anti-invasion force it was pathetic in the extreme.

It was the May 2nd, 1544, and the day before, an appalled Central Scotland had wakened to the news that a vast English fleet of no fewer than two hundred sail was in the Forth making for Leith. Soon the thunder of its cannon, and the lesser answering boom of the port's own artillery, reinforced the dread news to all with ears. There had been no warning. All knew that one more English invading force was again battering its way north under the Lord Eure, through the Borderland. The banner of the Lord High Admiral of England flew from the flagship. King Henry, this time, was not nibbling at the cherry.

Arran and David Beaton's desperate attempts to collect an army had resulted only in this scratch crew. Home had the main forces at their disposal guarding the Lammermuir and other Border passes against Eure, while the west-countrymen divided themselves between watching Dacre across Solway and Lennox in Dumbarton. More men would come in due course, especially from the Stewart lands in the Highlands.

The Regent was in a state bordering on distraction. Never had his fatal quality of indecision shown to worse effect. Moreover he had no experience of warfare. The Cardinal, in full armour, was more of a warrior than he, but he also had little practical knowledge of large-scale hostilities. Huntly and Argyll were the most experienced commanders there. Above the pounding of their own horses' hooves, the dull rumble of distant cannon-fire reached them intermittently on the east wind.

Surmounting at length the north flank of Corstorphine Hill, they came in sight of Leith and Edinburgh both. A pall of brown-black smoke drifted towards them from the former; but so far the capital looked as usual, with its great citadel soaring above it serenely — a comforting sight.

They had sent word to the Provost of the city to muster the citizens, and to the Hamilton lieutenant-governor of the castle to aid and arm them — Arran himself was the Keeper. But with what effect they did not know. The Provost, Otterburn of Reidhall, with Douglases ever too close at hand, was of the English party and tinged with reforming zeal. There was some doubt amongst the lords whether to make for Edinburgh itself, or directly towards Leith. Arran was for the former, relishing the security of the castle and its artillery; but Huntly advised the latter, to get to grips with the enemy, if possible, while he was still disembarking. David threw in his weight with the Gordon, and they hastened towards the sea.

They were nearing the hamlet of Drylaw when one of the Hamilton scouts returned with the grievous word that while the English warships continued to bombard Leith itself, the transports with the soldiers had sailed a mile or two further west to Granton Craig, and there the Earl of Hertford, one of Henry's most able but savage commanders, had disembarked no fewer than twelve thousand men. These were even now converging on Leith from behind.

Shaken by the revelation of the numbers involved, the Regent was again for turning south to Edinburgh. But Huntly thought otherwise. He boldly urged an attack, behind Hertford, on his beachhead base and transports at Granton sands. Again David backed the veteran soldier, and without enthusiasm from most, they rode on to Royston.

From that coastal height they could see the little haven of Granton, dwarfed by the huge concentration of tall English transports standing off-shore. The sandy beach was crowded with men and stores, and there was a great ferrying of small boats and barges from the ships.

Huntly pointed. "Rafts!" he exclaimed, in his grating voice. "Cannon on them! He's no' waited for his artillery, the man.

331

In one charge, see you, we could clear yon rabble on the beach. Capture his cannon. Then turn them on his back. As he attacks Leith. Splendour of God — we could!"

It was a bold and unorthodox proposition, but at least with possibilities of success. Almost without debate, and before their presence there could be discovered by the enemy, the Scots were thundering down upon the unprepared shore parties working on the sands.

As Huntly had foretold, it was all over in one headlong charge. The English went down like ninepins before the calvalry. Trapped against the sea and amongst the litter of stores, they had no least chance.

Amidst all the miscellaneous gear and trappings of a great army, there were perhaps a dozen cannon of various calibres already landed. This was a notable prize for the Scots. As their so suddenly victorious troops rounded up prisoners, smashed-in small boats and looted what they would, the leaders argued the next move. David was for continuing with their previous plan — getting the guns teamed up behind horses and following up Hertford at once. Arran thought that they should smash the cannon, or otherwise make them unusable to the enemy, and get away before Hertford had time to come back upon them. Argyll urged that they do neither, but leave Leith to its fate, hopelessly outnumbered as they were, and take the artillery by a round-about route to Edinburgh.

But Huntly had a new idea. Those transports anchored out there were a magnificent target. Unable to fire at the shore for fear of killing their own people, they were at the mercy of shore-based cannon.

It was a brilliant notion — although the noise of any bombard-ment was bound to bring Hertford's force back in haste. All agreed that it should be tried — but for no prolonged period. And they must be prepared to break off and away when their scouts warned them that the English army had turned back.

Time was wasted seeking for cannon-balls to fit the individual pieces, and suitable powder, amongst the captured stores. Also in finding men sufficiently knowledgeable to fire the weapons. In the end Huntly himself, Argyll, and a number of other leaders, turned cannoneer and five pieces were brought into service.

After a few false starts, great cheers greeted the first crashing discharge.

Whether they did as much damage to the shipping as they hoped for, it was hard to say. Certainly they created enormous confusion and panic amongst the transports, but how many ships were actually destroyed was another matter.

It was all inspiriting work—but David Beaton was uneasy. It was using up precious time. He would much have preferred to assail Hertford's unprepared rear than to face his front, turned about and hurrying back.

When scouts brought word that, in fact, two forces of the English were now hastening in this direction, David used his authority to insist on an immediate cease-fire and withdrawal—in which Arran only too thankfully concurred. It seemed that Hertford had in fact split his army, one half going on to invest Leith, the other heading south direct for Edinburgh. Alarmed by the cannonade behind, both were now moving back, and from different angles.

Anxious that their modest force should not be trapped between the sea and two larger bodies, David urged that a roundabout retiral on Edinburgh was now the only course. Although cannon might be invaluable in a static battle, in an action of movement as this must be, their painful lack of mobility could be nothing but an encumberance. Against the advice of many, he detached a small number of their least dashing troopers to escort the cannon westwards, by unobtrusive ways, to safety. Then, sternly ordering that none were to hamper themselves with booty from the beach, a start was made for the capital, three miles to the south, on a circuitous course to the westward.

Topping the coastal ridge, they discovered that their way was barred. Hertford's intelligence was evidently better than theirs. He must have heard how pitifully few were their numbers, and spread his net accordingly. From this ridge of Wardie, the intervening shelving ground between them and the city lay like an open map. And reaching across it from east to west, in two great arcs, was the English array, spread in widest formation, covering mile after mile of the land. The two arcs were near to meeting, closing.

They were not trapped yet—but were not far off it.

As all around men exclaimed and cursed, David looked at

333

Huntly. "My lord," he jerked. "What will they expect us to do?"

"Bolt for the west," the veteran Gordon answered unhesitantly. "Whereon their cavalry will turn into column and ride us down, extended in flank as we would be."

"Aye. That then is what we must not do. And since they are bound to be short of cavalry, coming by ship, where will they have placed their horse? On the extreme wings, for that very reason. Look — you can see it from here! So — the centre! And the joining of two hosts must ever be the weakest point."

"You are right, by God!" Huntly shouted. "The centre it is, my friends. Tighten together. Not at first, but as we ride. As I signal." Without awaiting the Regent's word, he whipped out his great sword, and held it aloft. "A Gordon!" he bellowed. "A Gordon!" And dug in his spurs.

It was a prolonged charge — for the two forces were more than a mile apart at the start of it. To the English it must have looked like a crazed gesture of desperate suicidal bravado, for the Scots line was spread out thin indeed, and charging ten times its number. Everywhere the miles-long English front rippled to a halt.

Perhaps halfway across the undulating farmlands the Scots line began to change shape and character, in answer to Huntly's sign. The flanks drew inward, the centre closed up. Soon it was no longer a line but an amorphous but swiftly moving mass. Almost imperceptibly, however, the mass shaped itself into a spearhead, Huntly at the very apex, closely supported by the Cardinal, the Bishop of Orkney, Argyll, Arran and the other leaders.

Too late the English commanders perceived the intent, and trumpets blared all along their front. The main cavalry concentrations were on the extreme flanks, the tips of the crescent, and nothing could get them to the centre in time. Only the bowmen could save that front from the full impact of the concentrated charge on a very narrow area.

The English archers, as ever, were magnificent; cool, steady, efficient, showering their shafts with almost unbelievable speed and accuracy. But the point of the flashing Scots spearhead was composed entirely of lords and knights in full armour, poor marks indeed for arrows. Few men fell.

The archers evidently were given orders to concentrate on the horses — and here they had more success. But the range was now shortening swiftly.

To the fierce yelling of slogans the Scots crashed into the English foot at the very point where they were weakest, where the two formations met. Pikemen, halberdiers, arquebusiers and archers went down under the trampling hooves and flashing swords. Hertford himself, with many of his captains, was spurring along from the extreme right, but could nowise reach the point of impact in time.

There were only brief minutes of fierce and confused smiting, thrusting and slaughter, and it was all over. The Scots were through. Not all of them, but the vast majority.

David Beaton found blood running down the blade of his sword on to his hand, and scarce knew how it came there. The English line was a shambles behind them.

But only a very small part of that line. None needed to have this significant fact pointed out. It has been a splendid manœuvre, and the Scots force was no longer trapped. But it represented no sort of English defeat. There were still more than ten thousand undefeated men behind the panting thousand.

There was obviously no point in seeking any further encounter, at this stage. They would not surprise the English twice. Hertford was a more experienced commander than any in Scotland. Indeed, already he was fanning his extreme east wing cavalry out southwards, fast, using them as a screen to get between the Scots and Edinburgh.

Seeing it, Huntly pointed. "We'll no' can make the city!" he cried. "A plague on them — we'll no' get through now!"

"What, then . . .?" Arran faltered.

"West," David said shortly. "Linlithgow. To gather our strength. We can do no other. And quickly — before their horse on that side cut us off."

"He's right," Argyll, slightly wounded in the wrist, declared. "Back to the west again. And try pick up the cannon."

There was no option. They pulled their horses' heads half-right, and settled down to sheer hard riding.

In tactics the day had been theirs' — but in strategy the invaders still had it all their own way.

That pattern continued, until a comparably large and dis-

335

ciplined force could be brought against them. Which demanded time, indeed. Leith resisted to the last, and was sacked and burned. The good folk of Edinburgh manned their walls gallantly but hopelessly. They sent their Provost Otterburn out, under a white flag, to try to negotiate with the invaders. But Hertford scornfully told him that he came as a soldier, not an ambassador, and his king's command was to lay waste the land and to bring back to London the child Queen and that devil the Cardinal. When Otterburn, white-faced, came back and told his fellow-citizens that, advising surrender and the handing over of the castle, initial shock and consternation was succeeded by cold anger. Otterburn was hooted out, a new Provost was summarily elected, and, man and boy, the burghers stood to arms.

It was a useless gesture, pathetic had it not been valorous. Hertford's veterans of the French and Low Country wars, mowed down the citizenry like standing corn, and in a few hours the ancient grey city was ablaze, the great pall of its smoke clearly visible at Linlithgow, eighteen miles away.

But the castle, under Hamilton of Stenhouse, held out. Hertford, of course, was now ill-supplied with artillery, and the fortress's cannon far outgunned him. Even when the armament from the warships at Leith were laboriously trundled up to the city, Hamilton's great cannon, including the mighty Mons Meg, outclassed them. In savage wrath, Hertford turned on the population of Edinburgh and gave over what was left of the town to three full days of terror.

In the midst of it, because Lord Home and his war-scarred mosstroopers had been hurriedly withdrawn from the Borders to stiffen the raw assembling Scots host at Linlithgow, another English force of four thousand horse managed to reach the Capital, under Lord Eure. To celebrate this triumphal junction of forces and access of cavalry strength, and to carry out an important part of Henry's orders, since Edinburgh itself now had little left to ravage, large-scale and systematic raiding of the surrounding countryside, the fertile Lothians, became the order of the day. Never had that fair land suffered as now it did.

Although word of this deliberate and merciless devastation reached Linlithgow quickly enough, it was not until over a week had passed, and the Scots mobilisation was beginning to show worth-while results, that the full significance and potentialities of it all burst upon David Beaton. It was the furious arrival of the Regent's father-in-law, the Earl of Morton, and sundry other Douglas lairds from the Lothians, unexpected visitors indeed, that opened his eyes. They were stammering, wild-eyed, with wrath, outrage and resentment. The English had sacked Dalkeith, six miles from Edinburgh, Morton's own town. His brother's house of Dalmahoy was also in ashes. Kilspindie, Angus's uncle's castle in East Lothian, was a ruin. As was Whittinghame and Spott and other Lothian houses. Also Blackerston and Evelaw in the Merse. The devils were making no difference between Douglas and other men!

Eyes gleaming, David managed to get Arran away from his wife's angry sire. "Do you not see it?" he cried. "We are saved! Or I am much mistaken. The fools have done for themselves what *we* could not do! They have given us the Douglases. Or enough of them to save us!"

"How shall Morton's two or three hundred save us, man?"

"Morton is the least of it! See — an edict proclaiming the release of Angus and the Douglases from their summons for treason. To be published abroad with all speed. A courier to Angus at Tantallon telling him so. Urging him to make common cause with all men against the brutal invader. He will ignore it, safe in Tantallon — but most of his lairds, less well protected, will not! Noise this loudly, so that all shall hear it. The English in especial. Then we ride with Douglas banners in the forefront of our array — however few Douglases may be behind them! I swear that Hertford will not fail to perceive his mistake!"

In fact, it was the Lord High Admiral, Lisle, who, fretting inactive in his warships at Leith, smelt danger first. David, a Fife man and more sea-conscious than most, conceived an additional gesture. He gathered together a miscellaneous flotilla of craft from the little ports up and down the Forth, decked them with improvised flags bearing the conspicuous Red Heart of Douglas, and sent them to manoeuvre off North Berwick and Tantallon, at the mouth of the Firth. Lisle's outposts promptly reported it, and that prudent admiral, envisaging the danger of being blockaded in the estuary by a fleet under Angus, weighed anchor and with such of the transports as were still sound, made for the security of deep water and the open sea.

When they heard of it, the Scots array—it would be inaccurate to call it an army, even yet, though now perhaps ten thousand strong—moved forward from Linlithgow with much display, especially of Douglas participation, although with no great haste. At the same time, David sent spies forward into the Lothians to spread the word that the Border Douglases under Cavers, Sheriff of Teviotdale, and Drumlanrig, were heading north to attack the English rear.

Hertford and Eure, faced with a long overland march to England, disconcerted and unable to tell truth from rumour, took the wise course. They abandoned Edinburgh, turned south by east, and took the coast road for the Border, burning Seton, Haddington, Dunbar and Renton on the way. They made a vicious journey of it—but in five days they had crossed Tweed, and the only English soldiers left in Scotland were dead ones.

It was a stricken land they left behind them—but still an unconquered one. Something else was left behind—a copy of written orders from Henry Tudor himself. They ran as follows:

"It is His Majesty's pleasure that you put all to fire and sword, burn Edinboroughe town, so rased and defaced when you have sacked and gotten what you can of it, as there may remain forever a perpetual memory of the vengeance of God lightened upon them for their falsehood and disloyalty . . . sack Holyroodhouse and as many towns and villages as ye may conveniently . . . sack Leith and burn and subvert it and all the rest, putting man, women and child to fire and sword without exception where any resistence shall be made against you; and this done pass over to the Fifeland and extend like extremities and destructions . . . not forgetting among all the rest so to spoil and turn upset down the Cardinal's town of St. Andrews, as upper stone may be the nether . . . sparing no creature alive in the same, specially such as either in friendship or blood be allied to the Cardinal . . ."

David Beaton wrote to King Francis, acquainting him with the news and pleading for a diversion across the Channel.

Chapter Twenty-seven

IT was hot, plaguey hot, in the great refectory of the Charterhouse of Perth, the place stank of perspiration, stale food and spilt wine, and the flies buzzed in a steady drone. Outside the leaded windows the sun shone from a cloudless sky. Gazing up at the dark beams and rafters of the roof, David Beaton's mind slipped frequently to the wide grasslands or Melgund of the sparkling waters of Lunan Bay — slipped, but always came back. Would that his thoughts might stay there.

Others, it seemed, were not plagued as he was, having to listen to all, to be concerned in all. At his one side, the Patriarch Grimani slept frankly, indeed snored a little — but then, he would not understand a word that was being said in the broad Scots dialect, even though it was mainly on his behoof that the entire affair was being staged, that he might have a satisfactory account to take back to His Holiness in Rome.

The Patriarch was by no means the only one who slept, as the clerk's voices droned on and on, in tune with the flies. Crichton, Bishop of Dunkeld, one of the three judges of this Diocesan Inquisition, had not opened his eyes in half and hour, even when the accused had been changed and a new trial begun, his assent in the previous judgement and sentence being taken for granted. William Chisholm, Bishop of Dunblane, president of the court, was not asleep — but it was to be doubted if his mind was on what was being said, the heat, the monotony of the proceedings, the humdrum nature of the offences, the dull voices, and the excellent dinner they had had, all contributing. The third member of the tribunal, their host, the Prior of this Carthusian monastery, looked more lively undoubtedly, being not a little awed by the company he was keeping. Moreover, it behoved him to show due zeal in this matter, for his predecessor, the Prior MacAlpine, who called himself by the presumptuous name of Machabaeus, had had to flee the country for heretical failings. Even his eyelids drooped occasionally, however.

At the Cardinal's other side, the Regent was not asleep, frequently and loudly as he yawned. He was bored, no doubt —

but Arran had a capacity for inanition, for doing nothing at all, which David envied him — for he himself had to listen, unfortunately, when words were being spoken, however dull, repetitive or even fatuous, were the words. How often he had wished that he could ignore the human voice and turn wholly to his own much more worth-while thoughts.

The diocesan procurator, a friar named Spence, was surely the most long-winded and uninspiring of men, concerned to drag out his prosecutions to the last syllable, in tribute to his own importance and presumably to impress his illustrious spectators. All the charges were practically identical, against wretched parish priests and friars, infected by the reformers, and guilty of possessing forbidden English Bibles, preaching heresy and the like; others, animated by their own cupidity or lusts, of oppressing the poor, claiming exorbitant burial fees, or seducing their parishioners' wives. It was poor, petty stuff to sit through — but the Church had to be put in order if it was to survive. And that all men — including the Pontiff in Rome — should see that this was being done, the Cardinal-Archbishop himself must needs go round these diocesan inquisitions, and as often as possible take the Regent with him. This was the only redeeming feature, as far as David was concerned; it was part of Arran's penance for previous backsliding.

David was gazing upwards and pondering how best he might allay the growing bad feeling between Arran and Mary of Guise — or, more truly, between their supporting lords — when his mind was jerked back to immediate matters by the mention of a name — a name that might almost be said to be haunting him, these days. The present accused, a sharp-faced and voluable friar named Keillor, charged with concocting what he called a dramatic mystery, a play to be performed in public, satirising the prelacy as persecutors of the true disciples of Christ and using the Jewish priests and Sadduceees of the New Testament to represent them in his play — this sorry spinner of uncouth and deplorable words had suddenly mentioned the name of Wishart. He had attended the preachings of Master George Wishart, here in Perth a few months before, he declared in answer to a question from the prosecutor, and had been inspired by them to arrange a performance of his mystery in the church at Dollar . . .

David sat forward. George Wishart again! Everywhere he

went, in these inquisitions, the name cropped up—Lanark, Ayr, Dundee. Even in Montrose, only a few miles from his own Arbroath Abbey. Wishart was fast becoming a major menace to the Church, traipsing the country, preaching, exhorting, pointing the finger of accusation—and always under the protection of the English party, in the personal company of the greatest of them, the Earls of Angus, Glencairn and Cassillis, the Lords Somerville, Maxwell, Sir George Douglas, and above all, that devil Crichton, Laird of Brunstane, a known spy and hireling of Henry Tudor. Time and again David had sought to lay him by the heels—but always he had escaped him, surrounded by an iron ring of lords' men-at-arms. He had a great two-handed sword carried before him, they said, wherever he went, even into the pulpit.

Wishart's name troubled David Beaton personally as well as politically. The business of King Henry's plot to assassinate him had been traced to Crichton of Brunstane—since when that Lothian laird had been watched carefully. A letter to him from one of Henry's secretaries had been intercepted—and had intimated that a fellow-countryman named Wishart was being sent from London to assist him in the murderous matter. This had been two years before, and David had no proof that it was the same Wishart. But the name was not a common one—and George Wishart was frequently in Crichton's company and more than once reported as staying at his house of Brunstane, near Penicuik. David did not judge him as the sort of man who would lend himself to assassination—however furiously he prophesied the forthcoming doom and damnation of the Cardinal—but others were less sure. Patrick Barclay was convinced that he was deep in the plot—and certainly he had dwelt in England for long, and even taught at Cambridge. Moreover, the assassination plot had recently been revived again, they knew, on King Henry's detailed personal instructions.

Proof of Wishart's link with this conspiracy was not necessary, of course, for his arrest and trial. He had been openly distributing the forbidden English Bibles, against the decree of Parliament, and preaching against the Papal link and prayers to the Virgin Mary, the invocation of saints, and the doctrine of purgatory. His case was crystal-clear. But—so was the scale of his protection.

David was still preoccupied with George Wishart when the Bishop of Dunblane suddenly grew tired of Friar Keillor, halted his flood of words, declared him guilty of heresy in the first degree, sentenced him to burning on the Castlehill of Edinburgh at a date suitable to the authorities there, and called the next accused, his co-judges grunting agreement, thankfully.

The new prisoner was a man of a different stamp, a twinkling-eyed, rubicond cleric of some standing, the sort of individual that David Beaton deplored to see in this situation and whom he could have used rather for the Church's improvement — Dean Thomas Forrest, Vicar of Dollar and Canon of St. Colm's Inch. He was not technically an incumbent of this diocese of Dunblane at all, coming under the authority of David's own archbishopric of St. Andrews; but because he had provided the premises at Dollar as scene for Keillor's performance, and encouraged that foolish friar in his heretical activities, permission had been given for him to be tried here, after the other.

Bishop Chisholm, who evidently knew Forrest well, sat up and changed his manner to one of coarse joviality. "Man, Thomas," he declared, "here's a bonnie state o' affairs! Ill company you're keeping this day, by the Rude! What's all this? I'm surprised at the likes o' yoursel' standing there. On siclike a charge. Man — this is no' the place for the likes o' you."

The Dean smiled. "My lord — I confess I could scarce more agree with you! Yet — perhaps any cause which brings me into the pleasure of your lordship's company — not to mention that of my lord Cardinal and my lord Regent — is always a matter for congratulation?" And he bowed all round.

"H'mmm. Aye. well." Dunblane scratched his tonsured head. "May be. But these charges — they're fell serious, man. I'd have esteemed you to have mair sense. They could roast you, mind! This of the play-acting — it was plain foolish. Yon Keillor is an ass, a man of no substance, a wordy carle of no breeding. Anyone can see it. Could *you* no'?"

"I perceived that he lacked certain attributes of gentility, my lord," the other admitted. "But then, so did most of our Saviour's apostles! Some may even have been a little foolish, at times. Have you not yourself thought so? Moreover, the chief priests and Sadducees, whom his little mystery declaims against, were never favourites of mine. I think you might even have enjoyed his play, my lord!"

"Tut, man! M'mm. There are other charges." Dunblane

looked down at the paper before him, wrinkling his bushy brows in fierce concentration. But his ability to read was less than the occasion demanded, and he had to turn to the long-winded prosecutor. "The other charges, I say, Master Spence," he said loudly. "But, a God's name, be brief about them!"

Friar Spence, bowing profusely, read out the indictment. Dean Forrest was accused of, amongst lesser offences, questioning the right to levy tithes — and of restoring to the poorer members of his flock those already levied; of preaching consistently to his parishioners — an activity abandoned almost wholly to friars and those in monastic orders at this time; of exposing the mystery of the Holy Scripture to the vulgar in their own tongue; and of teaching the Lord's Prayer, the Ten Commandments and the Apostles' Creed to all and sundry, again in the vulgar tongue.

"Aye, then," Dunblane said, at the end of this recital and before the prosecutor could elaborate. "D'you hear that, Thomas? Folly, like the other. What d'you say to it, man?"

"My lord — I cannot in honesty deny any of it. Nor desire to. So I conceive that I will save a deal of your precious time if I admit it."

"Sakes, man — you confess it? Confess to a burning matter, the likes o' this!"

"I said admit, my lord — not confess. You yourself will admit there is a difference? Come, confess it, my good Bishop William!"

"Ha! You were ever nimble wi' your tongue, Thomas. Ower nimble, it may be!"

Chuckling, Crichton, Bishop of Dunkeld, dug his fellow-prelate in the ribs. "Our Thomas's agile tongue will maybe choke him yet — eh, Will?" he suggested. "Oooh, aye."

Even the Prior of the Charter-house found himself bold enough to smile at this sally.

"Confess or admit," Dunblane went on grimly, "you'll need to recant. Or if you would prefer it, Thomas, repent. Or retract. Or burn your own faggot, man. That is — if your faggot's no' to burn you!"

"I fear not, my friend. Neither one nor the other."

"But . . .'fore God, man — you must! Declare yoursel' mistaken. In error. And we can save you. Some small penance. A man like yoursel' will no' burn for siclike a cantrip? It's beyond all reason."

"My own views entirely, my lord. Beyond all reason!"

343

"Then you do retract? Confess . . . admit yoursel' in error!"

"Alas, no. That I cannot do. For I would but do the same again, I fear. I conceive what I have done to be nothing less than my duty, as spiritual shepherd of my flock. Jesu Christ said 'Feed my sheep'. His sheep, I vow, need food for more than their bellies. They need it for their minds and souls. I seek to give their minds the food of the gospel in words which they can comprehend. God willing I shall continue to do so. I cannot believe that I err in that."

"Stab me — another o' them! You too have been smitten by the man Wishart, it seems? Is that it?"

"I think not. I have heard him, yes — but I do not agree with all he says. I do not rail against the Holy Father. I do not deny the authority of the Church. I but do my duty according to my lights."

"*Your* lights, man!"

"Yes. Or perhaps I vaunt myself. Say, in the light given to me — largely by the reading of Saint Augustine."

"Augustine . . .! God save us!" Dunblane's jaw fell, almost comically, and he shook a helpless head.

His colleague of Dunkeld took up the matter on a rather different level. "Come now, Master Forrest," he said genially. "We are reasonable and practical men — as I swear are you. These lights of yours are not in reason. You must admit that it is too much to preach every Sunday — too much for human powers! Yet that is what you would bring us to in the end, dear God! A flood of gibbering words! By the Mass — you'd have folk thinking that even prelates must start preaching! And where would we be then?" His laughter was rich.

The Dean bowed. "My good lord — many would be the better for your words, I swear!"

"Na, na. Spare them that! And as to this reading, see you — it's a thing that could well lead the ignorant into great error. Once set tongues a-wagging, and who knows what the Devil will find for them to read!"

"In Holy Writ, my lord?"

"Och, man — if you can find, of course, any good epistle or gospel which sets forth the liberty of Holy Church decently, I'll no' say but what you might read it to your flock. But . . ."

"My lord Bishop," Forrest declared solemnly. "I vow that I

344

have read carefully through the Old Testament and the New, and have yet to find in the whole compass of them one *evil* epistle or gospel! But far be it from me to claim omniscience in the matter. If your lordship will point out any such that are not good, I will be sedulous in avoiding them, in future!"

"Nay, Brother Thomas!" Dunkeld laughed. "My joy—that I cannot do! For I am contented with my breviary and pontifical, and know neither the Old Testament nor the New. And yet, see you, I have come on not indifferently well, have I not?" At the general laughter, the first the court had heard that day, the Bishop added, chuckling, "Take my advice, my friend, and leave these fancies—else you may repent them when too late!"

"I am grateful for your lordship's notable advice," the Dean acceded smiling. "But I fear that my neck is still stiff in obduracy. I cannot and will not recant or deny what I conceive to be my bounded duty."

Chisholm of Dunblane raised his head. "Enough of this!" he cried. "Here is a man clearly bent on his own destruction—as well as that of others. Does any here perceive cause why that destruction should be denied him?" He looked across at the Cardinal.

David Beaton, gazing straight ahead of him, did not so much as flicker an eyelid.

"So be it. Thomas Forrest, man, I declare you guilty of practices forbidden by Holy Church, and heresy in the first degree. You will suffer death by burning on the Castlehill of Edinburgh on a day to be decided. And may God have mercy on your thrawn soul!"

There was a long moment of silence. Then the other bowed. "That is my prayer also," he said calmly. "I do not deny your authority, in this, my lords—but I do pity your judgement. I bid you a good day."

As he turned away, Dunblane called out. "Have you more for us, Master Prosecutor? I think you have."

While the crowded refectory was still agog with exclamation and comment, five more prisoners were herded in, together— their appearance enough to create a new stir of interest. Even David Beaton, moved as he was by the last interlude, eyed these with some astonishment. He had heard that there was a case being brought for a special reason, concerned with trouble in

Perth not strictly ecclesiastical, heard before this court for good reason; but he had not looked to see such curiously uninspiring and feeble scapegoats as these.

There were four men and one woman, all evidently of the poorer type of townsfolk, bedraggled, dirty, unkempt, one of the men little better than a cripple, another obviously of low mentality. The woman held herself best of the five, a swarthy, gipsy-like creature, no doubt of Highland stock. It was strange indeed to see non-clerical accused.

The Regent leaned closer to David. "What are these kennel-scrapings?" he demanded. "Must we waste our time with such as these, Cousin?"

"I do not know who they are, or with what they are charged," the Cardinal admitted. "But William Chisholm has scrutinised all cases for this hearing, and is not the one to trouble himself, or us, with profitless labour. Have patience, my lord. We may yet be . . . edified!"

The Bishop of Dunblane was looking at the newcomers with undisguised distaste. "Who have we here, Master Spence?" he wondered. "A sorry crew, by the Rude!"

"Sorry yes, my lords," the procurator agreed. "But nowise lacking in wickedness. Nor in the greater iniquity they represent."

"Ha! Then they belie their looks, sirrah! Let us have the meat of it."

"They are William Anderson, Robert Lamb, James Ronald and James Finlayson, indwellers in this town of Perth. And the woman is Helen Stark, wife to the accused James Finlayson. They are known to be part of a shameless company in this city who work openly and impiously against Holy Church, a company which contains many more lofty citizens than these, and which seeks to impose heretical teachings on others."

"So. These then are but exemplars, representers? Of greater sinners?"

"Aye—but there are ample charges to condemn them, each and all, of themselves, my lord," the friar said quickly. "I have many witnesses to swear that alone and in concert these have spoken against the Holy Father, despitefully used the figures of certain saints in this town of Perth, openly at a meeting rehearsed the Lord's Prayer in the vulgar tongue. And worse, flagrantly broke the Lenton Fast. Indeed, these miscreant and abandoned men profaned Good Friday last and its sancity by eating a goose on that holy day!"

"Save us all — a goose!" Dunblane ejaculated. "Tell me, man — how did such as these *come* by a goose to eat? On Good Friday or any other?"

The procurator smirked. "That, my lord, may be a matter for another court than this. It is believed that the goose was stolen."

"Ha! Umm. You tell me that! Here are ambitious sinners, by the Rude! And the woman? No doubt she *cooked* the goose?"

"Yes, my lord. But we have worse than that, I think, against her. I have witnesses, the midwife in especial, to attest that in her recent labour of childbirth, this Helen Stark refused resolutely and contumaciously to pray for the aid of the Virgin Mary, insisting presumptuously in calling upon the Almighty direct, in the name of Jesus Christ, and thus did shamefully spurn and reject the Mother of God!"

"D'you say so! A proper besom, indeed! Though I swear she doesna look it!" Dunblane snorted, and considered the five accused. "You — you have heard the charges against you. Do you confess or deny them? If you deny, I shall call witnesses. If you confess, there is no need. What do you say?"

The five unfortunates looked from him to each other in helpless incomprehension, partly bewildered, partly sullen. They said nothing.

"Come, now — how do you plead?" the Bishop demanded, frowning.

One man shook his tangled head, and the woman crossed herself. That was all.

"You!" Dunblane pointed a finger at the headshaker. "Did you eat this goose? On Good Friday? Or no? Speak up."

After a few moments, biting his lip, the man nodded.

"Aye. Well." He pointed at the woman. "And you? Did you refuse to call on the Blessed Virgin, in your pangs? Or did you no'?"

She swallowed. "Aye, lord," she got out. "But . . . nae offence, lord. I . . . I but cried to God's son."

"So! And who are you, wretched trull, wilfully to reject the blessed intercession of Our Lady?"

She blinked, but found no more words.

347

The Bishop shrugged. "The charges ar'na denied, then — but confirmed. The matter is clear. I see no need for further deliberation." He glanced, eyebrows raised, at his two colleagues.

Both shook their heads.

"Aye, well. To sentence . . ."

"I think, my lord, that you might hear one witness, clear as the case may seem to be."

Dunblane looked up, and coughed. It was David Beaton who had spoken, from across the room. "Yes, my lord Cardinal. Very good. Aye. A witness as you say . . ."

"I suggest a witness of some substance, if this is possible. The prosecutor said that these unfortunate wretches represented a greater inquity than themselves, if I mind aright. Perhaps some small confirmation . . .?"

The Bishop drew a hand over his mouth. "As Your Beatitude wishes. Although . . . it might be better for such to be heard privily."

"Better for whom, my lord? These accused?"

"Ah. H'rr'mm. Master Spence — call the witness, Charteris of Kinfauns."

There was an audible gasp from all around. The Laird of near-by Kinfauns was an unlikely figure to be drawn into the case of such as these, a prominent man of standing in more than local affairs. He was known to be contending for the provostship of Perth, an office which had been more or less hereditary in the family of the Lords Ruthven. The present lord had assumed the position automatically on his father's death.

Charteris came in, amidst a considerable stir, bowing to the Regent and Cardinal rather than the court, a handsome man of middle years, bravely attired, a hand on the hilt of his sword — of which, this being purely an ecclesiastical court, he could not be required to divest himself.

"Sir," Dunblane greeted him. "We are informed by the good friar here that you may be able to aid us in establishing the guilt or otherwise of the panel before us? Out o' your own knowledge. Aye, and goodness."

"Certainly, my lord," the other declared briskly. "They are black guilty, one and all."

"Aye. Uh-huh. To be sure. That is good, sir — excellent. But . . . we shall require corroboration. Aye, corroboration. In

348

especial in the matter of, of what lies behind the wicked and shameless behaviour of these folk. You understand me, sir?"

Charteris nodded, and glanced enquiringly round the room. "You wish me to go into that? Here?"

"Well . . ." Dunblane looked over at the Cardinal, who nodded curtly. "Aye. Proceed, sir."

"Very well, my lords. These men, and this woman, are but a token. For many. The first-fruits of an ill harvest. That they may serve as a warning to others. Chosen that this fair Saint John's Town of Perth may be cleansed. From error. Aye, and from treason also."

At that dread word many sat more upright on their seats.

"Proceed."

"There is a party in this town, my lords, working contrary to Holy Church and to the realm, both. Evil men, led by he who calls himself Provost, the Lord Ruthven himself. They have a large following, in especial amongst the baser sort. They brought the man George Wishart here. Lodged him in Ruthven's own house. Had him preach to meetings of the people, with armed men at his back. High and low. Men of property – and such as these! They are wicked and deceitful men, blasphemers, heretics, working against the Church . . ."

"You said treason, man!" That was the Regent, his first intervention.

"Yes, my lord. In the English pay. They scheme to put down the young Queen. And make the Earl of Lennox King in her stead."

"Lennox, by God!" Arran was on his feet.

"Aye, my lord Regent. Lennox is married to Angus's daughter. And so is Ruthven's son. They are linked in marriage. Ruthven's sister is wed to Erskine of Dun, who set Wishart on his wicked way. They are all of a kind. And you . . ." Charteris moistened his lips. "You are to die, my lord! For . . . for returning to Mother Church. Likewise the Cardinal. Then the way will be clear for Lennox . . ."

"Fiends of hell!" His knuckles gleaming white, Arran raised clenched fists high. Shouting for his guards, without a word or a glance to any others there, he stormed out of the refectory.

Concern and consternation at the abrupt departure of the Regent set the court in an uproar. Even Charteris was alarmed at the reaction to his testimony, and eyed the door nervously. Only David Beaton seemed unperturbed. Indeed, he smiled slightly, and signed to Dunblane to continue.

He was, in fact, entirely satisfied. Charteris' story might be true or it might not — but there was certainly enough in it to serve David's purposes. Ruthven had been a thorn in his flesh for long — but because he had formerly been a member of Arran's party, and notable well protected in other regards, David had been unable to touch him. Now, thanks to Charteris' ambitions for this provostship, he believed that Ruthven's barb could be withdrawn. So small and simple a matter. Moreover, Charteris was linked with the Lord Gray, another of the dissident English-party nobles and a close adherent of Angus. With a little manipulation, Gray might be usefully detached. Ruthven was Sheriff of Perthshire, as well as Provost of Perth — an office of considerable profit. Gray had large lands in Perthshire . . .

It looked as though his prevailing upon the Regent to attend this modest Inquisition had been amply justified.

In the circumstance, William Chisholm interpreted the Cardinal's signal as an intimation to wind up the proceedings forthwith. With scant ceremony he thanked Charteris for his witness, and dismissed him, that laird by no means lingering about his exit. Then, equally unceremoniously, the Bishop declared all five of the panel guilty of heresy, condemned the four men to death by burning and the woman to be drowned, and ordered their removal for prompt execution. He rose to his feet, signifying the adjournment of the court — a highly expeditious performance.

For once, David Beaton was taken by surprise. He had not expected this abrupt termination to the proceedings. His object gained, he would have preferred the wretched prisoners to be let off with some minor punishment, however technically guilty they might be. The last thing he wanted was a crop of unnecessary martyrs. These would have served as an example and warning, without the death penalty. And, not being clerics, there might even be some trouble over the Church's authority to burn them — especially with Ruthven still Sheriff. On the other hand, verdict and sentence proclaimed, for him to interfere and overturn it would gravely undermine the authority of his diocesan and lower the prestige of the Inquisitions, at a time when at all costs that must be maintained. In a cleft stick, David cursed the brash William Chisholm, albeit beneath his breath.

His raised voice, however, gave no hint of all this. "My lord of Dunblane — my thanks for your devoted labours as preses of this court," he called. "And you, my lord of Dunkeld and my lord Prior. One small matter. Burning is too notable and distinguished a fate for such as these, is it not? To burn Thomas Forrest — and also these poor wretches — would be incongruous, I think?"

Dunblane, stepping down from the dais, paused, scratching his head. "Umm. Aye, my lord Cardinal — I daresay you ha' the rights o' it. To be sure. Master Spence — hang them, see you. It's fell easier, too! Aye, so be it. Hang them. This court is closed."

Later, in the Spey Tower, overlooking a deep pool of the Tay as it wound through the town, David had pleasure as Chancellor of the realm, in affixing the seal to the Regent's edict deposing the Lord Ruthven from the offices of Provost of Perth and Sheriff of Perthshire, and ordering him to put himself in ward under pain of treason, forthwith. With a deal less pleasure he mounted to the tower's parapet-walk to grace with his Primate's presence, if only for a few moments, the judicial drowning of Helen Stark in the pool, and the hanging of her husband and the three others on the bank near by. The woman, still with her babe at the breast, made a great fuss about being parted from her unattractive mate at the end — but this contiguity was the best that Friar Spence evidently could do for her. At least they were within sight — and should enter eternity approximately together.

The matter of purging Holy Church had its complications.

Chapter Twenty-eight

"You may safely venture forth, Master Cardinal!" Mary of Guise called out, though with modulated voice. "All danger is over-past. Save to my reputation!"

From behind the long heavy curtains of the Queen-Mother's private boudoir in Stirling Castle, David Beaton stepped out, somewhat flushed of face.

"It was to preserve Your Grace's reputation the more surely that I hid myself," he declared, a little stiffly.

"I said it was foolish — had you but heeded me." Mary sighed. "Still more foolish to leave your red Cardinal's slippers peeping out from beneath the curtain! The eyes of the Lady Reres near popped from her head at the sight!"

"Oh! Indeed. M'mmm." David tugged at his little beard.

His companon laughed her warm throaty laugh. "Be not so crestfallen, Monsieur Davie! No great harm is done. My ladies are discreet — at least, so I believe. And Lady Reres is your own niece. Besides . . . gentlemen who linger in ladies' bowers should not grumble at the consequences!"

"Madame — of your charity, let us speak seriously!" the man said, with an asperity that was highly unusual for him. "I only sought you here because I had to speak with you alone — and that becomes ever more difficult, I find. Your lords throng you so close. And your ladies are like a flock of chattering starlings!"

"Mary-Mother! I believe that you are jealous!" the Queen accused, dimpling.

"Highness — a truce to this, I pray you. I came here for more than such raillery."

At his tone, Mary of Guise looked concerned. "My friend — you are not offended in me? Wrath with me?" she asked anxiously. "You are not losing your love for me?"

"Does it look like it, Madame? In this your privy bower? I but would have your full attention . . ."

She shook her head. "Of late I have sensed a change in you. You are less kind. More sharp. Are you so with all? Or is it only myself?"

"Your Grace cozens me! Such a thing is unthinkable."

"No. I think it is since the trouble with Arran. You blame me for that, still, is it not? I was foolish, perhaps. But the man is insufferable. Arrogant and pompous, yet a fool and a bungler. Both. To claim to rule my daughter's kingdom! And me with it . . .!"

"Scarce to rule!" David amended, more mildly. "Say, to preside over!"

"True. *You* do the ruling, Monsieur Davie. While Arran but struts and postures."

"Is it not a suitable arrangement? The realm has benefited by it, I think. Madame – do not frown. I know that your many noble friends would have you as Regent in place of Arran. So, by God, would I – were it a simple choice! But it is not. The realm must be maintained as near to unity as may be, in the face of the ever-present English threat. Some would accept you, a Frenchwoman, as Regent – but others would not. We need the Hamiltons – and, so long as your daughter remains a child, we need Arran, the heir to the throne. Better that he should be an arrogant Regent, supporting the child Queen, than an arrogant contender for her throne!"

Mary sighed. "Always you are right, of course!"

"Not always," he said. "But in this case there are no two ways to it. That setting up of your own Parliament, here in Stirling last November, was folly. I could not support it. I know it was the lords' advising – but it had to fail. I had to support Arran's true Parliament in Edinburgh – even though fewer lords attended it. Doing so, I may have seemed to desert you for him. But only so could I hold the realm in a semblance of unity – the French party, the Church party, and the Hamilton party, against the English faction."

"Yes. I see it now. It was a mistake. I listened to Argyll and Huntly. They hate Arran. I am sorry, my friend. But that is long past. Yet you still hold it against me, I think?"

"No. Not so. Empty your mind of that, I beseech you. See you, it is not meet and seemly that I should speak of my affection for Your Grace. That you must perceive for yourself. But this I do declare – that if it is necessary that we cleave to Arran, loving him not, then it is a round score of times more necessary that we cleave to each other, you and I! In love and duty. Always. For the child Queen's sake. For our own. For Scotland's sake. And the Church's."

She reached out to grasp his arm. "There we speak with one voice, old friend! Me, I promise never again to doubt your goodwill. Nor, if I may, to give you cause to lessen it."

"You are kind, gracious," he said, smiling. "It is a compact, then?"

"Agreed. Now – the close tidings you have brought for my ear alone?"

He grimaced. "It is about the same Arran. He has redeemed himself, in some measure. In the Borders. After his shameful defeat in November at Coldingham, when the Douglases deserted him, and Eure's English scattered his force like chaff—now, he has had a notable victory. At Ancrum Moor. Largely because the English defaced the Douglas tombs at Dryburgh. Home and Buccleuch aiding. Eure and Layton are both slain. There are a thousand English prisoners—the dead as yet uncounted. The remnants of the enemy host have fled back into Northumberland. Once again there is not an English sword in Scotland—save for our own legion of traitors!"

"But this is splendid news! Excellent. But . . . why did you not shout it aloud? For all to rejoice over. Why keep it close, thus?"

"Because it was not Arran who sent the tidings. One of my own men in the Regent's train brought me the word. It would not do to anticipate Arran's messenger!"

"Ah, so! You keep a watch on my lord Regent, then, Monsieur Davie?"

"I keep a watch on everyone prominent in this realm," he assured her simply.

"Even myself, I warrant?"

"Even Your Grace's royal self." He bowed. "But that pleasure I reserve for *myself*!"

She laughed again. "You should have been a Frenchman!" she said. "Preferably a noble Frenchman—whom I might have met a dozen years ago!"

They eyed each other for a long moment, silent.

Turning to the window, he went on. "I have other news also. From France. A force of ten ships and three thousand men is on its way. From King Francis. It is less than I had hoped for—much less. But welcome. And necessary. For this defeat at Ancrum will but spur Henry to greater efforts. We may be sure of that. God knows, Scotland will have no peace while that monster lives! Nor I any safety."

"More . . . more threats to your life?"

"Aye. Or more proof of the immediacy of the threats. Another letter intercepted. From Hertford, who is assembling still another army at York. To Crichton of Brunstane again. Requesting to know what the man Wishart has done with the £1,000 sent him—in the matter of killing the Cardinal! Saying that it is His Grace of England's most stern command that this be accomplished without further delay. That he is sending an English agent, by name Forster, expert in the business, to second Wishart's efforts. The Earl of Cassillis' name mentioned, as privy to the plot."

"Oh, Davie . . .!" Mary's voice quivered. It was the first time that the man had noticed her calling him that without the Monsieur. Suddenly before his mind's eye was a picture of Marion, using the same phrase.

"Never fear," he assured. "I take precautions. I never ride abroad with less than a hundred of a guard. I have spies in every kitchen that feeds me. No stranger or doubtful man may approach me without escort. It is devilish cramping and ill to thole . . ."

"This Wishart? It must be the preacher. Why do you doubt it? It is folly, with your life at stake!"

"I doubt it only because of what the man is. I met him once. He comes of a Strathmore family, Wishart of Pitarrow. His father was Justice-Clerk when Angus ruled. He is a bigot, a determined enemy of the Church, and in English pay. But I deem him sincere, according to his lights. An, an honest traitor! But no assassin."

"And on such slender belief you hang your life?"

"I' faith, I have little option! I would lay him by the heels if I could — for his other offences. But he ever eludes me. He also takes his precautions! Going better protected than do I! And a deal more secretly. Not that his actions are secret — only his comings and goings. Did you hear? Only last week he roused the mob to riot in Dundee. Against the Church. The houses of the Black and Grey Friars both were sacked and pillaged. But he was gone before the Sheriff's men arrived. The Sheriff is the Lord Glamis, of course, and not to be trusted."

"If this is not the same Wishart, what other is there?"

"It is a small family, certainly. But he has brothers, cousins. I ever seek to resolve the matter."

"This Laird of Brunstane, then? Crichton, is it? A proved traitor and spy. Why do you not take him, at least?"

"He is of more worth to me, as he is. Knowing his treachery, I can watch him. Hope that he will bring me to the one Wishart or the other! Free, he is a guide; held, since he has powerful friends, he could be more trouble still. But his time will come!"

The Queen-Dowager shook her head. "You are strange men, here in Scotland. In France, my good Guise brothers would not act so — or fail to act! All these enemies would have their heads

355

off, long since! It is such a tangle of evil! And all stemming from that devil, Henry Tudor. An ogre in the guise of a king! To think that he would have had me in his bed!" She tossed her head. "At least, there I might have made an end of him! And done Christendom a service. Perhaps served Scotland better!"

David smiled. "It is Henry who makes an end of his partners, is it not? Rather than his wives!"

"Hitherto. But he has not yet wed a Guise!"

He sketched a flourish with his arm. "There is still time, Madame! You are a free woman, unwed. Henry would have Katherine Parr's head off, the same day he received your least suggestion of marriage!"

"And I would be permitted to go to him, sirrah?"

"Perhaps. But over my dead body, to be sure!"

"I thought so. Although, you tell me, he is ailing?"

"Aye. My spies at his Court are at one on that. He is so great and gross that he can scarce move. His mind is deranged, beset by ill humours, so that he sees enemies and assassins in every shadow. But—the pity of it, they are only shadows! And his disintegration is a slow progress! To Scotland's sorrow."

"You . . . you never considered to hasten it? You, with your spies."

At her tone of voice, he wrinkled his strangely unlined brows, and shook his head. "I have many sins to my discredit, I fear—but not that one! I am no more assassin that I conceive George Wishart to be!"

She nodded. "I did not think otherwise. But—what is to be done, then? Must we ever bear Henry's spleen, awaiting his death, helpless? There are ten Englishmen for every one Scot. And every fourth Scot a traitor, it would seem!"

"No, no. Every fourth noble, perhaps. But the folk are leal, true. Never doubt that. It is the greedy, treacherous nobles. As ill a crew as ever burdened a land. That is why, above all, Scotland *must* hold to the Church. Since the lords will not give the people the lead that they need, the Church must. Henry knows it, and so bends all his ire against the Church."

"And you, Monsieur Davie, are the Church! You alone. So you must die!"

"Aye. I am the Church, God help me! It is for this reason that I *am* the Church. That I have worked to make myself so. Else, heaven knows, I am no churchman! It is a race between Henry Tudor and myself."

"God grant then that you win that race!"

He inclined his head. "Meantime, we prepare once again the weary business of warding off Henry's next attack. Be sure that it will follow this Ancrum defeat, with the greater speed and fury. The pity that King Francis is sending only three thousand. They say Hertford has already some thirty thousand at York. I would go to France myself, to show Francis the need. But I dare not leave Scotland for so long. And there is no time, I fear." He drew a long breath, almost a sigh. "Mother of God — I could do with a rest from it all!"

"The day you rest, David Beaton," Mary of Guise said slowly, levelly, "Scotland is lost!"

Chapter Twenty-nine

THE Provincial Council of the Clergy, meeting in the church of the Black Friars in Edinburgh's Cowgate, sat in appalled silence as the tale of woe was unfolded, even the clerk's voice choking with emotion as he read.

". . . the Abbey of Kelso also sacked and burned. Abbot held for ransom. All brethren dead, and much of the people. All houses, granges, granaries and orchards fired. Eight hundred horses, three thousand cattle, six thousand sheep, slaughtered or carried off. The Abbey of Jedburgh sacked and thrown down. Abbot nailed to his own door. All farms and settlements burned. Town of Jedburgh and fourteen villages rased to the ground. Three hundred horses, four thousand cattle, seven thousand sheep lost. Abbey of Melrose burned. Abbot escaped. All chapels, dependencies, farms levelled. Nine thousand horses, cattle and sheep taken. Abbey of Dryburgh destroyed, with all pertinents and pendicles. Beasts lost, five thousand. Priory of Coldinghame sacked . . ."

David Beaton, who had heard most of it already, listened frozen-faced. Henry's answer to the Battle of Ancrum. Hertford's savagery on this invasion of 1545 surpassed all previous records. He exultingly wrote to his royal master that so much damage had not been done in Scotland by fire and sword in the last hundred years. Even his own English soldiery were said to be shocked and disgusted. Almost it made David wonder whether Scotland would have been better off to have submitted to the tyrant? To have become a humble vassal of Henry, and been spared his mad rage. Had his own life's work been a mistake? Had he cost his country dear, instead of saving it . . .?

Sombrely pondering, David found Patrick Barclay at his shoulder.

"My lord," he whispered. "News! Brunstane has arrived secretly at the house of Cockburn of Ormiston, in Lothian. And George Wishart with him!"

"Ha! Wishart! At Ormiston, you say? A dozen miles, or more. The word is sure, is it?"

"The parish priest sent the message, as sure. One Hepburn."

"Hepburn, eh? One of Bothwell's clan. A treacherous crew. But hating Douglas. And not of the reformers." David bit his lip. "We must seize the chance, true or false." He rose, signing to the Archbishop of Glasgow to take his place in the president's chair. He followed Barclay out, as the clerk continued the recital of horror.

"Where is the Regent?" he demanded, in the vestry.

"At the castle. Assembling men to go to the aid of Home and Buccleuch, who hold the hill passes against Hertford."

"Aye. Send to him — no, go yourself. My services to him and, will he detach a large body of horse, and ride with it to Ormiston, with all speed."

"You have your own guard of six score waiting here, my lord. Surrounding this church . . ."

"Not enough. Wishart has ever the protection of his lords. In Douglas country like Lothian . . . Tell Arran that I will await him near to Ormiston village." David paused, frowning. "No — Arran is ever slow, hesitant. And Bothwell is Sheriff of Haddington. See, Patrick — get my lord of Bothwell. He is at Holyroodhouse. He is a scoundrel — but he will act faster than the Regent. It is in his bailiwick, and the word has come from one of his people, this Hepburn. Moreover, Bothwell and his tail of cutthroats riding through Lothian will seem strange to none. Whereas the Regent and myself will set all tongues wagging. Brunstane and Wishart might be warned. Escape."

"Aye. Bothwell to bring Wishart here?"

"No. Too dangerous. We would have a riot on our hands. See — I shall ride for the Lord Seton's castle, at Seton on the coast. All know he is my friend. It will be dark before I reach there. Then, in darkness I shall strike inland. For the tower of Elphinstone, on its high ridge. I shall wait there, for Arran. It is but two or three miles from Ormiston. If Bothwell requires help, he is to light three fires. You have it? Three fires together. I shall see them from Elphinstone Tower, across the valley. If the Douglas rally, Bothwell may require all the aid the Regent and I can bring him. It is understood?"

"Aye," Barclay nodded. "Pray God we get him this time!"

David sat, in rich half-armour, in the lamp-lit Hall of the great square keep of Elphinstone that towered above the long hog's back of ridge separating the vale of Tyne from the coastal plain of the Forth. With only partial attention he listened to the talk of his burly host, Sir Gilbert Johnstone, from his seat in the deep embrasure of one of the south-facing windows, while ever and anon he turned his head to gaze out across the deep dark gulf of the Tyne valley. One or two pinpoints of light winked across there, in the sharp frosty air — but nothing that could be mistaken for three fires lit close together. Two miles away across the void the house of Ormiston lay secret in its woodlands. Would this attempt misfire, as had all the other efforts to trap George Wishart?

David had one hundred and seventy men waiting in the courtyard below, keeping warm as best they might, for it was a bitter frost for early December, Seton and Johnstone having provided fifty between them. How many Bothwell had managed to gather for his endeavour, he did not know. There was no sign of Arran, as yet. To arrest one man, even in a strongly held house, this might seem crazily excessive. But the dread castle of Tantallon lay about another ten miles to the east; and Sir George's house of Dalkeith half that to the west. A thousand men might be insufficient if surprise was not achieved.

A stir and shouting from below interrupted Sir Gilbert's monologue, from before the great log-fire, on the sins of his Douglas neighbours.

"The Regent," David said. "Go receive him, friend Johnstone."

But when presently Sir Gilbert returned to the Hall, throwing the door wide, it was not to usher in Arran but the Earl of Bothwell and Hepburn of Waughton. Between them they held another man. Roughly they thrust him into the warm lamp-lit room.

Still-faced, David rose to his feet. "So-o-o!" he said, on an exhalation of breath. "We meet again—after twenty years!"

The other bowed stiffly. "I could have wished in better company, my lord." And he glanced left and right at his captors, who jerked him the more fiercely in consequence.

"Pray unhand Master Wishart, my lord of Bothwell," David requested. "My thanks for your successful errand. But, we are not here dealing with some cattle riever or cut-purse!"

"No—with a forsworn traitor, my lord Chancellor!" Bothwell answered strongly. But he and his colleague let the other go.

David was surprised by the man's appearance. He remembered him as little more than a boy—and had built up in his mind the image of a fiery zealot, a thundering prophet of doom and damnation, as were so many of the reforming preachers. But George Wishart was still boyish-looking—even more so than was David Beaton in fact, and of a very different sort of youthfulness. He was broad-faced, of an open, indeed freckled countenance, frank-eyed, with a crop of fair curling hair. He was of stocky, muscular build, his carriage upright but unassuming. Only his dress, wholly black, approximated to the accepted pattern.

David drew a hand over his mouth. "Be seated, Master Wishart," he invited. "You wear your years lightly, I perceive."

"As do you, my lord." Faintly the newcomer smiled. "Which implies no great credit. To either of us!"

"Sir Gilbert—wine, I pray you. For my lord of Bothwell, Waughton . . . and Master Wishart. It is a cold night for riding, as I know."

"My lord Cardinal—had I deemed that you sought this treasonous plotter for wining and fair discussion, I vow I'd have haled him straight to the Regent!" Bothwell growled. "Arran will have it otherwise, I warrant."

"Perhaps, my lord . . ."

"I remind you, Earl of Bothwell, that I consented to come with you, without unseemly struggle, solely on your word that

I would suffer no hurt," Wishart intervened quietly but firmly. "Do I detect a change of tune, sir?"

"You said such a thing, my lord?" David asked sharply. "On whose authority? Not mine. Nor Patrick Barclay's. That is certain."

"My lord," the Earl said coldly. "I am Bothwell. I do not require your authority for every word I speak. Or any man's." Then he shrugged. "But—the fellow lies. I have made no such promise. Have I, Harry?"

Waughton grinned. "Hepburns do not bargain with such as this!" he said briefly.

"I leave you to judge whose word you should accept, my lord Cardinal," Wishart commented dryly. "But . . . from your own words, I fear I must take it that you *had* intended me hurt?"

"I intend you not hurt but a fair trial."

"Fair . . .? The quality of your trials is known, my lord! I deny your authority to try me for anything. In especial, the preaching of God's holy word."

"My authority is sufficient." David shrugged. "Or, would you prefer to be tried by my lord of Arran, the Regent? In *his* courts? For treasonably accepting English gold in Scotland? For inciting the Queen's lieges to burn and destroy sundry monasteries? For working with those who plot my murder . . .?"

"I do not plot your murder, sir! I abhor the shedding of blood. Even yours!"

"I thank you! Such charges are the Regent's affair—the province of the civil courts. The ecclesiastical court is but concerned with matters of heresy and doctrine. In such, I assure you, your trial would be fair indeed. As Chancellor, I can permit you the choice."

"My friends may well dispute your authority and powers, sir."

"Possibly. But, praises be, your treacherous friends do not yet have the last word in the matter!"

"Nor do you. The last word is with Almighty God!"

"Ah, yes. Undoubtedly. Then, we shall await His verdict, shall we? Meantime humbly acting according to our inadequate lights!"

"Mocker! Blasphemer!" George Wishart did not shout the words, as some would have done, but spoke them quietly, almost sadly, as though in duty.

Another commotion downstairs heralded the arrival of the Regent, at last.

They all rose as Arran came stamping into the Hall, rubbing his hands and complaining of the cold. At sight of Wishart he looked somewhat put out.

"Is that the fellow?" he demanded. "Have I brought five hundred men for that!"

"I took him from Ormiston with less!" Bothwell observed dryly.

"At the price of a safe-conduct!" Wishart added.

"A lie!"

"Eh? Safe-conduct? What's this, a-mercy?" Arran looked around them.

"My lord, there appears to have been some mistake," David told him soothingly. "A misunderstanding. Master Wishart claims to be in some measure injured. We must discover the rights of it."

"Injured—by God's eyes! This . . . this felon! Sitting there, supping wine! Like any honoured guest!" Stepping forward abruptly, the Regent swept Wishart's goblet from the table to the floor with a blow of his arm. "Johnstone, man—hale this rebel down to your deepest pit, where he belongs. Would you have him breathe the same air as honest men? The morn I'll ride with him to Edinburgh. Now—away with him. Then bring me meat and drink, a God's name!"

"My lord," Wishart protested. "I have Earl Bothwell's promise. If I do not return to Ormiston this night, my friends will know what to do!"

"Then they'll must needs come chapping at the gates of Edinburgh Castle for you, you limmer—for that is where I'm taking you. Johnstone—hence with him, I say!"

As their host led the prisoner away, David Beaton murmured a final word. "You may perceive something of my point, Master Wishart, when I offered you a choice of courts!"

Although the Banqueting Hall of St. Andrews Castle was packed, there might have been only the two men in that great apartment as far as the principals themselves were concerned. It had been the same throughout; prosecutors, accusers, witnesses, testifiers, came and went, but these two, David Beaton and George

Wishart, had eyes only for each other. Almost they seemed to ignore the flood of words that eddied around them, judge and accused both. In theory, of course, there was a veritable host of judges, for the entire convocation of prelates and clergy called for this 28th March constituted the court; but in fact all saw it as a personal issue between two men, and acted accordingly. Which was, strangely enough, the last thing David had desired. Only too clearly he perceived the danger to his name and reputation, possibly his life, in this trial – the probability that it would be claimed generally as mortal spleen against the man whose name had been linked with threats against his safety – even though no hint of such plots had been so much as mentioned throughout the charges. David had tried hard to convince the Regent to appoint a judge, as representing the State, who might share the responsibility; but Arran, for once, had not lacked decision. And now this vast courtful of judges somehow consisted only of spectators. Sole liability and onus had settled with grim inevitability upon his own scarlet shoulders.

When at last the complicated indictment was finished and the chief prosecutor sat down, a long silence ensued. It was with almost a physical effort that David Beaton roused himself from the strange inertia and reluctance which gripped him – but even so his eyes never left those of the other man.

"Master Wishart," he said at length, quietly, almost softly. "You have heard. What have you to say?"

The prisoner shrugged. "What is there to say, my lord? What lies between us is beyond all words. None knows better than yourself that this is not a trial. It is but a public condemnation. You but in many words accuse me of doing what all men know that I have done – of preaching the Word of God to God's people. I can and do deny the motives you impute to me. But the teachings I can no more deny than the fact that I breathe God's free air."

David nodded, brooding expression unchanged. "There is no question, then, as to what you have done. Nor is there any question but that you knew the penalties imposed by Holy Church upon those who deliberately act as you have done. Can you deny that you did not know that an excommunicated priest of the Church who continues to offer the sacraments to others is punishable by death? That the distribution of English Bibles is not only a heretical offence against the Church but a treasonable offence against the realm, both punishable by death? That your other admitted offences, of preaching against prayer to Our Lady, against invocation of saints, and the like are acts of heresy and merit the same penalty?"

"Merit?" the other repeated. "I leave you, my lord, to judge what penalties these actions *merit*! But — how can I deny knowledge of your penalties when in public preaching in half the cities of this land I have declared what would be my fate if and when you and your like should take my poor person?"

"In other words, Master Wishart, you of a purpose set out to embrace martyrdom?"

The accused frowned. "Not so. I declared the rigours of my fate, should I be taken. But as your lordship knows, I took all due steps to see that I was *not* taken! Successfully, over many months. Until your forsworn Earl Bothwell betrayed me."

"You deny, then, that you seek martyrdom?"

"I do. But if martyrdom is thrust upon me, I shall embrace it with humble pride, and what courage God gives me."

"Aye. Fortunately that will not be necessary."

Wishart's eyes widened a little, and he opened his mouth to speak. Then closed it again.

"Martyrdom will not be thrust upon you, my friend. If you die, it will be because *you* would have it so. Not this court."

"What mean you?"

"I mean that mercy is of God. And God's Church is ready to show mercy even to so determined a foe as you have been. Repent, and you shall be received back into the body of the faithful, with full absolution for all that you have done."

There was a stir throughout the crowded hall of the castle.

Wishart bit his lip. "How can I do that?" he cried.

"You can, without difficulty. After all, you have done it before!"

The other stared at him, hands gripped tight together.

"In the English city of Bristol, in the year 1538, you were tried before the ecclesiastical court. Your friend King Henry had not then turned wholly apostate. You were accused of preaching against prayer to the Virgin Mary. You confessed, and were condemned for heresy. To be burned. But you recanted. And thereafter, before all men, burned your own faggots in front of the church of St. Nicholas in that town."

If there had been a stir before, it was eclipsed now as men exclaimed and commented at this hitherto secret information.

Wishart looked down at his white-knuckled fists. "I was but a weak and foolish young man. Of twenty-five years," he said thickly.

"You acted more wisely then, than in the seven years since passed!"

"No. Not wisely. Only feebly, shamefully. I shall not so fail again." He raised his head, and stared back at the Cardinal.

That man met his glance long and expressionlessly. "So," he said, at length. "You refuse to recant?"

"I do."

David's sigh was apparent to all. "Do you put forward any reason, Master Wishart, why due sentence be not passed upon you?"

"I do. I say that the Word of God is the sole rule by which I have been guided and may be judged. As it should be the sole exemplar and authority of every man who accepts the teaching of Christ. It follows that I am bound to refuse and deny all that Holy Scripture condemns, and to attach no importance to any matters it leaves in obscurity. The dogmas of the Pope and your Church, therefore, for which no authority is to be found in God's Word, I cannot accept. I declare outward ceremonies which leave the heart unaffected, insufficient for salvation, and the hearing of confessions useless." Speaking with a fierce and urgent determination, as though he drove himself on, the words tumbling from his lips now, the prisoner glared round at all the ranks of appalled faces. "The doctrine of purgatory, I condemn as false, Christ Himself assuring us that after death the soul immediately passes into immortal life and felicity. Fasting and the sacrament of the Lord's Supper, I uphold, but . . ."

"I rejoice, Master Wishart, that you uphold something of the teachings of Holy Church!" David interrupted grimly. "I asked for reason why sentence be *not* passed upon you. Not why it should! Out of your own mouth you condemn yourself, do you not?"

"Rather I condemn you!" the other shouted. "I denounce your doctrine for which you burn men, as pestilential, blasphemous and abominable, not proceeding from the inspiration of God but the suggestions of the Devil! I say that . . ."

In the uproar that drowned his further declamations, David eyed the man with perplexity and a kind of grieving disappointment. Hitherto he had been contained, dignified, lucid, appearing scarcely to be moved by the proceedings, master of himself. Now, suddenly, all was changed and he was but a ranting bigot. Whipping himself up to crude defiance. It must have been the glimpse of a way out offered him in the suggestion of recantation. The temptation had been real. Now he must drive himself to the stake, to prove it otherwise.

Wearily David raised his hand; at last the hubbub died away. "So be it," he said, his voice level, flat. "Since you will have it so, needs must. I declare you, George Wishart, guilty on all charges, and in the name of this court condemn you to suffer death by burning forthwith, at the forecourt of this Castle of St. Andrews. Between now and sundown." Abruptly he rose to his feet, as he saw the man before him blench. "To be strangled by the neck before committal to the flames," he jerked, and turning, strode from the hall.

Shortly dismissing his attendants, even Patrick Barclay and Gilbert Ogilvy, David settled himself to watch from the castle window. The execution was to take place in the castle forecourt, and so swiftly after sentence, for the same reason that the trial had been held in the castle itself — that there should be no rescue. Wishart's powerful friends, so assiduous about protecting him hitherto, were not the sort to shrink at this. The date of the trial had been kept as secret as possible, but with so many clergy involved something of it was bound to have leaked out. And with the Earl of Rothes himself, Sheriff of Fife, showing leanings towards the English-reform party, anything might happen.

Already a great crowd had gathered — but there looked to be nothing of threat about it; just the usual unthinking throng, avid for the spectacle. To think that men and women should choose to come and watch such unlovely proceedings! And yet, seeing him at this open window, in his kenspeckle scarlet, would not all assume that he likewise was as eager as any for the sight of his enemy's death? When he would in fact rather be anywhere else than in St. Andrews this March afternoon. He could, of course, have ordered the execution to take place in private, and absented himself – but that would have been partly to defeat the object of it all. George Wishart's death must serve as an awful warning, and be seen to be so by all.

At least the crowd's ghoulish pleasure would be curtailed. That was something that he had been able to do for Wishart, as for those poor wretches at Perth. Although, if he was honest, perhaps the curtailment was as much in his own favour as that of the victim; to shorten his own ordeal of watching. The strangling would not be pretty, but it should be swift.

His men were still putting the finishing touches to the scene as Wishart was led out – for of course it would not have done to have set up the apparatus of death before the trial was concluded, and speed was now essential. It would be dark in three hours. And to wait until tomorrow would give the dissident lords time to assemble their strength.

The faggots at least were dry, of that he had made sure. If he had to burn men, he hoped to do so more efficiently than had his uncle. They were piled up methodically around the tall greenwood stake, in steps and stairs. Near by was a brazier with a welldoing fire of glowing coals, and alongside it a gibbet stood, its chain and dangling hook swaying a little in the breeze. David was thankful that breeze was from the south-west; at least he would be spared the smell.

George Wishart came out with a firm step between his guards, head held high, a noosed rope around his neck and an iron chain around his middle. The executioner came forward to receive him. On this occasion there were to be no time-wasting and unnecessary ceremonies and formalities. David could not forbid the condemned man's customary address from the scaffold, of course – but he hoped that he would keep it brief.

All in position, the captain of the guard glanced over towards the Cardinal's window, and David raised his hand.

Wishart climbed the steps of his scaffold, under the gibbet, without assistance or the least hesitation. If he looked southwards, towards the long ridge that cradled St. Andrews, and from which any deliverance must come, from his higher vantage-point, it was only for a moment. He knew now, as did all others, that no rescue could be in time to save him, on whatever scale – for St. Andrews Castle was now as much a national fortress as an archiepiscopal

367

palace, and every cannon in its armoury was trained this afternoon on this forecourt, with the gunners standing by, their matches and fuses in their hands.

The prisoner turned towards the watching crowd. "My friends, he called, his voice strong, vibrant. "You are here to witness the folly and the shame of men. It is my prayer to the Almighty that you may not be offended at the Word of God by the sight of the torments brought upon me, its preacher. But rather to love it, and to suffer persecution likewise, if it is necessary — although I pray that it may not be so. For this night of darkness, I say, is near its end."

So clear and calm was his enunciation that David Beaton, a hundred yards away, could hear every word. He was well-pleased that his enemy had recovered himself, and would, it seemed, die like a man. Anything else would have been but shame on all.

Wishart went on. "Gladly I declare to you that freely and fully I forgive all my enemies. Even including the judges who have unjustly condemned me to this fate. In especial I forgive him who sits at yonder window, in his pride! He knows not how soon shall be his fall from the same lofty place — but I tell you, and him, that it shall be so. Mark my words well. I declare to you that I shall not long precede him before the tribunal of the Judge who judges righteously!" And he thrust out a hand more accusing than forgiving, towards the castle window.

From his chair, David inclined his head in wry acknowledgement.

The executioner now moved forward, up the steps, and there on the scaffold, fell on his knees before his victim, begging forgiveness also — an unreheased incident which caused some stir.

"Most willingly do I tender it," Wishart said, and raising him up, actually kissed him on the brow. "Be of good courage, my friend, and do your office. You have received token before all that I forgive you."

Then he too knelt, and in a loud voice cried. "Oh, Thou saviour of the world, have mercy on me; Father of Heaven, into Thy hands I commend my spirit." Three times he said this, and then, rising, bowed to the red figure in the window, and turned to the executioner. "I am ready, friend," he said.

As the murmur of the crowd rose, the hangman hitched the hook of the gibbet into the chain around Wishart's waist, and bobbing a kind of bow, began to wind the handle of the winch.

Creaking and clanking, the condemned man was raised up, trailing his neck-rope behind him. He had some difficulty in keeping himself upright. At its full height, the operator twitched the rope over the arm of the gibbet, and secured the end deftly to a peg. Then, suddenly jumping back, he released the winch-handle.

There was a brief rattle as the chain ran out through its pulley, and then a snap, as the body dropped and was brought to a savage halt by the rope around the throat. The snap might even have been the neck breaking, for by the odd angle of head to hanging body, it seemed as though this had been successfully achieved.

What had been George Wishart dangled there, twitching and jerking. But swift as the change had been, it was extraordinarily complete and comprehensive. Somehow the hanging thing no longer looked like a man. Or even a corpse. Abruptly the blue-eyed, curly-headed boyish-looking preacher was no more than a twirling, sagging bundle of black clothing on the end of a rope.

Peering up, the executioner smirked, and drew a hand across his own throat, in eloquent signal that the first part of his task had been accomplished with notable efficiency.

An angry animal growl rose from the mass of the spectators, thus drastically cheated of their sensation.

The hangman lowered the inert body, and with the aid of two of the guard, climbed with it up over the faggots to the stake. Since it would by no means stand up, they tied it to the green wood in approximately a sitting position, slumped to one side. Torches, lit from the brazier, set the pyre alight at the first application. The flames that shot up from the tinder-dry bundles of brushwood were as effective as the rest. In a matter of moments all was engulfed in red fire.

Many of the citizenry had already turned away, disgruntled.

David Beaton waited for a little longer, still-faced. Then he rose and making just the suggestion of a bow, to the forecourt, also turned and walked away.

As he paced the corridor, making for his own chamber in the Sea Tower, an officer of his guard spoke to him.

2A

"It was featly done, my lord Cardinal," he said. "The man died well."

"Featly, indeed," David acknowledged evenly. "He died well, yes."

Chapter Thirty

THE clatter and stamp of innumerable horses' hooves, the clank of armour and the shouts of command, brought a new and unprecedented clamour to the quiet precincts of Melgund on its high tableland. Marion Ogilvy sighed as she waited for David, within the splendid doorway beneath her own initials in stone, her lovely face anxious.

He came to greet her, arms out and smiling—but there was a strain about his features, a tension, which caused him to look more nearly his forty-nine-years, and which brought a stoun to the woman's heart that was like a physical blow.

"Dear heart!" he cried, and made to take her to him, then thought better of it, with the scores of watching eyes at his back. "Joy to see you! Joy to be here again . . .!"

"Aye, Davie dear—joy! But . . . is it joy that made you bring all these? Here, to Melgund?" Askance she looked past him to the thronging men-at-arms, who could not have looked more foreign to that serene and peaceful place.

"I am sorry, lass—it had to be. I dare not ride without them, meantime. Wherever I go, they go. Too many seek my life. But—I shall quarter them at a fair distance. Never fear, they shall not intrude . . ." He turned, to take Isobel, the youngest, into his arms, whilst Elizabeth and Margaret curtsied, and his sons bowed politely.

He kissed each girl, and held out his hand to their brothers. James and Alexander took it, but George, the eldest, turned away abruptly.

Brows raised, David showed his surprise. "Why, George?" he said. "What's to do? Are you not glad to see me?"

"No," the youth jerked. He was a tall, good-looking young man of nineteen now, taller than his father indeed. "Would that I were!"

"Geordie!" Marion cried, pain in her voice.

"Why, son! What do you mean?"

"I mean, my lord Cardinal, that there is blood on your hand!" the youngster exclaimed, and hurried away, rejecting the still extended hand.

David winced, as though he had been struck. "Dear God!" he whispered.

The other young people, all save little Isobel, turned, embarrassed and unhappy, and drifted away.

"Davie! Davie, my love—forgive him!" Marion pleaded. "Do not heed him. He has been listening to tales. The land is full of them . . ."

The man stared at her, through her, without seeing her. "My own son! My first-born!" he breathed. "Flesh of my flesh . . .!"

Biting her lip, she shook her head, wordless.

A cough from behind them turned them around. Gilbert Ogilvy stood there, in half-armour like the rest.

"Aye, Gibbie—come in," David said vaguely, frowning.

"Gibbie! I did not know that you were here," Marion greeted her now grey-haired and somewhat portly brother. "But—you are welcome indeed. Always you are that."

"I have come to wed your daughter, Marion. David would have it so."

"Wed . . .? But, I thought . . . her father . . .?"

"I conceived it better. Wiser. That Gibbie should do it. A truer priest!" David looked down at his hands, sombrely. "I was right, it seems. These hands! With blood on them!"

"My dear! My dear!" Marion said. "Geordie is but a boy, yet. He does not understand . . ."

"At his age, I was fighting Scotland's cause in France!" the man said harshly, and strode into the great house, leaving brother and sister alone.

Later, when they were together in their own room, David challenged her. "You said, I think, that the land was full of tales? As to me. My blood-guiltiness."

"Idle stories, Davie. Meat for gossiping tongues."

"Yet such as my son will listen to, and believe!"

"He roams the country now. They all do. I cannot tie them here, at Melgund. Young folk will not bide quietly at home . . ."

"The tales?" he interrupted her. "What do they say of me?"

371

She looked down at her twisting fingers. "Oh why, Davie — why did you have to kill those poor folk at Perth?" she burst out.

"So! That is it! Marion — there has never been a realm in all this world that did not require men to die for it. Few, or many, that more might be spared."

"That unhappy woman! With child at her breast. Was that truth? What harm had she done?"

"None. Save to be who she was, and where she was, that day."

"And so your drowned her, tied like a dog, they say!"

"I . . . shall we say, I did not save her?" He was frowning blackly.

"The same thing, is it not? When you could have done so. You, who bear more authority in this land than any one man has ever done!"

Sombrely he eyed her. "You believe that I would have let her drown, if I had not conceived it necessary? For greater benefits than the life of one unfortunate woman? Or the wretched men? Marion — in the government of a realm a man is caught, as in a cleft stick. Frequently he must choose between performing the lesser of two or more evils. Those poor wretches had been selected — how, and why these, God knows — because Perth town was in a state of revolt. A warning had to be given, an example made. Even so, the day was scarcely saved. For the forces against me, against the Queen's government, are strong, ruthless. So strong did Ruthven deem himself that he defied the Regent's edict deposing him from the provostship and sheriffship, and sought to hold the town against the Crown. Sixty men died in the fighting he occasioned. Yet I have heard no accusation of blood-guiltiness against my lord of Ruthven!"

"That was war, honest fighting . . ."

"It was treasonable revolt. Against his own Queen. In favour of Henry Tudor . . ."

"And against your Church!"

"My Church — and yours!" he said quietly.

"Oh, Davie — there lies the root of the matter! It is because you are a churchman that men blame you. That you do all in the name of Christ's Church. You should never have become a churchman!"

"Were I not, woman, Henry Tudor would rule in Scotland

today, and burn thousands, as he does at Tyburn. You would bow to proud English governors. And there would be no Church —only sad Lutheran preachers and fierce Calvinists spouting hellfire and damnation! Would you have it so?"

"No." She shook her head, unhappily. "No. But—could you not have achieved this without the fire and the rope?"

"Men being men, I could not. Would that I could." He gripped her arm. "Marion—do you not understand? Even you? So often I have told you. How shall I show you it? While there is yet time?"

She looked alarmed, eyes widening. "Time? While there is time? What do you mean?"

He drew a hand over his brow. "It is nothing. Heed me not. No matter. It is but the life that I lead. With so many threatening my death. Henry's time grows short—and he will have my blood, first, if he can. I said that a realm demands the lives of men. I do not grudge this realm mine. But—only if I know that *you* understand! I care not what men say of me. But you, Marion Ogilvy, must comprehend. I am a sinner, God knows. I have nothing of the saint in me. But this I have—I love my country. And I love you. Say that you understand, my dear!"

She threw her arms around him. "Oh, Davie—that I understand! My love, my love—never fear it. Forgive me if I seemed to fail you."

"Your understanding I must have," he repeated. "Or . . . or it is all but as the wind across this Melgund!"

"Yes, my heart—yes. But—is my poor understanding so important? So long as you have my undying love?"

They clung to each other, and in time found the comfort that had never failed them.

The Great Hall of Finavon Castle, four miles to the west, was not so fine as that of Melgund, but it was slightly larger—and size was important this day. For not only were practically all the nobility and gentry of Strathmore, Angus and the Mearns present, with wives and families, but inevitably a large contingent of the Cardinal's guard must be therein also, to keep watch on the others, however much of a corporate spectre at the feast they might seem; it was inconceivable that none of the guests present would be untainted with heresy and disaffection.

Nevertheless, it was not because of space and size that the festivities were being held here, rather than at the bride's home. Marion's desire that Melgund should remain inviolate, remote, its peace preserved from prying eyes, was the true reason for the reversal of the usual custom — and one with which David entirely sympathised. Since he was paying for all, anyway, it made little difference — even though Margaret herself, and the other young Beatons, might have preferred otherwise.

At the dais-table, at the top end of the packed Hall, David turned from conversation with his host, to glance at Marion, on his right. Shining-eyed, eager, looking little more than a girl again herself, she was smiling to her daughter over the separate little table where she sat alone with her new husband. Margaret was looking comely indeed, sparkling with youth and a king's ransom of jewellery, gorgeously gowned, a radiant bride; but her mother, nevertheless, was far more beautiful, the most lovely creature in that great and crowded apartment, simply dressed as she was in silver-grey taffeta that set off her fairness most surely, her only adornment the huge blood-red ruby which David had brought her so long ago, and which had never had public wearing until this day.

"You are satisfied, my dear?" he asked her, quietly.

Happily she turned to him, to take his hand beneath the board. "Oh yes, Davie — yes! All is as it should be. So good. So right. Is not Margaret bonnie? And happy. She esteems her bridegroom well. That is a great joy. She told me that she finds him handsome — although, to be sure, I scarcely see it!" Marion laughed. "But then, *my* taste is otherwise! For fair and slender men, not great dark giants!"

Ruefully David looked down. "Less slender than once, I fear!" he said. "And hair thinning. I show the years. Whereas you — you could be the wench I chased across the Braes of Airlie, lang syne! Aye, and would chase again . . ."

"Hush, Davie Beaton! This is Margaret's day — not mine! Remember it. And that you are a Prince of the Church. And Chancellor of this realm. Your days for chasing women long past. Now, I am told, they chase you! Perhaps they always did? Was not that why I won you? Only because me *you* had to chase!" With part-laugh, part sigh, she added. "These two have not chased each other. They have done as do most — what they are told. But . . . I think they will be happy, nevertheless. Do not you?"

"I pray so. But who can contrive happiness for others?" He could not say that he had planned today more for the mother's happiness than the daughter's.

As though she read his thoughts, she answered. "You *have* contrived it. For me. Here and now." She gestured around them. "All this. Right and good and as it should be."

That was something of a kind exaggeration perhaps—with those hundred keen-eyed and watchful armed men lining the apartment walls, and another hundred and more standing to arms outside amongst the larger throng of guests and tenantry for whom there was no room within. And with David's personal French cook, who travelled everywhere with him, to first prepare and then taste every dish that was set before his master, and who now stood unobtrusively behind, amongst the men in armour. But, such matters apart, everything was as it ought to be, the day had gone well, and she was content. Not least in that she recognised that this was David's last and most notable gesture of contrition and restitution towards herself for the great wrong he had once done her.

Marion's daughter, and his, was now wed, legitimised and bearing the name of Beaton, not Ogilvy, to David, Master of Crawford, eldest son and heir to the Earl of Crawford, chief of the Lindsays, and senior earl and peer of Scotland. Moreover, her dowry was enormous, princely, the greatest ever known in the land, freely given. The scale of the wedding celebrations would have done credit to a king. Countess of Crawford Margaret would be, with precedence only below the Queen herself—Marion Ogilvy's daughter by David Beaton. It was enough.

The Earl, somewhat drink-taken, was beginning to demand the bear-baiting and similar delights, and David reminding him that the bride's health was yet to be drunk and some small eloquence customary, when Patrick Barclay materialised at his shoulder, as was so often his trying habit and duty.

"Urgent tidings, my lord!" he murmured. "Henry's fleet is embarking Hertford's army at Newcastle. Some ships are already at sea. Sailing north. Spies say that this time it is not Leith they make for, but St. Andrews!"

"Damnation! Once again!" David groaned. "And St. Andrews?"

"Aye. The word is that Henry, hearing of your lordship's projected journey to France to gain more troops, would strike first. The Cardinal's death is Hertford's prime command!"

"David!" Marion had heard that last. "No! Oh, God—no!"

"You say that some ships have already sailed?" David's fists were clenched. "Then—I must be up and doing!"

"No, Davie! Not—not into certain danger! Again!" Marion protested. "You will not go . . .?"

"I must, my dear. Think you I can sit here, while Henry's ships sail against us? Against my own town and castle of St. Andrews?"

"But you will put your life in their hands! What they desire. Stay here. Give orders and plan as you will—but do not go to St. Andrews."

"You forget, lass. I am Chancellor of Scotland. Would you have the realm's chief minister to skulk and hide, with the enemy at the gates? No—I must ride. And at once."

"Then this time I shall come with you!"

"That you will not, my dear. What could you do? You could serve no purpose at St. Andrews. Here you can, and do. See you—I shall steal away quietly. None shall know. None *must* know. Do you want all here spoiled? Yourself, you said that this is Margaret's day. She must have it as little marred as may be. If I slip out, and you remain in your chair, she will suspect nothing. Till later. Then you must say that some matter of state required my attention . . ."

"Dear God! And I was so happy . . ."

"You will be happy again, my heart." Grimly he smiled. "It comes to me that this is not the first marriage celebration that I have had to leave in some haste! Now, Marion lass—smile, I say! Look your most lovely. For me, as well as all these others. That I leave you so, your beauty a bright joy in my mind."

Lips tight, she nodded. She produced a wan smile.

He could not kiss her, or make any evident leave-taking. Tensely they gripped hands beneath the table.

"Shall I inform Dean Gilbert?" Barclay asked.

"Gibbie?" David looked down the main central table to where

376

Gilbert Ogilvy sat in close and appreciative company with Elizabeth, Prioress of Lunan, plump but merry. "No," he decided. "Let him be. Besides, it would but attract notice. The same with these men of the guard. They must stay where they are. I shall take some few of those outside. The rest must follow later." He rose. "God keep you, Marion, heart of my heart!" he murmured. "These hearts are not parted, now or ever, whatever the state of our bodies. Smile, now—and fear nothing."

She did not speak, and such smile as she produced shone through tears.

David turned, and strolled to the door behind the dais-table, Barclay following him. His scarlet figure betrayed no hint of urgency or crisis. In the doorway he spoke briefly to an officer of his guard who stood there. Then he glanced back. Marion's head was turned, looking at him. She was beautiful. For a long moment they gazed at each other. Then he strode for the stairway.

David and Barclay, with two score of the guard, were drumming their way down Strathmore and had almost reached Inverarity when a single rider, red-faced and breathless, caught up with them. It was Gilbert Ogilvy, still in the canonicals in which he had officiated at his niece's wedding, but with an armoured breastplate hurriedly fastened on top. With only a grunted word he took his place at the Cardinal's right as they pounded on.

The May night's quiet gloaming was settling on the land when the ferry from Broughty Craig put them down on the North Fife shore.

"Here we part," David said. "You, Patrick—ride for Stirling. Inform Her Grace. And the Regent. All leal forces to be rallied. The watch on the Douglases and their friends strengthened. The main array to assemble at Stirling. Warn Argyll, at Castle Campbell, as you pass Dollar. He to command, since Huntly is in the north. If Arran has gone to Edinburgh, send after him. You have it?"

"Aye, my lord. And you?"

"Gilbert here will ride round all leal Fife lords and lairds. Requiring them to assemble, with all their power. To defend these coasts. Myself, I go on to St. Andrews. If the castle is to withstand assault from the sea, it must be strengthened. Earthworks.

Sand. Ditches for forward cannon. The harbour must be closed. This I shall see to. Go now, both. And God speed!"

They went their destined ways.

There was no word yet of enemy shipping being sighted along the coast.

Chapter Thirty-one

IN the early morning of the 27th of May already some workmen had congregated in the castle forecourt, the same where George Wishart had died, waiting for the drawbridge to be lowered —for the Cardinal had commanded that work on the defences must go on day and night so long as there was any light; and at this time of the year there was little darkness in Scotland. The fact that a providential if unseasonable storm was said to have dispersed and turned back the English invasion fleet, was not being allowed to affect the work; Henry Tudor's determination could be taken as proof against all such set-backs.

Even so, the appearance of one of the quality at such an hour, waiting amongst the labourers, could have aroused considerable speculation; but Norman Leslie, Master of Rothes, was well known to the gate-porters; he was a friend of the Cardinal's, despite his father's religious backsliding, and in fact was under bonds of manrent to him, for certain feudal properties held of him. He had indeed been in conference with the Cardinal here the provious evening. The porters allowed him entrance, with his two servants, without question, when the drawbridge clanked down into position.

A little later, but still before five o'clock, with the next batch of labourers arrived James Melville of Raith, with three servants, seeking first the Master of Rothes, and then an interview with the Cardinal, as soon as his lordship should be risen. The senior porter sent his companion to enquire about this—but scarcely had the man gone than a group of nine more workmen arriving together, all turned upon the remaining porter. Armed and armoured as he was, he was taken by surprise. He was stabbed by several hitherto hidden daggers, and his body pitched down into his own moat. Of the newcomers one was John Leslie,

378

brother of the Earl of Rothes and uncle of the Master; another young Kirkcaldy of Grange, son of the former Lord Treasurer under the Douglas regime.

The Master was waiting for the new conspirators in the Inner Bailey. Kirkcaldy went to secure the private postern; and others, under direction, hurried to lock and bar sundry doors. Then the Master led them across to the great Sea Tower, wherein lay the Cardinal's personal quarters.

Workmen were already toiling hereabouts, shovelling sand, into large wooden bunkers suspended over the walls, which would protect the masonry from cannon-fire from the sea. A cry of alarm from one of the pseudo-labourers, and a pointing downwards over the outer wall, soon brought the guard from the foot of the Cardinal's stairway, round the corner, to peer over likewise—and to be knocked on the head and tossed down the cliffs below, to the very spot where once David Beaton had made love to a kitchen maid.

Nothing now prevented the conspirators from hastening up the twisting turnpike stair, leaving four men to guard its foot. At the door to the Cardinal's bedchamber, they were halted. It was locked. They knocked.

David Beaton's voice answered, enquiring who was there.

"Friends," the Master called. "All is well, my lord. This is Leslie."

"It is early for friendly calls, is it not?" came from beyond the door. "And not all Leslies are my friends!"

"But this is Norman. The Master, my lord. Fear nothing."

"Norman is my friend, yes. But—how do I know that it is Norman? Your voice sounds strange, a little . . .?"

"My lord Cardinal—how can you doubt me? I was with you but last night. We talked of my property of Easter Wemyss. And now—now I have brought you tidings. Of the English . . ."

"Ah." The other voice sounded closer to the door. "You must forgive me, Norman. So many seek my life. I grow sadly suspicious, I fear. But I'll have Norman Leslie in . . ."

They heard the key being turned in the lock.

So soon as the door began to open, the men on the landing threw themselves bodily against it, naked daggers already in their hands.

David Beaton, unclothed save for a bed-robe he had thrown

about him, staggered back with the impact. Eight or ten men surged into the room, and slammed the door shut behind them.

"So-o-o!" Still-faced, David confronted them. "It *was* Norman Leslie! and others!" Eyes on those wicked knives, he stepped back, and sat down on a chair, drawing his robe closer about him. "Well, Norman? Your business?" His voice, though thick, was steady.

It was not the Master but his uncle, John Leslie, who spoke. "Here is our business!" he said harshly, raising his dagger, and stepping forward.

Eyes widening, and shrinking back involuntarily, David gasped. "Would . . . would you slay me? Thus? A priest . . .?"

"Aye. This shall be your priest!" And Leslie lunged over him, and smashing down David's upraised arm, drove his steel deep into the bare chest.

Choking, the victim doubled up, so that Leslie had difficulty in wrenching out his weapon. As men exclaimed, shouted and jostled, one, Peter Carmichael, thrust forward to assist. Since he could not now reach the breast, he plunged his dirk into the bent and heaving back instead. With animal-like yells the rest of them rushed forward, pushing and struggling, to finish the business.

All save James Melville of Raith, a laird of middle years noted for his sober piety. Standing back, he raised a strong and commanding voice, in protest.

"Wait you!" he shouted. "Heed me. This is not how a godly deed should be done, my friends! Stand back! Back, I say! Would you spoil all with your haste? Impatience? Leave be, in the name of God!"

Strangely enough, they did pay heed to him. One by one they straightened up, moving back, to stand in a ring, panting hoarsely, around the jerking body that sprawled half on the chair, half on the already blood-spattered floor.

Men do not die so readily and so quickly as is conveniently assumed. David Beaton, bleeding from a dozen wounds, yet somehow managed to raise himself approximately upright on the chair, groaning, blood-bubbles forming at his lips. His eyes sought to focus.

Melville raised his sword to point it dramatically at David's heart. "This work and judgement of God, although it be done in secret, ought to be done with greater gravity!" he declaimed. "Let all things be done seemly, in the sight of our Maker." He jerked his steel point. "Careful Cardinal, Prince of Darkness — you are on the way to the eternal fires of judgement! How are the mighty fallen! Wicked pride lies humbled! God is not mocked! Priest of wickedness — repent!"

David's lips moved. With obviously enormous effort, he found words. "I am . . . no . . . priest. In truth. Your . . . steel . . . strikes . . . other. This realm. All . . . all is lost!" He slumped sideways, snoring thickly.

"Lost, aye!" Melville cried. "You are lost, miscreant! Slayer of the innocent! Repent, therefore. While you may. In especial, repent of the shedding of the blood of God's gentle servant, the holy George Wishart, to avenge whom we are sent by the same great God!" The man's voice rose almost to a scream. "Wishart, aye! Repent, if you can. And remember — this mortal stroke I deal isna the blow of a hired assassin, but the just vengeance fallen on an obstinate and cruel enemy of Christ and the Holy Gospel! God in Heaven, receive thy blackened soul!"

And powerfully he drove forward with his sword-point, straight into the victim's heart. Twice, thrice, he withdrew and struck again.

David Beaton, Prince of Holy Church, Primate and Chancellor of Scotland, toppled over, taking Melville's sword with him, and fell to the floor, dead.

"Glory be to God!" Melville cried. "Glory! Glory!"

His less pious colleagues fell upon the body.

Historical Note

THE Cardinal dead, his slayers had little difficulty in disarming and putting forth the remainder of the reduced guard, driving out the workmen, and securing the castle. Thereafter a large crowd assembled outside, with the Provost and the Town Guard, demanding to see the Cardinal. The conspirators brought the still-naked body to the castle-walls, indecently, indeed unprintably, maltreating it before all, and then hanging it by an arm and a leg allegedly from the same window from which David had watched George Wishart die. The body thereafter was put in a chest, packed with salt, and left unburied for months.

The killers retained St. Andrews Castle, joined by other militant reformers including John Knox, until over a year later, a French fleet was able to bombard them into submission.

Meantime, Henry the Eighth died only a few months after Beaton. On his death-bed he called Hertford, now made the Protector Somerset for the new nine-year-old King Edward the Sixth, and bound him to continue the offensive against Scotland with fullest severity. The battle of Pinkie followed, a major disaster for Scotland, and so concerned were the Scots for the safety of the infant Mary Queen of Scots that she was removed from Stirling to an island in the Lake of Menteith, and thence to France, where she remained for thirteen years.

Edward of England soon died, and his elder sister, Bloody Mary, becoming Queen, turned England back to Catholicism, and to some extent the pressure on Scotland was at last raised. Mary of Guise had now replaced Arran as Regent; and oddly enough it was under this sister of two Cardinals that the Reformation came at length, and comparatively peacefully, to Scotland, as it were twenty years late.

Marion Ogilvy, Lady of Melgund, lived for almost another thirty years, dying in 1575.